The Collected Stories

Autumn Blossoms

Praise for the Author

Broken Melodies

"*Broken Melodies* is a poignantly written tale that will find resonance in a nation where family dynamics are paramount and where warring parents and broken homes are becoming increasingly familiar."

Rediff Get Ahead

"Kottary's novel indicates a rich creative imagination and immense skill at weaving together disparate strands."

Sunday magazine

"Pacy, emotional, humorous and realistic ... the novel is an easy read and keeps one hooked."

Indian Express

"There is no doubt that Kottary knows both the milieu and the inner landscape of her characters."

Deccan Herald

"Kottary proves to be a solid storyteller building strong characterisations. Her sense of visuals is strong and her prose lends itself to very vivid pictures in the reader's mind."

Rediff mail

"*Broken Melodies* is a deeply moving novel about the search for beauty in our lives."

Indian Express

"*Bikhre Sur,* Gajra Kottary ka Hindi mein anuvaadit upanyas, bagair kisi ho-halle ke, generation gap, stree chetna, aur stree mukti jaise muddon ko naye sirey se behes mein laata hai."

Sukhanwar: The Hindi Literary Magazine

*

Once Upon a Star

"Kottary's offering shows an insider's view of an industry where drama seems to be a daily buzzword."

Indian Express

"Behind Bollywood, beyond Bollywood ... a compelling page-turner that looks at celebrity lives and the costs and collateral damage of stardom."

Namita Gokhale, writer and co-director of Jaipur Literature Festival

"Over the years, Gajra has sensitively and realistically portrayed women and their lives. She displays a very fine writing style."

Anupam Kher, actor, teacher and motivational speaker

"I can't stop marvelling at this story told with grace, warmth, nuance and unrelenting self-respect."

Feroz Abbas Khan, theatre and film director

"An insider's view of the world of cinema and the many faces of an industry where fame is fleeting and everything is as real as it is dramatic."

Society magazine

*

Girls Don't Cry

"Gajra's book is a thought-provoking saga that portrays the vitality of eliminating irrational stereotypes and adaptation in this dynamic age. Kottary's work blends the modern with the traditional while walking on the path of righteousness."

The Times of India

"Unputdownable – a novel about truly brave women."

Ruchita Mishra, author

"Gajra weaves a riveting tale of how at heart, the dreams, hopes and aspirations across three generations of women in a family remain constant."

Kirron Kher, actor and parliamentarian

"Each page, each character has a story to tell – the book instils the belief that the journey we take is forged by the decisions we make. It has the power to make the reader laugh and cry at the same time."

The Times of India E Times

The Collected Stories

Autumn Blossoms

FOREWORD BY ANUPAM KHER

GAJRA KOTTARY

Om Books International

First published in 2023 by

Om Books International

Corporate & Editorial Office
A-12, Sector 64, Noida 201 301
Uttar Pradesh, India
Phone: +91 120 477 4100
Email: editorial@ombooks.com
Website: www.ombooksinternational.com

Sales Office
107, Ansari Road, Darya Ganj,
New Delhi 110 002, India
Phone: +91 11 4000 9000
Email: sales@ombooks.com
Website: www.ombooks.com

ISBN: 978-93-5376-997-0

Printed in India

10 9 8 7 6 5 4 3 2 1

This book is dedicated to my mother, Maya

'Her name means an illusion
She was as real as real can be
Making my every joy her own
She lived vicariously, through me

Trusted me when I wasn't worthy
Just for her illusion, I try my best to be'

CONTENTS

Section II

Reflections in Water

Section III
The Mirror Does Not Lie

ACKNOWLEDGEMENTS

Rare are the editors who nurture their authors as Shantanu does. For whom books are not only about commissioning and editing, but are bridges to creative relationships that commit for life. That's the reason why, when he moves publishing houses, like the Pied Piper of Hamelin, authors follow him wherever he goes.

They don't make them like Shantanu Ray Chaudhuri anymore. I am blessed to have found him. Thank you, Shantanu, from idea to fruition, nothing would have been possible in this collection without your enthusiasm and ideas.

I also thank HarAnand Publishers, Jaico Publishing House and Storytel India for graciously allowing me to include the stories I wrote for them earlier, in this collection.

FOREWORD

Anupam Kher

Any anthology of short stories, running into 500 pages as this one does, is always impressive. It is testimony to the amount of love and labour the writer has put into creating the plots and fleshing out the characters in each story. Gajra is a fine storyteller. She weaves her stories from here, there and everywhere. On these pages you will find tales about a new bride's fantasy, the existential frustrations of a crusader's wife, the dilemma of a chic MBA in publicly recognising her homespun parents, an award-winning journalist who finds her campaign gone awry, a danseuse realising that a guru must do more than merely teach, and many more. Loveless marriages, noisy neighbours, the sane insane, and angst over self-worth and sexual identities are not left out.

Gajra writes women-centric short stories which detail their distinctive orientations and philosophies against the backdrop of a range of human emotions. I once asked her why she confines herself to women. "Aren't you leaving out the menfolk in your stories?" Her reply was pithy. "Because men too are more interested in women than in themselves!"

In the three decades that I have known her, Gajra's professional trajectory has been in constant motion. Quite apart from writing these short stories, she has published four novels, written over a dozen television serials – most of them long running – and even associated on the script of the odd film. In between all this creativity, she has managed to raise two well-brought-up children who are now adults.

The stories in this book are slotted into three sections: tales about women's relationships with men, their equally complex relationships with other women and lastly, their relationships with themselves. I particularly like the concept of the last section. Whether we are men or women or any of the other categories listed in current times, I am of the opinion that it's the relationship which we have with ourselves that defines everything about our lives. That belief is the title of one of my best-selling books, *The Best Thing about You Is You*.

For the men out there, please don't think that there's no room for you in this collection. In fact, I would recommend that men read Gajra's stories too – to understand women better (of course it's possible!) and to understand the ironies and singularities of life itself. And also to smile along and be taken aback in equal measure as I was while leafing through her narratives.

I wish Gajra all the best for the success of this lifetime collection of her stories.

SECTION I

The Yin and the Yang

A CLEAN SLATE

A little tempering of the dish
A little tampering with him
It's not deceit that I wish
Just render life a little less grim

"It is easier to make the break now ... You're only six months into the marriage – so the wound will heal quickly," the counsellor told her, his voice full of genuine concern.

"But maybe if I continue my attempts for just a few weeks more ... maybe giving it some more time will..." Bhavna began.

"So that you feel you did your utmost and only then gave up on it?" said Dr Jha.

This man is amazing, thought Bhavna. He was voicing her thoughts – right down to the exact words they were framed in.

"Mrs Bhavna Mehta, you have been coming to me for three months now. Despite my ... and I'm sure your entreaties too, Mr Mehta has never come here with you. He doesn't even want to admit that he ... or your marriage is faced with a problem. Mrs Mehta, as your counsellor I can now safely say that my priorities have shifted from saving your marriage, to saving you. So far you have been the only sane partner in this marriage, and now you need to get out of it as fast as you can if you want to retain your sanity."

"I realise that, doctor. But it's just that I would never have dreamed that one day my marriage would fail," said Bhavna.

Bhavna darted a look at Dr Jha and her eyes spilled over.

"These are exactly the thoughts they all feel ... All those women who can see the writing on the wall that's proclaiming the end of their marriage but refuse to read it. You are not alone in what you're going through. Nor are you to blame for it in any way," Dr Jha said, staring piercingly at her, a look that convinced Bhavna that Dr Jha was a hypnotist and not a counsellor.

"A man who comes home drunk almost every day ... passes out soon after and then wakes up his wife in the middle of the night to force himself upon her night after night – with no apologies either in the morning ... with not a loving or appreciative word for her in all these six months? He's definitely not worth it. I don't think you need to be so harsh on yourself, Mrs Mehta. You deserve much better that that. You better start doing so too ... You have already tried your best. Now, you have to take the difficult decision to walk out," Dr Jha continued as he walked her to the door.

*

Bhavna reached home and started putting some of her clothes and her most precious ornaments into a small suitcase. Just a little less quickly and a lot more neatly than heroines in Hindi films stuffing their belongings into their suitcases any which way do when they leave home.

Despite Dr Jha's assurances Bhavna was afraid. She was afraid of herself. And afraid that as more and more time elapsed from her visit to Dr Jha, the effect of his resounding words would diminish and she would not be able go through with the step she was contemplating. She shut the suitcase and looked at the phone. Should she inform Papa she was coming back home or just land up there?

After a bit of thought Bhavna realised that it would be difficult to explain the situation to him properly over the phone. Better to leave ... just plain and simple L-E-A-V-E, she thought, still staring at the phone, which came to life suddenly as if driven by her stare. She picked it up gingerly.

"Mrs Mehta..." It was Ranganathan, Alok's colleague, on the line. "There's been a freak mishap at the site today about an hour ago." Ranganathan hesitated. "Erm, er, sir was overseeing the work from the ground floor ... I was standing and taking notes right next to him ... when a construction worker who was on the first floor accidentally dropped a brick. It fell on sir's head. No ... no... there was no bleeding ... That's the funny part but I guess it didn't fall from too much of a height. The only thing is that sir fainted on the spot so we brought him here. I'm calling you from the hospital but you don't worry, Mrs Mehta, he's almost conscious now. You can come to City Centre Hospital. He's in Room No. 24."

Bhavna lifted the suitcase from the bed and put it by the side of the cupboard ... so it would be as unobtrusive as possible. No, her plans to leave would not change but in the interest of social and humanitarian considerations, they would only have to be somewhat postponed.

*

Half an hour later, Bhavna stood outside room 24 at the City Centre Hospital talking to Dr Bhargava who had been attending to Alok.

"You will be the best judge in this matter, Mrs Mehta. As doctors what really worries us a little in cases of head injuries is when there is no apparent outward injury as has happened with your husband. Even a CAT scan sometimes doesn't give us the best idea about possible internal injuries or other damage to the brain. The brain is such a complex organ, you know," he said. "As of now Mr Mehta seems fine and normal to us ... but it is your close observation in the next few hours that will confirm that no memory loss or gap has occurred as a result of this impact. We'll come back to you in a while. But please remember that we're all there to help you, Mrs Mehta, and will do our best, come what may."

Bhavna walked towards Alok's room gingerly. He looked up at her and smiled. A smile more warm than she'd ever got from him in the last six months. Alok extended his hand and clasped hers warmly. He winced in pain at this slight movement, and held his head above his left ear. She noticed the bandage.

"Does your head hurt?" asked Bhavna, concerned.

"No ... but this bandage on the ear does. The top of the ear tore just a little when the brick fell," he said, turning his head to show her the damage. "The doctors realised it just a while ago."

He remembers everything, thought Bhavna, shivering a little. Then she reminded herself of the humanitarian cause and walked closer to him. She hesitated a little, then extended her hand and stroked his hair sympathetically. He shut his eyes as if in relief.

"I love you very much, Bhavna," he muttered. "You're the most beautiful and innocent wife in the world and I'm the luckiest man in the whole world to have you."

Bhavna stared at him with disbelief. This did not sound like her husband talking.

"Bhavna, come and sit next to me," Alok pleaded as he patted the space on the bed beside his legs.

She sat where he beckoned her to.

"Bhavna ... I'm slightly confused about this but ... I think I haven't done much for you in all these months. You deserve a lot of happiness ... and I'll give it all to you. Do me a favour, Bhavna, when you go back home, call Ranganathan and tell him to book us two tickets to Goa for this weekend. I'm definitely going to be out of here by then. We'll have the time of our lives there," Alok said, his voice full of childish glee.

For six months she had hoped for, waited for and fantasised about something like this. But he had never ever spoken or behaved with such affection. And yet, right at this moment, hearing his loving words ... his coarse behaviour, the past few months came rushing back at her. Was she supposed to forget all that? Does this make it all right? Bhavna felt the bile rise in her throat. She suddenly felt very cold. This was certainly not Alok.

Bhavna rushed out of the room and to the basin as her stomach churned and heart beat fast. She splashed water on her face and felt slightly better.

"Is everything all right, Mrs Mehta?" It was the concerned voice of Dr Bhargava. "And what about your husband ... what do you think?"

"He's good. He's unbelievably good." Bhavna smiled.

"Are you sure, Mrs Mehta? Please don't jump to any hasty conclusions. Take your time but be sure to check for any kind of memory lapses. The earlier they are brought to our notice, the earlier we can decide on a course of action or medication, the better it will be for him. Maybe you could try and jog his memory a little to be completely sure," continued the doctor.

"No, there is no need to do anything. I want to take him back home right away, doctor. He doesn't need any medicines," said Bhavna firmly.

"As you like, Mrs Mehta," said Dr Bhargava.

Bhavna no longer needed Dr Jha to give her the strength to do what she now needed to. She herself was strong enough to know what she had to do. She was not going to unpack that suitcase now. It would certainly be useful to take to Goa.

A DECISION AT LAST

With more than a hint of pride
She dithers, she is a woman after all
Always letting the man decide
Right to the end, the final call

"It has become a part of your cultural DNA, you suffer from an almost pathological wish and need to be dominated," Shekhar had yelled in disgust at Kajol a few months after they were married. She had broken out into a fit of giggles. Such a complete gender role reversal in their thought processes. Shekhar was an ardent votary of women's empowerment and to that end, in their early years of marriage, had often encouraged her to try and take a lot of decisions on her own. But she had simply refused to heed his wishes.

It was not that Kajol hadn't tried. But time and again she had realised that she was simply helpless. The more choices Kajol had, the more bewildered she became. The moment she was faced with a decision to make, it was as though she could see, in her line of vision, a series of lanes and alleys fusing and merging into one another. She felt like a magnet being pulled in so many directions at the same time. And so Kajol always ended up begging Shekhar to decide for her. It made life so much easier and lighter. She always felt like a soaring bird the moment she shifted the awesome responsibility of decision making to him.

Over the years of course there had been some improvement. From not taking any decisions, it had at least graduated to Kajol helping certain decisions being made. Well, at least those that could be classified as the "smaller issues of life". What outfit to wear for the Sharmas' anniversary party … what new dishes to order from their favourite restaurants … whether the children ought to join a new extracurricular activity or not … nothing earth-shattering that could alter the course of life, but she had at least started to give her views. But even then it was finally always his call. And she was relieved and thanked god for that.

Shekhar often complained to her that though she performed all the duties of being a wife and mother satisfactorily, he worried for her. She was like a third child for him … loving, innocent but someone who simply refused to grow up. Shekhar had imagined a more tough and equal life partner … like what his mother had been to his father. But gradually both had reconciled to her indecisiveness, as loving partners in a marriage usually get used to each other's idiosyncrasies. For it is also true that despite all notions of an equal partnership, the best marriages and partnerships are those where one partner accepts the superior wisdom of the other on one issue or the other. One thinks and declares, the other does, and peace and happiness reigns in most such homes.

In any case Shekhar always thought right. Kajol could not remember one time in these ten years when they had regretted any decision he had taken. When he was so blessed, how did it matter that it was he who always decided, she had told Shekhar often.

"It's important to have an opinion, and a viewpoint, even if it sometimes proves to be wrong. How long will you depend on me to take all the decisions about our life?" he had asked just last week, irritated when he had had to decide the brand of the new washing machine that they had to buy.

"Forever," Kajol had said and given him a hug. Thankfully, as always, he had been assuaged. She couldn't help it, but this was exactly what Kajol felt. Deep in her heart she knew that his concern was genuine and in the rightness of things.

She thought that was that and that Shekhar wouldn't be irritated with her on this issue anymore. But that afternoon when he came home early from work, with a plan to take the family for a surprise weekend vacation, he asked her to decide where they should go.

"Anywhere," she said, smiling at him, hoping it would work as usual.

Shekhar seemed irritated as he disentangled himself from her arms.

"It's not funny," he said. "There's something seriously wrong with you, Kajol."

"Oh Shekhar, not again … I thought we had worked this out between us," Kajol said.

"What's the problem, Kajol? Does it take the strength of Bhim or the wisdom of Arjun to decide whether we should go to Mahabaleshwar for the weekend or just go up to Marve? Forget it. I'll wait for the kids to come from school and tell me. Today I had actually wanted to surprise them … just bundle them into the car and not tell them where we were going … but never mind now."

"But why don't you decide as always, Shekhar. We'll go anywhere. The idea is to take this weekend break and be together. Why are you making such a fuss this time?"

"Why don't you understand, Kajol? I feel guilty always deciding for everyone. Anyway, let the kids come home and decide. I want them to start thinking for themselves from the right age. Otherwise, they'll end up like you. And what's more, they might never be able to change their minds and habits later as you haven't been able to," he said bitterly.

"Mahabaleshwar," blurted Kajol as Shekhar almost scalded his tongue with the first spoon of soup that he had been stirring absent-mindedly. "I've decided that we should go to Mahabaleshwar."

Shekhar got up from his chair and took Kajol off from hers. He twirled her around as she giggled. Jai and Tanu walked in just then and stared in disbelief, then jettisoned their satchels and joined in.

*

In no time at all suitcases were packed and they hit the road. It was like a scene in the movies ... the romantic drizzle ... miles of fields that resembled a sea of green ... the car deck blaring *"You fill up my senses"* ... two beautiful children dozing in the backseat. And then, like the proverbial twist in a screen tale, the car skidding to avoid a speeding truck in front. The cold scrunch of twisted metal followed. Then silence.

*

Kajol looked with glazed eyes at Shekhar sleeping peacefully, clinging on to life with the help of the life support machine ... the oxygen mask over his mouth ... tubes all over his arm ... the ECG machine connected to his chest. The hospital sheet covered him up to his ribs and the only evidence of the gory accident were the caked lines of mud and dried blood in his hair.

Her mind was numb and yet abuzz. It was she who had decided to come to Mahabaleshwar and the decision had gone so wrong. So very wrong. This was exactly why she always hated taking decisions ... but no one had ever understood how justified she was. This time even Shekhar hadn't.

"Have you taken a decision yet?"

Kajol nearly jumped out of her skin. No it wasn't Shekhar asking.

She turned around. It was Dr Verma.

"I know, ma'am, this is a very tough decision. But this isn't getting anyone anywhere. We wouldn't be recommending this if there was even the faintest chance of recovery. Your husband is in a coma, he's alive only ... only due to these..." Dr Verma waved his hand, indicating the medical paraphernalia attached to Shekhar. "You must give us permission to pull off life support soon."

Another decision? How could Kajol tell them she could not take this decision? No, she certainly could not, she would not.

Kajol broke down as she looked at Shekhar. "Don't make me go through this, Shekhar. Help me, Shekhar, help me," she cried.

Tears flowed down her cheeks and more kept clouding her eyes, leaving the visage of the slumped Shekhar a mere blur before her eyes. The tears seemed unending ... Shekhar had never been able to ignore them – they had always been her ultimate weapon. But now, he lay completely unaffected. But wait ... didn't he?

Yes, miracle of miracles, he seemed to be responding! Kajol wiped her eyes quickly. She couldn't be wrong. She was sure that she saw Shekhar's hand move. She rushed to tell the doctor. A miracle ... it had to be a miracle.

The doctor conceded that it had been a miracle all right. Shekhar's hand had jerked at an angle that had pulled off the oxygen mask. Two gasps later he was gone.

He had taken the decision for her yet again.

ALL FOR THE GOOD CAUSE

The big battles are for him to fight
I only keep the purse strings tight
An iron fist, my velvet glove hides
Wars are won by the worldly-wise

In these times when a prosperous city man is forty-five, he is not supposed to look a day beyond thirty. And five years ago when my Abhigyan was that age he didn't look even that old. I remember watching him fondly from the front door every morning as he got into the backseat of the grey Ambassador at 9:20 sharp to be driven away to work. It was the one time in the day that I saw him from far enough to really know how handsome he still looked.

But then that had been the time that he was only *my* Abhigyan. The husband I loved … the father of my children Maneka and Pranay. He did not yet "belong to the people" then as he does now.

The man that lay before me at this moment was not mine alone. I had to remember and remind myself of that so many times a day. He did not even look much like the Abhigyan I knew.

In the last five years, he had aged twenty.

It was not a disease, a calamity, or the excesses of a corrupt lifestyle. None of these. It was due to what he often called, when interviewed by admiring journalists, "the turning point in my life".

Abhigyan had always been philosophically inclined – and had insights into life and its problems like few had. It was a quality that mesmerised all those who came in contact with him. It was a rare person – amongst his half-score staff at the ministry where he worked – who had not turned to him for advice at some point or the other in those twelve years that he worked there. And those were the twelve most beautiful years of my life too.

How beautiful they were I realised only much after they had long passed. At that time I was often irked at how few of his off-duty hours Abhigyan had gradually started to spend at home. True that the children were now old enough to be almost completely on their own. True also that romance in our marriage had somewhat dulled. In fact we both had often talked of how our lives needed refocusing ... only I imagined that we'd do this together as we'd done all the earlier years of "focused parenting".

I thought that we'd read together, go for long walks, maybe get to know each other's fantasies and perhaps even help them come true. That's what "refocusing" meant to a foolish woman like me. For I did not want to admit or accept that my man was meant for a larger purpose in life. That I should be grateful that his midlife crisis did not lead him into the arms of another woman. But led him to the forefront of a fight for justice, for people he had earlier never even had anything to do with.

The tribals of the Teesar district of Uttar Pradesh were protesting the cutting down of some of their forests for a road that would help connect the district to all the prominent towns of the state. The state government claimed that it would change their lives for the better while the environmentalists with a handful of tribals were convinced it would be their nemesis.

It was true that previous examples of the effect of such developmental projects went to show that dispossessed and displaced families never really came back strong enough to be on their feet. And so this time, Swami Dhireesh, a social figure of the region, was determined to give the government a run for their ideas and spearhead a movement to oppose the road plan tooth and nail.

Abhigyan was then deputy secretary in the Public Works Department. Given his ability to deal with and convince people with his oratory and persuasive skills he had been pushed forward by the department to deal with the Swami ... and hopefully win him over to compromise, so that work on the road construction could begin.

I still remember the date. It was 19 July 1996. Abhigyan had shared his state of mind with me that morning before he left to meet Swami Dhireesh.

Swami Dhireesh was a man he had long admired and hoped to meet. I also knew that there were few men that Abhigyan actually looked up to. He admired Swami Dhireesh for being one of the few men who had not donned saffron robes to escape from his ability or conviction to do something for society. Abhigyan had explained to me that the Swami was so much like the social reformers of previous centuries like Swami Vivekananda and Shri Rabindranath Tagore, for whom the espousal of social causes was as important and perhaps linked to their personal quest for spiritual salvation.

Abhigyan's anticipation at meeting Swami Dhireesh that morning had however been tinged with the realisation that his mission was to convince him to abandon the campaign to lead the tribals. He shared his state of mind with me. And the only way I could help him out was to counsel him that it would be all right if he didn't succeed in his expected line of duty. What would be would be. Privately I was sure that Abhigyan, unable to espouse something that he did not believe in one hundred per cent, would come back mission unaccomplished. I would never have dreamed however that that would be the day he would find his life's mission.

Abhigyan returned in the evening looking preoccupied. I had learnt not to intrude upon him in those initial few hours of his return from the office. He usually opened up much later and on his own. But that day he slept early. The next morning he woke up early too and asked me over our morning cup of tea whether I loved him enough to stand by him in any kind of times to come.

"Of course I do and I will," I had said and he had looked relieved.

I had meant what I had said. But it was much more than I had bargained for. Abhigyan resigned from his prestigious IAS post that day. The next day he left us all to live life like the tribals whose cause he had completely crossed over to and whose lifestyle he felt he must adopt if he were to truly empathise with them.

A few weeks later Swami Dhireesh moved back to his headquarters to lend his name to another cause. So Abhigyan was left alone to become the messiah of the tribals. He moved into the cottage near the Beenwa River where they looked after him as one of their own. Abhigyan had insisted that Maneka, Pranay and I live in a small flat that he had bought for us a few kilometres away. Money was very tight but Abhigyan said that that was a good thing, for Maneka and Pranay would now perforce have to toughen up to face life.

Life changed rapidly over the next few months. Abhigyan locked horns with the very people that he had once worked for. He went on several fasts at various points in the agitation, and that combined with the legal steps that he took on behalf of the tribals had succeeded in stalling the road construction work now for almost four years. The tribals, their cause and Abhigyan became international media entities ... and thanks to them Teesar became a tourism hotspot.

Everyone told me that I should be proud of Abhigyan whose selflessness and ideals were now beginning to be compared to those of Gandhi. My Abhigyan? Were they really talking of him? I often wondered.

It is the fifth day of his fast unto death. I've been in this tent staring at him in his stupor-like state for three days now. Maneka and Pranay have been coming and going but otherwise managing pretty much on their own. Their friends go to parks in the evening and discos at night. But my brave children work part-time and even cook themselves a spartan dinner at night if I am late in returning from the tuition classes that I take. They haven't yet protested too much against this toughening up. Nor have I. It's not easy to do that when the entire nation considers you the family of a national hero.

And the hero lies before me at this moment. His hair coarse and dry. The lips that once transported me to ecstasy are now chapped and bleeding. The deep warm breath that made me secure all night is now hot, raspy and short but I'm grateful it's there at all. The paunch that was an endless source of mirth for Maneka and Pranay was now sunk, his ribs visible and his skin stretched somewhat loosely over his bones. All the hundreds of hours I'd spent cleaning and cooking the best of food to nourish his flesh and blood have come to nothing, as the cause has sucked at his very form.

The doctor told me clearly this morning that Abhigyan's life now hung only by the slender thread of his willpower. And it is only I who know that that thread might be slender, but unfortunately it was very stubborn!

Yes, I dare to say unfortunately, because it is this very willpower that is going to make it difficult for Abhigyan to give in and end his fast if the state remained firm in their stand. That, incidentally, was another truth the minister had told me three mornings ago, for now that the Supreme Court verdict had ruled in the government's favour, all that they would have to contend with were the emotions of the people and the media and the conviction of Abhigyan.

The minister had told me that everything was in my hands now. The project would be going full steam ahead anyway, but since the contractors would be happier to work without fear of controversy or revolt they had requested me to convince Abhigyan to concede so that the tribals would do so too. Not only that, they had promised to contribute a percentage of their budget towards any other cause he might want to fight for if Abhigyan did concede.

The contractors had come to me every morning in these last three days and I had honestly pleaded that I had no influence over Abhigyan's decision to call off his fast. That was the truth but it didn't seem so to them. "Bhabhi-ji, surely he will give in to your wishes if you convince him to," the grey safari suit had said. "Just think about it … we'll come again later."

Abhigyan opened his eyes slightly. I noticed that his pupils moved involuntarily from side to side along his upper eyelid. I held his warm hand. I noticed that his thumb stuck stubbornly to his palm, trying but failing to respond to my touch. The doctor had said this was a sign of severe dehydration.

He seemed to be looking at me … if that's what looking could be called without the pupils in place. And I could see our future in the glaze of his blank eyes.

I can see myself sitting in this tiny hut with folded hands as hordes of people float past me whispering words of condolences. Then Pranay and Maneka come to my rescue and take me back to our small home in town.

Maneka, the girl we had once planned to send to Harvard, has given up her studies. Pranay no longer plays football, the game he could once kill for. They are lovely children, only I am a wretched mother.

"Abhigyan?" I whispered into his ear. "They have agreed to everything."

Abhigyan pressed his hand against mine. I knew he was asking, "Are you sure?"

"Yes, yes, Abhigyan … have I ever lied to you?"

This time his hand jerked to say, "No, of course I believe you."

"So have this and leave it all to me," I said, lifting the cover from the glass of water kept by his side. I helped him rise slightly and put the glass to his lips.

"No, no, only a little right now … it must go in slowly," I said even as I watched him clench the rim of the glass with his teeth, his hot breath causing bubbles in the water.

"That's enough for now. You rest awhile," I said as I helped him lie down and then got up to leave the room, looking at him one more time.

The news of Abhigyan breaking his fast spread like wildfire. Within minutes, grey safari suit had come with the bag of contributions from the contractors which he handed over to me to manage and use for the cause of my choice.

I bade grey safari suit goodbye, warning him to be discreet for a while about what I had accomplished for him. Clutching the bag I peeped into Abhigyan's room one last time. He was surrounded by his beloved tribals, one of whom was patiently feeding their hero some fruit juice teaspoon by teaspoon. His eyes had begun to focus and it was as if they were looking for someone. I knew he would be fine in course of time ... but by then his eyes must not find what they searched for.

I turned away and walked out of the hut. Maneka and Pranay were walking towards me, fear writ large on their face.

"How is Papa?" Pranay asked.

"He's going to be fine. He has ended his fast. But we can't see him now ... we are leaving for Delhi right now."

"But why?" asked Maneka.

"So that we can live our lives," I said as I turned both of them roughly by their shoulders to ensure that they walk with me, and not towards their father. Nonplussed, the children did my bidding.

"How can we leave like this, Ma? We haven't got anything with us. Let us at least pack our bags at home? We'll need at least a few basic things wherever we go," Maneka spoke again.

I clutched the bag of money that I now held even more tightly. "This is all we shall ever need again, my children."

ANYONE'S BLUNDER

Life forgave him in the end
But she could never do so
And so their world could never mend
From fate's cruel blow

I

Her hands trembled as she flipped through the thick album. Slowly. Taking time over each photograph. Each photograph was familiar; she had seen then several times, but today, Srishti was searching for something else. The problem was she didn't know what.

She stopped at her favourite picture.

It was a family photo, of her parents, younger sister and herself, taken many years ago. They had been on a vacation and Srishti had been just four at that time. It was one of those pictures, radiant with sunny laughter and carefree smiles, an advertisement for happy families.

Right now, her eyes were on her father's face in the photo. Abhay looked amazingly handsome, bright and contented in the picture. Srishti's sister Adya, barely two-and-a-half, sat in his lap busy figuring out a toy whilst the photographer aimed, and Srishti herself was wedged between her parents, saying cheese as hard as she could.

Srishti looked at Papa's face again. No, it wasn't possible, she thought. That call must have been some kind of prank. Or…?

Her thoughts snapped as she heard the front door click open and shut. Ma was here. Srishti could access the album only when Disha was not around. Quickly, she shoved the album back in the drawer. Her heart racing, she hurried out to the hall.

"Hi Ma. Long day?" Srishti said, offering her sunniest profile. She knew that Ma tended to be edgy for a while after returning from work.

Disha sighed as she sat on the sofa. "Hi darling. Yes, I *am* tired."

"Let me get you some water," said Srishti as she proceeded to the kitchen, avoiding eye contact with her mother.

*

At the dinner table that evening, Srishti was quieter than usual and Disha, though tired, couldn't help notice.

"What is the matter, Srish? Something wrong?"

Okay, so this is it, thought Srishti. She fiddled with her soup a bit, as if drawing courage from it, took a long breath and finally managed to blurt it out. "Ma, is Papa really dead?"

Disha froze. The fear of the unknown crept up her spine. She tried to appear normal. "What kind of question is that, Srish? I've told you everything."

"That's *why* I'm asking, Ma. I know what *you* told me. You told me that when Adya died, Papa passed away because he was too heartbroken. But … but today … someone called. She asked me to inform you that Papa is in…" Srishti couldn't bring herself to complete what she was saying.

"Sandhya called?" Disha sprang up from the chair. Her face was turning pink now and she was suddenly very uneasy. "Did she say anything?"

Srishti looked up in surprise. She had never seen her mother like this.

"Yes, that was her name. How did you know ... and who is she?"

Disha ignored the question. "What did she say?"

"She said Papa is ill and may go any day now. And that we should go and see him once. When I said that my father had been dead for seventeen years, she asked me to tell you what she had told me..." She looked at her ma closely, eyes searching Disha's face for answers.

Disha was silent for a while. When she spoke, her voice was curt. "We don't need to go anywhere. If she calls again, tell her to stop calling."

*

Once in her room, Disha could no longer hold back her tears. As she sat down on the bed, her heart beating wildly, a wave of helplessness swept over her.

She had sat on this very bed seventeen years ago, her eyes burning, empty of tears. Abhay had stood a little away, head bowed, silent tears spilling down his stubble.

She had turned to him angrily. "Why did you kill my baby?" she shouted, hysterical with pain. "Why? Why weren't you more careful?" She clutched his shirt and shook him, her nails digging into his flesh. "You didn't care, did you, Abhay? How can you just stand there not feeling anything ... after what you ... No, Abhay, I won't be able to forgive you. Not today, not tomorrow. It's over for us."

As she vacillated between helpless wrath and bitter guilt, Disha hugged Adya's teddy bear tightly and cried. Her body shook with long, racking sobs.

Abhay had stood motionless, paralysed by the horror of that morning.

They had been on a weekend vacation in Goa. Abhay had received his annual incentives and was thrilled with the rewards. Their cottage at the resort extended into a sprawling private beach, a heaven of clean white sands dotted with the tallest palms they had ever seen. Disha had been very happy with this unplanned break. She had gone with Srishti to the nearby flea market, while Abhay had stayed back, playing with little Adya on the beach. In a while, when Adya became cranky with sleep, Abhay cuddled up with her in one of the low hammocks tied to the trees. He didn't remember when he dozed off next to her.

Waking up with a start at some commotion, he noticed that Adya was not with him. Abhay ran frantically towards the beach, where a small group of people were gathered near the sea. His heart sank when he sighted Adya's little head bobbing up and down the waves. He ran through the waves in panic, swam and searched, but even as he found her, he knew that he had lost her.

Disha could never forget. There was no reconciling with what had happened, and the pain kept growing like a monster inside her, threatening to swallow her.

A numbed Abhay tried his best to salvage the situation but it was futile. Their lives spiralled out of control, and all that remained were painful, silent scars. Since there was no resolution to the pain and the guilt, the only way out for him was to try escaping it.

One day, the servant brought back Abhay's morning tea and told Disha, "Sa'ab is not in his room." Disha walked to his room, locked the door and sought to begin life afresh. Or so she thought.

*

Lost in her thoughts, Disha missed the sound of Srishti's footsteps in the room. Srishti kept her hand on her mother's shoulder gently and sat next to her. When Disha looked up, Srishti saw years of buried pain surfacing in her eyes. She looked like a lost child. For the first time in her life, Srishti held her mother like a baby as she cried and told her daughter the truth.

As they sipped tea together the next morning, Srishti's eyes welled up involuntarily as she asked Disha, "Ma, will we go and see Papa?"

Puffed eyes staring at the table cloth, Disha said. "No, I won't. I won't be able to."

"But Ma, he's dying! Don't you think…"

Disha was suddenly bitter. "No! I can't think! I stopped thinking years ago, Srish!" Her voice hoarse with an impending burst of tears, she said, "Maybe I would have if he still loved us. But he…" The tears had begun to flow again. "But he doesn't. It's only Sandhya for him now."

Srishti became quiet. There was no point arguing. She was gentle in her next request.

"Will you let me go?" Before her mother could say anything, she added quietly, "I want to see Papa."

*

As Srishti disembarked from the bus at the small beach town near Panaji, the breeze carrying the smell of the sea blew hard into her face. Bringing back hazy memories of that day seventeen years ago. She kept trying to push away the discomforting vagueness of her thoughts. Srishti looked at her watch. It was way past noon. There was no time to check in somewhere. She hired a car straight to Deepdaan hospital.

She entered the quaint hospital building and walked up to the reception manned by a middle-aged woman.

"Abhay Dheer. Which room is he in?"

The lady first looked up through her spectacles and then down into her worn-out register. "Room number 23. You may go with the ward boy." She called out for one and the young lad led her up a wooden staircase to a wide corridor. Somewhere in the middle of the corridor, he stopped in front of a room and gestured inside. Srishti kept her bag just inside the threshold and stepped in a little further.

On a bed in the middle of the room, lay a man in his early fifties. Pipes and needles extended from his body to a couple of devious-looking machines. From a distance, he looked like a frail bundle under white sheets, with only his head propped up straight on a pillow. Srishti instantly knew that broad forehead and that jawline from the photo. It was unmistakably him. A surreal blankness engulfed her. After the last few hours of purposefulness, she didn't know what to do next.

"Srishti?" A voice from behind surprised her. She turned around to find a woman standing. She was in her mid-forties, slim, her oval face framed by slightly greying hair tied in a loose bun at the nape of her neck, her skin spotlessly wheatish. She was wearing a pastel cotton sari. The look was simple yet attractive. Her voice was exceptionally calm. So was her demeanour.

Srishti nodded and even before the woman introduced herself, Srishti knew that this was Sandhya, the lady who had called the previous day. Sandhya walked up to the bed and motioned to Srishti to sit on the nearby stool. Now that she was closer, Srishti could see his face clearly. It was still very handsome, she thought. The lines, the sunken eyes and the pallor notwithstanding, a quiet charisma exuded from his face.

Sandhya touched his forehead lightly. She dabbed it with a white kerchief and then took his hand in hers. She looked at him for a few long moments. There was an awkward silence as Srishti watched them both. She was an outsider, aware of the affection between two close people before her, and she suddenly felt a twinge of envy at not being part of this picture. Her thoughts broke when she heard Sandhya whispering softly, "Abhay, open your eyes, see who has come to meet you."

Abhay stirred and opened his eyes very, very slowly. His sight fell first on Sandhya. She smiled at him and continued, "See, I told you your angel will come." Her eyes gestured towards Srishti sitting on the other side. Abhay turned his head slowly and looked at Srishti.

His eyes, tired, looked at her in a strange way, caught between disbelief and incomprehension. Srishti couldn't feel anything, as if her heart had suddenly stopped beating. She thought she saw a pale light in those eyes, like a faint streak of recognition and then the very next second, the flicker went out.

A tear trickled down Sandhya's face.

As if in a trance, Srishti stared at Abhay's face, wondering about the unbearable weight of absence.

II

Srishti signed the hospital papers in a daze. The staff was kind enough to get the body transported to the cremation ground. Sandhya spoke to the pandit as Srishti watched silently, not knowing exactly how she could be useful. Sandhya seemed to command respect among the people she interacted with. She went about the various tasks required with a serenity that Srishti found strangely comforting. Yet, she was overwhelmed by a weird sense of resentment. *Why am I feeling like this? I've hardly met this woman a few hours ago. Then why is she affecting me so much?*

As the time for cremation drew near, a stream of people began joining them for the rites. By the time the pyre was arranged, a small crowd had collected all around. Srishti noticed a young woman talking to Sandhya. Later, the same woman came up and spoke to her.

"Abhay-ji was a very nice person. Extremely generous ... the kindest soul ever in dealing with children. His piano lessons were amazing. My daughter will miss him."

Srishti smiled. "Thank you."

The pandit called upon Srishti to light the pyre. She came forward and executed his instructions step by step. As she lifted a burning piece of wood, her arms felt numb. She lowered the piece onto the stack of wood.

The pyre smouldered and smoked till tiny yellow and orange flames burst into articulate form. As the flames licked the air, they grew and crackled hungrily, taking Abhay into their blazing fold and freeing him slowly, surely and finally.

Srishti's eyes smarted with smoke and the pain of helplessness. Sandhya stood by her side all the while. They hadn't spoken much so far.

Dusk descended and the skies melted into dull blues and purples. Srishti and Sandhya stood with their hands folded as the visitors went past them offering their condolences. Some stopped and spoke to Sandhya, expressing their regrets.

One particular gentleman, hands joined together sincerely, was very grateful. "Sandhya-ji, it was because of you that we came in contact with a wonderful person like Abhay-ji. For whatever time he lived he did so much for the community here. If there is anything I can do, please let me know. God give you strength to cope with your loss."

When the last person had gone, Srishti, who had been hearing the prayers and blessings, looked at Sandhya. But Sandhya was lost in her thoughts, eyes downcast. Srishti took a last look at the remains of the pure and picked her bag to leave.

"How will you go?" Sandhya asked.

"I'll take a bus. I know the way now."

"Hmm ... won't you stay back for another day?"

Srishti looked at her sharply. Sandhya smiled.

"I mean ... won't you like to see where your father lived ... and how?" The last two words hung heavily in the air between them.

"I don't think so. In any case, it was not just *his* house," she blurted, despite herself.

She had barely taken a few steps when Sandhya called out, "Srishti, please take his ashes with you."

Srishti looked half over her shoulder, but then moved on, without answering.

Sandhya waited for her to disappear out of sight. She gathered the urn and asked the driver to take her home. The home which would never be the same again, she realised.

Once she reached the white-and-blue house near the beach, she stopped in the portico just outside the main door. This would be the first time in seventeen years that this house would be without Abhay. She stood there, urn in hand, like a child about to enter school for the first time.

Manohar, their faithful housekeeper, opened the door. "Sandhya beta, how long have you been standing here? Come on in or else you'll catch the evening chill."

Sandhya moved towards the door. Manohar stepped out and stood before her. "Here, give this to me," he said, taking the urn from her hands. Seeing Sandhya hesitate, he assured her, "Abhay will always reside in this house. But beta, you can't bring this inside. You will hurt him if you do so."

He had cared sincerely for this house, Abhay and Sandhya all these years. He choked up as he hung the urn on the peg on the wall that he had readied.

Sandhya walked in and sank into the sofa gratefully, suddenly very tired. After a whole day of reining in her emotions, she felt tears roll down her pale cheeks tentatively. Manohar watched her from a distance.

"You should eat something. And retire early today. I'll lay the dinner table," he said with concern. Sandhya nodded. Manohar arranged the evening meal at the table. As he placed the last bowl, Sandhya told him, "Keep plates for two, Kaka. I'll just come." She walked to the bedroom.

Manohar looked at her, but she had already gone inside. Just then, there was a knock at the door. By the time Sandhya came back to the living room, having changed her clothes and washed her face, Srishti was sitting next to the grand piano kept at the other end of the room while Kaka was busy at the table.

"I knew you would come here, beta." Her voice was always calm, noticed Srishti, removing her hand from the piano.

"This is Abhay's. This is where he gave piano lessons to children," continued Sandhya. "Kaka, make some tea for us please. We'll have dinner a little later," she added politely. Then she proceeded to ask Srishti, "Have you informed your mother that you are staying back another day?"

"Yes, she knows," Srishti said, sounding as noncommittal as possible.

"Come, I'll show you Abhay's room."

Sandhya proceeded to lead Srishti up the stairs. She stopped at a landing upstairs where two rooms were built next to each other. She stopped outside the first, opened the door and stepped inside. Srishti followed. It was almost dark inside with the moonlight sifting through the drawn curtains just slightly. Sandhya switched on the lights.

Srishti let out a small cry as she gaped at the walls. They were plastered with huge blow-ups of herself and her sister Adya, when they were four and two respectively. There were some books, a midsized bed and more photos, but the poster-size pictures of Abhay's two girls were undeniably granted supreme status. Involuntarily, she moved closer to the walls and stared. Each nerve in her body was tense.

Sandhya showed her the couch near the window. "When Abhay would drink a lot, I didn't leave him alone. We would sit on this couch and talk. He would always start crying and eventually rest his head on my lap and doze off. And I would sit and look out of this window till dawn."

Srishti's eyes were beginning to well up. She felt just that hint of anger rising in her. *Ma should not have hidden such a big truth from me. She should have given me a chance to know Papa.* Life could have been so different if she had known him.

"Can I ask you something?" Srishti knew she couldn't stop herself anymore. When Sandhya nodded, she went on, "Did Papa marry you?"

Sandhya smiled. As if she had known all along that Srishti was going to ask her this.

"No, he didn't," she said, rummaging through the cupboard looking for something. "He was too much in love with Disha. Not that I expected it. For me, Abhay was a godsend, an added purpose apart from my singing. We knew each other well, but we never wanted anything from each other."

There was something rather matter of fact in the way Sandhya said this, as if this was the most natural thing in the world and that anything else would have been an abomination, that made Srishti let out a long-drawn sigh.

Srishti watched as Sandhya extracted a diary-like book from the cupboard and brought it to her. She turned to the last page and took out a folded paper, handing it over to Srishti. Srishti sat on the couch and unfolded it. She read:

My dear angel,

The pitter-patter of your tiny footsteps haunts me each day as I carry the burden of the moments left in my life. My life? Strange, but "my life" is such a misplaced idea for me. When I know that my life resides in you, your mom and our Adya.

I know Sandhya will contact you when I'm gone. And this letter is my last chance. To seek and gain forgiveness. Both from Disha and from you, my angel.

Adya went because I was careless. If your mother is angry, she has every right to be. I love Disha madly and have never loved any other woman. I never can. I have died and lived a million deaths each day in the last seventeen years, knowing that I have hurt her irrevocably.

My fairy, don't ever blame your ma for anything.

I wanted to know you, see you, hold you, but was scared. Scared to come back and see the resentment in your eyes. Scared at the prospect of seeing contempt on Disha's lovely face.

Forgive me, angel. Ask Disha to forgive me. Please scatter my ashes where our baby Adya took her last breath.

Your papa.

Srishti's brimming eyes spilled over. The veneer of control collapsed, as the tears grew into sobs. Sandhya watched for a few seconds, then put her arms around the tender twenty-one-year-old. When Srishti did not protest, she held her more firmly, like she would have held her own daughter. After two days of confused emotions and blankness, Srishti gave herself up to the comfort in Sandhya's arms. She was ready to go home to Disha.

III

The morning mist trapped the warmth of the sun. Srishti woke up with a start. Her feet reached for her slippers. She couldn't find them. Just then, somebody knocked on her door. When she opened it, she found Manohar standing outside with a tea tray.

"Kaka, I can't find my slippers."

"Like father, like daughter," said Manohar affectionately, keeping the tray on the side table. "Look on the other side. You must have taken them off there last night."

And indeed they were there. Kaka smiled indulgently at her and went away, asking her to come down for breakfast in half an hour.

Later that day, they made their way to the beach. Leaving the car on the road, both women walked down the beach barefoot, Sandhya holding the urn of Abhay's ashes. At a distance, Srishti could see the cottages where life had irrevocably changed for them seventeen years ago. She looked at the waves, a mixed bag of feelings permeating her senses. The moments that had altered the course of her family's life were frozen here.

Sandhya took her to a patch of rocks a little into the waves.

"This is where Abhay used to sit," she said. "He used to come every Sunday and just sit here, sometimes with me, sometimes alone. When he was here, he never cried. He was very still."

Srishti stared at the impatient waves. As she settled over the rocks, she was overwhelmed with the feeling that Abhay had suffered so much silently. She got up and took the urn from Sandhya's hands. She faced the sea, arms extended and closed her eyes for a few seconds. *Papa, this thought is for you. I love you, Papa.* Then carefully, she bent over the rocks and tilted the urn towards the hungry waves.

Almost at the same moment, a hand appeared below hers, cupping it in its palm. The touch was not a stranger's. She turned and saw Ma kneeling beside her, hands outstretched towards the urn.

They gave Abhay over to the sea. The grey ashes bobbed on the surface for a few seconds before sinking into oblivion. A few grey particles swirled back towards Disha, before they were carried afar again.

After they had kept the urn aside, Disha and Srishti sat back and watched the sea. They were still, very still, like Abhay had been.

COUPLE GOALS

When love begins to fray
In the mundane everyday
How does one begin to restore
What was, for today and evermore?

"Well, the long and short of it is, we got married two years ago, and it turned out to be the biggest mistake of our lives. So here we are, for the mandatory marital counselling session before we can mutually agree in court to put an end to our marriage."

Visibly irritated, Neha swiped through pictures on her phone, showing them to the lady sitting across her. In stark contrast to her mood, the pictures Neha was skimming through were beautiful. It was hard to believe that such a place existed on earth, that someone hadn't generously painted over a regular picture of a beach with magnificent blues and greens for the water to produce those stunning visuals. As Neha swiped through them one by one, the photos of a beautiful seaside resort showed up, complete with pools and cottages out on the waterfront.

"I can't think of anything I want to do less in the world right now than go here," Neha said.

She locked her phone and put it away on the table, facing downwards. Then moved it around a bit till she was satisfied it was placed perfectly. She looked up at the lady sitting on the couch facing her. Spectacles, but very obviously not with zero-powered lenses, lending a sort of impersonal touch. She wore a crisply ironed grey shirt and black trousers, the lack of colour matching the lack of any emotion on her face.

"The pictures look lovely though. Gramworthy, I think they're called nowadays?" commented the counsellor, smiling.

"Yeah, that's going to be a lot of fun, posing with that idiot. And that is if he manages to show up."

Neha gestured to the empty space beside her on the couch. Anish was late. As always. Neha began to tap her foot nervously on the floor, something that she often did when restless. She noticed the framed degrees hanging on the otherwise featureless walls behind the counsellor.

"SANGITA PENDSE, M.D."

A couple of medals and awards here and there, photos clicked at lectures and presentations, and the mandatory plant adorned the room. Everything was perfectly aligned and she couldn't find a single fault in the arrangement. Dr Pendse, however, kept looking at her with a half-smile, as Neha continued to beat a regular rhythm with her foot.

"How are you, Neha?" asked Sangita.

"I'm fine, absolutely fine, doctor. And besides, this is about both of us and our marriage, isn't it? Not about me…"

"True, but I don't see anyone else here, do I?" said Sangita gently.

Neha turned to look at her phone, but it was quiet; no long buzzes of a phone call, no short buzzes for texts explaining that Anish was "just a few minutes out". She wouldn't have been surprised if Anish had forgotten about this session.

"What should I say?" Neha asked.

"How about beginning by telling me about the situation you find yourself in, right now."

That was unexpected. Neha sat up in her seat and straightened her perfectly creased shirt.

"Well, we are completely different people with different personalities. He's very, very lax when it comes to his personal life, and I don't think he takes anyone seriously, or for that matter anything, aside from himself and his work priorities. It's really disrespectful ... and ... ummm ... insensitive."

Neha glanced at the phone by her side. It kept mocking her with its silence. Still no buzzing.

"And the thing is, I know that he chooses to be this way, because I've seen him at work, and on set. He's always sharp, never a minute here or there; nothing escapes him. People are actually on their toes around him at work because of how on-it he is."

"And were things always like this?"

"No. Things were great in the start. Of course, I understand that there is always the intoxication of a new romance that masks all conflict, isn't there? As much as we fought, things were really exciting in bed. And out of it."

Neha paused, unaware of the slight smile on her face.

"Now, however, it's really debilitating, and I just can't deal with it anymore. He knows how hard it's been for me growing up; I've always had to look out for others. I was completely drained, taking care of my mom all those years after Dad passed. He knows that sometimes even I need someone else to be responsible and look out for me for a change..."

Neha paused again. Her voice was quivering a little, but she held it all together with a deep breath.

Talking about Mom and growing up often did that to her.

Dr Sangita Pendse reached out for the tissue box kept within reach, but Neha raised her hand to gesture for her to not bother.

"How does Anish feel about this?" Sangita asked.

They were interrupted by a knock on the door.

Neha gritted her teeth, and subconsciously, her body stiffened. She was already prepared for the excuses to flow.

"Well, let's find out now, shall we?" asked Sangita.

*

Anish let himself in, breathing heavily, and rushing in with his characteristic sheepish smile.

"Hi, doc, sorry, sorry I'm late. I was video-calling my sister and she was trying to make me choose the backdrop for the wedding reception, asking me what colours would look best on camera for the video. Can you believe it? Had to take the stairs so the call wouldn't get cut."

"Not a problem, Anish, please have a seat," said Sangita, her lips betraying a hint of a smile.

Anish glanced at Neha, who looked straight ahead.

"Hi," he said, and sat down carefully at the other end of the couch.

It was as if suddenly, someone had spread an uncomfortable blanket of silence over the room, and Anish looked at Dr Pendse for some indication on how things were to proceed. He could sense the cold draught from the other end of the couch.

"So, Anish, Neha was showing me pictures of Krabi, where your sister's wedding is being held," said Sangita.

"Yeah! Quite insane, isn't it?"

Dr Pendse glanced at Neha, who was barely managing to keep her boiling anger under the lid. Anish realised that he had clearly missed out on a lot of the conversation.

"I mean yes, well. It's a beautiful place; that's why Anuja was so insistent we have it there."

"And are you looking forward to it?"

"Yeah, sure! I mean she's my baby sister. Okay, not such a baby obviously, but I'm excited about the wedding."

"And what are your thoughts about travelling with Neha?"

Again, that blanket of heavy silence made its presence felt. Anish felt a bit uncomfortable, not knowing what he had missed, and what Neha had said to Sangita before this.

"Yeah. So, Anuja is marrying this guy called Siddhant. His parents are pretty conservative even though he's super chilled out, but frankly no one in either of our families knows about the ... err ... problems we've been facing over the last two years. She's requested that we don't reveal anything to anyone till the wedding is over, because aside from my own parents, we don't quite know how Siddhant's parents would react to the thought of their son marrying the sister of a divorcee and all that typical rubbish. You know what I mean, right?"

"So basically, because of that 'typical rubbish,'" said Neha, forming air quotes around those words, her voice heavy with frustration and anger, "we are going to have to pretend to be a happy and deeply-in-love couple for the three days of the wedding."

"And why do you think you aren't this happily and deeply-in-love couple?" Dr Pendse looked at Anish for an answer.

"Look, doc, it's not like I don't have my flaws, but our relationship has just boiled down to her pointing them out to me again and again, and becoming a source of nagging and annoyance. I've explained that yeah I am sloppy and forgetful in my personal space, but that's only because life and work are honestly stressful enough. But no, she has to have it her way."

"What exactly do I have to have my way, Anish? When have I had my way in the last two years? Have you ever remembered anything I've asked you to do? Our anniversary for that matter? When *you want* to do something, you go ahead and do it. When *you want* to remember something, you remember it. *You want* to talk, you talk ... *you want* to remember to show up or show up on time, you do it..."

"How will it make a difference anyway? Because all you do, Neha, is nag me all the time like some nanny. When was the last time you appreciated anything I did at all?"

"When was the last time you did something for me worth appreciating, Anish?"

"All right! Time out now," Dr Pendse interjected.

Neha and Anish settled further into the very comfortable sofa, feeling a bit silly. They realised they had made a fool of themselves in front of the counsellor.

"So, yes, clearly we have unresolved issues here, which we can definitely work on, but considering that both of you find yourselves in this situation, how can we reach some sort of understanding so that the two of you have a peaceful few days in Krabi?"

Anish and Neha looked down like schoolchildren being ticked off. All of a sudden they were scared to say anything at all.

"Nothing like that, doctor, I've put up with this for two years. I think I can do three more days for Anuja."

"And when do you leave?" asked Dr Pendse.

"Late tonight."

*

The international terminal was a lively place for one a.m. Backpackers and people in formals were rubbing shoulders at the check-in lines, while hordes of people waited outside the terminal, watching their friends, family or loved ones depart.

Neha was making a mental checklist of essentials as she made her way towards the self-check-in counter, with her ticket and passport in hand. The hand sanitizer was accessible, her toothbrush was handy, and so was Anish's since he had predictably forgotten it at home.

"Neha! Come, come quick!" Suddenly Anuja caught hold of Neha's hand and pulled her towards a bunch of people whom she slowly recognised. Dipti and Shashank, her close friends. They were all smiles and holding up a phone to take a selfie. Neha sighed as she followed Anuja. The pretence had begun.

"Neha! So good to see you! Come quick," said Dipti, making way for Neha. Everyone adjusted their angles, and Shashank turned the camera just a bit, so that the light fell evenly across all their faces. Neha was acutely conscious of the attention they were drawing; after all they were at the check-in counters but behaving like they were outside a club. Where the hell was Anish?

"Wait, wait, wait!" Dipti exclaimed, and started pulling out something from her bag. Shashank grumbled to her about getting late for check-in, while Anuja gestured towards Neha asking where Anish was. Neha rolled her eyes and shrugged. Anuja sighed, put a hand on Neha's shoulder as if to say, it's okay. He'll make it.

"Here!" Dipti pulled out a tiara and a sash that said BRIDE-TO-BE in the brightest purple possible. Great, thought Neha. Even the people who hadn't been looking at the group before were doing so now. Anuja laughed and put it on, and Neha, in her office formals, looked rather out of place in the selfies that followed.

"Chudail! I can't believe you started off without me!" Anish's voice hit Neha like a punch in the back of the head, but as it turned out, he was talking to Anuja instead.

"Gadhe, any later and I would have had to take that flight without you."

"Hey guys, what's up, what's up..." Anish went around greeting Dipti and Shashank in his usual bro-hug style, and stood near Neha rather self-consciously, awkwardly pecking her on the cheek when he was sure that Dipti and Shashank were looking.

"Couldn't have come any later?" she whispered in his ears.

Anish gave her an irritated look, and turned around in defiance.

"Guys! There is a problem!"

"What?" asked Shashank.

Anish pulled out a half-filled bottle of Cafe Patron from his bag. It was Neha's favourite.

"We can't take this past security, can we?"

Shashank laughed and looked at Dipti and Anuja.

"Shots!" they shouted at the same time, pulled the already self-conscious Anuja towards them and started passing the bottle around. Dipti made it a point that all of them take suitably large gulps of the bottle. Neha was terrified that they would get caught but before they knew it, they were all well on their way to being very drunk indeed, and soon, on their way to Thailand as well.

*

As soon as they switched off the seatbelt sign, Anuja, who was sitting in the row in front of Neha and Anish, turned around and faced them, kneeling down on her seat.

"Anu, this better not bloody be you wanting to throw up now."

"Shut up, bhai, I'm fine, why are you whispering?"

Anish pointed to his side. Neha had fallen asleep already, and slowly, her head had slid down onto his shoulder. Anuja started laughing but controlled herself. She was still wearing the tiara on Dipti's insistence even though it had slipped halfway down her head several times by now. The alcohol had definitely kicked in.

"You guys look so cute together, you know?" Anuja slurred as she smiled.

"Anu, shut the hell up. I swear I would've punched you if I could move..."

Anuja laughed even harder but muffled it. Anish fumed but couldn't move, for fear of Neha waking up. The whole sight was too much for Anuja. She took out her phone and took a picture as Anish refused to pose and glared at her.

"Come on ya, bhai. Be nice. This one could make it to the album. You promised, no?"

Anish forced a smile, and made it a point to snap out of it as soon as he possibly could, once Anuja had taken her photos. Anuja hurriedly sat back down in her seat as she saw the airhostess gesturing towards her from the end of the aisle.

*

The pictures really didn't do Krabi much justice. It was even better than she had imagined, thought Neha, as they made it to their hotel room. Of course Anuja would have wanted to have the wedding here; she had always been a "beach bum" as Anish had put it. Anish dumped his bags in a corner and walked straight up to the French windows, spreading them wide open, and soaked in the sight of the vast expanse of water that their room looked out on.

"I don't remember the last time I saw the sea so clean..."

"Hmm..." said Neha, as she laid out her suitcases neatly and placed her shoes in a corner of the room. Three days, she thought. Just three days of this now. She glanced at him standing there in the balcony of their room and began organising their things. She kept his bags neatly next to hers.

"Your toothbrush. You had forgotten it at home. I'm leaving it near the sink."

"Hmm," he said, still rooted at the window. "Listen, there's this place here close by called the Emerald Pool which should really be seen in bright sunlight, so I'm going to head there now. It's in a forest."

Neha stared at him, incredulous. Could he not see what she was doing?

"Do ... you ... want to come?"

"No, Anish, I want to unpack, and settle in and make sure we're all set for this three-day performance we have to put up."

"Neha, we're not going to have any time later to check out the island. I'm just offering..."

"We're not here on a honeymoon, Anish, or some sightseeing trip..."

"I know that! Geez, would you chill for just a second?"

"I was perfectly 'chill' till you started talking nonsense. We have only three hours in which to rest and be ready for the evening."

Anish looked at her. It was always like this. She was just waiting to pounce on him. Nothing he said now would make anything better in any way. He turned on his heels, and walked out.

"Yeah, walk away, Anish! Like always. Easier that way than having nothing else to say, isn't it?" she said, struggling to keep her voice down.

She threw the hotel towel at the door he had already shut behind him, but as soon as she saw it fall to the floor she picked it back up, dusted it and hung it back on the towel rack.

Her tirade was interrupted by the buzzing of her phone by her bedside table.

Anuja had sent her a picture from the plane last night, and she wanted to punch Anish's stupid smiling face.

*

"He's here! Guys! Welcome shot for the brother of the bride!" said someone.

"And another one because he's late!" called another voice.

So much for wanting to make a quiet entrance. Before he knew it, Anish was surrounded by people he had never met before, and with more bottles of alcohol in his face than he usually stocked at home. Of course, he was more than happy to oblige. A whole evening of pretending to be deeply in love with his wife would need some liquid fortification.

"How nice of you to join us, did you get lost in the forest?"

Neha walked towards him once the crowd had cleared. *Here we go again,* he thought. But wow, did she look stunning in that beautiful dress! The emerald green of the skirt against the sands bathed in gold from the lamps close by was offset by the smooth bronze of her skin. It actually looked like the perfect shot.

Anish shook the thought out of his head. Was the alcohol kicking in already?

"For your information, the forest was amazing. I'd show you pictures but you're clearly more interested in folding bedsheets and unpacking toothbrushes."

"Play nice boys and girls!" Anuja said from behind, walking up to them. Siddhant was with her, and greeted Anish with a huge hug.

"So good to see you, bro. I see my friends got to you before I did..." he said, gesturing to Anish's welcoming committee who had found themselves another victim in the distance.

"Well, it's good to see them having fun before all the parents arrive tomorrow," said Anish, glaring at Neha.

"Bhai, can I borrow you for a bit? Cool thanks," said Anuja, pulling Anish to the side before he had a chance to respond.

"What's wrong with you?" she asked him, in a tone that was a complete contrast to how she was speaking a minute ago.

"What?"

"You guys are supposed to act like everything is okay, right?"

"Yeah, that's what I'm doing, in case you hadn't noticed. What do you expect me to do? Snog every time someone looks our way?"

"Shut up, bro. I'm not talking about Neha. I'm talking about you."

"What about me?"

Anuja glared at him, making her smoky-eye makeup really pop. She could shut him up like no one else.

Anish walked over to Neha with two rather dangerously proportioned and filled-out shot glasses.

"Really?" Neha commented.

"What really, one is for you..."

"What? No please. I've had enough yesterday. This is turning into some sort of music festival weekend scene," grumbled Neha.

"Look. We've been asked to put on a show, right? Let's just make it a damn good one for Anuja, okay?"

Neha rolled her eyes and sighed. The music grew louder as everyone started hitting the dance floor. Anish joined in, playing referee for a dance-off between the bride's side and the groom's side. Neha, too, was not one to be left behind for once, Anuja and she putting on a real challenge for Siddhant's side, with Anish following suit. Anuja, ever the clever one, pushed Anish and Neha close together, and for a few brief moments, they were lost in the music, the flow. They closed their eyes, shutting out the noise; for a while they were oblivious to the world.

As the night wore on, the crowd thinned out. Slowly Siddhant and Anish helped the few overenthusiastic drinkers back to their rooms, while simultaneously poking fun at each other's drunkenness.

"I don't know how much time I will have with you these next two days, bro, but I'm so glad you guys came so early on. Can't tell you how much it means..." Siddhant was slurring, but still very coherent.

"And, cue ... tears on three ... two ... one..."

"Brooooo," slurred Siddhant.

The two of them laughed at each other once again, and with some considerable difficulty found their way back to their rooms. Just as Siddhant was about to head into his, he stopped Anish and gave him a hug.

"Bro, it's damn inspiring to see you two still so into each other man. I was scared, but like, it's possible, right? Happily ever after happens, right? Like the ever-after part of it?"

Anish stood in the silent hallway of the hotel, knowing that just a few doors away he was probably going to have another argument with his wife as soon as he walked in.

"It does, bro. It does..." he said reassuringly.

Neha was fast asleep when he entered the room. Anish tried to be as quiet as possible, and tiptoed around.

He entered the bathroom, and found that his toothbrush, favourite cologne, and shaving kit were right there. As he stared at himself in the mirror he wondered if he had been stupid in telling Siddhant what he did. Two more days, he thought. Just two days.

While her head was buried deep inside the pillow and her eyes were shut, Neha wasn't asleep at all. She lay down on the bed with her shoes on, to make it look like she had passed out. She just wasn't in the mood to talk to Anish, or even look at him for that matter. She waited patiently for him to turn in, but then she felt her shoes coming off. One by one.

Really, Anish? she wondered silently.

She watched with her barely open eyes as he placed them neatly by the side of the wall, and then turned off the light. Whatever it was, it was just two more days.

*

Neha opened her eyes in the morning to find her arms around Anish. She was quite alarmed, but moved gingerly to avoid waking him up. She pulled away, but got a hangover pill and kept it by his bedside.

Smoothly done, she thought. If they could avoid each other like this, the next couple of days could pass by without any incident. In a rather cheerful mood, despite being a little heavy-headed, she made a coffee and before she knew it, she was out of the room, and on the way to the banquet hall of the hotel for the mehendi ceremony, right on time.

But right outside the hall, she felt her phone buzz with a message.

It was Mom.

A few hugs and smileys, and then: *Thanks for arranging the health check-up, beta. Just done. Hope the Crab Island is fun with Anish! Love, Maa.*

Neha squirmed at the second part.

Krabi, Maa, Krabi. And yeah, all is good. Love and hugs.

Fun with Anish? If wishes were horses, and all that...

*

The hall was beautifully decorated with flowers all round, and their fragrance filled the air with an aroma that made everyone forget about their hangovers for some time. As they got closer to the front end, the smell of mehendi became more and more pronounced. Anuja looked resplendent in an elegant silk sari. Her parents had finally made it, and looked tired, but beaming with happiness at the sight of Neha.

She touched their feet, and they embraced.

"*Jeeti reh, beta*! Where is that nalayak?" asked Maa-ji.

"*So raha hoga, aur kya?*" said Anish's father.

"I'm not surprised ... Anuja was showing us the pictures from last night's party," said Maa-ji

"Yes, Maa-ji, it was a lot of fun, we really did miss you and Dad..." said Neha.

"Oh, nonsense. These beachside parties are all for your lot."

Neha had always loved Anish's parents, reminding her of the family that she had yearned for so much her entire life. Acutely aware of how silly and immature their son could be, they had treated her very well indeed. She would miss them a little bit, she thought.

"Come, beta, let's get some colour on those hands now, yes?" Anish's mother pulled her away.

*

"And a five, six, five six seven eight and one two three four five six seven eight ... yes! You guys are getting the hang of it now..."

The choreographer was being especially strict with them. None of Anuja's friends and family were trained dancers, and there were barely a few hours to go before they would be on stage.

Still standing like a scarecrow to ensure the mehendi did not get smudged, Anuja bellowed, "Come on, guys, we can't let Siddhant's side win. You guys will go home after this but I'll have to listen to him rub it in for the rest of my life, okay?"

Anish and Neha were standing together right at the back, trying their best to not be seen, and also to avoid eye contact with each other as much as possible. They stood around awkwardly, as a familiar song started playing.

"Shit," said Neha as she recognised the song.

"Yeah, do you remember?"

Of course she did. "*Roop tera mastana*", the same song they had danced to on their own wedding sangeet together. Anish looked to Anuja across the room with an expression that said he would punch her face if he could. She just shrugged as if to say, what are you going to do about it?

"Listen, do you think if we just do the steps properly he'll let us go soon?" asked Neha.

"Yeah, let's try," said Anish, pulling Neha by the hand towards the front of the room. They started moving with the rhythm. Both of them somehow had it nailed down to perfection. Right foot over left, the cross, the hand catch and pull. The twirl and arm wrap, followed by the spin in the air. The perfect landing, the switch of hands as he held her at the small of her back, and pulled her back up for the final pose. As they stared awkwardly at each other for a second before breaking away, they realised they had lost track of the hooting and cheering and clapping. Anuja looked on with happiness, and the choreographer took off his Yankee's baseball cap and bowed in acknowledgement.

"Okay, so we know the steps, you think we can go now?" Neha asked sheepishly. She wasn't used to being the centre of attention in a room.

"Go now? Hell no, Ma'am! You and Sir are killing it, so you're going to help me teach it to everyone else here!"

Neha gave Anish the death stare.

*

But kill it, they did. Later that night, the "side of the bride", as the extremely enthusiastic anchor had called them, put up a great show. Siddhant joined towards the end of their performance and brought everyone else as well. Anish was being his usual popular and entertaining self, choosing to dance with all the aunties and becoming the darling child of the wedding. Anuja and Siddhant were shining, looking radiant together, and just for a moment, Anish looked at them from afar, putting his own problems with Neha aside, and felt a tinge of nostalgia. His baby sister, kiddo, was leaving for good.

But the moment didn't last too long. The infamous "welcoming committee" had pulled him to the floor and put him in front of Neha again. Damn, he thought, she really did look beautiful in the sari, looking up at him like she was asking a question with her eyes. As he tried to shake the thought away, they started playing their song once again, and shouts of "Once More! Once More!" rang in the air.

And once more, they nailed it.

His hand on her waist, he pulled her close, with everyone hooting and cheering and laughing, timed with her long and wavy hair swaying around and covering his face. He pulled her in with the twirl, and then the pose at the end, when she leaned on him and he held her. Their faces were so close, they felt each other breathing.

And for just a moment, their lips touched.

They jumped apart as they became conscious of everything around them. The hoots grew louder, but Anish and Neha didn't speak to each other for the rest of the night. As the parents, uncles and aunts slowly left the venue, the music grew louder, and the party went on.

*

As Neha supported a swaying Anuja on her shoulder in the hallway, Anuja kept calling out to Anish, and calling him a fool.

"Anu, you want to throw up? Not here, Anu, we are almost in your room," said Neha.

"No! I'm fine. I just want you to listen to me," insisted Anuja.

Neha looked around to make sure no-one was around. The bride being a drunken mess in the deserted hallway of the hotel was not going to be a pretty picture.

"Yeah, sure, Anu, can we go to your room and talk?"

"No! Sis, please. Let me speak here," Anuja pleaded.

The childishness didn't surprise Neha. Anuja and Anish were siblings after all.

"Okay. Sure. What's up?"

"I know I've never said this enough to you, sis, but you've inspired me, always," Anuja mumbled.

Neha was still on the lookout, but saw that Anuja had sort of steadied herself against the wall and was standing up straight.

"But like, the way you are, the way you've been brought up, the way you've taken care of your mother alone..." Anuja continued. "You know, before you guys got married, I used to think that there was something definitely fishy about you. Like, how can someone be so damn perfect all the time and so nice and so good at heart? Like, you know, how Bhai says, black in the lentils and all?"

Anuja sat down on the floor, and Neha sat down next to her. The mehendi had almost completely flaked away, and the design on her hands was vivid and dark. Neha wondered if there would be any lemon and sugar in Anuja's room to apply through the night and make it pop even more in the morning.

"But I don't know, sis, you really are that nice, you really are that person."

Anuja got up slowly with the help of the wall, and Neha was springing up like a dart, ready to support her.

"I want Siddhant and me to be like the two of you..."

"Shut up, Anu. Why would you want to curse your marriage the night before the pheras?"

"I mean it, sis! You guys are awesome, really awesome, and really good for each other. Like the whole world can see it, except you two ... So yeah, I want us to be like the two of you, but definitely not so stupid that we can't see it."

Anuja started laughing, but seeing Neha's sad face, stifled her laughter.

"Sorry, sis. I've said too much." They stood facing each other, awkwardly silent.

"Hey, come here, let's hug it out, okay?" said Anuja as she nearly fell on Neha in an embrace.

"I love you, sis..." Anuja whispered.

Anuja broke away and started walking back to her room. Neha began to follow her.

"No! You go. I'll find my way and you find yours." Anuja laughed as she skipped towards her door. Neha stood right there, in the now silent hallway.

*

Siddhant had warned them that the baraat would take its own sweet time.

"Should we check for next year's mahurat then?" Anish had joked.

But Anish and Neha certainly weren't laughing now. They'd been waiting for an hour while the dholaks from the baraat seemed to come closer to the hall at a snail's pace, but of course, everyone was all smiles, and so were they, for all the relatives to see.

The kids at the wedding were sent with messages to the baraat to hurry, as they were running out of time.

"I wonder if they have it all figured out, stealing Siddhant's slippers and everything..." Anish said, but Neha was tight-lipped. One more day to go through with this act.

"I'll go check on Anu," he said.

"Hmm..." said Neha.

As Neha stood there waiting, Siddhant came closer into view. He was beaming with happiness; even under the heavy turban, it was evident. But something else caught Neha's attention; he was wearing a very familiar sherwani.

It was the same one Anish had worn on their wedding day.

Neha's jaw dropped. This couldn't have been a coincidence.

"Looks familiar?" Anish's mother winked at Neha, and made her way to the entrance to get ready for all the greetings.

But Neha was thrown back to two years ago. Anish had looked so handsome that day. She remembered wanting to hold his hand, and not leave his side at all. Just the sight of him that day had made her smile uncontrollably. Even the photographers didn't have to ask her to be more "cheesy".

In Anuja's room, Anish was reliving the same moment as well.

Anuja was in the same deep red-and-gold lehenga he had seen on Neha on their wedding day. He had come to ask her if everything was alright, but there she was, his little sister, and he remembered all he had felt that same day in his own life. He knew she had been sneaky with this, and planned it all along. He would've been so annoyed with her on any other occasion.

But right now, a tear made its way down the side of his face.

"Bro, what the hell is wrong with you?" Anuja laughed out loud.

"Huh? I … nothing. Is everything okay?"

"I should be asking you that," Anuja sniggered. "How do I look?" she asked twirling around.

"A lot like the most beautiful woman I know…"

Anuja smiled, and winked at him, before making her way to the mandap.

*

It was uncanny, like reliving that entire experience. The pheras, the jokes they cracked while taking their vows, the sneaky handholding that went on, on the mandap, between the two of them, even the way Anuja and Siddhant were whispering to each other.

Anish and Neha stood side by side, and it wasn't forced. Here, at the dusk of their marriage they were seeing its sunrise being replayed before their very eyes. They weren't even aware of their tiredness any more, and time seemed to have stood still. Their fake smiles were gone, and they just took in all they could there.

It was going to be their last day together now after all … Wasn't it?

Everyone cried at the bidaai, but Anuja held on to Neha in an embrace the longest.

As the happy couple made their way back to the hotel in their rather subtly decorated car, all of Siddhant's friends came to say their goodbyes with promises to connect and keep in touch.

Anish's parents were in tears. Neha wanted to hug them and console them. She remembered her mother being inconsolable on the day of her wedding, but she thought, better not to. It was time for them to go.

Back in the room, Anish and Neha were silent. She sat on the bed. She should've been relieved, but she wasn't. Anish walked around the room uncomfortably, and then chose to stand outside, taking in the last views of the sea. Change was coming; he could feel it.

He walked back inside, and saw that Neha hadn't started to pack, let alone even mentioned it. He began to tidy up the things around the room. His shoes went into the laundry bags from the hotel, and were swallowed up by his suitcase. His dirty clothes that were dumped in a corner were all rolled up and sectioned off in bags to be packed into his suitcase.

"Can I pack your shoes too? I have some space."

Through the surprise she found herself nodding.

"This body wash that you've brought along, it's almost over. Can I just leave the bottle here?"

"Sure."

"And I'll wipe the shampoo bottle after..."

"Anish!"

He looked at her. For two people so hopelessly tied up in emotional knots, their voices were somewhat lacking in passion.

"Just stop, okay?"

"What? I'm just packing everything..."

"No! Enough. There's no need to."

"What? What is wrong with you? You're the one who is so insistent and suddenly when I'm doing..."

She got up from the bed and faced him. Her eyes were red, and had welled up with tears. Anish was silent. The only sound that broke the stillness was her heels falling from his hand. They looked at each other. She did look so beautiful in that sari, and he didn't feel like shaking that thought from his head.

They came closer together. And before they knew it, their lips were locked together. He pulled her in closer and she ruffled his hair as their bodies, so comfortable with each other, closed the gap between them.

It was all too familiar, and they had been there before. The fights and the fiery lovemaking that followed and masked all their irritation.

But this was different. Tears rolled down his face on to hers as they continued to hold each other. They could feel each other's heartbeats. She nestled her head on to his neck, her favourite spot in the whole world, she used to call it. Her hair tickled his nose, as they breathed in and out together, holding on to each other tightly, but also their memories.

*

Siddhant and Anuja made their way to the reception the next morning, rather worried.

"Did you see them at breakfast?" he asked her.

"No! They didn't make their flight either, I checked. God knows what's going on," said Anuja.

"Ah, yes, Ma'am, err … Miss Aaahnujaa?"

"Mrs," corrected Anuja with a smile.

"Ah, yes of course! There was a note for you left here," said the receptionist.

Anuja snatched the note from the receptionist's hand.

"*Dear Anuja,*" she read out loud. It was beautiful cursive writing. Had to be Neha. "*I'm sorry. Anish and I won't be making it to the reception tomorrow. We have a little honeymoon of our own to make it to, Love, your best big sis.*"

HELLO, GOODBYE

What was it about her
You saw that eluded me
That her heart was clear
And that I could not see

Sonam Kapadia sat alone in a corner booth of Café Chiaroscuro, the mellow rays of the setting sun casting a warm glow on her face. She twirled the silver ring on her finger idly, her eyes vacant and mind burdened with a thousand thoughts. It was a small diamond, much smaller than the one on her earrings even, but it was the one Suyash had bought her with the payout from his first major contract.

That was twenty years ago.

The air was thick with the smell of freshly brewed coffee and baked bread, though their usual allure was lost on her today. As she gazed out nervously at the sea of faces on the other side of the glass windows of the café, her daydream was interrupted by a message from Ahana, her daughter.

All okay? Please keep us updated, waiting anxiously. x

Waiting for Divya, she texted back. Then added: *And Ankush?*

Here, came the swift reply.

At eighteen, her daughter Ahana was the light in her life. Strong and independent and used to growing up in the absence of her entrepreneur father, sometimes she made Sonam wonder how she had raised such a wonderful and bright girl. Sixteen-year-old Ankush, however, was a different story, choosing the most unruly ways to live out his rebellious teenage years. Sonam had begun to feel that the absence of a father figure ever present through his formative years was beginning to show its effects. Today, she feared that absence would only grow, perhaps indefinitely.

It had been a week since Sonam had received a call informing her of the same over a muffled voice on the phone.

"One crore, randomly numbered notes, all in cash, no police," was the demand, and it had shaken her to the bone. Not because it was a huge amount of money – the Kapadia textile business had been flourishing for some time – but because of the shock that something she had thought happened to people only in films, had happened to her husband. When Suyash hadn't come home the previous night, Sonam had thought nothing of it; he had often worked late into the night and had, in the last few years, been treating his home like he would a hotel. Often, just coming in to shower or sleep, he saw less and less of his wife and children. Sonam had come from wealth, but he had not. She had often wondered if it was this hunger and ambition that made him work incessantly, more than would be required to provide his family with a comfortable lifestyle.

But alas, it wasn't all because of his work. Today, she was waiting for the woman her husband loved.

Her eyes darted towards the entrance to the café as a gust of wind nudged the door open. She caught a glimpse of Divya, the woman who had lived in the shadows of her family life for years, now cast into the light by a cruel twist of fate. Divya carried a bag that held more than just cash; it was filled with the key to Suyash's freedom.

Sonam studied her with a sense of dread and curiosity. She noted Divya's slender frame, her sharp features softened by the gentle evening light. The woman was indeed beautiful, in a delicate, ethereal way. Sonam felt a pang of insecurity, the painful memory of the day she discovered Suyash's infidelity resurfacing.

She had found a hidden stash of love letters and photographs, and it was the raw emotion in Suyash's words that had stung the most. A passion long lost from their marriage, discovered anew in another woman. Doubling her antidepressants and the odd anxiety pill didn't help. She knew she had hit rock bottom when Ahana offered to start yoga classes with her in the mornings. Was she already being mothered by her own daughter?

Perhaps it was something every woman in her phase of life had to deal with, a lack of relevance as her children grew up and out of needing her constant presence in their lives; Ankush had made it clear to her several times. But to see that she was no longer the one her husband wanted, while she had built her world around his, was one pill she could not swallow. But all of that had to take a backseat. The ransom call made her turn to the one woman she did not want to interact with, Divya. Having been his assistant for more than a decade, she knew the ins and outs of the company, and had become his right-hand woman in running Kapadia Textiles.

Divya slid into the seat opposite Sonam, her eyes showing a mixture of defiance and apprehension. She looked older, the stress lines etching deep grooves on her youthful face. She clutched her bag a little tighter, her knuckles pale.

"Hi Sonam, are you doing all right?" Divya asked, seeing and knowing that Sonam wasn't.

"I'm fine, thanks for asking," said Sonam, "and thank you for taking charge of doing this for us."

Divya had been tasked with finding the funds within the company, and making the largest cash withdrawal in their history without drawing too much suspicion.

"Sonam," Divya began, her voice trembling slightly, "there's something you should know about the company."

Sonam stiffened. This woman had snatched away her husband's affection, and now she had the audacity to patronise her about his business? But before Sonam could retort, the shrill ring of the phone sliced through the awkward silence. It was an unknown number, and when Sonam answered, it was the same muffled voice that had sent a chill down her spine a week ago.

"The construction site behind the parking lot of the Palladium Mall. You have eight minutes..."

The gravity of their situation started sinking in. Sonam felt her mind swirling with dreadful scenarios, and her heart started racing. This was what happened in the movies, and it seldom ended well in them. She was sure this wouldn't end well in real life either.

Divya, in contrast, exhibited an unexpected determination, snatching the phone from a stunned Sonam's hand.

"Wait!" she said to the voice.

"Who are you? I said nobody else!"

Sonam was livid. Was Divya going to put her husband's life at risk by sabotaging this?

"No police," she said, feigning confidence. "I am Suyash's assistant who got the funds from the company," she continued, avoiding Sonam's glare as she introduced herself.

"What do you want? I said eight minutes!"

"I need to hear Suyash's voice, how do I know if you even have him with you?"

There was a long silence at the other end of the line, and Divya feared she had made a deadly mistake. She put the phone on speaker, and held it out in front of Sonam, who was still in a state of paralysed shock.

The next voice they heard was Suyash's. His voice was weak, but the underlying emotion was unmistakable. "Sonam..." he said, and the name hung in the air like a plea, a testament to their shared history.

Divya's grip on the phone tightened, her knuckles whitening. The mention of Sonam's name sent a shockwave through her. She had known, of course, that Suyash would never leave his wife and family, but hearing him call out to Sonam with such raw vulnerability felt like a punch to her gut.

Sonam, meanwhile, sat in shocked silence, the situation playing out in front of her like a bad dream. Her husband had been kidnapped, his life hanging in the balance, and here she was, relying on the woman he had cheated on her with to secure his freedom.

As the call ended, Divya looked at Sonam. For the first time since she entered the café, she saw not the scorned wife of her lover, but a fellow woman ensnared in a complicated web spun by the man they both loved. She took a deep breath, her decision to leave Suyash and his world behind cemented further by the heartfelt plea in his voice when he had called out to Sonam.

"You need to go, Sonam, we don't have much time," said Divya, an urgency in her voice as she handed Sonam the phone and the heavy bag she had been carrying.

"Aren't … you coming with me?"

"No, Sonam. You heard him, you have to go alone. If I come and he suspects that I'm a policewoman in plainclothes, or anything like that … Suyash…"

Of course. Even in times of crisis, Divya could think straight. It had always been one of the things that Sonam had admired about Suyash. She really had become so dependent…

"Okay … Thank you, Divya…"

Before Divya turned to leave, she handed a white envelope to Sonam. "After things go smoothly."

"I'll hand it to him," said a confused Sonam.

"No, Sonam, it's for you," said Divya, struggling hard to keep her voice even, before she left the café in a hurry.

*

The construction site was abandoned. The workers had left their shift just minutes ago. Sonam felt extremely uncomfortable. The sun was setting in the sky and the dust and mud from the terrain she found herself in were all over her feet and the bottom of her dress. Her hand was already a little tired from carrying the heavy bag of notes. Strange, she thought, she didn't actually know what carrying around a crore of rupees physically felt like. She couldn't care less though, as she began to look around for signs of Suyash, or a black car that would perhaps show up mysteriously...

As if to answer her thoughts, her phone rang, almost startling her into dropping the bag.

"Leave it there," the voice on the phone said.

Sonam began to look frantically around her. How she wished she had Divya's presence of mind right now. The light was fading as she tried to look for signs of Suyash.

"Where is my husband?" she demanded.

"In the parking lot you just came out of. Bay 58."

Sonam didn't have to be told twice. She did exactly as she was told, and ran as fast as her expensive flats would allow her across the muddy construction site. She sprinted across into the parking lot, almost drawing the attention of the security guards, and began frantically looking for signs directing her to number 58.

There, in the golden hue of a Mumbai winter sunset, she found Suyash. His face, usually so full of confidence and vigour, was pale and drawn, eyes heavy with fear and relief, and a gag over his mouth to stop him from screaming. He was sitting on the floor, his hands and feet tied together, but more importantly, he seemed unharmed.

The sight of Sonam brought tears to his eyes, as she embraced him, frantically untying the knots and freeing his arms and legs. She didn't know how long they held that embrace.

"Are you okay?" asked Sonam, battling through her tears.

"Yes," he said. "Don't worry, love, I'm fine, and you? The kids?"

Sonam instantly pulled out her phone and dialled her daughter's number. Ahana answered almost instantly.

Sonam watched as Suyash tearfully spoke to his children, and remembered the note that Divya had handed her. Something in her told her to open it then and there, and she couldn't resist.

> If you're reading this note, I didn't have the time to explain it to you in person. I wanted you to know that the company is not doing as well as it may seem. The money that you used to pay for Suyash's freedom was not from

the company at all; the company has no money to spare. We are barely breaking even at the moment. Suyash was afraid of looking like a failure to you and the kids, and so he never told you any of this. A few years ago, when the company was doing well, Suyash invested some of the money into a few apartments, and he transferred the ownership of one of them to me last year. It is a lot less than what the flat was worth, but we needed the cash and I had no choice. It was for Suyash.

But this is for you. I know that I've caused you pain, but I don't want to. I know Suyash will never leave you for me, and I can't live as "the other woman". I'm leaving this life behind, and your lives as well.

I'm sorry for the inadvertent hurt.

Divya...

As the words washed over her, Sonam felt a heavy silence envelop her. The woman she had once despised for her beauty and charm had shown courage and selflessness beyond comprehension. It was as if a veil had been lifted from her eyes, revealing Divya not as the "other woman", but as a saviour, a woman bound to her by the threads of love, sacrifice, and an unexpected camaraderie.

Dusk had swiftly given way to night. In that quiet parking lot, under the watchful gaze of the rising moon, Sonam held the note. The echoes of the past still lingered, but they were slowly drowned out by a newfound respect for the woman who had unshackled herself from the chains of love and duty to save a man who could never truly be hers.

"Sonam ... Sonam!" said Suyash, his voice shaking her out of her reverie.

He handed her phone back to her, as she embraced him once again. She had missed this feeling of his presence so dearly.

"Can we go home?" he asked softly in her ear.

"Yes ... Yes I want to go home..."

INSANE AND ABLE

Condemning her to hell
With her wrath he did not reckon
He'd have done well
To remember a woman scorned

Anjana had all the time in the world now to reflect and philosophise. In fact she really had nothing better to do, for her beseeching, crying and bouts of hysterical insistence that she was normal had left everyone at the asylum unmoved. If anything, it had made the doctors and attendants over there even more convinced that she was indeed a mental patient. For all of them knew with experience that every lunatic genuinely believes that his is the sole voice of sanity in an otherwise loony world and thus he makes sure that this voice is heard. In just a few days here Anjana had realised this and had therefore stopped remonstrating.

Forced to be a quiet observer, Anjana had also stumbled upon another ironic realisation – that true happiness was to be found only in the minds of the insane. The insane, who were the sole inhabitants of their own private universes, did not depend on other people for their happiness. Sane people who did were more often than not unhappy. Going by the same logic, Anjana was completely unhappy, and therefore completely sane. She was surer of this fact in the asylum than she had ever been in the world of the sane outside.

Anjana bit her lip at the thought of how much easier she had made Vishwa's task. That's what landed her here today ... her constant and honest admissions of feelings of inadequacy and inferiority when she had been with him. She looked all around her, as if to belie the disbelief she felt even now at having landed here.

Except for her, each one of the eleven inhabitants of the dorm were fast asleep. The pale moonlight streaming in shafts through the two windows seemed to bounce around the room, reflected by the cream-coloured night suits that each of the women wore.

Ever since Anjana had passed out of boarding school, she had never imagined that she would have to spend a night in a dormitory again. For she had married soon after and this was hardly the sort of place one would associate with a woman who had a husband and a child.

Yet here she was, in the prison of the mind, where sleep had eluded her every single night in these last few weeks, just like it had today. By now she had even lost track of time – it simply stretched in a vast endless sea in front of her, marked only by the ripples of her constant incomprehension at how and why her world had fallen apart in this last year.

It was just about a year ago that she had returned home from hospital with her newborn son Arush. She had hoped so much that Arush would be able to bring colour to their pale lives as a couple and that they would help them finally feel like a family. Arush had made her feel so wanted. He was the first human being who made his preferences for her so loud and clear that she felt like the most desirable woman on earth.

In those early few weeks it had seemed that she was nothing except a mother. A feeling she had smugly accepted until that fateful afternoon when she realised that her motherhood had come at a price.

Anjana had just started nursing three-week-old Arush. She could hear her sister Gudiya, who had come from Bangalore to be with her for a few weeks after her delivery, clearing the vessels in the kitchen after lunch. She herself was sinking into a delicious nap even as Arush continued to suckle at her breast. She was vaguely aware that she must soon sit up and hold Arush upright to make him burp, but sleep overtook her. And it was only when she felt a sticky wet feeling on her chest that she awoke suddenly.

Arush had thrown up his feed and spluttered helplessly in his own vomit. A panic-stricken Anjana picked him up and ran, shouting for help, towards the spare bedroom which Gudiya had been given.

She burst the door open and stood transfixed. A naked Vishwa strode upon Gudiya, making love to her as she moaned with pleasure. Anjana screamed and ran back to her room. She put Arush on the bed and stared at him. He had recovered by himself and showed only telltale signs around his mouth of the mess he had made.

Anjana wiped him vigorously – almost as though she were wiping away from her mind the scene that she had just seen. But that was not to be. For the more she tried, the more the import of what she had seen that afternoon sank in.

Now it all made sense to her. Gudiya preferring to manage Anjana's house rather than attend to her when she was in hospital, the indulgent glances that Vishwa gave his sister-in-law, her insistence on serving Vishwa his meals fresh and hot. It was not Gudiya's girlish enthusiasm for living up to responsibilities. It was Gudiya's discovery of passion with Vishwa. The lust of a polio-afflicted girl who had not been able to find a timely and legitimate outlet for her desires for want of a suitable groom.

After the initial shock, Anjana came to terms with the fact that she might be able to forgive Gudiya her sin. She was so young after all, and more importantly she was her own kin. It was Vishwa she found more difficult to forgive – firstly for being a man and therefore more in control of the situation, and secondly for the timing and object of the deceit.

Forgiveness as an issue however did not even arise, as Anjana was soon to learn after the discovery. For having discovered a certain magic of passion together, and already having been damned for it, Vishwa and Gudiya together decided that they did not need Anjana's lifelong martyrdom. They needed instead to have her out of the way, in order to rework their future together – after all, everything was fair in love and war. And this was both! And so it was due to their efforts that Anjana was at the asylum today.

It was amazing how quickly Vishwa had been able to medically certify Anjana's "madness". If she chose to remain silent as to the cause of her prolonged postnatal depression, the doctors would concur with Vishwa that she was in chronic and therefore dangerous depression. And if she took the risk, as she did on two occasions, to reveal the double betrayal as the cause of her shattered feelings, she was marked out as a hallucinating schizophrenic. Either way, Vishwa and Gudiya walked away with all the sympathy, for having to manage her poor son Arush, who now had to be kept away from a "dangerous" mother. It was therefore decided by professional opinion that Anjana should best be kept confined in the interest of both mother and child.

*

Oh, how Anjana ached for Arush, whose birth had brought nothing but trauma in its wake for her. How she longed to hold him upright as she used to and feel the soft down of his head as he chewed her shoulder to indicate his hunger. How she longed for him to grab at her breast and drain her until she felt as dry and thirsty as an Indian summer.

Anjana opened the first two buttons of her nightshirt and ran her hands over her breasts to relive the sensations that she had just been thinking about. But her touch was like an insult to them and made her feel even more barren than before. Not only was it impossible to come anywhere near what the real thing had been, it also made her cringe and feel ashamed of herself. What if someone saw what she was doing at this moment? They might be justified in concluding that she was really loony. A lunatic who had to satisfy her ache to be touched by feeling up her own self.

Anjana recalled her last few days at home. In Gudiya's eyes she had rarely seen the guilt of helpless want. She also still had too many memories of Gudiya as the pathetic little sister of her maternal family that overshadowed the justifiable hatred she felt for her now. Anjana realised that she wanted no vengeance on her own flesh and blood, beyond denying her the one whom she wrongfully lusted for.

But Vishwa? A man who had fed like a vulture on one sister's faith and another's vulnerability? His words to the doctor still rang in her ears and burned them. "Imagine the crazy insinuations she makes. She's certainly a mental case to talk about her own sister like that. She just doesn't know what she says and does," he had said, admitting her here.

Anjana wished for the nth time that he would die as horrifically as ready meat for the vulture whose soul she knew he actually possessed. And he deserved no mercy, for his meat was certainly not the same as her own flesh and blood. If only she would get one chance to wreak vengeance on him today she would do so. What stopped her was not a fear of punishment. It was only a lack of opportunity. For now she had nothing more left to lose anyway. Nothing much, except missing knowing her baby Arush growing up.

Would Arush ever know the truth about her? Anjana certainly hoped so. She did not know how, but someday, somehow, she did want to be able to tell him everything. It was the one hope that refused to die in her pining breast. She could not afford to die, if only for Arush and his future alone.

Anjana pulled the sheet up to her neck and shut her eyes. But shutting off the world did not drive away the quiet desperation that was now her constant companion. She soon opened her eyes, got up from the bed and walked to the small window to the left of her bed. She felt the breeze caress her face and teasingly ruffle her coarse hair as though it was attempting to break the morbid stillness of her life. The pages of the calendar fluttered with a crackle and then settled again. Anjana looked at the picture of

Gandhi-ji – his toothless, beatific grin looking in her direction, and her eyes fell on the words printed at the bottom of the picture. "Find purpose and the means will follow". Easier said than done, thought Anjana, but true nevertheless. She would have to find a focus if she was to last out until Arush came of age, and she would have to find it fast.

Anjana searched hard and found it soon enough. Found it in fact the very next morning in the form of Snehlata Deshpande's new scheme for the women inmates at the asylum.

Snehlata had been appointed the warden of the asylum only two months ago. Known for her radical thinking, she had declared to all those associated with the place that she believed in finding positive solutions to the most pressing practical problems they were having there. Now she had found one to solve the perennial problem that the asylum faced in attracting staffers to do the poorly paid labour-intensive jobs in running the place. If the inmates themselves could be guided to do the jobs, it would not only keep them fruitfully occupied but also help them earn some money.

Snehlata gathered all the thirty-five inmates of the home in the courtyard one morning and explained her plan. She announced that she would guide and review their work and also make sure that the money they earned was put aside in their accounts, which they could either give their dependents, or save up for themselves to use when they left the asylum to face the world outside.

For most of them gathered there, Snehlata's rehabilitation plan was just a new rule they would have to follow. It was only Anjana who walked up to her, her eyes full of gratitude and appreciation, for the focus that the plan had just given her life. Snehlata, taken aback by Anjana's intelligent response, only stared hard at Anjana. Something unspoken passed between the two of them that moment and a bond was formed.

Snehlata knew that Anjana was not like everyone else. And in the forthcoming weeks she was vindicated in what she had felt at that moment, without even once discussing it openly with her. Anjana came to be entrusted by Snehlata with the most trustworthy job at the asylum – that of running the kitchen. In no time at all she took it over completely. From morning until dusk, Anjana rushed about, chopping, cooking, cleaning and directing the five women who had been assigned to assist her. It was something she was used to doing, for she had run her home with Vishwa with remarkable organisation and competence. Until that dark day.

In a few weeks' time Anjana came to symbolise the success of Snehlata's rehabilitation scheme. She became a virtual exhibit for both the inspection staff who occasionally visited the asylum, as well as for the few relatives of the inmates who sometimes called on them. She was an embodiment of hope and the living proof that a mental patient could lead a fruitful and dignified life and maybe even recover and heal.

And then one day Vishwa came visiting. Snehlata led him proudly into the kitchen to watch Anjana who sat on the floor finely shredding her way through half-a-dozen cabbages with utter concentration, totally oblivious of their presence. Vishwa watched silently for a few moments.

Snehlata prodded him to stop hesitating and they walked towards her. Anjana looked up at Vishwa's forlorn face. A wave of anger lashed at her. She knew that he had only come to size her up and check whether her condition was conducive to his future plans. She listened quietly as he pretended to brighten up when Snehlata praised Anjana.

The unsuspecting Snehlata told him that at the rate at which Anjana was making a positive impression, she might soon test to be completely normal and therefore be allowed to go home. She added that they would all miss her at the asylum, but that Anjana surely deserved better.

Vishwa looked confused as Snehlata goaded him to go closer to Anjana and talk to her. Snehlata turned to walk away a few yards, to facilitate the hesitant and tender husband-wife intimacy that she thought might follow. Vishwa had no option but to comply and went closer to Anjana. Snehlata smiled contentedly as she neared the exit door. But stopped dead in her track soon. A bloodcurdling scream rent the air.

She turned around, horrified to see Anjana repeatedly stabbing a screaming Vishwa with her kitchen knife, and watched aghast as he slumped to the ground in a pool of blood upon the pile of shredded cabbage.

"This is the man who said I was mad, when I wasn't. And he's paying for it now. This proves that I'm mad, doesn't it?" she screamed as she drove the knife again and again into Vishwa who lay there with a stunned look on his face, feeling the life slowly draining out of him. Snehlata ran towards Anjana and pulled her away from him as Anjana continued ranting. "It is your gift of madness, Vishwa, which has today enabled me to wreak vengeance on you, without any fear of punishment," she continued, as she threw the blood-soaked knife to a corner.

"I'm a certified mental case. How can I be punished for this when in my madness I don't even know what I say or do? Didn't you yourself say that about me, Vishwa? Answer me, didn't you?" she hollered.

But Vishwa did not answer.

IT HAPPENED ONE DAY

Grief suits a woman
Wearing her vulnerability on her sleeve
While quietly reels the man
As silently he grieves

The alarm for six o'clock was yet to go off but Suparna was already awake, staring at the windows. It was a cloudy winter morning. How different was this December for her in Delhi. She no longer awoke happily to the sounds of morning tea, the bottles of milk at the door, the newspaper. Nothing had changed since last December, and yet everything had. She dragged herself listlessly out of bed, feeling sick at the thought of returning to the world from the dull stupor of sleep.

The first thing she became conscious of every morning in the last four months was her daughter's absence. And it was no different today. The now familiar, dull churning at the pit of her stomach was a sensation that would be her companion all day long and subside only when she would escape into sleep – at night.

Ruchi, little Ruchi, had gone forever ... she was dead. Gone ... at five years of age ... in a gory school-bus accident. A load of chattering children – unaware of their fate, in a few seconds nothing more than a bundle of twisted, mangled bodies ... life had never been the same again.

Ruchi, Suparna's little baby – where must she be now? Ruchi, born partially deaf, had found it difficult to live the life of a normal child. But with help from family members and the hearing aid, she had learnt to cope. With Ruchi and eight-year-old Akshay, the budding cricketer, life was filled with a quiet, everyday happiness ... until that fateful afternoon that had snatched Ruchi away from them all. Her friend Aditi's words rang in Suparna's ears. "God recalls his loved ones early..." Hollow. Devoid of even the lazy comfort of a platitude.

Ruchi, loving innocent Ruchi, was sleeping in the arms of the heavenly father? Suparna stared at the piercing eyes of Ruchi's favourite doll. They seemed to shine beseechingly at her in the pale light of dawn that filtered into the room.

The alarm rang, shattering the morning quiet. Before Suparna could stretch out her hand and shut it, Ashish had already done so. The same Ashish about whom she would often joke that even the blowing of a trumpet could not awaken him. He was such a light sleeper now ... or maybe he had been echoing her thoughts all this while...

Routine took over as she went about her morning chores. Tea, breakfast, helping Akshay pack his bag, packing lunch for Ashish and Akshay – so much to do. After both of them left, she sank weakly into a chair. She had no spirit to go about the rest of the housework. There had been a time when she would enthusiastically pour over a cookbook, go shopping in the mornings, or just potter around her plants on the terrace ... but these days she barely went beyond the bare essentials. It all seemed so pointless.

Looking listlessly out of the window, she wondered if she might be better off with a job ... and not be haunted by memories of Ruchi in every corner of the house. Maybe that was the reason why Ashish still looked so much at peace at the end of the day, while she felt no better than crumpled rag. Not once had he suggested dinner out or a play. In fact, the first thing that he would do after getting home would be to go and lie in bed, and stay there till dinner, idly staring at a newspaper or some point on the wall. He made no demands on her and his concern for her showed through very often. Even Akshay tried not to be demanding and boisterous.

Suparna's thoughts were abruptly disturbed by the sound of the doorbell. It was a saleswoman, selling one of those unknown varieties of washing powder no one in their senses would buy. She politely refused to buy any and saw the woman look crestfallen as she bent down to pick up her bags. But before Suparna could shut the door, she noticed a strange sight behind the saleswoman.

A spastic and deformed child, a little girl, her face both grotesque and innocent, her eyes reflecting the sadness of her mother's humiliation. She seemed five or six years old and the woman was finding it difficult to carry her along with so many bags. Suparna didn't know what to make of it, but before she could react, the woman hesitatingly enquired, "Madam, could you give us a glass of water to drink?"

"Will you have a cup of tea?" asked Suparna.

The woman followed her inside and sat down on carpet, cradling her daughter over her crossed legs. As Suparna poured the tea in the kitchen, she heard the mother and daughter in communication. The mother was talking to her as though she were a mere baby and the daughter was gurgling back in reply. Suparna felt a warmth envelop her. She was hearing happy sounds in her home. She was not alone.

As they both sat sipping the tea, Suparna could no longer contain her curiosity and asked, "Why do you carry her around like this? After all she must be making it difficult for you to move around."

"Madam, my husband deserted me when this child was born deformed. He said I was a witch. Now I have to work in order to support her and myself, but I can't leave her in anybody's care. She's too much of a burden. Nobody likes her and nobody is ready to look after her. And you know, madam, because of her I'm not as mobile as the other salesgirls. See, today I haven't sold anything..." She trailed off, her face devoid of any emotion.

Suparna looked at the child who was now smiling at her, drooling from the corner of her mouth with the effort of doing so.

Suparna felt a lump in her throat as she murmured, "You could leave her here sometime, when you're doing the rounds of this locality..." She was surprised at her own offer. She had spoken instinctively and without forethought. Perhaps she had been moved to sympathy or perhaps...

The woman gave her a warm smile. "No, madam, thank you so much. It's enough for me to know that there are still people like you in this world who understand our sorrows," she said, as she put the cup down with a clatter. "Thank you for the tea, and by the way, why don't you buy a packet of my washing powder." She smiled.

"All right," said Suparna, returning her smile. "By the way, what is your name?"

"Kirti Gupta," said the saleswoman, handling her a packet.

As Suparna saw the figure of Kirti Gupta, and her burdens, recede further and further along the lane, she wondered ... *This woman has lost so much ... What keeps her going?* Thank god, she herself had a lot to live by, despite Ruchi. But was she really living it ... living for the other people she still had with her?

When Suparna went about her work in the kitchen that evening, she felt as though that dull ache in her stomach wasn't as unbearable. The doorbell rang and she proceeded with a light step towards the door.

It was Ashish. She gave him a tired smile and saw him look a little bewildered. They sat down to tea and he proceeded to pour it. She took the teapot from his hand and said, "Let me do it."

Her words had a strange effect on him. She saw tears well up in his eyes. Soon he was crying like a baby ... tears of sorrow – that he could now afford to reveal and shed – tears of relief at her new strength. They came gushing, and she did nothing to stop them. For he deserved his turn now. As he buried his face in his hands, embarrassed at this outburst, she saw that his hair was greying in many patches. She hadn't even noticed it all these days.

Tears welled up in her eyes. It was a sorrow she had not been sharing with him ... nor was she aware of his. Suparna got up and hugged him tight. She felt small, intensely aware of her preoccupation with her own sorrow.

Late in the evening, Suparna sat with Ashish in the bedroom. It was quiet and peaceful. She was tired of having cried so much. As Akshay sauntered into the bedroom and snuggled between his parents, Suparna smiled lovingly. And as she smiled, Ruchi smiled back at her, through the eyes of Akshay, and through the eyes of Ashish.

PAPA

The first man in a girl's life
This love has no equal
Come hail, come storm
She'll love him despite all

"No! It's *not* okay! It can't be okay all the time!" Shefalika's angry voice rose, drowning Subodh's attempt to pacify her. "You don't understand, Subodh. You never will. It's useless!"

"Shefali, it's my bread and butter! I can't neglect it for heaven's sake!"

Shefalika smirked. "Huh! Except that we hardly get any bread out of your earnings for months."

Subodh looked hurt. "Now don't start that all over again!"

"Why not, Subodh? Why not?" She came closer to him and lifted her finger accusingly. She lowered her tone and spoke with a menacing lilt. "I had warned you. I had asked you to think a hundred times before chucking that cushy job. You didn't listen to me. Now, when things are not going as planned, you do nothing but overwork and neglect Tanya and me!"

"It takes time, Shefali. Being on your own is serious business. It's not a nine-to-five job."

"Oh! And how much time, Subodh? Days, months, or years? And how many years? And what happens in the meantime? Tanya stops growing up? Or I hold all moments in temporary freeze till you come back and give us time, and which may not even ever happen?"

Subodh stood with his arms folded across his chest, eyes riveted to the ground. He took a deep breath and, unfolding his arms, took a step towards Shefalika.

"Shefali, I didn't mean to..."

"Enough! Now don't ridicule my sentiments by giving me false excuses. You could have given us all the security we needed, if only... if only you would have had the sense to *not* quit that job!"

"Fine! Fine..." Subodh snapped. "If that's how you feel about it. Go to..." he stopped abruptly as he turned and saw Tanya standing in the doorway.

Shefalika followed his eyes.

It seemed Tanya had been watching them for some time. Neither had noticed when she had entered the house and been silent witness to their heated squabble. Not that it was something new to her. The frequent arguments between her parents were a reality. She looked at each of them sharply, picked up her schoolbag and walked towards her room without saying anything. She slammed the door shut.

Shefalika was visibly upset, more with herself than with anything else. Her eyes watered as she picked up some files and put them in her bag. It was the same story. Every time she tried to avoid a quarrel with Subodh in Tanya's presence, she failed. Tanya was invariably always there. It hurt to know that her daughter was suffering and bearing a pain that she didn't deserve.

Shefalika looked at Tanya's closed door. For a moment she toyed with the thought of going in and talking to her, but discarded it immediately. She knew Tanya. There would be nothing but stubborn silence right now from her. Helplessly, Shefalika slung her bag on her shoulder and, without looking at Subodh, walked out of their home.

Subodh sank into the beanbag with resignation, holding his head in his hands.

In her room, Tanya sat on the bed, allowing her thumping heart some time to settle down. The suffocating smoke of a damp unseen fire within her numbed her senses. Each time Ma and Papa quarrelled, she was engulfed with this weird feeling that everything was crashing around her. Her heartbeat galloped in panic and she felt dizzy. She wondered whether her parents had any idea how she felt right now.

Subodh's eye caught the time in the wall clock. Though he was relieved that Shefalika had gone, the awkward quietness which hung in the air was troublesome. He contemplated for a few moments, then got up and arranged three plates on the table for lunch. It was then he realised Shefalika had left already. A twinge of guilt hit his heart.

He knocked on Tanya's door and put on a cheery tone.

"Tanya! Time for lunch..."

There was no answer.

"Tanya!"

He was about to reach for the knob, when the door opened. Tanya looked at him coldly and walked out. She went and sat at the dining table without a word.

Subodh served her meal and his too. They ate quietly.

"How was school?" Subodh tried to break the ice.

"Okay."

"Hmm ... You submitted your project?"

"Hmm."

Tanya looked up from her plate.

"Papa?"

"Yes, honey?"

"Why do you irritate Ma so much?"

Subodh was tongue-tied. He let out a deep sigh.

"I'm sorry, beta."

"Still, I want to know ... *why* do you?"

Subodh looked at his fifteen-year-old daughter. In a nanosecond flash, her cherubic two-year-old image crossed his head. A hundred sentiments flooded him. There was so much to say. He felt the words on his lips, but they betrayed him even as he tried to manifest them.

"Maybe I'm not her type. Maybe I'm just not good enough ... that's what she says and that's the truth I guess. Maybe..." Subodh paused and shrugged his shoulders. "I don't know, but honey, I really wish I knew. I really do." Subodh felt his throat going heavy and he got up abruptly, avoiding Tanya's gaze.

"Papa?"

"Yes, beta?" he asked her while he kept looking the other way.

"Can't you take up a regular job instead of doing your own thing? Or maybe do both?" begged Tanya.

Subodh looked at her. He had swallowed his tears by now. He went up to her and pecked her on the cheek.

"I have to rush to the studio. Catch you in the evening, darling."

He didn't see the tears that welled up in Tanya's eyes as he walked out of the door.

Later, the maid was surprised to see two unfinished plates of lunch on the table. When she went to check on Tanya in her room, the young girl was asleep. That was odd, she thought, because Tanya hardly napped in the afternoon. The maid touched her forehead. Everything seemed okay. She left quietly, without disturbing Tanya.

When the maid had gone, the last big tear slipped from the closed corner of Tanya's eye and trickled on to her pillow.

*

Shefalika bumped into Karan in the office elevator.

"Hey! Where are you since morning? No call either?" he asked cheerfully.

Shefalika smiled to hide the strain on her face. "Took half a day off. Bad headache. How's the print campaign shaping up?"

"The team is waiting for your approval on some designs. There's a meeting at two with the client. Hope you're feeling okay now," he said with concern.

"Of course!" said Shefalika. They had reached their floor. As she and Karan stepped out of the elevator, she added, "See you at two then."

Karan stood watching her till she disappeared behind the frosted-glass door of her cabin.

*

Subodh switched on the lights in the studio and hung the keys. He went straight to his Nikon camera sitting on a tripod in the middle of the room. As he adjusted the settings, he remembered something. He went to the chest of drawers in the corner and began searching.

"Where are those photos?" he mumbled to himself.

"Which photos, sir?" Sameer, his assistant, had entered the studio from the adjacent room.

"The landscape snaps we had to dispatch to *The Traveller*." Subodh pulled out the last drawer. "Here it is." He fished out the parcel and was about to shut the drawer when the gold-and-red album kept there caught his attention. Subodh took it out. He kept it on the desk and turned to Sameer.

"Here, get this going. Right away."

Sameer left with the parcel. Subodh sat at his desk and opened the album.

It had photos of their wedding. He stopped at their first twosome photo during the wedding rituals. Shefalika was draped in a traditional deep-red sari, glowing in her bridal finery and bliss. He stood next to her with his arms around her shoulder, smiling brightly at the camera. It was Shefalika's favourite wedding portrait because, as she said, it epitomized the fulfilling contentment experienced by two people in love.

He sat back and closed his eyes. His thoughts traversed back to the time when he had met Shefalika alone after their engagement.

"You're a man of few words, aren't you?" Shefalika had quizzed him on his reserved demeanour.

Subodh had smiled gently at her and replied, "Few, but weighty words." He paused and added slowly and surely, "Don't worry, I'll serenade you with silence too. You'll love it, I promise. True romance need not always talk."

He had looked into her big beautiful eyes with such romantic élan as he spoke, that Shefalika had been swept off her feet. She loved his quiet style.

But time had layered that magic with gradual dust as life moved ahead. Shefalika was caught juggling a busy advertising profession and a hectic home schedule. Subodh gave up his cushy job as a photographer in a big media house to be on his own dream-wagon. The struggles grew, and so did the miles between them. Tanya came and for a while promised a miracle, but soon the enchantment of parenthood was sucked into a humdrum existence.

Shefalika needed a shoulder to lean on, someone with whom she could share her own struggles in a demanding profession. Subodh's entrepreneurial endeavour, however, precluded him from offering the shoulder she needed more often. It did not take time for his quietness to turn to negligence in the routine matters of life. So far as Shefalika was concerned, her "man of few words" had metamorphosed into one who offered little emotional succour either. Neither remembered when the complaints grew into insensitive arguments pulling them apart.

Subodh's phone buzzed.

"Subi ... I'm sorry about the morning." It was Shefalika.

After a moment's silence, Subodh said, "It's okay, Shefali. I'm sorry too." He paused for a moment. "Will you be home early today? Tanya was quite upset."

"Yes, I will. Don't worry. See you."

In the evening Shefalika found Tanya in her room, doing her homework. She tiptoed quietly behind her and hugged her.

"My baby!"

Tanya turned and hugged her back.

"Ma! I have a plan! You have to listen to this."

Shefalika laughed. "Yes, darling. Tell me. What is it?"

Tanya's eyes were sparkling with excitement.

"Ma, it's your anniversary after a week. Let's go out for dinner!"

Shefalika tried to conceal her disappointment.

"Papa is very busy dear. He'll not be able to make it."

"Ma! Please!"

Shefalika smiled indulgently at her daughter. "Okay. We'll all go out. You figure out how to convince Papa."

"Yes!"

*

The day arrived. It was a beautiful morning. Shefalika felt light. She waited for Subodh to wish her. He was rushing out for work when he remembered. He hugged Shefalika hurriedly.

"Many happy returns of the day, Shefali," he said and went away to work. Shefalika stood there, feeling the familiar irritation creeping up on her, but she had promised Tanya she would not react to anything and just wait for the evening.

On Tanya's insistence, she draped a pretty blue silk sari and wore extra make-up.

In office, Karan entered her cabin and stared at her, mesmerized. When she looked up, he was embarrassed. "You're looking beautiful," he managed to blurt out.

"Thank you," said Shefalika nonchalantly. "It's my anniversary. I mean our anniversary, Subodh and mine."

Karan sat opposite her.

"Lucky guy."

Shefalika smiled wryly. "Huh! Ask me ... I know better."

Karan caught the sad hint in her eye but she hid it behind her next question. "So what's the schedule today? Please update me."

*

Evening fell. Tanya and Shefalika waited at the Regency lounge for Subodh. He was supposed to be here an hour ago. Shefalika was getting impatient.

"What did you tell him?" she asked Tanya.

"That we're having dinner here tonight," Tanya hissed.

"I told you he wouldn't come. Some important work, more important than us, must have come along. Darling, I told you we should have remained at home."

Tanya tried Subodh's number. It was switched off. Half an hour later, when Subodh had not arrived, Shefalika got some food parcelled and drove them both home.

When Subodh entered the house at 1:30 in the morning, he went straight to their bedroom. Shefalika was not there. He went to Tanya's room and peeped in. Shefalika was sound asleep next to Tanya. He shut the door as quietly as possible and crept back to his room. Within minutes, he had crashed into deep slumber.

The next morning, Tanya rose early and proceeded to her parents' room. It was cold inside. The room was full of damp morning chill and Subodh, unaware of anything, was curled up on the bed, the blanket thrown away at a distance carelessly. Tanya walked to the window and shut the panes. She turned and stood watching Subodh for a moment. His face was lined with a stubble and the dark circles under his eyes appeared a shade deeper, giving him an exhausted, worn-out look. Tanya sat on the edge of his bed as quietly as possible and kept looking at him. When she got up, she pulled the blanket over his curled frame and walked out.

When she was leaving for school, Subodh was still asleep.

The air over the breakfast table was stiff. Shefalika, dressed for office, ate her toast slowly. Subodh came and sat at the table.

"Good morning," he said calmly.

Shefalika didn't answer. She waited for the apology. Subodh began munching on his cornflakes. Shefalika glanced at him. She thought he looked a bit haggard.

"I think you've forgotten that we were waiting for you at dinner last night," she said curtly.

Subodh didn't look up.

"I know that. I got entangled in a problem at work. Didn't find time to call either, presumed you would manage."

Shefalika got up abruptly. "You presumed! You presumed what, Subodh? That our anniversary dinner ought to be complete without you? That Tanya's heart was broken to pieces as she waited for dear Papa to arrive? Someday you'll presume that we don't live with you anymore!" Shefalika was shouting at him, her eyes smarting with angry tears.

Subodh sat stone-like, no expression on his face.

"What problem, Subodh? Tell me. Let me see how big a problem stopped you from attending your anniversary dinner."

Subodh remained quiet.

"Tell me!"

Subodh didn't answer.

"Fine! If that's the way you want it, that's the way it will be!" Shefalika stormed out of the house.

*

It was two in the afternoon and practically all staff had gone for lunch. Karan rushed into the conference room with a bunch of papers to be arranged for a meeting later in the day. As he entered, Shefalika got up from her chair and hurriedly wiped her eyes.

"Oh, I'm sorry! I didn't even know you were here," said Karan apologetically.

"No, no, it's okay. Please carry on. I was just taking a break." Shefalika tried to hide her embarrassment and began moving towards the door. Karan noticed the puffed eyes and heavy voice.

"Shefalika, will you wait a second?" he asked. Shefalika stopped where she was. Karan came around the big oval conference table and stood in front of her. "Are you okay?"

Shefalika looked up at his handsome face with empty tired eyes. There was something in the way he spoke to her that wrenched her heart. Sharp tears sprung up shamelessly as she strained to figure out an answer. Karan took her by the arm.

"Shefalika, listen ... tell me, what has happened?"

Shefalika reined in her teary deluge bravely.

"I am full, absolutely fed up of trying so hard. He never listens to any advice and then … and then…"

Shefalika was overwhelmed by a fresh burst of emotion and shaken by intense sobs. For a moment, Karan was unable to fathom what to do. Shefalika's vulnerability stirred in him a deep protectiveness. He put his arms around her hesitantly. When Shefalika rested her head on his chest and continued to cry, Karan held her more firmly.

A few moments later, Shefalika disengaged herself and looked at Karan, somewhat embarrassed and confused. Karan smiled at her.

"I'm sorry, Karan. But … Thanks a ton."

Before Karan could say anything, Shefalika exited the room.

*

In the following days, Shefalika and Subodh hardly spoke to each other. Shefalika slept in Tanya's room. Subodh was more withdrawn than earlier. He came home when the lights had gone out and rose each day when everyone had left.

For Tanya, the situation was an emotional tornado spiralling out of control. She felt the dizziness overwhelming her days and nights. It had been five days since the anniversary debacle. She hadn't had the chance to speak to Subodh even once. Every morning, she got out of bed earlier than usual and slipped to his room secretly. Every morning, she would cover him with a blanket and shut out the cold, sit on his bed, hoping that he would open his eyes and comfort her anguish. She wanted him to tell her why he didn't respond to Ma affectionately, why he didn't care to ask her anything, about what she felt as his daughter, or why she thought he should talk to Ma. Every day, she went to school simmering with questions.

She sat on the school steps one day, lost in thought.

"Let's go, Tanni. Chemistry practical in five minutes." It was Kaveri, her friend.

As they walked to class, Kaveri asked Tanya, "What's the matter? Why are you so gloomy these days?"

Tanya was terse. "Nothing much. The usual."

"You mean your parents?"

"Yup."

Kaveri put her arm around Tanya's shoulders. She didn't carry the conversation forward. She knew Tanya would cry if she asked more.

*

The next Monday, Subodh sat in his studio alone, trying to conceptualise an important campaign. Around mid-noon, a courier boy arrived and handed him a fat stamped envelope. Subodh opened the seal and pulled out some papers. For the next few minutes, he stared vacuously at what he saw.

They were divorce papers.

He entered home at eight that night. Shefalika was seated with Tanya on the couch in the living room. They stopped talking when he came in. Tanya looked at him nervously, her wide eyes holding a world of trepidation.

She got up and ran to Subodh.

"Papa!"

That is all that she said. Her words melted into a hundred tiny sobs as she clung to Subodh, face hidden in his chest.

Subodh held her tightly. He looked at Shefalika who remained seated on the couch, eyes downcast. He walked to the nearest chair, holding Tanya, and sat down. He let her sit on his lap and rest her head on his shoulder as she cried uncontrollably. They sat like that for how long, he didn't know. After a while, Shefalika came up to them and told Tanya gently, "Let's go to your room, beta. Come."

Tanya got up shakily and let Shefalika take her by the arm. She looked at Subodh who was watching her.

"I hate you, Papa. You don't love us. You could have handled everything but you didn't. I hate you," she whispered intensely.

Shefalika took her away.

*

In the days following the encounter in the conference room, Shefalika had consciously avoided proximity with Karan. There were moments when he was on the verge of asking her how she was, but she always managed to kill the effort by bringing up an important professional task or debate. It was as if she had recoiled tighter into a shell she had accidentally ventured out of that day.

Shefalika was working beyond office hours one day, when Karan knocked on her door. She motioned him to come in.

"Hi," he said casually.

"Hi," she answered without looking away from the computer screen.

"Why are you avoiding me?"

The directness of Karan's question jolted Shefalika for a second. Gathering her wits, though, she readied herself to answer, when he sat down on the chair opposite her and spoke in a calm, clear voice, looking straight into her eyes.

"I am not going to wait for an answer, because I already know it," he said.

Shefalika watched him intently.

"Shefalika, there comes a moment when someone in our life enters a private moment and shares our pain. That is what happened to us that day." He was silent for a few seconds and then continued. "Sharing that one moment doesn't always mean intrusion. At least not for me. I know what you're scared of. All I want to say is that no matter what we shared, I am not going to put conditions on your letting me in. That's not the way I look at it. Neither will I ever expect anything more than what you share."

Shefalika began to say something. Karan stopped her.

"Don't say anything." He got up and walked up to the door. Before moving out, he turned and said, "If you want to, you know you can rely on me. That's a promise."

Karan went out. Shefalika slumped back in her chair, her senses tingling with what she had just experienced. She was amazed at how Karan had read her mind without a word spoken by her. A warm secure sensation enveloped her tired mind. She smiled to herself.

*

The next morning, Shefalika found Tanya in her room, weeping silently. She held her daughter in a tight hug. Fifteen minutes passed by and Shefalika kept holding her till she was calmer. When Tanya overcame her sobbing fit, Shefalika took her hand in her own. She spoke with difficulty, fighting back her own tears as well as she could.

"Look at me, Tanya, and tell me the truth. Whatever you honestly feel; don't say anything to please Ma. Have I ever made you feel unwanted?

Tanya looked into her mother's eyes.

"No, Ma."

"Have I ever missed any school meeting and let you down?"

"No … Ma."

"Have I ever said I will not listen to you?"

"No, Ma."

Shefalika began crying.

"I also need attention, Tanya, the way you need it or anybody else needs it. And I've been searching for it too. Your papa is not able to give it to me. I don't know why. I have waited for a long time now, but I don't know why he couldn't care less. I'm not happy with him. I need to go. *We* need to go. This situation is not making any of us happy."

Tanya stopped crying.

"Yes, Ma, I understand," she said with some difficulty.

Shefalika hugged Tanya tightly and didn't let go for a long time.

"You can always come and visit Papa as much as you want to. I will never stop you. But we need to go from here, Tanya. He doesn't need us anymore," Shefalika whispered as she held Tanya.

"Yes, Ma. That's right. We need to go," she whispered back.

*

"Where will you go? After all, you're not alone. Tanya is with you. Let me at least..."

"No! You will not do anything! I have made all arrangements." Shefalika refused to listen to Subodh. "We will have to live separately before divorce is granted. I'm moving into a vacant flat which belongs to Karan."

"Karan's flat?"

"Yes. Why? What's wrong with that? He's a terrific friend, and I think you know that. I trust him. It's okay."

The following week saw a flurry of activities. Shefalika and Tanya had to pack their belongings and the task inched forward to completion, a little bit each day. Every day, Tanya packed some of her things. Everything went inside boxes; clothes, books, favourites. Each time the maid asked her if she wanted to keep something in a box, she would feel a confusing burden on her heart. This was not something she had bargained for. Why had God given this to her? She wanted her parents to live together.

Subodh was not at home most of the time. He came in and went out erratically. One evening, Shefalika and Tanya were having dinner when the phone rang. Tanya took it. It was Sameer, Papa's assistant.

"Is Subodh sir there?"

"No. He must be in the studio."

"Studio? I'm calling *from* the studio. He's not here. In fact..."

"Yes, what were you saying, Sameer uncle?" Tanya asked.

"He's not been here for the last week, ever since that prestigious R & S campaign slipped from his hands."

"Oh! Papa lost that campaign? I didn't know! When was that?"

"Sometime in November, 27 November, in fact." Sameer hesitated. He had revealed something he shouldn't have.

Tanya's heart skipped a beat. Ma and Papa's anniversary date.

"I'll let him know that you called. Bye."

She kept the receiver down.

"Who was it, Tanya?" asked Shefalika when she came back.

"Sameer uncle. Wanted to know where Papa is."

Shefalika raised her eyebrows and kept quiet.

*

The day of departure arrived.

Tanya packed the last of her things and sat alone on her bed. Shefalika came into her room.

"Ma, can I go to the roof and be there for some time?" asked Tanya.

Shefalika was about to refuse when she noticed the forlorn look on Tanya's face.

"Okay, but hurry up. Karan will be here after some time."

Tanya went up to the roof. She sat on the stairs which divided the lower roof from the upper portion. Half an hour later, Tanya descended and went straight to her room where Shefalika sat waiting for Karan. Shefalika smiled at her.

"Come here. Give me a hug," she said affectionately.

Tanya hugged her, then looked up at Shefalika's face.

"Ma, can I talk to you?"

"Yes, of course, darling," Shefalika answered sweetly.

"How are you feeling right now?"

"Well … a little relieved. Sad and relieved. And the rest … I don't know."

"Karan is a very good friend, isn't he?"

"Yes, you've met him. Don't you like him too?" Shefalika looked at Tanya.

"Yes, I do," said Tanya. "Ma, you'll be very happy after we leave, won't you?"

"I'll try to, beta. *We* will try to. Yes, I think everything should be okay."

Tanya fell quiet. She got up and sat on the sofa kept against the other wall, at a distance.

"Ma..."

"Yes, darling?"

"I want to stay with Papa."

Shefalika looked up at her, surprise writ all over her face.

"What! But why?"

"I want to."

Shefalika hurried up to Tanya near the sofa. "But why? Come on, Tanya, this is not a time to be childish, you're not a baby anymore."

"No, I'm not. That's why I want to stay with Papa. I can manage."

Shefalika's expression softened and she spoke to Tanya gently.

"Tanya, I know you will miss him. I know you love him too. But Tanni, you know him. He can't take care of himself! How will he take care of you?"

Tanya got up and faced Shefalika.

"I will take care of him," she said determinedly.

"But Papa doesn't need us! Can't you see?" Shefalika threw up her hands in despair.

"How do you know?" countered Tanya. She stood calmly.

Shefalika stared at her daughter. She didn't have an answer.

Tanya continued. "Ma, you have me. You have Karan. You have a job."

"So?"

"You are a much stronger person than Papa. You are on your own and you know how to look after yourself." Tanya paused for a second and looked away towards the window before continuing. "Papa doesn't know how to look after himself. You will manage, he might not. He will be alone if both of us go. I can't leave him alone."

"But Tanya..."

"I'll take care of him, Ma. He needs me more than I need him."

"Tanya ... he never comes home on time. How will you manage to live with him?"

"He has gambled his whole life on making a mark in his field. Today his feet are on shaky ground. But I know he will be okay when he gains stability in his work. And I'm sure he will get it one day. But he needs to be looked after till then. And I will do that. I want to."

Shefalika was speechless. The maid came in to say that Karan was at the door waiting for them.

Shefalika kissed Tanya on the forehead. With moist eyes, she gave her daughter a big warm hug and smiled at her. Tanya smiled back.

"See you, beta," Shefalika said softly.

"See you, Ma."

Tanya watched her mother walking away from her.

RETURN TO INNOCENCE

When her love's labour's lost
He will know, love comes at a cost
She will love till the end of time
Her love knows neither reason nor rhyme

Ritu squealed with laughter as Jatin lifted her in a joyful hug and twirled her around. When her feet touched down, she hid in his warm embrace. Jatin cupped her face in his hands lovingly and kissed her forehead. She clung to him and wouldn't let go, overwhelmed by a fierce desire to be protected.

There was a loud crash.

Ritu opened her eyes and lay in bed for a few seconds, her comprehension clouded with fading remnants of the dream just gone. The muffled memory of the crashing sound suddenly became sharp and she got up with a jerk. She ran to the bathroom.

Her favourite mirror frame lay on the floor in three jagged pieces. She looked at the wall where it had been hanging. The nail which had held itself precariously for so many days had given way. Good grief! *Now I'll have to get this fixed, and there's no time,* she thought. She grabbed a broom and began brushing aside the broken glass into a corner. Regretting that she hadn't got the wall repaired earlier, she bent and picked up a fragment of glass gingerly.

In silent dread, Ritu brought the piece of broken mirror slowly before her face. She looked at her reflection in it. The face which stared back at her killed the last dreamy flutter in her heart. Her eyes moistened as her thoughts grew despondent. No, this unimpressive image could never draw somebody as attractive as Jatin. She was a fool to even dream of such proximity with him. Ritu snapped out of her sad reverie and hurried to get ready for another day at work.

When she reached office late morning, the staffers were pouring in one by one. She passed Jatin's cubicle and found it was still vacant. Keeping her bag on her desk, she proceeded towards the coffee machine.

"Ritu!" His voice arrested her steps like magic. Ritu turned and saw Jatin walking quickly in her direction. As his six-foot frame surged towards her, her heart leapt in anticipation. He was closer to her now and she hid her thoughts behind her best professional smile.

"Hi Jatin! Early today?" she asked briskly.

"Had to be. Need to discuss something important with the boss today," Jatin replied as he joined her.

Ritu was not listening. Her mind raced, her face flushed. This was the same Jatin she had worked with for the last four years in this newspaper. Their ascent to fame as responsible, fiery journalists had been the result of their shared passion on stories unearthed together. The professional comfort in their mutual dealings was a known fact in office and so was their dependability. Yes, this was the same Jatin, but it was she who had changed. For the last six months, unknown emotions had seeped through her hardened mind, conditioned to be a tough reporter and nothing else. Never before in her four years with him had she felt so conscious of his presence.

They had filled their cups with coffee and Jatin was narrating the account of an unusual scoop he had managed the previous day.

Ritu nodded as he spoke, without hearing a word. They had now reached his desk. Suddenly, Jatin brought his face very close to her ear. Ritu felt the familiar, nervously sweet sensation crawling up her back. These days, every time he was physically near her, this overpowering awareness of him threatened to sweep away all the professional protocols she had at her disposal. Now again, as she felt his warm breath on her skin a secret shiver travelled through her flesh.

"We're going to Kashmir," he whispered.

Ritu snapped out of her stupor and broke into a grin. She and Jatin had been pitching for a feature on victims of terrorism in Kashmir. Now that the approval was through, they would have to leave in a day. Ritu was pleased. Nothing made her happier than a new story to cover.

At home, while she packed her things hastily, Ritu's heart throbbed with a vague unease. Would this official trip be her personal turning point too, she wondered. Maybe in the environs of Kashmir, away from the familiarity of known colleagues and routine reporting days, she would be able to gather the courage to bare her sentiments for Jatin. Maybe the fear of rejection inside her would give way to the recklessness that occasionally assailed her with intensity. Maybe he would be able to see beyond what he saw every day.

*

The valley was stirring to life when they reached the mountain road leading to the army base where they had to camp. Cutting across the town of Srinagar, their convoy, accompanied by army personnel as escorts, left a trail of noise and dust on the sparse settlements dotting the outskirts. Ritu noticed a couple of young Kashmiri women standing at the side, waiting for them to pass and staring at them with big kohl-rimmed eyes. Jatin and the two other colleagues cast a long appreciative look at them, then glanced at each other and smiled.

A pang of wistfulness leapt at Ritu's heart at the rustic, mesmerising beauty of the women. As long as the dusty trail allowed her to, Ritu kept staring back at them. Her knotted emotions raised their heads in self-comparison. Here she was, a successful woman who knew her way in life, who could rough it out as much as any man could in her profession and who commanded tremendous respect from her peers. And yet, each moment of male attention was but a mirage for her. Her professional confidence dwarfed every time she looked at a mirror and saw herself; she felt so insufficient, so lacking.

As the women receded in the distance, the reporter in Ritu discarded the wave of envy and set her logical, rationale side to the forefront. She began thinking how these women were like an oasis in the fearful, barren landscape spread over endless miles across the valley. It was difficult to internalise how these people lived amongst the constant fear lurking in every corner of their lives.

Jatin, Ritu and their small team were welcomed brusquely by the commander-in-chief at the base. They were led to their tents by a soldier who gave them curious glances now and then despite attempts to appear stiff and uninvolved.

Soon enough dusk was falling. Ritu stepped out of her tent after a short nap and noticed Jatin at a distance, near the high fencing. He was holding a pair of binoculars.

"What are you doing?" she asked.

Jatin turned to her and smiled. "Just watching the mountains and the picture-postcard houses. This is such a beautiful world, isn't it?"

Ritu came and stood beside him. She took the binoculars from him and looked through.

"Yes," she said. "This is an awesome place. Can't believe so many people are being killed here almost every day."

Jatin shook his head. "Which reminds me, the team has to meet in an hour in my tent. We need to start work from tomorrow."

"Yup, sure, see you in an hour."

The team met and discussed the next day's plans. They would be together the first day, scouting the terrain for victims' families and recording experiences. The second day onwards, they would split and repeat the schedule.

*

At the break of dawn, Jatin, Ritu and two photographers set out towards the nearest cluster of human habitat. With them were a couple of army staffers. The commander had given them details of certain victims they could interview, with a warning to be cautious despite security approval. At a couple of posts, they had to flash their I-cards for entry. Finally, they made their way into the nearest village. The sun had risen to golden warmth but the cold air muted its rays, casting an eerie gloom over the valley's ethereal beauty.

They interacted with the people. People, who were scared to open their doors, but were gradually persuaded to do so. Sometimes, it was the army with them which succeeded, sometimes plain requests tagged with identity cards. There was suspicion flashing in each eye. Mothers, wives, sons, babies, victims of human barbarism, with tales of torture unleashed on them in the name of god. Tears flowed freely after the ice was broken. Ritu noted details furiously, recorded and rerecorded sordid accounts of despair at a hidden war sucking the life out of god's heavenly abode.

Back at the base, Jatin was quiet over dinner. Later, he sat outside his tent smoking a cigarette, sending whiffs of smoke towards the sky in circles. Ritu watched him from a distance. His faint silhouette stroked the nascent love in her heart. She smoothened out her rough stray hair with both hands and went and stood beside him. Jatin looked up.

"Sit."

Ritu sat down and pulled her shawl over her shoulders tightly. She waited for him to speak.

"You know what, Ritu? I was just wondering how many years have gone by. We have been cracking stories for four years together, and I another two years before that. So much strife, bloodshed, warfare; nothing has changed over the years. When will all this end? When will people like us be without work?"

Ritu loved this philosophical side of Jatin.

"Yes, Jatin ... It has been long. But it is not for us to control the fate of humanity. We can only do our job, which is to tell the world the truth."

Jatin remained quiet. Ritu kept looking at his handsome features in the dim light of the stars. These stars appeared so close here in Kashmir, it was like she could reach out and touch them. She prayed silently and thought, *this is it. I have to say it now.* In her mind, she rehearsed what she was going to say.

*

"Jatin..."

"Hmm?"

"I wanted to say something..."

"Tell me."

"I..." she started shakily. Her heart was palpitating wildly. Beads of perspiration broke out on her brow.

"I have feelings for you..." Her voice came in fragments. She realised with a start how ridiculous she might be sounding. How do people do these in books and films?

There was a fleeting surprise in Jatin's eyes, which immediately dissolved into an intent look laced with curiosity and affection.

"I have had feelings for you. I mean ... I think I love you. No, Jatin ... the truth is I love you deeply ... But ... but this is the first time I'm saying it..."

Ritu stopped when she saw Jatin shifting position. For a second, she thought he was about to walk away but instead he came closer to her. He was all attention. He took her hand in hers. There was a long quiet moment which stood guard between them both. Then it went away and Jatin sighed.

"Ritu, I'm glad you told me. I am very fond of you. Very. It's been a long association." He looked up at the stars again.

"I value your commitment at work. And you know what? You are everything a man could wish for. Dependable, responsible, caring, focused, intelligent..."

Ritu's heart was beating wildly. She knew she was at the edge of her dream and it was about to happen. She raised her eyes to look into his. Jatin cleared his throat.

"Ritu, I love you too..." He paused. It was like eternity as Ritu held her breath and waited.

"But Ritu, that love ... is more a fondness ... I value you. You are my buddy, my friend in crisis, and that means a lot to me. In fact, I've never seen you in a romantic light. But trust me, it's better that way, because I wouldn't trade a friend like you for love. Your ... your..."

Ritu sprang up on her feet and ran. Hot tears ran down her face and blinded her with searing pain. She ran away, even as Jatin called out to her, "Ritu! Ritu! Listen to me...don't go away! Ritu!"

*

"Ritu! Hullo? Where are you? You were about to tell me something!" Jatin was waving his palm in front of her face. Ritu snapped back to the present instantly and realised that what she had just imagined had drained away all her courage. Years of staid existence crawled up and smiled mockingly at her. She remembered how she would cry when no boy would ever ask her out in college. An image of the broken glass and her ugly reflection pierced her head like a monster. She faked a smile at Jatin.

"Nothing ... I forgot. I'm so tired; my brain isn't functioning at all. Will tell you tomorrow, or whenever I remember..." She got up on her feet and pretended to yawn. "Goodnight then. I'm really sleepy," she said and began walking towards her tent.

Jatin called out to her, "Ritu!"

She looked over her shoulder. "Hmm?"

"Thanks for being there."

"Hmm."

Ritu resumed walking and the first tear of frustration ran down her cheek in the dark. Inside her tent, she snuggled in her quilt and cried herself to sleep.

*

The second day was an early one too. Jatin set out in one direction with his colleague and Ritu left for another demarcated territory with her photographer.

In the evening, when Ritu's jeep drove back to the base, she felt anxious. She was really longing to meet Jatin after the whole day. She hoped she would be able to muster enough courage the coming evening to say what she felt for him.

As the jeep approached the camping tents, she noticed the base commander standing with a posse of soldiers around a big bundle-like object on the ground. As they came closer, Ritu realised with horror that it was a body, covered by a white sheet stained with blood.

She was stricken with fear. She got down from the jeep quickly and looked at the commander with questioning eyes. Jatin's face swam in front of her. Scary thoughts surfaced in her mind. Before the commander could say anything, she rushed towards the body and knelt beside it. She threw open the sheet and cried. It was Jatin's companion. His blood-soaked body was marked by several gunshot wounds. Ritu noticed his camera at a distance, mutilated beyond recognition. There was no roll in it.

She shut her eyes in panic. She knew that there was more to come. The commander came up and stood next to her. She looked up at him, scared at what she was going to hear.

"Jatin has been taken hostage by the terrorists. That is what the driver told us," he informed her stoically.

Ritu could feel time coming to a standstill. All the noise around her stilled. She rose from the ground. The commander continued, "We don't know where he is. We expect some communication from the terrorist group. Simultaneously, we shall gather information as quickly as possible ourselves. Let us wait and see. Please try and keep calm."

Ritu waited in agony the whole night. She should have gone with him, she thought; maybe she could have saved him. After a fitful night, she woke up early, heart in her mouth. Somebody was tapping on the canvas tent door.

It was the base commander. He was carrying a phone. Ritu's editor-in-chief wanted to speak to her.

"Ritu, if you want to come back, we'll arrange everything," said he.

"But Jatin, sir? We can't leave without him."

"Don't worry about that, we will do our best ... Jatin is our boy. We have contacted the home ministry. The army has been ordered to launch a hunt for Jatin. But it's not going to be safe for you there now."

"Never mind, sir. Jatin and I are in this together. I can't leave without him. And sir, he is a good friend too. I need to find him myself. Please."

The editor paused. "Okay, Ritu, very well then. I will speak to the commander. You take care and keep in constant touch."

The commander took the phone from Ritu and went away.

Over the next two weeks, Ritu went about the tasks she had come to Kashmir for, recording interviews, collecting information, researching her subjects. In the dead of night, when the base was mostly asleep, she sat and wrote her stories. When fatigue would overcome her, she would stop and close her eyes. Each time she shut them, her mind would wander to Jatin. She wondered how he was and prayed that he was alive and well.

*

Jatin opened his eyes and saw a young woman standing with her back towards him at a distance. His vision was hazy and the throbbing pain in his leg was the sole reminder of what had happened. The last that he remembered was that he had been shot in the leg during the terrorist ambush and he had dropped to the road. He looked around and saw he was in a cottage. The woman was still busy in the corner.

When he tried to move, pain shot up in his leg sharply. He winced and let out a cry. The woman turned. She walked to his bed.

"So you're awake now. Here, take this medicine."

She put her arm below his head and lifted him with some effort. She placed a glass of green concoction to his lips. Jatin gulped it down with distaste and lay down exhausted. The woman sat beside him and began checking the wound on his leg.

She spoke again while she dabbed his wound with a liquid. "In case you're wondering how you came here, those jehadis brought you here."

"Those ... meaning? What about you?"

"I'm a hostage like you. They killed my family and brought me here."

Jatin studied her carefully. He noticed that she was quite young, in her mid-twenties maybe. Her delicately etched features belied the suffering she might have gone through, and her slender body was dressed in a fitted Kashmiri suit. Her face had an impersonal expression. She never looked at him directly and was curt in her answers.

"What's your name?" he asked, hoping to get some information out of her regarding his whereabouts.

She looked at him without a smile and said, "Razia."

*

Two weeks after Jatin's kidnapping, there was no communication from the terrorists. Each day, Ritu would speak to the commander about the progress made. He promised her his men were doing their best, but they had nothing to report.

Jatin's memories haunted her like never before. His absence had added fuel to her smouldering heart. Her tough demeanour belied all that she was going through. She yearned for him and was desperate to know where he was. She regretted that she hadn't told him about her true feelings for him the night before he was kidnapped. She promised herself she would do so, whatever be the outcome, when they brought him back.

A few days later, the commander walked into her tent at evening. Ritu kept aside her pen and stood up, anticipating something positive. He smiled.

"We have located the region where Jatin is likely to be. We will launch a rescue operation by day after."

Ritu's heart flooded with hope. When the commander had gone, she stopped working and lay back on her bunk bed, savouring the news. A renewed lease of love surged through her. She looked dreamily at the roof of the tent. She would go with the battalion; be the first to hold Jatin. And this time she would tell him everything.

Suddenly she sat up. Her mind was teeming with thoughts. The hope she had found anew transformed into a device. If she could participate in the rescue and save him, he would realize and surely appreciate that she had stayed back for him. He will surely be touched by the fact that she had risked her life for him. Could gratitude make way for love and acceptance? Ritu felt it could. Her genuine concern for Jatin's life had found a motive too. So what if the motive was a selfish one? Why would he say no to the woman who saved his life? For a moment, she chided herself, but the desire to possess an ever-elusive love overcame all doubts. *Love has its own fallacies*, she thought.

The thought was warm, and gratifying. The pain of longing subsided a little with it.

*

The rescue operation was planned to the last detail. The commander was hesitant about her joining the convoy. Ritu, however, was adamant.

"You will be depriving me of my duty if you stop me," she said.

"But this is a dangerous affair."

"I'm not new to dangers."

"I don't have permission."

"I'll get it from the ministry through my newspaper. Jatin is a colleague. It is my moral responsibility to be there personally when he is rescued."

Ritu got the approval to accompany the rescue unit.

*

Jatin twisted his hands in an attempt to free them a little but they were tied behind his back so expertly that he could make no headway. He sat on the bunk bed and watched helplessly as Razia struggled similarly on the ground, with the chain around her feet tied to the bed. The jehadis had informed them the previous night that the Indian army might conduct a rescue attack in two days. They wanted to leave no room for escape. If they couldn't handle the attack, all hostages would be killed before final defeat.

There was a rumbling in the skies. Jatin and Razia strained their necks to see out of the window what it was. The rumbling turned to thundering. Confused, they wondered what was happening. They heard shouts outside and Jatin could recognize the sound of overhead choppers. There was a sudden furore around them and then big thudding sounds, followed by more shouts and the running of feet.

A terrorist barged into the hut, a rifle in his hands.

"The Indian army is here! You!" He pointed at Jatin. "Don't move!" The man then threw his rifle on the floor and proceeded to tie Jatin and Razia around their arms, ensuring that they became additionally immobile. When he grabbed his gun and rushed out, Jatin's face lit up with hope.

The air attack blended into a ground one. A shell hit ground near the wall of the hut and exploded thunderously. Jatin, with his feet free, rolled on to the ground and under the bed.

"Razia! Quick, try and move under the bed! We need to protect ourselves till the army finds us."

Razia dragged herself to where Jatin had managed to hide, her feet still chained to the leg of the bunk bed.

Both crouched there for the next twenty minutes, praying fervently that the army would be able to locate them. Gunfire raged outside. Razia shut her eyes tightly, mumbling Allah's name.

At a safe distance from where the rescue attack was being executed, Ritu sat low in an army vehicle with the base commander. The war sounds were nothing new to her. Jatin too was trained in basic safety rules and she knew that if he was here, he would try and protect himself till they found him.

"When are you going to send these men to search the huts?" she raised her voice above the noise so that the commander could hear her.

He gestured with his hand, asking her to wait.

Ritu jumped out from the vehicle. The commander was aghast.

"No! You stay here! It's dangerous there! Please!" he shouted.

Ritu ran. She ducked under when the gunshots roared, she dropped to the ground when there was no tree to hide behind; but she ran till she had reached the patch of land behind a row of huts. She pulled out the crumpled piece of paper from her trousers. It was a map of this terrorist settlement. She put her finger on the encircled part. This was it. Her bulletproof jacket and heavy army shoes were weighing her down, but she sneaked up cautiously to the entrance of one hut and threw the door open.

There was nobody there. Some empty vessels, an unfinished meal and some empty cartridges were all she found. Ritu ran out frantically and entered the next hut. No one again. Her heart sank. What if Jatin was not here at all? She entered the third hut and fourth. All were deserted, with things strewn across but no human life. There were two more. She entered the next.

Ritu looked around. One wall had almost collapsed. Yet close to it was a bunk bed with a green sheet spread over it. She turned to leave.

"Ritu!"

She stopped dead in her tracks and spun around. There was Jatin, trying to wriggle out from under the bed. Ritu rushed to him and helped him out, her heart beating wildly. Jatin slumped against the bed, exhausted with the effort. Razia also crawled out on her elbows and sat a little away from him, the chain around her feet dangling with the struggle.

Ritu's face was smudged with soot. Her eyes scanned Jatin's face. She broke down and hugged him tightly. Jatin smiled.

"I knew you would come with the army. I knew it." Jatin had difficulty speaking, but his face had lit up.

For a brief second, Ritu felt everything had stopped. The gunfire, the shelling and chaos around, the happiness, the sadness, everything. She just sat and stared at Jatin.

"Quick! Ritu, untie me fast. We have to get out of here!"

Ritu began struggling with the knots on the rope cutting into his flesh. Jatin saw Razia trying to release her feet at the same time. He said to Ritu with urgency in his voice, "Ritu! Help Razia first! She needs help."

Ritu was confused. Seeing her questioning eyes, Jatin explained quickly, "This is Razia. She is also a victim. She looked after..."

Ritu cut him short impatiently, "Okay, okay, let me untie you first, Jatin!"

"No! First untie Razia! I can't leave her here!"

Ritu looked up at him. Something about his voice sounded odd.

A shell exploded near the hut's door.

"Ritu, you know, if it had not been for Razia, they would probably have killed me. She told them to spare me. I owe my life to her, Ritu. I ... I can't leave her here. Please untie her first so that I'm sure she's free."

Ritu's hands stopped where they were. For some reason, what Jatin said, and the way he said it, filled her with a sense of unease. With a woman's unerring instinct, she knew that something had changed, though she could not quite put her finger to it.

Ritu looked at Razia, who smiled back at her faintly. For the first time, Ritu became aware of how beautiful Razia was. Even in the middle of the madness around them, Ritu couldn't help experiencing a pang of envy. No one deserved to be this beautiful – definitely not in a conflict zone, in the middle of a war. Her eyes travelled back to Jatin. He was squirming to get free from the tangle around him.

Ritu rose from the ground and stood transfixed like a statue. She had paled behind the soot and her eyes were smarting. The smell of gunpowder hit her nostrils.

"Ritu! Hurry!" Jatin was screaming at her.

Her eyes were fixed on Jatin for a long moment.

"Ritu! What is the matter? What are you waiting for! Come on, they'll be here any minute now!"

Razia had stopped struggling with the chain and watched Ritu, not able to understand what was happening.

Ritu turned and began walking back to the door. Alone.

"Ritu! Ritu! For God's sake! What's wrong with you? Help us!"

Ritu had reached the door. She stopped and pulled out a small miniature mirror from inside her jacket. She looked at her reflection in it. As she opened the door of the hut cautiously, she threw the mirror onto the floor. It crashed into a hundred pieces.

She walked out of the door.

RETURN TO ME

To do right
To do it properly
Ah! It bites
And it's so costly

Mansi ran through the sheet of rain as fast as her feet could carry her. The cool sting of impatient raindrops lashed at her face, trying to temper the anguished fire inside her but in vain. Up the rising and descending roads of the hill town, and then through narrow alleys opening into the arms of wider lanes, she stopped when she reached the white mini-bungalow she knew so well. She stared at the main door which was ajar, beckoning her warmly to come in. A little unsure she was, but her heart nagged her till she burst into a short run over the steps and then stopped abruptly at the door, her eyes feasting on the most beautiful sight they could expect to see inside.

Nihaal sat on the couch in the hall. Nihaal, her friend, her constant companion even when far away from her. Her childhood personified. His grandmother was fussing over him and his parents sat nearby on adjacent chairs, his mother speaking into the phone animatedly. A small crowd of cousins sat scattered near his feet and around him. Everyone was speaking to him at the same time and Nihaal was trying to answer them one by one. In the commotion, Mansi stood statue-like, soaking in the truth, gazing at Nihaal without blinking, her tangled breath heaving in and out and her clothes clinging to her frame in wet creases.

Nihaal noticed Mansi and smiled. His mother Anjana disconnected the phone and rose from her chair excitedly.

"Mansi! Look, he has come back after so many years!" she exclaimed, and then seeing Mansi's condition, immediately caught her by the arm. "My god! How drenched you are! Come on, child, change into something before you catch a chill!" she said and whisked Mansi away. Mansi smiled back at Nihaal as she went inside.

She came back, having changed into a cotton salwar kameez, her damp hair open on her back in clumped streaks. The eager cousins had dispersed and his family, though around, was not in the immediate vicinity. Nihaal got up when he saw her. The rain outside had ceased by now.

"Walk?" he asked simply.

Mansi nodded in a daze as they both stepped out.

They walked as the silence between them got accustomed to their proximity. A little away from the houses dotting the area, they approached the spot of ancient foliage which had been the destination of their innocent childhood jaunts. Mansi stopped at the huge tree with a thick trunk. Its sturdy branches had always sheltered Nihaal's escapades from school during those times.

"Nihaal, do you remember this place?" whispered Mansi.

Nihaal looked at the giant tree. His eyes flickered with fondness but then he suddenly looked away. "Yes, of course. How can I forget the place where I romanced my violin and sang freely to the winds?" he said sadly, and resumed walking.

Mansi discerned the catch in his voice, but preferred to ignore it cheerfully.

"And when your whole family was searching for you, I always, always lied for you, and also came and told you here that you better run home fast!" Mansi burst out laughing at the memories of mischief they shared.

"Yes. You were always my buddy, my greatest friend. You'll always be," said Nihaal, head down as he kept walking. He glanced at her and threw a wan smile. Mansi was caught unawares as she blushed at this sudden compliment.

She wondered why she blushed, because it had never happened before. Nihaal's presence, even in her adolescence, had never overwhelmed her. She took a deep breath and looked at Nihaal. He was lost in his thoughts.

"What's the matter, Nihaal? You've returned after so much time but you're just not your usual self."

"Am I not?" Nihaal asked curiously. He paused. "Hmm ... don't know, maybe I've just got used to city life so much that ... It's been a long time, Mansi. Things have changed. Or..." He trailed off.

"Or?" Mansi persisted.

"Maybe it's I who has changed, I'm not sure," said Nihaal gently, and his eyes smiled at her.

Mansi shivered as the wet breeze ran over the landscape. A newborn awareness coursed through her. She stole a glance at Nihaal. Something fundamental had changed about him. When he had left for Mumbai, he possessed a boyish charm, a raw impatience. Today, he appeared so very grown up. His features had matured into quiet, still lines. Suddenly, she was conscious of the broad shoulders under his casual shirt, the sheer maleness of him. His eyes carried a calm depth every time they met her, unlike the mischievous spark they showed earlier.

Nihaal walked Mansi home an hour later and left. She watched as he disappeared around the corner. She stood there for a while, basking in the glow of having retrieved her childhood friend from time, something she had lost hope of often in the past.

*

Three years ago when Nihaal had packed his things and left for Mumbai, to make it big in the world of music, all he had with him was a dream and the burden of opposition from his family. Mansi saw him off at the station. Nihaal had thanked her silently, his eyes riveted on her as the train chugged away, till she was no longer visible. He was unaware of the tears she had fought back to keep his motivation alive. Neither did he know of the flak she had faced for encouraging him to escape to his dreamy ambitions.

As Mansi sat on her bed at night, her heart was bursting with new-found colours she couldn't comprehend. She had missed Nihaal terribly. To see him again was a magical wish fulfilled, but this nascent surge flooding her heart was a mysterious stranger. Accompanying this mystery was the vague unease she had felt earlier in the day. Nihaal had changed maybe, like he said. Maybe it was the awkwardness of the intervening years. She didn't know, and right now, she didn't care either.

*

Mansi visited Nihaal after teaching at the school next day.

"Hi!" she said brightly as she walked into his room, surprising him. He was standing near his desk, searching for something. He looked up for a brief second.

"Hi," he replied and went back to whatever he was doing.

Mansi scowled.

"What is it, Nihaal? Where is your energy? Why are you so quiet and morose?"

Nihaal stretched his lips in a forced smile.

"Nothing, Mansi. I told you, I've just become quieter, that's all. I'm the same guy at heart."

"No you're not!" she retorted. For a moment, neither spoke. Mansi ensconced herself on the armchair. As she kept her books on a stool near her, she asked him casually, "And by the way, when are you scheduled to go back?"

Nihaal didn't answer as he continued sifting through the papers and books. Mansi got up and went to his side. She kept staring at him. He finally met her gaze.

"I'm … not going back." He hesitated, eyes fixed on her face.

"You're not going back? But what about your singing career?"

Nihaal shuffled his feet. His eyes went back to the books scattered on the desk and stayed there for a few moments.

"Aw … that?" he said in a dull tone. He sighed. "Well, it's been a three-year struggle, I've not done much anyway. I don't feel like pursuing it anymore."

Mansi stared at him in disbelief.

"And what, may I know, are you going to do *here?*" she tilted her head to her side and asked him pointedly.

"Anything." Nihaal grimaced. "I'll teach like you. Maybe join some local office or … or have a business of my own."

Mansi began laughing. Nihaal looked up at her, puzzled.

"You are going to have a *business?*" The sarcasm in her voice was cutting. "*You*? Who hated the very thought of sitting in a shop whole day and selling cloth or whatever?" She sat on the edge of his desk and continued smiling. She picked up a book casually and flipped through the pages. She turned to face him.

"Nihaal, tell me the truth."

"I *am* telling you the truth."

Mansi shook her head helplessly and stretched her arm to keep the book back on the desk. A photograph slipped out from between the pages and fluttered to the floor. Mansi picked it up. Nihaal watched her, at once stiff and cautious.

It was a photo of Nihaal and another young girl, on stage, singing into mikes held in their hands.

"Who is this?"

Nihaal didn't answer. He had begun keeping some books back on a shelf. Mansi went up to him and flashed the photo in front of his eyes.

"Who is this?"

Nihaal glanced at the photo casually.

"Oh this? I think this is when I sang for a show in honour of the members of the Blind Association. And this was the female lead in the duet we sang."

Nihaal went to his bed and pulled out his shoes from under. "I have to rush to a friend's place. See you later."

Without casting as much as a glance at Mansi again, he wore his shoes and hastened out. Mansi kept looking at the photo for very long. Before leaving, she kept it back in the same book it had fallen from. She went looking for Anjana aunty but the cook said she had gone to the market.

Throughout the evening, the photograph kept popping up in her head. A vague unease consumed her. Was Nihaal hiding something from her? Three years of struggle and he didn't want to go back? Mansi found that strange, given the passion with which he had departed from this tiny hill town. How could he just chuck up a budding career and return home without realising his dreams? The flurry of questions pushed her into a disturbed sleep.

Mansi was busy for the next few days at school. The children in her class were participating in a programme and the rehearsals were on. She couldn't squeeze in a single moment to meet Nihaal, as much as she wished to. The day after the programme was over, Mansi came back home and ate a frugal lunch. She switched on the TV and surfed mindlessly as she reclined on the sofa. Soon, she had slipped into a warm, comforting nap.

"Mansi, see who's here." Her mother was calling out at her. Mansi opened her eyes to see Nihaal standing before her. She brightened up immediately, sat up and flashed a big happy smile at him. The television was still running on a low volume.

"I'll get some tea for you, Nihaal," Mansi's mother said affectionately and left for the kitchen. Nihaal sat next to Mansi.

"How've you been? I thought you had disappeared," said Nihaal lightly.

"I had actually. But I'm back to eat your head now, don't you fret," she said with a twinkle in her eye as she got up and adjusted her hair.

Nihaal smiled. It was a tired smile, a defeated one, one that irritated Mansi, but she resisted saying anything since she was seeing him after so much time. A patch of wordless air hung between them. Mansi looked at him carefully. Nihaal was staring at the TV screen absent-mindedly. She noticed the dark circles under his eyes. He was dressed carelessly and his hair was dishevelled. The disorientation shadowing his face was painful to see.

A singing contest was being aired on the channel playing at that moment. Mansi got up and raised the volume of the TV slightly. Just then her mother called out to her.

"Mansi, come here and help me!"

Mansi turned to Nihaal. "I'll just be back."

She went inside. Her mother had arranged two trays with tea and snacks. They carried them together to the living room. When they entered the hall, Nihaal was not around. Her mother kept the tea and left.

"Nihaal!" There was no answer. "Nihaal, Nihaal! Where are you?" called out Mansi. Still, there was no reply. Mansi pursed her lips in dismay and bent to keep the tray on the table. As she did so, her sight fell on the television screen. Her attention was drawn to what was showing there.

A music video of a melodious song was playing on the screen. Interspersed with the story told in the video, the female singer's image was flashing in and out between the various shots. The image looked very familiar and Mansi wondered where she had seen that face. A few seconds later, the penny dropped. Of course! This was the same singer whose photograph she had seen in Nihaal's room the other day.

Mansi's heart sank. There was something about this girl that Nihaal was hiding. She was sure of that now. She sat down and kept watching the video. The girl's looks were glamorised in the video, but even through the make-up, Mansi noticed she was quite good looking. She appeared to be in her mid-twenties. When the video ended, Mansi switched off the television, wore her slippers and rushed out.

Instinct told her where to go and find Nihaal.

When she neared the giant tree, she stopped dead at a distance. Nihaal was sitting underneath, his face hidden in his folded knees. Mansi walked up to him, worry clouding her face. Nihaal heard the dry leaves crumpling under her footsteps and looked up instantly.

Mansi was horrified. Nihaal's face was washed in tears. His glazed eyes watched her painfully for a split second before he rested his head back on his folded knees and sobbed like a lonely child. Mansi's eyes moistened too. She had never seen Nihaal in such grief. She rushed to him and instinctively rested her arm around his shoulder. She was motionless as he continued to cry. Gradually, he became calmer. When he was totally spent, he kept his head on his knees but turned it so as to look at Mansi.

Mansi smiled at him lovingly. She took his cold hand in hers and sighed.

"What is it, Nihaal? Tell me," she whispered gently.

Nihaal was silent.

She looked at him sharply without flickering her eyelids and asked, "It's that girl in the photo, right? Isn't it, Nihaal?"

Nihaal's eyes said yes. Mansi took him home. She led him straight to his room and sat him on his bed.

"Okay, now tell me everything," she insisted.

Nihaal told her his story, about finding love, about betrayal, about his sinking career. Niharika was the love of his life, till she refused to consider him his partner because she was afraid of her parents. She wed a wealthy man's son to fulfil their wishes. Unable to cope with this, Nihaal's career went downhill rapidly. He came back to escape the heartbreak, but in vain.

As she listened, Mansi was overcome by a deep sorrow. A sense of loss so deep that it unnerved her. A terrible anguish swept away all vibrant colours inside her, and led her to a barren land where she stood alone, miles of undulating desert surrounding her. She knew she had lost something she had not even recognised so far.

After Nihaal had told her everything at home, she compelled him to lie down and rest. She pulled up a blanket on him and sat by his side, holding his hand till he dozed off. When she was sure he was asleep, she disengaged her hand gingerly and tiptoed out. As she shut his door quietly and turned, she found Anjana standing in front of her.

Anjana had tears in her eyes. She looked at Mansi knowingly. Mansi's wall of restraint crumbled and she hugged Anjana. A flood of hot tears overcame all her resolve and she broke down in Anjana's motherly arms.

When she reached home, Mansi was drained to the core. She nibbled at her dinner, much to the chagrin of her mother, and retired to her room early on the pretext of being tired. She bolted her door from inside and went and stood by the window. The grey moon sat on a bunch of fragmented clouds, its rays illuminating their seat subtly. As the moon sailed away, Mansi looked up at it and said, "If you knew, why didn't you tell me not to begin dreaming?"

Her tears blurred her vision so that she couldn't see the moon anymore. She walked to her bed and lay down, letting the pillow soak her sorrow, whispering to herself over and over again, "Yes, Nihaal, I love you. And I will get you back on your feet. I will." And she slept.

*

Somebody was shaking her by the shoulders in the morning. She got up abruptly, her heart beating wildly. Her mother peered over her.

"Nihaal is unwell. He is in hospital. Anjana called."

Mansi sprang from the bed and got dressed as quickly as possible. Her head was hurting but there was no time for that. She reached the hospital in half an hour. Nihaal's father was talking to a doctor. Anjana sat outside the room on a bench. She rose as soon as she spotted Mansi.

"What happened?" asked Mansi.

"He just fainted in the morning when he was trying to get up. The doctor says his blood pressure is low."

Mansi sat on the bench and comforted Anjana. Anjana was almost delirious as she mumbled to herself, "Don't know why he is like this. If Niharika has married somebody else, why should he remember her so much? What is wrong with him, Mansi? He doesn't eat or sleep properly. He doesn't talk to anybody..." She paused and looked at Mansi. "...except you." She continued, tears streaming down her face, "Only you can do something, Mansi. Please help him. Talk to him. I can't see him like this."

"Everything will be okay, Aunty. Relax," Mansi assured her, and squeezed her hand comfortingly.

When she went inside the room, Nihaal was asleep. His pale face was drawn in a haggard shadow, as if he had suddenly grown older in one month. Her eyes beginning to smart again, Mansi turned towards the door to leave, when she heard him saying something in his sleep.

"Niharika..." he whispered. "Niharika?"

Mansi went outside quietly.

Nihaal's father had gone to work.

"Aunty, I need to go to Nihaal's room."

"You don't need to take permission. Is there anything you need?" she asked.

Mansi looked at Anjana. "I think I should call Niharika. Maybe she can talk some sense into him."

Anjana dismissed the idea. "Don't be foolish, Mansi. She has a world of her own now. Why would she do that? She might end up hurting Nihaal even more." She waited a long second before adding, "And what about you...?"

"What about me, Aunty?"

Anjana took Mansi's hand and held it protectively between her palms.

"Mansi, I have seen your pain once. Why do you want to hurt yourself again? Why do you want to speak to Niharika for Nihaal? You can take care of Nihaal ... let time heal the scars. That's all he needs." Anjana's eyes brimmed over.

Mansi smiled and put her arms around Anjana. Resting her weary head on her shoulder, she insisted, "If he is mine, he won't go away, aunty. Please let me. Please. I know what I'm doing."

Anjana sighed and hugged her back. She went home to fetch some things and Mansi waited at Nihaal's bedside. When he opened his eyes, she grinned at him.

"You scared the crows out of everybody, you jerk! How are feeling now?"

Nihaal gave her a faint smile but felt too weak to respond. He just stared at her with gaunt eyes, a pale shadow of his earlier self. Mansi remained with him till about noon. Anjana came back to the hospital around the same time. She entered the room and placed her hand lovingly on Mansi's head.

"Go home. Take a break and come back in the evening," she said. Mansi smiled. Before leaving, she took the keys of the house from Anjana.

*

In Nihaal's room, Mansi scanned all his diaries, but couldn't find Niharika's number. About to give up, she pulled out Niharika's photograph and turned it over. There was a Mumbai number scribbled at the back.

When she dialled the number at night from outside the hospital, a young voice took the call.

"I wish to speak to Niharika," said Mansi.

"Yes? This is Niharika."

Mansi gulped. "Hi. This is Mansi, Nihaal's friend."

There was a strained pause.

"Yes?" came the reply finally.

"Nihaal is not well. In fact, he is very unwell..." And then she told Niharika everything.

"Can you please come and talk to him," Mansi begged.

Niharika hesitated and sighed. "But ... how will that help, Mansi? Look, I'm married now. I told him I cannot see him anymore..."

"Yes, I know," Mansi interrupted her. "But at one time, you *were* in love with him. You shared dreams together. You went on to fulfil yours, he lost touch with his, simply because he couldn't handle it all. Tell me honestly, you don't want him to hurt himself like this, do you?"

"No I don't ... trust me."

"Then please do something about it. He is squandering his life. Please come and talk to him, if only for the sake of bringing him back."

There was silence at the other end. "Okay, I'll come."

*

Two days later, Mansi picked up Niharika at the station. Dressed in an off-white kurta and trousers, she was a picture of elegance and grace. Her lustrous hair fell on her shoulders bouncily and gave her that unique glamorous look. Mansi took her straight to the hospital.

Niharika entered the hospital room with Mansi and gasped. Nihaal, who lay on the bed with closed eyes, was just a shadow of his former self. The lines on his face made him look sick and wasted. Niharika felt sorry for him. Mansi watched as she sat beside his bed, tears smarting in her vacant eyes.

Nihaal stirred and woke. At first he couldn't comprehend, and kept looking at Niharika blankly.

Mansi propped him up. Nihaal looked at her. Mansi gestured at Niharika and smiled. When realization dawned, he smiled weakly, but still couldn't utter a word. Mansi left them together and walked out. She met Anjana outside who accosted her and asked her, "What is all this, Mansi? What was the need of calling her here?"

Mansi rested her hands on Anjana's shoulders and looked into her eyes.

"Trust me, Aunty."

*

Later, Mansi took Niharika to her house. She introduced Niharika to her parents as a common friend of Nihaal and hers. After dinner, she and Niharika sat in the balcony. Mansi was contemplative and calm.

"You're Nihaal's childhood buddy, aren't you?" asked Niharika.

"Yes. I've known him for a long time."

"And known him well too?" Niharika smiled. "It must be really nice to have somebody to call a permanent friend in these fickle times."

"Yes, that's true. I can rely on Nihaal anytime." Mansi paused and braced herself. "Niharika?"

"Yes?"

"You *will* help Nihaal understand that he needn't fritter away his life just because you people didn't get together? Can you tell him that he needs to realise his unfinished dreams?"

"Yes, of course, Mansi. That's why I'm here. I'll try my best. In fact, I told him as much at the hospital. Life doesn't stop at one place or with one person. Don't worry, he'll be fine. We'll talk it out. And then he has such a wonderful friend in you. I'm positive he'll be okay."

*

Nihaal returned home two days later. His grandmother was thrilled to see him. His gaggle of cousins surrounded him once more. There was a joyous air around the house as everybody talked and joked to lighten Nihaal's mood. Niharika joined in the banter once in a while.

After a noisy half hour, Anjana chased away the cousins. "Off you go! Nihaal needs to rest now." When they left, Mansi helped Anjana settle Nihaal in his room. Nihaal looked at Mansi affectionately. His eyes spoke of a life stirring back to normality, and of gratitude. Mansi and Anjana left him with Niharika on the pretext of preparing tea. In the kitchen, Anjana cornered Mansi.

"How long is she going to stay, Mansi?"

"Another week," answered Mansi.

"I still don't understand. How can she help Nihaal now?"

"Because they made music together. She knows his dream by heart, and understands. She has the power to make him see how important his unfinished dream is. He'll be okay."

"And you?"

Mansi went red in the face. Her eyes welled up.

"I'll be okay too..." she stuttered. "If Nihaal is okay. Once Niharika talks to him, I'm sure Nihaal will be better. And when she goes back, it's Nihaal and I, Aunty. Just he and I. I can wait for him, I really can."

Anjana turned her around to face her.

"You really love him, don't you?"

Mansi's lips quivered. Anjana hugged her tightly.

"You are such an angel. God bless you, my child."

*

The days and nights flew past. Niharika was scheduled to return in a week. Mansi did not visit Nihaal during that time. She diverted her heartache into a project with her class. The children loved her dearly and when she was with them, she relinquished all feeling of pain to a comforting devotion towards them. She kept calling Anjana to monitor Nihaal's progress. The news that he was much better thrilled her and heightened the secret anticipation of conveying her feelings to him very soon.

Seven days later, Mansi gathered a huge bunch of flowers and reached Nihaal's house. She greeted grandma in the hall and went inside. As she approached the door of his room, strains of laughter spilled over to her ears. It was Nihaal!

Mansi was elated. She had not heard Nihaal laughing like this ever since he had returned. She hurried and stopped at the door of his room. She stood watching him silently from the door. He and Niharika were in splits over something. She cleared her throat.

"May I?"

Nihaal beamed at her.

"Hey Mansi! Come on in! What a good time you have arrived at."

Mansi glowed happily at joy in his voice.

"Look at you! You are so much better! Nihaal, please, now don't indulge in all those theatrical antics like before, or else I'll never come and see you again," she mockingly chided him as she handed over the flowers.

Nihaal smiled. "Thanks to you, Mansi. If you hadn't contacted Niharika, I would have continued to harbour all those misunderstandings inside me."

"Great," exclaimed Mansi. Turning to Niharika, she said sincerely, "Thank you so much, Niharika."

Niharika returned her smile. Nihaal took Mansi by the hand and made her sit next to him.

"Now ... I have something to tell you!"

Mansi pursed her lips and knit her eyebrows in pretend surprise. "Let me guess, you are returning to Mumbai to pursue your singing!"

"Smart girl. But that's not the whole of it."

"Aha! Okay, tell me fast," replied Mansi promptly.

Nihaal glanced at Niharika who smiled. Mansi thought there was something about the smile that she could not quite place but she was too keen on hearing what Nihaal had to say. He looked at Mansi.

"I..." He paused.

"Yes?" Mansi asked curiously, enjoying his childlike demeanour.

"I..." he began again.

"Yes, Nihaal? Come on, stop teasing me now," Mansi said impatiently, punching him on the arm.

Nihaal started laughing. He stopped for a second and grinned at Mansi.

"Niharika and I are getting married ... very soon."

A flock of pigeons flew noisily just outside the window towards the horizon. The sun slipped down and it suddenly became darker in the room.

"But..." Mansi began, getting up to switch on the light.

"Hmm. I knew you'll ask. Yes, Niharika is already married. In fact, you can say, she *was*. Niharika, would you like to tell her the rest?"

Niharika smiled at Mansi, who was standing by the switchboard, hoping that the tension in her body was hidden from both of them, thanks to the failing light and the distance.

"Yes, Mansi, it's true that when you had called, I told you I'm married, but I didn't tell you that my marriage didn't last for more than a month." She paused for a moment and sighed. "Rahul and I just couldn't get along. In fact, I am already separated from him." She added with a smile, "Hopefully, we'll be granted divorce in another six months. Then..."

"Niharika and I will get back together once the divorce comes through," interrupted Nihaal impatiently. "So, Mansi, how was the surprise?"

Mansi burst into laughter. Nihaal went on.

"I still have to tell Ma. Mansi, will you help me?" he asked, a little worried.

"Yes, I will, Nihaal. Of course, I will," answered Mansi softly. She switched on the light. The room was flooded in a white luminous glow.

"Mansi, it's all because of you. If you hadn't called Niharika, we would never have cleared the air between us. And we would have probably never known that we were still meant to be together. Thank you, Mansi. Thank you so much." Nihaal's eyes welled up with tears of gratitude.

Mansi came forward, and cupping his face in her warm palms, kissed Nihaal on the forehead.

"I am so happy for you!" she said to him lovingly, looking into his eyes. Bustling with sudden energy, she said perkily, "I'll just be back" and went out. She went straight to the hall and looked around, taking a second to get a hold over herself. She took the stairs, opened the door on the right of the landing and stepped inside.

Anjana was engrossed in prayers in the small niche for the deities carved in a corner of the room. The smoke from the incense permeated the air. Anjana opened her eyes and turned to look at Mansi. Mansi fixed her gaze on Anjana's face and walked slowly towards her, as if scared that hurrying would somehow make her full heart spill over. When she reached Anjana's side, she sat down next to her. Their eyes met and held each other.

Mansi couldn't fight back any longer. She fell in Anjana's lap and let out a cry. Her sobs grew louder and racked her mercilessly as she kept her face hidden in Anjana's lap. Anjana caressed Mansi's head and put the loose strands of her pretty hair into place behind her ear.

When the storm subsided, she pulled her up and shook her gently. A lone tear trickled down Anjana's cheek. Mansi watched as a determined expression crossed the errant tear and Anjana gathered herself to get up from the floor.

Mansi caught her hand. She looked at Anjana with vacant eyes and shook her head wordlessly. Struggling to find her voice, she whispered to her, "Don't, Aunty. Please don't."

REWIND

Life does not offer a rewind
Our decisions do often bind
She learned of it the hard way
The choices we make, make us pay

Namrata pressed the rewind button again. As the tape whirred backward she stared for the umpteenth time at the jacket. SUDEEP KUMAR – HITS OF 1994, it read. She sighed as she looked at the picture of Sudeep smiling at her.

She had always loved his smile. It was a smile that reached right up to his twinkling eyes. And it was this smile that had drawn her so irresistibly towards him when they had been together in college.

There wasn't a song Sudeep sang that she did not love. There wasn't a magazine that wrote about him that Namrata did not file in her collection. And each time that he sang, Namrata felt he was singing just for her. He overwhelmed her with his vocal presence everywhere – on the radio, on television, in the movies, singing to her.

And each time he sang "*Ab bhi hai tera intezaar*", Namrata's eyes would fill up. Her heart would brim over with the love that she still had for him. Only it was a love which she realised had been selfish in its considerations.

She had waited five long years for him after they finished college in Ahmedabad. All through those years she had prayed fervently for him to make a mark in the uncertain world of Bombay's music industry.

She had prayed, for the sake of his own self and more than anything else so that he would be in a position to take her to live with him in Bombay.

But five years later, Sudeep still remained on the fringes of the music world. Yet he was not willing to give up hope. Like all hopefuls, he always felt that opportunity and fame were just round the corner.

At the end of those five years, Namrata had tired of his promises and his pleas for more time. She was only getting older and Sudeep did not have much stability to offer her.

On the other hand, there had been Akhil whom Namrata had lately started seeing. Yes, there wasn't that twinkle in his eyes but he had his own quiet charm. He was, also, an IAS officer. And at twenty-five, for Namrata the need to settle down seemed so much more compelling than the urge to seek a life of adventure.

Namrata still remembered the day when on one of Sudeep's visits she had explained all this to him. She recalled vividly the pain in those once twinkling eyes as she had walked away from him.

Soon she had got married to Akhil. It was a marriage she had gone into with limited expectations. It had worked out into a happy and stable relationship. But fate had willed otherwise for her. For, seven months after she was married, Akhil died in a gory car crash.

Namrata was back to where she had started – accepting what came her way as the will of god. But it was almost with an eerie coincidence that after Akhil's death, Sudeep came right back into her life. This time not in person, but through the success of his music. She heard his voice everywhere – sometimes singing songs of love, sometimes belting out songs of anguish. All of which she imagined were meant only for her.

If only, if only he knew that she was there for him. That she needed and wanted him more than anything and anyone in the world today. If only he would forgive her rejection and give her another chance.

Yet, Namrata knew that it was impossible. No self-respecting man would do what she wanted. Yet the temptation to see him and tell him. Maybe, just maybe life would give her another chance...

She felt ashamed at her thoughts – for here she was, a widow who ought to be mourning her husband, pining instead for a lover. A lover whom the whole world loved by now, and whom she had once rejected. Namrata tried to banish these thoughts and calm her mind but it was not easy. Especially now, as Sudeep's voice seeped into her whole being.

But what was this commotion outside that overpowered even his mellifluous voice. Namrata switched off the music and peeped out from the window. She saw a shiny black Mercedes drawing up outside the house of Sudeep's parents down the road followed by many people eager for a look at the boy wonder from their town who had done them all proud.

Sudeep got down from the car and opened the door for his bride. He put his arm protectively around her as they walked towards the entrance. Sudeep's mother performed the aarti for the couple and applied tilak to their foreheads. They bent down to touch her feet. His bride put her right foot forward across the threshold.

And Namrata took two steps backward...

SUCH A LONG JOURNEY

The more things change
The more they remain the same
Nothing changes
Yet nothing remains the same

The August Kranti Express was already on the platform at Bombay Central station. Cheerful maroon coaches, with curtains that sealed from view the windows of the air-conditioned cabins colloquially called 'dabbas'.

Smita looked at the passenger list outside the coach. Yes ... there was her name. Mrs Smita Raghavan. Thankfully the other seat in her cabin was to be occupied by a woman too. Mrs Priya Deshmukh. Whatever anyone might claim, the comfort value of being in the same coach as a woman on a seventeen-hour journey was much more than being with a man no matter what his age or status might be, thought Smita.

She carried her bag deftly at waist level as she walked sideways through the narrow aisle towards her berth and settled into it.

The other seat in the cabin was already occupied. Priya was a woman in her late thirties who seemed to wear her smartly cropped hair, slightly salt and mostly pepper, with quiet dignity. She had a no-nonsense air about her.

Priya looked intently at the twenty-seven-year-old confident and radiant Smita and smiled at her. Then she rested her left elbow on her bag as it leaned against the wall and looked out of the window. Smita followed to do the same with her right elbow resting on her bag.

"Anyone else with you?" asked Priya, turning away from the window.

"No, no one else. You too? You're travelling alone?" asked Smita.

"Yes, I'm alone too. By the way I'm Priya Deshmukh," said Priya putting her hand out.

"And I'm Smita Raghavan. Hi! It looks like both of us are together 'alone' in this cabin," said Smita with a chuckle, as she clasped Priya's hand.

"That's the advantage of travelling off-season," said Priya.

"Absolutely. I told my husband Pogy that this was the best time to travel for a woman alone – no rush, no crush. I'm so glad I timed it right," said Smita.

"I too always make sure that I avoid travelling during the holiday season. Of course my nieces and nephews get terribly upset because they're at school half the time that I'm there on holiday," said Priya.

"It's almost five o'clock now so I don't think anybody else is going to join us. Shall I draw the curtains?" asked Smita.

"Yes, yes, go ahead. Then we can stretch out our legs a bit more without getting self-conscious," said Priya with a smile. She proceeded to do just that, now resting her head on the bag she had earlier leaned on.

As she turned to go back to her seat, Smita looked (taking care not to appear as though she was looking) at Priya's hairy legs that became visible as her sari hitched up to her knees. Thank god she herself didn't wear saris – for unwaxed legs were among some of the most repulsive sights she could ever imagine.

"Do you live in Delhi or Bombay?" asked Priya as she settled herself a little more comfortably.

"Delhi," Smita replied. "I came to Bombay last week for a reunion of our school friends. We had a real ball this entire week. You're going to Delhi on a holiday?"

"Yes, I live in Bombay," said Priya.

As the train slowly chugged out of the station, Smita exclaimed, "Bon voyage, friend."

"Bon voyage to you too." Priya smiled back.

"Tell me, Smita, you're married, aren't you?" she said, her eyes focusing on the mangalsutra around Smita's neck. "Your husband ... he's a nice man I must say, to allow a young pretty wife to go on a week's outstation holiday without him."

It was a rather intimate statement for someone you had met barely ten minutes ago, thought Smita, a little taken aback before she proceeded to reply. "Yes, you're right indeed. He's a fantastic husband. In fact he is the one who encouraged me to go. He always tells me never to miss out on any opportunity for a new experience or change," said Smita with a smile as she visualised Pogy's smiling visage.

"You're either a very lucky girl, or you're just recently married," said Priya with a laugh.

"I don't think four years is too recent, is it? But yes, my husband is a really wonderful person and therefore I think I'm extremely lucky." She paused. "Isn't that the case with you too? I mean travelling without hubby?" Smita laughed.

"Well, yes, but we travelled away from each other much before this journey. I'm divorced now. It's been almost six years since. I know I still put Mrs as a prefix to my name, but that's entirely due to reasons of convenience. In fact I've even reverted to my maiden surname. I live alone and I love it – Bombay is a city that makes it possible," said Priya with a laugh. Every year or so I visit my parents, brothers and sisters in Delhi for a few days. That's about enough of a family scene that I can take at this stage of my life. Whenever I'm in Delhi for a little longer than a week, I yearn to come back to Bombay and be by myself again. It's been like this for a long time now," said Priya.

"It must have become like this after your divorce I think. Otherwise, few women from your generation would really choose to be alone. Divorce always makes one bitter and leaves one with a whole lot of pain and a feeling of defeat. I've seen these things happen really close. My husband Pogy too had been through a divorce much before we got married. I know the entire gamut of feelings that a divorcee goes through. Pogy's divorce left him withdrawn and alone ... it must have been the same with you too," said Smita, realising too late that perhaps she too had got carried away with her own thoughts, and unwittingly steered the conversation into very intimate territory.

But Priya took it well. She smiled back at Smita.

"You're an intelligent woman, Smita," said Priya. "What you've said is really the plain truth. After a divorce, it takes a long time to work the bitterness out of one's system. First the loneliness crushes you, but after some time it becomes a companion." Priya's eyes shifted from Smita's face to a vacant space on the ceiling, clearly chary of meeting Smita's eyes just yet.

"It's more difficult to get rid of the fear and bitterness if one is alone. It's easier when someone is there to help pull you out of the morass. I had to work on Pogy for quite some time before he was able to get back his faith in love and life again. But four years of marriage later, I must say that it's been worth every minute," said Smita.

"A second shot at love comes much more easily to a man than a woman. Women by nature are more cynical than men. Another big irony is that it's only after a woman for some reason loses her partner – it's only then that she starts discovering herself as an individual."

"Did that happen to you?"

"Yes, it did. He was such a double-faced person. We were equals in the same class in college when we fell in love. But after marriage the whole equation changed. He didn't like me going out – not even to work. He was very insecure. He treated me like a maid in the house. I took it all in the name of love. But when his eyes started to wander despite me fulfilling his demand of paying him and the home full attention, I decided that it was not worth it after all. Even after all the crushing of my soul, my marriage had proved to be a farce. So I thought I might as well salvage my soul. It was horribly painful doing it after five years of investment in my marriage. But when I think in retrospect today, I'm glad I had the nerve to do it when I did. If I had waited any longer I might not have been able to do it. One's resolves and strength do diminish with age. It was tough but I was able to put the marriage behind me."

"You're so right, Priya. In our country it usually takes a divorce or widowhood for a woman to start thinking of her own identity. Even a decade ago things were more or less like that. But times are changing, you know. More importantly, I think men are changing. They are finally beginning to realise that true happiness in a marriage depends on the woman's development as a person in her own right. She is not just meant to be an appendage to him," said Smita, the optimism of her own life shining through in the conviction with which she spoke her words. "Do you know, Pogy himself didn't want me to change my surname? He said it wasn't fair to me, nor to the family that had brought me up with such love and affection. He's so sweet!"

"Maybe you're right. Maybe men are changing, excruciatingly slowly though, but it's finally happening at least in your time. Good for you all," said Priya.

"Yes, but it's women like you who've come about half a generation before us who have helped it happen. All of you, who have paid a heavy personal price for your stand, have made men in general change for the better."

"I never really looked upon myself as a social reformer, but hey … your analysis does make me feel good, I must confess," said Priya bemused. "My stand, for example, was one that I took merely for selfish or rather self-respecting reasons. I for one did it to get out of this syndrome of my husband first restricting my opportunities for growth in the name of homemaking, and then making me feel inferior. Inferior to the women-of-the world with whom he got into one affair after another. I stood up for myself to prevent being corroded to a stage where I started to think of myself as a worthless human being."

"That's precisely what I mean, Priya. It is principled stands like these that have made men of today realise the importance of treating their women with the dignity that they deserve," said Smita. "Look at Pogy, for example. To be frank I was ready to forget my own ambitions and talents. I'm personally too laidback to make the effort to do anything of consequence with my life. But Pogy keeps pushing me out of my laziness to do something worthwhile. He says it's good for my sense of self-worth and for our happiness as a couple that I grow as an individual. He's proved to be right – for today my ceramics business is booming, and my success makes me feel so much more fulfilled as a person. It's all due to his encouragement."

"You're really lucky to have a husband like that. He's poles apart from my husband ... I mean my ex-husband, when he used to be my husband that is." Priya laughed.

"You know, Priya, at this reunion we had in Bombay I was telling all my friends about Pogy. At first they kept teasing me about having been wise enough to have chosen to become an old man's darling rather than a young man's slave – something most of them seem to have done. You see, there is an almost twelve-year gap between Pogy and me. But after they had all finished with the ragging, they admitted that they all envied me. Everyone said that I was one lucky woman. Pogy has really proved to be the most fantastic husband in the whole world," said Smita, her eyes shut tight as if to emphasise the sincerity of her statement.

"Some people do have all the luck! What I yearned for, you got so easily ... but then that's the way of the world. Isn't this why the most independent and individualistic of us believe in the theory of karma?" asked Priya with a calm smile.

"Yes, it sure does," said Smita. "I too have begun to believe in it of late."

"Dinner is ready," shouted the train attendant, peeping through the curtains.

Priya got up with a start, covering her hairy legs as she pursed her lips, taken aback and irritated at this sudden intrusion.

Smita, however, had sensed Priya's discomfiture and quickly taken the two trays from the attendant.

. "There's no point expecting etiquette from them. It's just too much for their class of people," said Smita with a frown on her face as she handed a tray to Priya.

"Thanks," said Priya, "both for the tray and for your alertness – for I did get very fazed with the attendants' sudden entry."

"No problem," said Smita as she settled herself next to Priya and they started to eat.

"The food has improved since I last ate it. At least the pulao tastes like pea and not kerosene pulao," said Priya, tucking it in with relish.

"You like the pulao? Why don't you take some of mine too? I'm off rice for the last two weeks."

"Weight management? You're slim enough already," said Priya.

"Well, frankly yes, it is," said Smita as she scooped out her rice and served it on Priya's tray.

"I'm sure Pogy likes you slim-'n'-svelte. Men sometimes don't say it openly but they don't like wives when they put on weight. Mine used to make such cutting remarks! Thank god, at least now I can eat what I want," said Priya, enjoying her pulao with gusto.

"No. Actually, Pogy doesn't hassle me about it. He says he'll always like me, irrespective of how I look. But I get unnerved at the prospect of putting on weight," replied Smita.

The two of them went on to complete the rest of the meal in silence.

Silence that was just as comfortable as their conversation had been a few minutes ago. As was their sleeping in the same cabin all through the night, gently rocked by the movement of the train as though they were babies in their cradles. Smita was amused by the sight and sound of Priya's snoring through the night. She seemed to have lost all her feminine qualities, along with the man in her life!

In the morning Priya looked on fondly as she saw Smita carefully making up her face and dabbing on perfume, obviously excited at the thought of meeting Pogy at the station. Later, they exchanged contact numbers and addresses in Delhi, promising to meet again. Both knew that each of them really meant what they said about wanting to keep up the association that had started with this journey.

It was 9:40 a.m. as the train slowly trundled into Hazrat Nizamuddin railway station. Smita pulled Priya's hand and led her to the exit door of the coach where they waited for the train to come to a complete halt.

"You've got to meet my Pogy. In fact if no one comes for you, you'll come with us. East of Kailash you said you had to go, didn't you?"

"No, no I'll manage. I've always managed. I'll definitely meet your New Age Man but no dropping ka chakkar today. I'll go on my own."

"Okay, okay, we'll see. But at least come with me right now. Yipee! There he is … can you see him? The one in the pin-striped blue shirt!" squealed Smita as she pointed her finger at the crowd.

Priya could not make him out as the train, still chugging along stubbornly, swept past a sea of faces, each of them bobbing their heads concernedly to identify the coach from which their loved ones would alight.

Smita hopped down from the steps, running energetically ahead, while Priya followed, hesitant and reticent to intrude upon this very private moment. She unabashedly hugged the man in a pin-striped shirt, with a salt-and-pepper mop of hair, who then broke free to stare at Priya.

"Priya, this is Pogy, Pogy, this is Priya. Priya and I have just been together on this short journey but it feels like we've known each other for ages," said Smita, failing to notice the hard stare that Pogy was giving Priya. Then she turned to Priya, who had been looking just as stony-eyed at Pogy.

"How have you been, Priya," asked Pogy softly.

"I'm all right. But you've certainly come a long way with Smita … I see," said Priya as she turned to a nonplussed Smita. "It's been a really long journey for all of us. Especially for him – from my Pratap to your Pogy. It's time now to say goodbye. Goodbye, Smita, and God bless you."

Priya nodded slightly at both Pogy and Smita, and walked away slowly with her bags.

THE FINAL ACT

All of life is an act
Sifting the fiction from the fact
Faking joy, feigning sorrow
Tools at our disposal to borrow

"Sir is very serious, Mrs Das. It is better if you come with Rahulji. We are all waiting for you both," said Nair, his voice quivering as he spoke. Chhaya heard the clicking sound of the phone being disconnected at the other end. Nair had put it down before she could ask any more questions. He was probably scared of the truth coming out if he spoke anymore.

But even without Nair saying it in as many words it was clear to Chhaya that her husband Amarendra was no more. She knew that this heart attack at fifty-six, in the middle of dictating notes to his faithful secretary Nair, had felled him. Perhaps it was just the kind of end he would himself have wanted – to die with his boots on and with as little emotion and in as clinical a manner as he had lived his life. Simply like the battery running out of a piece of electronic equipment. At least the fact that he had a heart attack proved that he had a heart, thought Chhaya, for that certainly wasn't the faintest of impressions that she had in all these years of being his wife.

It was certainly mean for her to be thinking this way, at a time like this. Chhaya sat on the settee beside the telephone. It was a moment that she had imagined and relived in her mind umpteen times in these last twenty-five years.

She had often wondered how it would finally happen, how they would bring his body home and how she would behave through all that would follow. Now that moment had finally come. It was time to put up the last act of the marriage drama that she had been starring in for a quarter of a century. But the problem was that like the finale of any good drama it would have to be a most convincing display of histrionics. Because all these years she had only had to put up a show for a few people around her. But this she knew was going to be the most trying performance yet. The "part" of her life, to be played at the time of his death. Today Chhaya felt like an amateur actress nervous at the prospect of facing a big audience for the first time.

Chhaya recalled the numerous times that she had been left alone to brood in their bedroom after a particularly bad fight with Amarendra. As soon as she would hear his car leave the driveway after the fight, she would bolt the bedroom door from inside. Then she would sit in front of the dressing-table mirror for a few cathartic moments. She would contort her face into possible expressions of grief at the imagined passing away of Amarendra. A couple of times she had genuinely tried to cry, to feel grief at his envisioned death, perhaps by remembering the few times that he had been good to her. But to summon enough reasons to miss him had always proved tough – actually nearly impossible – for her.

Alarmed at the cactus-like state of her emotions she had experimented with glycerin, onion juice, even the eucalyptus-based cold rub around her eyes, but they had succeeded in activating her tear glands only for a very brief while. Also, they would not be able to help her cry at the crucial time, for each of them were dead giveaways by virtue of their sight or smell. So this problem had gradually become one that remained unresolved, as did all other issues that connected Amarendra to her.

Why was she so sure that he would die suddenly? And that he would die before she did? Chhaya had asked herself these questions many times. She herself did not know why she was so sure that he would. For, while she had wished him dead many times, she had never even remotely gone to the extent of plotting his murder. The thought of his death remained only a fantasy bordering on wishful thinking.

Was this surety just a woman's gut feeling? Perhaps. But it was a gut feeling backed by the logic of reasoning. For Amarendra did not keep very good health. His heavy boozing and smoking, his middle-age paunch, his absolute apathy towards his diabetic condition and his philandering were all contributing factors. Most of all was the fact that he did not even believe in resolving conflicts. All of this was bound to lead to the end. And it was also bound to be sooner rather than later.

The time bomb had finally gone off today. And for Chhaya the moment to be reckoned with was here. Chhaya called out to her son Rahul. Twenty-three-year-old Rahul, who was the one good thing that had come out of her marriage to Amarendra.

Rahul was a protective son. He would not hear of taking her to hospital just then. "Let me take charge," he said, putting his arm around her. "I'll call you from there and let you know the situation."

Chhaya agreed because she knew that she needed time to prepare. Time to resolve, more than anything else, the issue of tears. For now, every conflict that she had had with Amarendra was only hers to resolve. Hers to resolve in whichever way she wanted to. She was finally going to be in control of herself and of the proceedings that were going to follow – indeed of the remainder of her whole life. It was an awesome and exhilarating feeling, one that she had not experienced in a long, long time. And yet to enable herself to savour it forever, she would first have to pretend to be the brave and grief-stricken wife.

Chhaya walked back slowly to her bedroom. She looked at the king-size bed brought twenty-five years ago along with so many other upper-class accessories that they had purchased when they had shifted into this huge flat. Chhaya pictured Amarendra and herself as they had lain beside each other night after night on either side of the bed, its ample space thankfully providing a safe distance between them.

Some nights in those early days she had been "taken" of course. Merely aberrations before Amarendra and she would both assume their normal positions on either side of the bed again.

Two years after some such aberrations Rahul had been born. He had come to occupy the space between them so conveniently that he actually succeeded in moving each of them somewhat away from the sides of the bed and more towards its centre, where he slept.

This was the only distance that Rahul ever succeeded in bridging between his parents.

He had slept between them until he was ten years old. By then it was almost certain that Chhaya would never need contraception again. By now Amarendra did not even "need" her as he did in the first few years of marriage. She had grown plump and dumpy. While earlier she had known that she was not someone he could really "show off" at the social dos that he attended, now, as he had caustically commented, she wasn't someone he could even merely "show".

There were so many others to fulfil his various needs, she had more or less accepted it this way. He didn't need her and he made that very obvious to her.

Chhaya looked at herself in the dressing-table mirror. It was the same mirror into which she had tested all those crying expressions. Her face was frozen now, and seemed incapable of any kind of expression. She found it difficult to meet her own eyes in her reflection in the mirror. She looked at the rest of her – cold, misshapen and dull. Yes, it was what stared back at her from the mirror that was the real reason, and not Rahul, that she had not left Amarendra when love had left them.

Who else would have her now? She had grown so used to the trappings and tags that being Amarendra's wife so easily accorded her. She was a woman of limited looks and talents and therefore had few options. It made more sense to stay on in the marriage, and therefore very long ago Chhaya had made up her mind to heed her instinct for survival.

In fact, survival as an art was something that she had learnt from Amarendra. She had learnt from him how to exist purely at the physical level. This was also in a way the greatest nirvana of all, something like a this-worldly preparation for the ultimate release of the soul by the next.

And so each day in these last few years had only been spent eating, sleeping, bathing, drinking, cleaning, sullying, breathing and being – daily chores that had been elevated to a state of meditation.

For Chhaya this meditation was disturbed only by all the emotions that motherhood had clawed out of her. Rahul's hugs and his tears, his wants and his fears – they consumed her days at first. Then, as he grew, they merely punctuated the silences in an otherwise meditative day. And in these last few years they appeared only like the rare rainbow on the colourless horizon of her existence. The truth was, now Rahul too did not need her in the manner that he had as a child. Only he did not revel and rejoice in this knowledge as unashamedly as Amarendra did.

In these last few years Chhaya had grown restive again. Like a sage unable to meditate anymore, she was full of questions addressed to herself that she had earlier put to sleep in the cosy lap of her practical wisdom. Questions about her whole life and its significance. A life now tired of its endless frontward journey, on a road where there were no turns at all. Until now, that is – when this strange moment had descended upon them all.

Chhaya sat still on the dressing-table stool. Even through the closed door she could hear the voices of so many people now. They had obviously been let in by their bewildered family retainer, Shankar.

"No, no, no, we can't let her remain inside. Never mind protocol at a time like this, we must go and get her from her bedroom."

That was definitely the voice of Mrs Nair. Chhaya felt the voices coming closer and closer to the bedroom door.

"It's all right. After all, Rahul asked us all to take charge and moreover to take particular care of his mother," said another voice righteously.

"Let's go to her, it's just not right to leave her to her own grief and shock. Sometimes people do dangerous things at such times – they can even harm themselves if they get too dazed by grief," Mrs Nair said, her voice full of concern as she proceeded to push open the door.

And as the door burst open, half-a-dozen women, arms outstretched, walked towards a frozen Chhaya.

"Oh my dear!" wailed Mrs Nair. Then, as if on cue, the others joined in, with each of their cries registering at different decibel levels. Mrs Nair hugged Chhaya tightly. Chhaya's face fell and she felt her heart sink as she heard the sounds of commotion in the hall outside, and the din of car doors opening and closing with rapidity in the courtyard. The moment was finally upon her – there was just no way for it to be wished away any longer. But as Chhaya realised to her horror, she was still not yet prepared to face things.

Each of the women now proceeded to hug her and each of them by turns said a few words to her. Chhaya seemed to absorb it all like a zombie, stony-eyed and unmoved.

"She's still in shock," she heard someone whispering close to her.

"He was such a nice man. Never harmed a fly. I pray for his soul to rest in peace and in heaven," said another.

Chhaya's eyes were still dry.

The women led her, supporting her hands and her back as if she was an invalid, into the hall.

Chhaya noticed with amazement how quickly the furniture and carpets had all been moved to the sides of the hall. How quickly everything had been organised to accommodate the farewell to the master of this home. Her gaze fell upon Rahul, Nair and the others as they entered through the front door, holding the poles of the stretcher with Amarendra's body on it. She then saw them lower the stretcher to the ground.

Rahul was now crying aloud. He cradled his father's head in his hand as the others proceeded to help in moving Amarendra's body to the ground.

Males of all shapes and sizes dressed in differing hues of white more or less surrounded Amarendra and blocked Chhaya's view. Then after what seemed like eternity she was slowly led towards him, and her torso was gently pushed to bend so that she could kneel beside his body.

Chhaya looked at Amarendra's face. The face of the man that she had grown to hate. It was the first time in years that she was looking at him so closely. Somehow, she hadn't imagined that his face would be crisscrossed by so many fine lines.

She could look at him now, as hard and as long as she wanted to, without the embarrassment of being caught doing so. And without worrying that by doing so she was giving him the vicarious pleasure of knowing that he still mattered to her. For he hadn't looked at her for ages, not even from the corner of his eyes. She always thought, and actually hoped that she would catch him looking at her as he had caught her doing so many times. But he had continued to ignore her.

It was no different today. He was still ignoring her but in a completely different way.

Now he would never ever look at her. He would never love her, nor ever hate her. How then could she live on without all that she had got so used to?

Sorrow finally crept up Chhaya's guts and seized her throat as she let out a hoarse cry. Her eyes, finally moved by the sounds from her throat, started to shed tears as animals shed their old skin. Tears that were so elated by the discovery of their own existence that they continued to flow from strength to strength. Chhaya let out a long sigh of relief. At last she had played out the last act in the drama of her life to absolute perfection.

THE PERFECT SWITCH

When the routine begins to itch
And the familiar you long to ditch
Be careful of what you desire
For the heart holds a mysterious fire

Who doesn't like a good love story? I do and I bet you do too. But true love stories are one of those things that are as rare as red diamonds nowadays. Red diamonds do exist, you know! The only reason we don't hear about them is, well, because they are rare! Just like true love stories. But I know one, and now that I have your attention, I'm going to tell you all about it. But I do have to warn you, it probably isn't quite what you're expecting.

Aditya was running late. Trust me when I say he was running late, in fact he was beyond late. He panicked yet again as he looked at his watch and pressed stop on the treadmill. It was eight already, he should have been home by now. His personal trainer looked at him questioningly but Aditya didn't bother with an explanation. The guy got his pay on time and that is all that should matter to him. And with Aditya's ripped body, he could afford to skip half an hour of exercise today for making it on time for work.

As he sipped on his protein shake and made his way outside the gym, women craned their necks to take a good look at him. Aditya was a hunk and he knew it. He liked the attention and at twenty-eight, with the amazing job he had as an investment banker with a leading firm, he got plenty of it, because he was good at his work.

As he pulled away in his Porsche a little later, he was still turning heads. He zipped past his posh gym and soon pulled into the exclusive residential building in which he lived. He had worked hard to earn his perks, and everything he had was a result of that. He even looked at his gorgeous wife Ayesha as a perk of the hard work he had put into his career. After all, why would Ayesha's family have married her to him if he wasn't the best of the best?

As Aditya rang the bell to his penthouse, Ayesha, four years younger to him, answered the door. It was a lovely and familiar sight. She was beautiful, he thought yet again, as she looked at him with a smile. But he didn't say it to her. He didn't want her to begin to compete with him in that department. Ayesha had been born with the proverbial silver spoon in her mouth. Her looks, pedigree and confidence had clinched the deal for Aditya. He loved to show her off to all his friends and colleagues.

She began to flutter around him, asking him what kind of juice he would like, what he wished to eat for breakfast and when he needed to leave, just like she always did. Familiar.

Aditya took one good look at her, dressed in her nightwear, and he could not deny that she was a stunner even in her bedroom clothes. He shushed her, telling her that there was only one thing he really needed to have before he went to work: her! And so, he did, just like they always did. Satisfying. But ... familiar.

As Aditya was being driven to work, his thoughts were on Ayesha rather than the meeting ahead. She was so perfect in the way she dressed, talked, cooked and even made love. He could predict it all. Familiar. Familiar? No. Boring!

Aditya hated the routine of it all. It should've been great, but now he was bored. No matter how good she looked, no matter how satisfied he was, no matter how lovely she was to him. No matter how perfect his life made itself out to be, it bored him to death. He wanted something new, and it wasn't going to be found in the stupid old poems Ayesha kept reading out to him while he pretended to listen.

*

"We and our existences are really non-existence; thou art the absolute Being which manifests the perishable." How beautiful and how true those lines were, Ayesha thought. Before leaving, Aditya had just asked her what they should plan for their anniversary that was coming up next month.

Ayesha had told him she was fine with anything he wanted to do. At her age, Ayesha had already travelled the world, seen it all, been everywhere. There was nothing she yearned for. She often wondered if this was all there was to be in her life. But yes, one thing that mattered to her was Aditya and his happiness. And the other thing that really mattered to her was what Aditya really did not care about, but she hoped she would make him come around to – a baby! Ayesha wanted to have a baby desperately, but Aditya felt that at this point in their lives, it would just be a hindrance.

She had tried to convince him a hundred times. How could he not see that the kicks one got from all the exclusive parties, the crazy alcohol, the innumerable designer clothes and accessories or the fancy wheels never lasted beyond one day, forget a lifetime. But a baby? A baby could change all of that, give the kind of meaning to life and love that nothing else could.

Ayesha was convinced that a baby would add back the missing spark to their marriage that lately Aditya had talked a lot about.

Maybe a baby would bring back Aditya's interest in her? But there was only one way to find out, and Aditya wasn't willing to budge on his stand. She sighed as she looked around the windows at the mall. Even what she saw nudged her to these thoughts as she caught herself window shopping in a baby clothes' store. Talk about the universe sending out messages ... only that she and Aditya seemed to be getting entirely different ones!

*

As Aditya looked around him in his office, he saw the same sight he was so used to seeing every single day. Through the glass walls of his cabin, people smiling, greeting each other the same way. How could they go about their routine every day without change? Surely they must have some source of excitement? Something that made ordinary life seem bearable? He daydreamed, imagining all of them piled up near each other in one orgiastic celebration of lust, no more fake smiles, but raw faces of passion. He knew that most of them were hooking up with each other. Married, unmarried, it didn't matter. And then he imagined himself walking into that pile, and felt his heart beat harder. New. Unfamiliar. Exciting...

No. Ayesha. This would be so wrong to her. Sure, he was bored, but he still loved her deeply. He would have to find another way. He drew the blinds in his office and opened the first file that lay in front of him.

And then it struck him! He had heard some locker-room banter in the gym earlier today. As he was in a hurry, he had dismissed it. But now, as he stared at the last quarter figures in a file, it hit him like a ton of bricks.

While showering, he had heard two guys discussing something that he had only read about earlier – wife swapping or, to be more politically correct, partner swapping!

Aditya was intrigued. Very intrigued to say the least. He wanted to know more. Needless to say, the file was relegated to the side as he opened a new window on his computer and let the internet educate him on a whole new subject. Exciting. Unfamiliar.

As Aditya was driven back home that evening, a new thrill animated his whole being. Here was a way to get back everything that he had lost. As he had pored over page after page on this interesting subject, Aditya realized that wife swapping does not need to be the taboo that people project it to be. Done the right way, it could be the elixir that relights the embers of every dying marriage.

Aditya had become so fascinated with the subject that he had found out all he could about it. In fact he had done little else that day. He now knew all the important details that went into the whole process and he even had found out about a place they could try this phenomenon at. As he set his eyes on Ayesha that evening, he knew that he was convinced. All he had to do now was convince Ayesha about it as well.

As exciting as the idea was, as Aditya stared at a bubbly Ayesha telling him about her boring meal with the hoity-toity ladies that afternoon, Aditya realized that it would be a very bold step. He asked himself if he was ready to share his wife with another man and the answer was a resounding no. The entry of another man and woman in their marriage would change the equation.

If he were honest with himself, Aditya would have really enjoyed sleeping with another woman. It would not even be like he was cheating on Ayesha since she herself would also have the freedom to sleep with another man. And that is where the problem lay. The fact that she would also sleep with another man.

"Won't you share your dessert with me, Aditya?" Ayesha's question jolted Aditya out of his reverie. He stared at the tiramisu that lay before him and then at Ayesha's eager face. No, this was definitely going to be too much for him to deal with. Ayesha was his and he could not think of someone else with her. He smiled sweetly and pushed the entire dessert towards her. She happily plunged her spoon into it and began to eat.

As Ayesha heard the gentle snores emanating from Aditya that night as he slept beside her, her thoughts wandered to her existence once again. It had been just another day, they had gone out for yet another dinner, made love yet again and Aditya had wanted to sleep right after it, never mind that she wanted to talk. When she thought of it, she never really had conversations with anyone. Sure she met a lot of people and they talked a lot, but those soul-stirring conversations that she really wanted, never really happened.

*

Okay. Once. Just once. He could deal with Ayesha being with someone else for one night, couldn't he? Aditya thought to himself the next day on the fourth kilometre of the treadmill. He could live with that, couldn't he? Maybe it would help rekindle their marriage? Besides it was Ayesha. There was no chance that anything could get out of hand. He intended to make full use of this chance…

What was wrong in that, thought Aditya. Wasn't he doing the right thing by trying to keep his marriage alive? Of course he was. His mind raced as he filled in the details on the secret website for the next meeting of this group. He couldn't quite believe he was going to do this. Of course, there was the small matter of convincing Ayesha, and that would have to be done when the time was right.

The right time presented itself sooner than he had expected. Aditya and Ayesha had gone out to dinner at the place of Aditya's friend and colleague Shweta. She was slightly older than Aditya and while she worked in finance, her husband Prabodh was an artist. They were not what one would expect of a typical couple. Wild and carefree in their thinking. Shweta was an open woman, one who did not mind getting friendly with other men. Ayesha always got a bit uncomfortable with Shweta's attitude and even the attention that Prabodh showered on her did not flatter her. On the contrary, it stifled her. But if she objected to meeting them, Aditya would always fly into a huff.

An incident started it all. While Ayesha was counting the hours to the time the dinner at Shweta's place would get over, Prabodh decided to show Ayesha his latest work. As Aditya had already seen it, Ayesha alone was led to Prabodh's studio to see the work. Even his paintings were beyond her, forget the man! Aditya knew, whichever way this went, he was in luck.

Inside the studio, Prabodh gazed at Ayesha, trying to explain the meaning behind some of his work. He stopped in front of one portrait of a couple making love, and came a bit close to her while explaining what he had envisioned for it. His gaze made her uncomfortable. He hadn't even laid a finger on her, but she felt him undressing her in his mind. It was a bizarre feeling, getting that attention from a man other than Aditya.

Seeing her squirm, Prabodh asked her why she was so uncomfortable. Sex was a basic need for everyone, he opined. He asked her if it wasn't a need of hers. Ayesha did not know what to say. She wanted to go back to Aditya and said so. That irritated Prabodh who accused her of being a prude. Convinced that this was the last place she wanted to be, Ayesha faked illness and wished to excuse herself.

The dinner that followed was awkward and silent. Ayesha squirmed when they were to say goodbye. As Prabodh was a little too cosy while giving her a hug, and so was Shweta with Aditya. Aditya was not happy. He drove rather recklessly on the way back, and said nothing. Ayesha tried to talk to him, but she might as well have been speaking to the dashboard of the car. She tried to put her hand on his and he jerked it away. She prepared herself mentally for their routine way having a fight. It was after all, familiar.

She apologised, explaining that she was uncomfortable and it didn't feel good being there, not that it was a judgement on the character of Prabodh and Shweta, but she didn't think that she could enjoy an evening the way they would.

All the while, Aditya drove back home as fast as he could, saying nothing, but breathing heavily. He could feel her unease next to him. Good, it was working. She was exactly where he wanted her to be. Soon she'd take it upon herself and want to make up for it, and didn't he have just the perfect solution…

He told Ayesha to shove her conventional mentality down the toilet as Shweta and Prabodh were well-travelled individuals who had seen the world and had some of the most exclusive friends, people who believed in living and letting live. He said she had no idea what she was talking about, or whom she was talking to, and that as a result of her bad judgement, he was made to look like a fool, and she a prude.

*

It was as they got ready for bed and Aditya picked up his quilt and pillow to sleep in the other room that Ayesha could take it no longer. She apologised profusely to him, even asking him if there was anything she could do to make him feel all right. Aditya knew that now the iron was hot.

He placed his pillow and quilt back on the bed, looked at her pleading face, and simply asked her to come with him for a party the next weekend.

Ayesha couldn't really believe what she was hearing. A party? Of course she would. She would leave right that minute if that's what it took to make him feel better and forgive her. She laughed through her sobs. She jumped on to him and hugged him, and waited for him to slowly undo her dress as she knew he would. It was all so ... familiar.

As they slept that night, cuddled next to each other, Ayesha wondered if all marriages were such hard work. She had the template of the marriage of her own parents in her mind, an easy-going and loving camaraderie between two people who were each other's best friends.

Ayesha's parents had taught her that it was okay to disagree as long as they never insulted the other for the way they felt about something. But increasingly Ayesha had begun to feel that she was always walking on eggshells around Aditya, worried about the next thing he would take offence at. But all was good now, they would go to a party together, they weren't fighting, all was good, she told herself.

*

The drive to Lonavala was scenic, as it always was, but that wasn't the main reason Ayesha was in good spirits. Aditya was like a happy little excited puppy, the way he had been in the beginning of their marriage.

Maybe it was a rough patch? Doubts always arose in a marriage. She was silly to think that Aditya was uncaring towards her. Yes, sure, he did not share her taste in music, but he was a banker, how could he? Perhaps she had been a little selfish in her own expectations?

Nevertheless, she felt grateful, and this time when she put her hand on his, he smiled and held it tight. Maybe this would be the trip where she could finally bring him round to seeing her point of view. Maybe they could finally have a baby together.

As night began to fall, they drew closer to their destination. The venue of the party was a huge bungalow at a secluded hill. They drove into the gates and were stopped by security. Aditya was asked to identify himself, their names were duly checked and then double checked. He was then asked to reveal a password and even the host spoke to him on the intercom.

As they drove into the compound, Ayesha wondered about all the secrecy for what was just another party. The driveway was long as they wheeled past sprawling gardens with a fountain and a huge pool in which people were swimming. There were huge zorbing balls in them, the kind in which people can get in. Except that there was a couple in one of the balls, laughing and giggling and playing with each other. There were drink counters everywhere and everyone was in high spirits. Just looking at them all cheered Aditya immensely. It was quite a sight, and the facade of the bungalow looked like no other house she had seen in this country, thought Ayesha.

The building itself was a modern villa with lots of glass and greenery everywhere. The place had been lit up beautifully, yet elegantly. Clearly the owners knew a thing or two about design and architecture. As they stepped out of their car, a valet arrived to park it and then, they were handed masks to wear. Ayesha looked at Aditya with a smile and he put on his, urging her to do the same, saying that it was for fun, reminding her of her promise.

Ayesha and Aditya entered the party where people were mingling with each other. She clung to his arm asking him where the hosts were. Aditya asked her to relax, distancing himself a bit from her. He told her that they were here to have fun and what better way to do so than begin afresh with a bunch of strangers? Some of the strangers were looking at her quite appreciatively, but no one was lecherous. Everything seemed too elegant for that. She kept wondering what this place was and what was going on, as Aditya made small talk with some of the other couples. She felt like dancing, and Aditya handed her another glass of wine.

Tables nearby were groaning under the weight of the food. None of the guests were on their phones. They were all just trying their best to enjoy the moment. All-in-all, after her appraisal of the place and the people, Ayesha felt a bit silly for panicking so much.

*

At the other end of the large hall, Viren hadn't been able to make himself seem quite at ease. Panic didn't look like it was going to be leaving him soon. He kept thinking why he was there, feeling out of place. As he looked at the masked men and women before him, a thought came unbidden to his mind. If they are so ashamed to even show their faces to everyone, why have they all come here in the first place? He quoted his famous lines of Rumi to himself: *Tear off the mask. Your face is glorious.*

His wife Saumya meanwhile had with her a young lady and was now introducing Viren to her. He could not remember a word of the conversation later but one thing was certain, the will to walk out of there had gone. Viren could not afford to break the promise, not if he wanted his marriage to work.

*

Viren was thirty, married to the twenty-eight-year-old Saumya. They had fallen in love in college. But Saumya came from a very different world from his. While he was from a family that had scraped some money to get Viren an education, Saumya was elite stock. She had grown up in different countries, living the life of the privileged. While Viren had to wonder about where his next fund for an education would come from, Saumya had no dearth of money to spend on the slightest need. Perhaps it was then only natural for opposites to attract.

But while Viren was prepared to let her go, knowing that she would never be able to live a life like his, she refused to forget him. In fact, the more Viren urged her to get on in her life, the more she came back only to him. She went against the wishes of her family and got married to Viren, and sure enough, soon even her parents came around to the idea of both of them being together. When Saumya's father met Viren after the marriage, he was quite impressed.

Viren, who was trying to work hard and support his family and Saumya, soon got the offer of an investment from her father. He did not know what to do but he did know that he eventually did want to start something on his own. The idea of accepting money and never returning it was alien to him, and so Viren began to work hard to set up his artificial-intelligence-based firm, and vowed to pay back every single rupee to Saumya's father.

But Saumya had soon got bored of her life. She had insisted on moving into a bigger home, a fancier car and all the trappings of the good life. Viren had just begun to work harder and while his relationship with Saumya was beginning to unravel, his business had begun to do very well. He had managed to return three-fourths of the loan made by his father-in-law and now looked forward to starting a family. Saumya, however, was in no hurry to ruin her figure, her peace of mind and her life, as she put it.

Their reason for coming here tonight was Saumya. She had promised she would think of planning a baby soon if Viren came away with her to the party tonight. Left with no other alternative, he had agreed.

He was cursing himself right now but he knew he would have to pay this price. As he stared at Saumya talking animatedly with the others, his heart skipped a beat. She was beautiful, but she was deeply unhappy with him. He was not the wild, experimental kind of guy she wanted in her life. He was a simple man, with simple needs and the deep-seated desire for a child or two of his own. He did not like to admit it, but apart from poetry, the only other thing he wanted from life was a daughter! But really! Was this the way he was going to have to convince his wife for a child?

Impatient and feeling out of place, Viren rose from his chair and walked to Saumya. He held her hand and pulled her away to the side. She was shocked to say the least. Viren asked her why they were here in the first place. Saumya was fed up. She looked into Viren's eyes calmly and said that they had decided that both of them wanted to do this and now they were here. If he wanted to renege on his promise and leave, he could but she was going to stay. On hearing these words, Viren withdrew his hand. Disappointment and resignation were writ large on his face. Saumya wanted this at any cost...

*

As the night wore on, Ayesha stuck by Aditya's side as if leaving him even for a moment would be her doom. Aditya was irritated with her constantly hanging around but he did not want to upset her by saying anything. Soon the host for the evening took matters in his hands by saying that it was that time of the night when they would get down to what they were here for, getting to know each other even better. He brought out a large glass bowl filled with car keys.

The host explained that now they would shuffle the keys and place them in a black velvet bag from which all the lovely ladies would pick out a key. The gentleman to whom the key belonged would have the pleasure of the company of that particular lady for the night.

Ayesha's world came crashing down. She looked at Aditya as if to reconfirm that this was all a joke. That they had merely come to watch this thing unfold like a movie. But he looked serious enough. She asked him how on earth could he even consider something so disgusting, but Aditya shot her a look and said that she had agreed to work on their marriage. This was how he was going to.

She couldn't even scream, or say anything, as her heart pounded inside her. After all she still didn't want to embarrass Aditya, but who was this man whose arm she was on? Did she even know her husband anymore?

Aditya was still talking, assuring her that these men were not going to force themselves on her, and that she was free to do anything so long as she was comfortable with it, but she could barely hear him.

Was he really going to sleep with somebody else tonight? Aditya nudged her forward when her turn came, and she picked a key from the bowl, numb. A man came forward, they were given the key to a room, and they walked down a hallway.

*

As Viren followed a young lady towards their assigned room, he had no clue how he would break it to her that he was not interested in sleeping with her. Ayesha's face was reddening as she walked. No, she would have to delay getting there. She let out a low scream of pain and clutched her ankle, pretending to have a sprain. Viren was instantly by her side. He peeled off the mask he was wearing and cast it aside, his entire attention on her ankle. Viren helped her up on her feet and lead her to a nearby sofa.

They dared not look at each other. Ayesha wondered when Viren would suggest that they head to the room. Viren on the other hand was rather glad for this incident. He called a bearer over and ordered two cups of iced tea, looking at Ayesha and asking if she wanted alcohol instead. She was pleasantly surprised. Iced tea would do.

As they sat in the deserted corridor, open to the outdoors, they could hear the flicking of the cicadas, the chirping of crickets. The night sky was a deep blue and the giant palms swept up a cooling breeze towards them. They could also see a huge pond from where gentle sprays of water swept towards them with the wind.

But all this serenity was lost on the only two people witnessing it for they were both in a terrible predicament, not of their own making. *Actually, I am responsible for landing up in this situation,* Viren thought to himself. Saumya was so used to getting what she wanted that she could not realize where to draw the line anymore. He thought of where she must be right now and of the man she had been left with.

Ayesha was, meanwhile, indulging in some self-pity. Tears clouded her eyes as she looked away from Viren. In any case, Viren looked lost in his own thoughts. As he heard a sniffle, he turned towards Ayesha assuming that her ankle hurt. He shrugged his shoulders and offered to assist her in some way if she needed it but she shook her head. That suited Viren just fine. As the bearer turned up with their iced tea, both took them tentatively, wondering how they could avoid turning up at the room.

She is a beautiful woman indeed, thought Viren. In other circumstances he could have complimented her, but in this charged situation, it was the last thing he would do. He quietly got her up and led her to the room. As Viren closed the door behind him, Ayesha was suddenly afraid. A closed door; it was as if her fate for tonight was being sealed.

She sat down on the bed gingerly, and Viren pulled up a chair against the table and set their masks on it. Awkward silence.

"Excuse me, I don't want to sleep with you," Ayesha blurted out.

Viren stared at her, open mouthed.

Ayesha was shaking with fear. The man looked strong, much like Aditya. Anything could happen. But he wouldn't hurt her. Would he?

"Sorry, please, I have nothing against you. I just … I have been dragged here by my husband…" She broke down.

Viren, still shocked, poured a glass of water and handed it to her. She kept apologising furiously, and he kept telling her, it was okay. A wave of relief washed over him.

When she had calmed down, he sat down next to her, and said that he was in the same predicament. His wife had dragged him here, and he had no interest in sleeping with other women, but that Saumya had promised him they could plan a child together if he let her indulge herself tonight. Even as he said it, he was shocked at how silly it sounded. He hoped this woman didn't think he was a fool. Then again, she was in the exact same position as he was.

He told her why he was indebted to Saumya and her family, and his business. Ayesha too opened up about her life, her worries, and today, with this stranger, she felt like she could open up about everything. This stranger, this chance encounter, it seemed more real than any conversation she had had lately.

They spoke about their spouses, their lives, ambitions, and thoughts. She shared that she would hate Aditya for some time for doing this to her, but eventually forgive him like she always had. She remembered at some point thinking, what a silly pattern of behaviour that would be.

"Do not feel lonely, the entire universe is within you..."

Viren's words caught her off guard. He stood over the coffee machine, beating the coffee and the sugar together, as Ayesha realised she had been staring out into blankness for a long time.

Rumi...

What was the chance?

"The wound is the place where the light enters you..." she said.

He stopped and turned around. There, at that moment, both of them knew that they had found a kindred spirit in each other.

Hours and hours of conversations with friends would not tell you anything about them, and tell them nothing about you. And a moment like that, thought Ayesha, could tell you all you need to know about a person.

*

They talked till morning, about everything in their hearts, their childhood, their dreams, their aspirations and hopes. They didn't know where time flew. They headed out to eat a humble breakfast of chai and poha at a tea stall. Ayesha looked beautiful in the morning sunlight, Viren thought, and she felt beautiful indeed, it had been a long time since she had laughed and smiled and felt that happy.

A day ago she would have never imagined herself seated across from a man she had met in such extraordinary circumstances and yet feeling so free with him that she could talk about anything, knowing he would be genuinely interested in it. He would never feign an interest that he did not genuinely feel. Her thoughts did wander to what Aditya must have been up to, that he may have had more fun in this one night than he ever had with her, but now, Ayesha did not feel like competing in that department anymore.

They made it back before time and in a while, all the other guests wearing masks arrived back into the hall. As Aditya saw Ayesha, he rushed to her, hoping she had not created a scene. But seeing her quite normal he said his goodbye to his partner and they left.

Aditya was expecting fireworks. He did not get as much as a sparkler. And strangely enough, this worried him no end.

*

Viren could tell that Saumya had had a good time. She was happy and chirpy today morning. That was certainly more of an exception than the rule. Saumya was only ever happy when she got what she wanted; he wasn't in a very giving state of mind. She had pushed him too hard and he had had enough. Saumya was surprised that he didn't bring up the topic of a baby at all.

Ayesha too did not want to have a confrontation with Aditya. What could she possibly say to a man who did not mind sharing his wife with another man as long as he got to have his fun? With all his good looks, his super-fancy successful life, Aditya looked nothing more than a glorified stud to Ayesha. The more she saw him that way, the more he seemed comical to her rather than scary or daunting. She still took care of him the way a wife is supposed to, but that completely trusting intimacy ... that was no longer something she felt she would be able to give him.

Sometimes, seeing her so normal, Aditya wondered if she had indeed had a better time than him with her partner that night. Aditya did not want to admit it but he felt jealous for the first time.

Slowly, Ayesha had begun to mentally compare Aditya with Viren in every little thing. Where Viren was gentle, Aditya was a brute, where Viren took a firm stand, Aditya was wishy-washy, where Viren refused to compromise on his morals, Aditya's were practically non-existent. In every aspect, Ayesha realised that Aditya behaved more like a spoilt kid than a grown adult. Actually, why call him a kid because kids were at least innocent. It was not like this was a revelation for her ... she had lived with him long enough to know this, but just had chosen to turn a blind eye.

*

Ayesha. She was all Viren thought about now. She consumed his thoughts. He had never felt such a connection with anyone. Yes, there was a time that he could have said he truly loved Saumya. Sure, he still did care for her but lately, he seemed to have outgrown it.

Saumya even asked him why he roamed around with a silly grin on his face ever since they had come back. Viren simply told her that the sight of her feeling content made him happy. She obviously did not believe him. So be it, he had no intentions of clarifying anything anymore.

With thoughts of Ayesha in his mind, he uploaded his Facebook status to say, "In a world where everyone wears a mask, it has been a privilege to see a soul." Another one of Rumi's jewels. It was all he could do to hope that she would see it and respond somehow.

While Viren enjoyed poetry, he had never wallowed in the sentimentality of it. Poets were crazy men who lived in a different world where they could afford to stay intoxicated in the thoughts of the one they loved. Viren could not afford such a luxury. And yet, Ayesha had had this crazy effect on him that all he really wanted to do was just think of her, reach out to her, to talk to her and get to know her. He hoped he was not the only one so affected, that she too felt something. It had to be. He really hoped for once that somehow, she would respond.

And respond she did. The conversation went from Facebook to over the phone. They would steal moments where they could speak, share lines of poetry, and laugh with each other. It was wrong though. Or ... Was it really?

*

Aditya often saw Ayesha smiling over something she read in her phone. Curiosity got the better of him but his ego did not allow him to peek through her phone. Seeing Ayesha happy bothered him. It bothered him a lot. He did not like the changes in his wife since the visit to Lonavala. He admitted to himself that the trip was meant to do good to him. He did have a good time that night, but that was it. This was supposed to do good for their marriage, but it seemed like Ayesha had been least interested in him after that night. For the first time in their marriage, he felt like he was way more into it than she was.

*

Saumya bore the visit of her mother-in-law with decency. This was the least she could do for him, since he had agreed to come for the party with her. Even her mother-in-law was surprised at all the attention and care Saumya showered on her. But what irked Saumya was that Viren had never bothered to ask her about her experience, nor had he bothered to tell her if he had enjoyed himself. She often saw him looking into his phone and smiling.

*

Quite oblivious to how they were affecting their respective spouses, Viren and Ayesha were just getting to know each other. He treated her like a lady and she realised that there were so many facets to this man. She found herself not with him but with thoughts of him all day long. Just knowing him had made her life beautiful.

Ayesha was sorely tempted to ask Viren to come and see her. But doing so meant acknowledging there was something happening between them. For the first time ever Ayesha was not ashamed of the way she felt for Viren. She did love him and wanted so badly to meet him.

Aditya tried to mend things between him and Ayesha. He still asked her to come for dinners and parties with him. She turned down too many and accepted too few. He sulked, threw tantrums and even tried to rile her but she had just stopped reacting when he was in one of his moods.

When he was spent with emotion, she would come back and ask him if he was feeling better and handle him coolly. Aditya had never seen this side of Ayesha and he did not know what to do with her. And, most importantly, this new, non-people-pleasing Ayesha was immensely attractive to him. He was beginning to fall in love with her, and he wanted her so badly.

*

It started with an innocent refusal one evening when Aditya asked her to come out to a party with him. Ayesha told him that she was not up to it and would rather stay home. Aditya asked her not to pretend, since all she would do even if she stayed home was stare at the phone. Ayesha chose not to fall for the bait and walked away. This got to Aditya. He was fed up seeing this ice-princess sort of wife who would handle all his tantrums so deftly without batting an eyelid.

Aditya then chased her, ordering her never to ignore him. One thing led to another and soon, he was so turned on by Ayesha that he was kissing her. He was rough, very rough. All the pent-up frustration of all these days was finally out and Aditya was very aggressive making love that evening. In fact, he was not making love at all.

Ayesha did not even know who this man was anymore. She bore the onslaught but it scared her. When he was done, she looked at Aditya and realised that she did not love him anymore. She was certain of it. As she saw the man she called her husband leave the apartment, she knew he had crossed the line today and there was no going back. She knew she was going to have to leave.

She picked up the phone, and told Viren that she needed to speak with him urgently. Boldly, without caring for what could happen of it, she said she loved him, and she needed to run away from her life. Viren was shocked to hear this out of the blue; he said if she hadn't said it first he would probably have never had the courage to. But he was so glad she did, relieved even.

They hatched a plan.

When the invite for the next partner-swapping event arrived, both Ayesha and Viren had excuses ready for not attending but allowed themselves to be coerced into going. As they drove up the now familiar drive to the villa, Ayesha shuddered remembering the last time Aditya had brought her here and thrust her into a wholly unfamiliar world. Wasn't a husband supposed to protect his wife?

As they wore their masks and entered the venue, Ayesha's eyes looked only for one person. And sure enough, she saw him in one of the corners, talking to a few people, Saumya by his side. They were all wearing masks but there was nothing fake about the look in the eyes of Viren and Ayesha when they saw each other.

Ayesha was getting a bit antsy as the time for the draw drew nearer. Though Viren had planned well, she hoped nothing would go wrong. Maybe she was imagining it but everything about tonight seemed less scary. Even Aditya looked more like a cartoon to her than anything else. After what he had done to her, she felt no remorse for what was about to happen.

When the draw began, Ayesha looked apprehensively at Viren. He gestured to her to calm down. The keys were picked, the people were coupled, and Viren and Ayesha walked away to their room once again, followed closely by Aditya and Saumya to theirs.

This time there were no mishaps on the way. They reached the room, both a bit nervous. Like the last time, they were both anxious, but this time for different reasons. When they entered the room, they took off their masks, and Ayesha hugged Viren tightly and kissed him. It lingered on, and they gazed into each other's eyes, and kissed again. He gently led her to the bed, but he didn't undress her at all, just held her close, caressing her skin.

Once again, morning arrived sooner than expected and Viren jumped out of bed as soon as the alarm went off. They had work to do. Ayesha rushed and got ready as Viren opened the door silently, careful not to wake anyone up. They tiptoed their way down the hall. What had looked like a beautiful setting the previous night was a mess in the morning. Ayesha smiled as she thought that it could be said of most of the revellers as well.

Viren picked up the do-not-disturb sign from their room, and hung it outside a door after latching it shut from the outside. They had seen Aditya and Saumya disappear into the room the previous night. It was silent, and they made their way to the parking lot.

Viren fired up his car, and waited for Ayesha, who seemed to be staring out into the woods. Viren gestured that they should leave, before someone woke up, but Ayesha waited. She picked up Aditya's car keys that she had sneaked out from the bowl, and threw them with all her might into the forest. She ran into the car.

"Let's just go," she said.

She had tears in her eyes as she looked at the man beside her. He handed her a small velvet box. She opened it to see a beautiful ring with a red stone on it.

It's a red diamond, he explained. They do exist, and they're the rarest of the rare, he continued.

I would've taken even a pebble from you, she said.

I know, and that's why. He smiled, knocked the car down a gear and sped off with her hand on his...

THE REVELATION

If turning a blind eye
Offers an illusion to live by
Life often does levy a cess
Every joy seeks its pound of flesh

"Kuhu! Finish your puja fast please! I'm getting late!"

Ajoy's nagging yell compelled Kuhu to mumble her prayers and get up hurriedly. When she reached the dining area, Ajoy was about to call out once more.

"What is it, Ajoy?" she asked calmly, almost maternally.

"I need another sandwich," Ajoy answered from behind the newspaper.

Kuhu raised the lid of the vessel kept on the table and took out a sandwich for Ajoy.

"It was right here, Ajoy, on the table," she said, trying to conceal the exasperation in her voice.

Ajoy put the paper down.

"How was I to know, madam? Thanks anyway," he said sarcastically. He munched on the sandwich, eyes on the paper, not once looking at Kuhu.

The doorbell rang. Kuhu opened the door and smiled at the flowers hiding the face behind them.

"Surprise!" Kiran was grinning warmly as she lowered the flowers and gave Kuhu a tight hug.

"Happy birthday, Mrs Kuhu Sen!"

Ajoy stood up from his chair and watched as Kiran came inside, followed by Kuhu. He looked a trifle embarrassed and just a tad sorry. He grimaced at his wife.

"I am sorry I forgot, Kuhu. A very happy birthday to you," he said abruptly before turning to Kiran. "Thanks, Kiran, for reminding me."

Kiran's expression was quite unpleasant. She nodded and smiled artificially. Ajoy gathered his things and began moving out.

"Okay bye. You two catch up. Will see you in the evening then."

Once the door was shut, Kuhu sighed happily and fetched a cup of tea for Kiran. Kiran sat at the table itself and Kuhu sat next to her. She noticed that Kiran was not smiling anymore.

"Hey! Where are you?" she asked, waving her hand in front of Kiran's face.

Kiran looked at her and pursed her lips. "Don't you get fed up of his attitude?" she said, irritated.

"You mean that he forgot my birthday?" asked Kuhu gently, and before Kiran could confirm, she said, "It's okay, Kiran. He came in late last night after a hectic day; must have slipped his mind."

Kiran was unrelenting. "There you go again. It's the same story always. I'm telling you, Kuhu, you let him get away too easily. It's not done."

Kuhu let out a long sigh. "Okay, I admit, I did feel bad. In fact, the way he disturbed my puja this morning was awful. It doesn't matter to him that I have a way of life. It's always about him, always. But…"

"But what, Kuhu?"

"I'm not expressive like you, Kiran. I'd rather he understood on his own."

Kiran was agitated. "He will never understand on his own! For your information, most men are like that!"

Kuhu laughed. "Here comes my Rani of Jhansi! Okay, okay, calm down now, and tell me what you will have for breakfast."

Kiran relinquished her frown and broke into a smile again. "Nothing. I have to rush. I wanted to wish you personally, so I took a detour."

Kiran left in a hurry, but not before extracting a promise that Kuhu would spend the evening with her if Ajoy didn't return on time.

Kuhu knew Ajoy wouldn't be home early in the evening. He had already told her the previous night about a special project consuming him and it was unlikely that he would change his schedule suddenly. So when Kiran sent her a message in the evening, she readily agreed to go out with her and her colleague Avinash.

*

Avinash was Kiran's new buddy in office. Both were together for most of their professional hours. Recently, their working relationship had spilled over into their personal arena too. When they picked Kuhu up and drove to a swanky restaurant nearby, Kuhu couldn't help notice the light-hearted camaraderie between them.

The conversation flowed freely. Avinash asked Kiran in jest, "So Kiran, when is your sun rising?" Both women looked at each other blankly. Kuhu started laughing. It dawned on Kiran a second later.

"You mean marriage? Hmm ... don't know, have to find the right man," she said.

"And that, Avinash, I've told her, is elusive. For all her practicality, she lives in a fantasy world when it comes to this issue," Kuhu said.

Kiran protested. "No, it's not just about a Mr Right! It's just that I can't stand it when men act condescendingly." She glanced at Kuhu. "Worse, when women take that attitude lying down, I think it is highly demeaning to themselves."

"Agreed." Avinash winked at Kuhu, who was smiling. "Tell me one thing, Kiran, are you a descendent of Germaine Greer, by any chance?"

"No again! I don't understand! If a woman has a viewpoint, why are men so threatened? It's just an opinion, it's not feminism! Yes, I *do* think that the man I marry should be able to give me time and genuine concern, not just dutiful finances and callous forgetfulness in the name of comfortable love!"

By now Kuhu was looking the other way. Kiran threw her hands in the air. "Oh forget it! What are we talking about! Let's just celebrate this occasion for now. There! The cake is here. Come on, Kuhu dear, blow your wishes towards god!"

*

When she tucked herself into bed later that night, Kuhu's thoughts wandered to Kiran. She and Kiran had been together for years; since school. They had always stuck to each other through thick and thin. What was intriguing was that the similarity between them was restricted to the letter 'k' in their names. But they complemented each other in a strangely fulfilling way which was as unfathomable for them as it was for others. But what mattered was that they knew each other like the lines of their hands. When Kuhu's parents passed away a couple of years after her wedding, Kuhu, a single child, had no one to turn to except formal relatives. It was Kiran who had pulled her within her circle and become her family. Kiran, for all purposes, was a sister to her. In fact she was everything to her.

Ajoy was more a companion of her routine existence. Just as Kuhu felt that she was a daily mundane matter for him. Kuhu came from a conservative Bengali family. The warped value of a woman being seen but not heard had long been ingrained in her genes. Her being wedded to an educated, modern and hardened chauvinist was the beginning of an uneventful life and the start of a lifetime filled with an overwhelming sense of suppressed frustration.

As her eyes were weighed down with sleep, her thoughts inched towards Ajoy. Ajoy had a nice cushy job which gave her materialistic security. He was absent-minded and insensitive towards her too often, but then she had been cornered into acceptance by the lack of an alternative in life. Maybe god intended things to be this way for her. After all he was all she had in the name of family now. And frankly she just did not have the guts to live life as boldly as her friend Kiran did.

*

In the morning, Kiran rushed out to the gate where Avinash was waiting in his car. As she settled in her seat, Avinash said, "Straight to the client meeting? And then maybe we could have lunch somewhere."

"Sure. Any particular place?" asked Kiran.

"Rangoli is good I've heard."

"Okay."

The meeting went well and Kiran was on a high. Avinash looked at her appreciatively.

"That was an awesome presentation!" he said.

"Thanks, Avinash. Your flawless research helped a lot."

"Lunch now?"

"Yes! I'm starving. And this one will be on me," said Kiran.

Avinash smiled as he drove on.

As soon as they had taken a table, Avinash began looking for a waiter. As he moved sideways to catch a glimpse of the reception, Kiran became a statue in shock.

Right behind Avinash, at some distance, sat Ajoy, with a young woman.

"Quick, Avinash, sit straight!" she whispered.

Avinash was puzzled. He raised an eyebrow and smiled mischievously.

"What, ma'am? Is this posture drill a part of the menu?"

"Shut up, Avinash! Do as I say!"

Avinash sat straight, wondering what was going on. Kiran shifted her sight slightly above his shoulder.

What bothered her was the air between Ajoy and the woman. She was smiling a lot and it seemed that he was explaining something to her. She was quite good looking and her clothes and demeanour smacked of an official air. However, the way they were interacting raised Kiran's suspicions. A moment later, Ajoy was laughing openly, his head thrown back. The woman looked at him affectionately. Too affectionately, thought Kiran. What followed horrified her.

Ajoy leaned forward and tapped the woman's nose playfully. He clasped her hand in his and planted a kiss on her palm, staring at her all this while.

Kiran got up and turned towards the exit door.

"Avinash! Get up!" she hissed.

Avinash followed her, terribly amused. "What happened, Greer of Jhansi?" he asked, as he kept walking behind her.

Before Kiran could answer, the manager had reached them. "Anything wrong, sir? You're not dining with us?" he asked with concern.

Kiran kept her face towards the door. She didn't want Ajoy to see her. Avinash thought fast.

"No ... yes, in fact ... not much ... madam here doesn't like ... doesn't like ... your..."

The manager was waiting.

"Your waiters!" Avinash finished his sentence with a flourish. The manager gave him a confused smile laced with controlled politeness. Avinash rushed out after the speeding Kiran.

In the car, Kiran was fuming.

"What the hell happened?" asked Avinash.

Kiran looked at him pointedly.

"Men!"

*

Kiran couldn't sleep a wink that night. She tossed and turned and raged inside. How could he do this to such a wonderful woman like Kuhu? And Kuhu; she must be blissfully unaware of what was happening behind her back. *I had told her to keep an eye on him, but she's done a damn*!

The first thought that hit her in the morning was how she would tell Kuhu about her discovery. Kiran was sure Kuhu wouldn't be able to take the news. She doubted whether Kuhu would actually believe her.

The phone rang. She lifted the receiver. It was Kuhu. She was crying.

"Kuhu! What's wrong? Why are you sobbing like this?"

Kuhu was barely able to speak. Kiran's heart sank. So she already knew. Kiran braced herself.

"He ... he didn't eat his breakfast. He just left in ... in a huff," Kuhu said in a broken voice.

"Hmm ... So?"

"He was angry that I'd not made his favourite vegetable for his lunch. But Kiran ... I-I haven't been well since yesterday. I couldn't get up on time. I..." Kuhu began sobbing again.

Kiran was relieved. She brought a stern note to her voice.

"Let him go to hell! Kuhu, give it a break! Why didn't you tell him about your condition?"

Kuhu wasn't listening. She cried bitterly. She was fed up, she said. Kiran consoled her as best as she could and promised to see her that day.

After lunch, Kiran sat waiting for Kuhu at their regular café, rehearsing repeatedly how she would convince Kuhu to take a stand for herself now. Kuhu arrived. She was dressed in a pink sari splattered with printed yellow flowers. Her hair was freshly washed and her characteristic Bengali dot shone resplendently on her lovely forehead.

There were no signs of the morning outburst on her face. Kiran looked at her curiously as she ordered coffee. They sat quietly for some time talking about this and that. Kiran noticed

Kuhu was evading the reason they had met for, and it puzzled her. When their mugs were empty, she broke the silent barrier.

"So?" quizzed Kiran.

Kuhu looked at her. She tucked a strand of errant hair behind her ear and paused.

"He called from office. He apologised for his behaviour," she said calmly.

Kiran was nonplussed.

Kuhu continued, "I'm feeling better. I'm sorry I alarmed you in the morning."

"Why don't you do something for yourself, Kuhu? How long is this going to go on?"

Kuhu sat with downcast eyes. "I know you're worried about me, Kiran. I'll do something, don't worry. I'll talk to him. Right now, things have settled."

"When will you talk to him? When I say? Do you know, I saw..."

Kiran stopped herself. No, she couldn't blurt out that part so easily. Kuhu would get hurt. No, she would have to find a way out to make it easier for Kuhu to handle the news.

Kuhu looked up curiously. "What were you saying?"

"Nothing. Forget it. Listen, I have to get to the office now. Take care of yourself. See you later."

*

Kiran was restless the whole day. She racked her brains no end but couldn't figure out a way to inform Kuhu about Ajoy's adventures and why she needed to pull him up. In any case, she wanted to get to the bottom of what she had witnessed at the restaurant. Kiran knew Kuhu needed help. And she also knew that there was only one person who could help her.

After office hours, she walked up to Avinash and pulled up a chair next to him. Avinash smiled.

"Hi GJ! So what can I do for you?"

Kiran glared at him in mock displeasure. She lowered her voice.

"A lot actually."

She narrated everything to Avinash.

A friend of Avinash, who had once dabbled in a private investigation agency, was roped in to garner more details about the woman Ajoy was dating. That, combined with Kiran's own discreet enquiries, confirmed her worst suspicions. Ajoy was having a torrid affair with that woman, who was a business associate in a subsidiary firm.

Kiran felt more confident about broaching it to Kuhu now. But she knew she would have to be tactful. Kiran visited Kuhu's home one evening. As they talked, Kiran asked casually, "How is Ajoy doing?"

"He's fine. Busier than before. But he took me out for dinner yesterday," Kuhu said pleasantly.

"Oh! That's nice," said Kiran, hiding her contempt of such a gesture from Ajoy. "Did you go to Rangoli by any chance?"

"No, we went to Atithi. Why?"

"I saw him at Rangoli the other day. Thought maybe he was patronising that place these days. The staff seemed to know him quite well."

"Oh! He didn't mention meeting you."

"He didn't see me. I was there for a business lunch; couldn't leave for a second. He too was with a lady. I thought maybe she was a client; didn't feel right about disturbing him."

"Hmm."

There was a pause. Kiran resumed, looking Kuhu straight in the eye. "Tell me honestly, Kuhu. If Ajoy would be seeing somebody else, how would you react?"

Kuhu started laughing. "C'mon, Kiran. If you're saying that the lady he was with…"

"No, I'm saying what if…?"

"I would talk to him about it, of course! What else?" Kuhu answered, a bit miffed.

Kiran was not impressed. "You know, Kuhu, you should question him more often. Asking a couple of questions need not necessarily imply suspicion. I mean you should just generally know where he is and with whom!"

"You're right. I will."

Kiran knew there was no point in trying to convince Kuhu, so she just let it be.

*

In the next few weeks, Avinash's friend passed on whatever he could gather regarding Ajoy's movements. Apparently, Ajoy frequented Rangoli for lunch every day. Kiran thought it would be a good idea to track him there once and bring him face-to-face with Kuhu. She called up Kuhu.

"Lunch today? At Rangoli? My boss is out of town and I'm a free bird. Thought we could catch up."

Kuhu was delighted. "Of course! Will be there. One sharp."

Kiran waited in the car outside the restaurant. Her watch struck one, one thirty and then finally two. Where was Kuhu? Ajoy had walked in with his ladylove half an hour earlier, arm in arm. When it was ten past two, her mobile rang.

"Kiran, I can't come! I've got a severe headache. If I don't rest, it'll blow up badly. I'm really sorry." Kuhu sounded really unwell.

"Oh, that's bad … It's okay, some other time. You take care." Kiran tried her best to hide her disappointment.

*

The woman in Ajoy's life was a marketing consultant working with his firm. Her name was Riya Pal. She was single and smart. She seemed to know her way with Ajoy. Kiran felt she should know where she lived. One day, she called up Riya's office. When she asked for her, the operator transferred the call.

"Riya Pal." Her voice was elegant and clear.

"Good afternoon, ma'am. I'm calling from 'The Florist'. We needed your home address for a personal delivery." Kiran tried her best to sound like a florist's clerk.

"My address?" Riya was bemused. "But the concerned person must have given it to you, right?"

"Well ... actually yes, ma'am. But the truth is ... I lost it. I'm really sorry, ma'am. Please don't complain about this. I might lose my job, ma'am. It won't happen again. Please?" Kiran couldn't believe she was fibbing like this.

"Okay, okay, relax. Take it down." Riya gave her the address and Kiran thanked her profusely.

When she related her histrionic display to Avinash, he almost fell off his chair in laughter. "You are marvelous, GJ! From today I'll call you GJA."

"GJA?"

"Greer of Jhansi-Actor." He guffawed. Kiran picked up a magazine and gave him a whack.

*

On one evening the following week, Avinash found Kiran in a foul mood.

"What's up, GJ?"

"Stop calling me GJ! As it is Kuhu has spoiled everything today!"

Avinash waited for her to settle down. Kiran went on, "It beats me. You know, Avinash, I went to see her last week. I fabricated a tale of how I had met Riya at some conference and how she happened to mention Ajoy and discovered that his wife is my best friend. I left her home address and number at Kuhu's table, on some valid pretext, since she is Ajoy's close associate."

"And then."

"I called today to find out. Kuhu had not called Riya. It's like she doesn't want to know anything about this woman, who practically lives with her husband the whole day. Beats me. Really does. How can she trust him so blindly?"

Avinash was looking at her intently.

"What?" Kiran asked.

"Stop giving her hints," suggested Avinash.

"What do you mean by that? She's my best friend. I can't see her squandering away her life for…"

Avinash interrupted her. "You better go and and tell her directly now, I say. Everything. What you know, what you don't. Simple. Just tell her."

Kiran looked at Avinash.

"Perhaps you're right."

*

When Kiran called Kuhu, she discovered that Ajoy was away on a tour. She called Riya's office. She was out of town too. Kiran drove down to Kuhu's place, who welcomed her warmly.

Kiran didn't hug her back. Kuhu persisted, "What is it, Kiran? Why are you sulking?"

"Ajoy is having an affair with Riya Pal."

Kuhu stopped where she was.

"He has been seeing her for three months now. I have known for the last one month."

Kuhu stared at Kiran blankly.

"He has lunch with her every day. He is showering her with public displays of affection when he tells you he is busy in a presentation. I gave you Riya's number, thinking you might be curious enough to know who this new associate of Ajoy was. But you thought nothing of it obviously."

Kuhu had sat down on the sofa. Kiran felt sorry for her, but she wanted to get over this.

"I had called you to Rangoli the other day because I knew he would be there with her. You could have seen with your own eyes."

Kuhu looked at her with blurred eyes. Kiran was really angry.

"I decided to tell you this directly today. Ajoy is away on tour, not alone, but with Riya. And right now, as I speak to you, he is probably in her arms in some hotel room! Do you understand?" Kiran was shouting at her now.

Kuhu sat silently, tears streaming down her face. Kiran walked up and sat beside her. Kuhu hid her face in her friend's lap and wept. Kiran caressed her hair and held her firmly. When she stopped crying, Kiran came to the point gently.

"Why didn't you speak to him, Kuhu? How can you live with him? Why don't you do something?" she said softly.

Kuhu continued to be silent. Kiran became impatient.

"Speak up, Kuhu! What is wrong with you? I told you..."

Kuhu sat up and held her hands up at Kiran.

"Yes! You told me this and you told me that!" she cried. Her voice dropped low. "You are telling me something that I already know."

Kiran was stumped. She was sure she had misheard.

"What! What did you just say?"

Kuhu turned to face Kiran. Their eyes met. She was slow and deliberate.

"I *know* that Ajoy is having an affair. I knew it much before you did."

Kiran was dumbfounded. She stared at Kuhu, amazed and shaken. The anguish, the painful concern, the want to protect; everything melted away into a very long moment of empty time.

"And you are okay with that?" she whispered, her brow knit in worried surprise.

Kuhu held Kiran's hand and took her inside her bedroom. She opened the wardrobe and pointed at some saris hanging neatly in a row. There were beautiful yards, silks and chiffons, in bright reds and pastel greens, and so many other hues. Kiran stared at them and then at Kuhu.

"Ajoy gifted me these in the last one month; every time he came back from a tour."

Kuhu picked a diary from her dressing table and opened it. She traced her finger down a page to something scribbled in her handwriting. She showed it to Kiran. It was an appointment reminder at the best spa in town for the coming week.

"He fixed this for me. He said I needed a break to just look after myself one full day."

"Ajoy said that?" Disbelief was writ large on Kiran's face.

"Yes! Kiran, look at me! Am I the same person?"

Kiran looked at her carefully. Kuhu was glowing. The dark circles under her eyes had lightened and she had a satisfied sparkle in her eyes which Kiran had never seen before. Kuhu walked towards the window and looked out at the sky.

"Every weekend, for the last three weeks, Ajoy has been taking me to the Ritz for dinner. He even danced with me the last time."

Kiran stood rooted to the floor, too dazed to understand what was happening.

"He calls me twice every day to ask me what I'm doing and how I am. The day he apologised for the quarrel, he took me to the doctor in the evening." Kuhu's eyes brimmed over.

"And ... and?" Kiran seemed to have lost her voice.

"And what, Kiran? He comes to me more often at night now. He tells me how beautiful I am when he makes love to me." Kuhu turned to face Kiran. "Last night, he said we should have a child."

Kiran was tongue-tied. Kuhu came forward and took her hands in hers. She was crying again; but a smile cut across the tears.

"A child, Kiran! A baby! My own baby! I've been dying to have one. Ajoy ... he finally said yes! Won't that be wonderful?"

Kiran's eyes welled up. She hugged Kuhu tightly and wouldn't let go. Kuhu held her and kept talking.

"I don't want to lose Ajoy now. I have never seen him like this. Yes, Kiran, I knew all along that he is not mine alone. But then ... nothing ever was, was it? Some are destined to pay a higher and maybe unfair price for their share of happiness. If Ajoy is a better husband to me today, it is because of Riya's presence in his life."

She paused before continuing.

"He gives me everything I wanted from him; love, lust, passion, care and affection. So what if it is a loan from destiny. I can create my own happiness with it. A ray of brighter hope will be mine when I hold my child. No, Kiran, I don't want to trade this unreal dream for the harsh reality written in my fate. Please, Kiran..."

Kiran disengaged herself from Kuhu. She wanted to rave and rant at her. Tell her that she could just not understand her. But she decided against it. It was as if she was all spent and had resigned herself to something she herself wasn't sure of. She went away, fuming inwardly, and plonked herself on the sofa in the living room.

Kuhu wiped her tears and walked towards the kitchen.

When Kiran went to see what she was doing there, she saw Kuhu making tea for her best friend.

TURNING POINT

Arriving at a fork in the path, turn,
And what life has to offer, meet,
Let all your certitudes burn
As you lose the ground beneath your feet

Ajoy was trying to lift his wife Shobha who had suddenly fainted. He had been complimenting her about her insight into human character when it happened. Poor thing, she was not used to his praise. Perhaps it was just a fainting spell. As he lay Shobha on the divan and turned on the fan, Ajoy's mind raced over the events of the day. Yes, he recalled standing outside Ms Sengupta's office in the morning.

"Ms Sengupta? May I come in, Ms Sengupta?" Ajoy called hesitantly, as he knocked on the door to her cabin.

"Come in," she answered.

From the tone of her voice itself, Ajoy knew that Ms Sengupta had answered him without the usual joie-de-vivre that had been characteristic of her mannerism as well as her spirit.

Of course Ajoy knew that she couldn't really be blamed for this. Not after what had happened at the office party last night.

Damn Shobha, he thought for the nth time that morning, as his mind went back to his wife while entering Ms Sengupta's cabin. He walked hesitantly up to her table.

She sat behind her table and looked at him silently for a moment. Then, with her hand still holding the pencil that she had been sketching with, she beckoned him to sit.

She looked even more beautiful when she was a trifle subdued like this than when she was her usual chirpy self. Ajoy noticed that the kajal outlining her eyes never ever spilled out and transgressed its limits – as Shobha's often did. Almost as if the kajal had a mind of its own and decided not to stray, lest it takes away from the clarity and depth of its beautiful subject. Ms Sengupta's lips, now hesitant to break into a smile, looked even more luscious, as the black mole perfectly in place above her right lip quivered as she spoke.

She brushed aside her burgundy coloured hair. Ajoy could not help wondering, as he settled into the seat opposite hers, what kind of man could possibly leave a woman as gorgeous and lovely as Ms Sengupta.

It was a thought that had not struck him earlier as emphatically as it had at this moment. For, in an advertising agency like the one he worked in, it was not unusual for men like him to be working alongside divorced or otherwise single women, without bothering to find out why they were so. And yet today, the thought was bothering him like it had never done anytime over the last year that she had been his art designer.

He knew that it was Shobha who was responsible for this heightened awareness. Shobha, and the jealousy and hostility that she had displayed towards Ms Sengupta at the office party last night. The incident had made Ajoy realise that Ms Sengupta's sensuous charm and single status made a lot of women like Shobha very insecure.

"I'm very sorry about last night, Ms Sengupta. I don't know what came over Shobha for her to behave the way she did. I wish to apologise on her behalf," he said, wondering what more he could possibly say on the matter at this juncture.

"You've been calling me Ms Sengupta long enough, Ajoy. Call me Jaya," she said. "It's all right, you don't have to apologise. It's not the first time that this has happened to me. A lot of married women feel very threatened by their husband's single-women colleagues. It's something I have sensed very often in these last three years that I've been single and working. I can't say that it doesn't hurt or affect me at all, but I think I can handle it a lot better now than I used to earlier. Earlier I would be completely shattered, but look at me today. I'm fine and back at work despite what happened yesterday."

Jaya was trying to be brave but Ajoy could see the sadness around her lips. How gracious she was being about the whole sorry episode. It was as if she epitomised all the feminine qualities that a woman could possibly possess. And to think that he hadn't noticed any of this through the entire year that they had been colleagues!

"I really don't know what to say, but I really feel so miserable. Ms ... er ... Jaya," Ajoy continued, wincing at his inability to find better words to express how he was feeling.

"Don't say anything more and don't feel miserable either. Let's not discuss this any further. For me you're still the colleague that you were. And a nice one at that," she added. Her lips finally broke into a smile. A smile, that as he had noticed earlier, went right up to her eyes.

The telephone rang and Jaya picked it up. She started to chat with a friend. Ajoy muttered a soft goodbye and left the cabin.

Somehow, Jaya's brave smile only made him feel much worse than the righteous tantrum that he had expected from her. He simply had to do something more than just accept Jaya's gracious forgiveness, forgiveness that had overwhelmed him completely.

Shobha had had such an easy life compared to Jaya, Ajoy thought. He had treated her well, unlike how Jaya's husband had probably treated her. She was also financially secure and actually revelled in Ajoy's status in social circles, more than he himself felt comfortable doing. Yet she always found fault in others, especially if they were women. There was always some deep, mysterious reason why she believed that everybody else had had a better deal in life than her. Of course this had nothing to do with her own self – nature and destiny, according to her, always conspired to give an advantage to others. Psychologists call that a persecution complex.

It was this that had prompted her to go up to Jaya the previous evening and acerbically comment that single women like her had no respect for institutions like marriage and family. She had made it worse by saying that more than other women, those having had broken marriages themselves, especially, thought nothing of breaking up the marriages of decent, happily married women.

It had started out as an academic discussion but developed into a pointed conversation. Given Shobha's tendencies to dominate, a monologue would be a more apt term to describe what that interaction had been all about. And god alone knew what else Shobha had said to Jaya. A stunned Ajoy had heard only bits and pieces of the exchange while trying to make polite conversation with one of their clients. But suffice it to say that Jaya, not being the sort to get defensive in the face of Shobha's aggressive posturing, had made a dignified exit from the party.

Ajoy had berated Shobha about it at home the previous night. Of course Shobha had only said that she was talking "general truths", and that it was Jaya's guilty conscience that had made her take umbrage. She had closed the argument with Ajoy by saying that in any case vain women like Jaya "deserved" what they got. Ajoy had realised that it was no use arguing with Shobha. She was just not the kind of person who would ever accept that she had done any wrong. And in recent months she was only getting worse, picking on people she had little to do with and becoming not just difficult to live with, but increasingly also a social embarrassment.

Ajoy knew that the situation was getting beyond repair. He could not imagine being able to put up with this all his life. He had already started avoiding spending time with Shobha, and knew that sooner or later he would have to muster the nerves to tell her that he wanted out of the marriage. Only, he would need to develop nerves of steel to issue the ultimatum to her and be able to handle its aftermath.

Right now of course he had to first fix the latest damage that Shobha had done. Jaya had handled all this with such exceptional dignity that Ajoy was determined it would not go unappreciated. He sat at his desk all day, planning his evening trip to Jaya's house armed with an apology card, flowers and what he definitely knew was her favourite perfume. Anais Anais.

It had been comforting to plan this trip. Cathartic even, to choose the right bouquet, the right shade of wrapping paper for the bottle of perfume, and write the apology card, with all of which he finally came armed to Jaya's door late that evening.

Jaya was overwhelmed that he had taken so much trouble and insisted that he stay on for dinner, an invitation that he was actually very happy to accept. For it meant that he would get to spend the evening away from Shobha.

It had the class of a wine-and-roses affair, never mind if what followed was only cheese sandwiches and instant soup. It was food laced with the aphrodisiac of the attraction and understanding that two misunderstood people had found in each other that evening.

In the event, Ajoy found more than just that. He found Jaya in his arms, and it took him some time to believe that she was really there. He wondered how he had mustered the courage to make the first move ... he had never thought he was capable of wearing his heart on his sleeve or being able to make his feeling known for any woman. And least of all to a woman such as Jaya, who was the epitome of elegance. What would have happened if something had gone wrong, or if she had not reciprocated his feelings? How would he have faced her the next day? He dreaded these thoughts. But there she was, and she was reluctant to let go of him. And that was all that mattered.

Ajoy could feel Jaya responding to him. She matched him stride for stride. Yes, more than anything else, after many years Ajoy enjoyed the feeling of controlling a woman physically and emotionally. He felt confident, he felt like a man.

Much later, as he stood on his own doorstep, Ajoy felt a cocktail of emotions coursing through him. Should he feel guilty?

Hadn't Shobha brought this upon herself? Did he feel anything for Shobha? Yet, she was his wife and how could he have done this to her? His head was in a whirl when the door was opened by Shobha who sized him from head to toe and launched into a tirade even before he crossed the threshold.

But this time Ajoy did not back off. He wanted to test his manliness again. What a great feeling it would be for his perpetually crushed ego if he were to score over Shobha! He stared at her hard, and in a gesture he had never tried on Shobha before, he raised his forefinger as a warning to her to stop. Shobha was startled.

Then, in a low voice he said, "You were right, Shobha, absolutely right. Single women like Jaya really do not respect marriage. How easily they entrap stupid men like myself with their charm and wit. But I love being trapped ... and I will always remember your insight into the darker truths of human character."

That was when Shobha collapsed on the carpet.

VIRGINAL FANTASY

Hey, the joke's on her please
So she lets it play
She knows how to be a tease
And he takes her breath away

Vaidehi lay on her side, her head resting on Mahesh's shoulder. Her forehead brushed against the stubble of his cheek. Every little while, his hand caressed the undulating curve of her hips, came up to her waist and rested there, as he drifted in and out of sleep. Then when she went back to lying on her back, his hand caressed the round of her breast and then came to rest on her stomach. And this after they had made glorious love already that night!

It was something he seemed to do almost every night since they had been married as though confirming the delicious reality of having his woman beside him all through the night. The pleasure of such a realisation was not his alone. Vaidehi too was delirious with happiness at this privileged position by his side. No amount of lovemaking was enough and she craved his every touch even when he had possibly done so only subconsciously. Every such caress would stir in her the delicious sensuousness of being a woman and she revelled in the sensation each time. It was a feeling so new and so exhilarating that she felt she could never ever have enough of it. Delirious and aroused, she felt that falling asleep would be a waste of time that could be so much better spent in experiencing these sensations. Sometimes, Vaidehi had to pinch herself to be certain she was his wife now. And that in a primeval sort of way, she too possessed him, as much as he did her.

Mahesh was a fantastic lover – gentle and passionate at the same time. Of course, Vaidehi had known no other man to be able to really compare, but even then she instinctively knew that he was good. After all, Mahesh had had plenty of experience with other women before he married her. He had been – to use his own words – "an intellectual playboy" before matrimony. He had often in a most blasé manner claimed to have lured the best of women onto many a bed or floor and on many a night or day, "of their own volition". Of course seeing her shocked and somewhat hurt face, Mahesh had promised her that all that had been a need- and opportunity-based lifestyle, and that with her entry into his life all that was a thing of the past.

"A man has his needs ... sometimes rather desperate needs ... and in my position, there are always ways of fulfilling such needs quite easily. But I was very clear that when true love struck, lust would not be allowed to lead it," Mahesh had explained to Vaidehi very early in their relationship. "And I think I was right," he had continued, "for I finally did find you to love."

He had said the same thing to her again, a few hours ago. And Vaidehi had smiled to herself. It was good to feel that she was the *real* one. The one that he loved, and not merely lusted after. Although Vaidehi had now realised that lust too was not such a bad thing after all!

Vaidehi smiled again at the memory of the first few days after marriage. She had been so gauche then. She did not know what went where or whether it was not a bit rude to keep her eyes and mouth closed as he kissed her all over. She used to look at him for approval all the time, and on one or two occasions she had even dared to ask whether she had passed muster. He usually always held on to her lovingly in the warm afterglow of lovemaking, sleepy and reluctant to talk. Frankly, she hadn't enjoyed sex the first few times. Much like the performance anxiety that men suffered from, Vaidehi suffered from response anxiety that was so typical of sexually inexperienced women.

Now, two months later, Vaidehi was so much more relaxed. In fact she had begun to feel absolutely magical sensations that she had never known actually reposed in her own body. And the more she became alive and uninhibited about them, the more love and passion Mahesh had gradually infused into their lovemaking.

It seemed as if in the last few weeks Mahesh had been lying in wait for her to develop a taste for and then get addicted to the passion that he realised he was capable of unleashing. Waiting, perhaps, for her to become as good as the lovers that he had known earlier.

It had been particularly beautiful today. For the first time, Vaidehi had openly moaned with incredible pleasure for an eternally long time as he made love. Mahesh had been both amused and pleasantly surprised, and had declared that this time she had been like the ultimate fantasy come true for him.

At first Vaidehi was happy to hear this. But later when she thought about it, she realised that he had certainly borne her earlier inexperience with fond indulgence. Actually he had been quite reassured by it, for it proved to him beyond the faintest doubt that she was a virgin. He had never said so in as many words, but Vaidehi knew that this was what he was really thinking. And once she knew that he knew, she felt even more virtuous about it. For contrary to the modern and somewhat fashionable pooh-poohing of the Indian belief that virginity is a gift to one's husband, she had come to believe that there wasn't a more accurate ancient psychological theory that was as relevant now.

But these days it was unfashionable to believe in this theory and Vaidehi was actually a fashionable woman. To tell herself the truth, her 'gifted' virginity had been nothing but a chance. Yet it had paid off handsomely for she wondered if she would have been as loved and cherished by Mahesh had she not been one. If she hadn't been fashionable she wouldn't have been able to love and cherish him, despite all the women that Mahesh had loved.

"Isn't it true that you wanted a virgin as bride though you yourself have made love to countless women?" Vaidehi asked.

It was not the first time she had asked him this question, and Mahesh would always be a little irked each time. And to be fair to him it was definitely an embarrassing question for any new husband to answer.

"They were not women I loved, but merely lusted for," he said rather emphatically as he first stroked her hair and then proceeded to play the drum on her cheek with his fingers. "You are the only one I love," he continued.

"You made love to them," she persisted. "After all, you cannot divorce feelings and emotions from the act of making love. Don't you feel love for me when you make love to me?" Vaidehi asked, her eyes shining indignantly.

"Of course I do. It's different with one's wife. But for a man, it is possible to just want to have sex with a woman without feeling any love for her. It's not like that for most women, therefore you will find it difficult to understand," he explained patiently, as if talking to a child.

"But those you made love to ... they were also women, weren't they?" Vaidehi asked, very sure that he would have nothing to say to that.

"Yes, but you have no idea what kind of women those are. They were not at all like what you are," Mahesh said. "They were not real women. They were women who were out for a good time, as much as I was, with no feelings involved. Do you think I would hurt a real woman's feelings? Trust me, I can make out within the first few minutes that I spend with her what a woman is all about," he continued with supreme confidence.

"Does that mean that only virgins are real women?" She was nothing if not persistent.

"No, it doesn't mean that. A woman could lose her virginity to a man she really loves, yet she may end up being someone else's wife. I don't say that that makes her a loose woman to her husband,"

Mahesh said weakly. "No, it certainly doesn't," he whispered, almost as if trying to reassure himself.

"Would you have fallen in love with me the same way if I had not been a virgin?" Vaidehi continued.

"Yes, I think I would have. I certainly didn't check that fact with you when we were getting to know each other. But to tell you the truth I was quite sure that you were," he said in a voice that showed that he was clearly tiring. Somehow Mahesh never liked too much of this bare-my-soul talk, Vaidehi had realised. And yet she just couldn't help but continue.

"I am sure that made you feel very good about me, didn't it?" she asked.

"Yes, it did," Mahesh replied, a bit testily. "However much a man may pretend otherwise, he does feel great if his woman is untouched by another man. I was not hung up on virginity, but it certainly had its appeal. It always does to all men. Yet I'll say this much – that if everything else about you had been the same except your virginity, I would still have married you. I mean it. I think it is not just a question of virginity for its own sake. Virginity to me implies a complete innocence of body, soul and mind. I think when a woman loses her virginity, a little innocence of the other aspects goes too. And innocence is ultimately a woman's most beautiful jewel. So I am not sure that the rest of you would have been the same if you weren't a virgin."

He had been patient enough so far with all her questions. Now he was too exhausted to want to continue the discussion.

"Let's stop this pointless discussion now. What's important is what finally happened, and what finally is, between us. Why bother about what might have been?" he said, as he turned to his side, rubbing his legs against her thighs.

"Is this not beautiful enough?" he asked, turning back.

"It is." She sighed. But it was actually only half the truth.

Sometimes she thought that the problem with Mahesh was that he was much too honest. Most of the time he did not say right and comforting things that might be slightly untrue. But the flip side was that he could be trusted so completely about meaning exactly what he said. Oh how she loved him! She knew that he was better than most Indian men though not the ideal that any woman could ever hope for. He was immensely loveable, charming, successful, confident, and yet so very honest and simple at the core. So very loveable. Whatever he might say, Vaidehi was sure that the women he'd made love to had really loved him, and had hoped he'd love them back. Little did they know of the theories of love and lust that roamed in his handsome head. Vaidehi was sure that for at least some of Mahesh's women, a hope for love was the moving spirit, and not the pure lust that he attributed to them.

But Vaidehi was a wife and she certainly had no sympathy for any of them. Oh how she hated the thought of those nameless, faceless women and the pleasures they received from him! The pleasures that were rightfully only hers. How dare Mahesh think that only a man wanted a wife untouched by another man! How she wished she could have him – untainted and virginal, as he had had her.

Mahesh laughed at the idea – that familiar indulgent, slightly mocking laugh. "But I never ever hid anything from you," he replied. "You knew all along about all these women, and the fact that I initiated all the encounters, with them playing willing partners. But that was all much before I met you. All of this has been over long since. It's simply not an issue anymore, darling! Why is it disturbing you so much now? It's no reflection on you, you silly little girl," he said, ruffling her hair. "And now will you please let me get some sleep tonight?"

Vaidehi felt so angry. Here she was – a real woman alive with all the normal feelings of love, hate, possessiveness and jealousy. But Mahesh seemed like he would never understand that she was neither silly, nor little, nor a girl anymore. Of course it was not possible for her to reverse his escapades, but once, only once did she want him to admit that he understood her feelings, no matter how absurd they sounded. For they were born out of love for him, an aspect of physical love that she had discovered only when she had known his body. If he could only realise that his past did hurt her, and only once, just once, acknowledge that he did regret it, she was sure that it would assuage her restless feelings. She knew that Mahesh was sensitive and capable of doing that, if only he was ready to acknowledge that it was not abnormal for her to feel this way. Vaidehi decided just then that she was somehow going to make him realise that.

There was only one way to do that. And that was to put him, for a brief while, in her shoes. Just to give him a taste of his own medicine, and to make him feel how the shoe pinched. Yes, that was now the only way!

"Mahesh," she whispered, and gently shook him from his sleep. "I have something to tell you."

"Tomorrow," he mumbled, irritated.

"No, Mahesh, I might not have the required courage to tell you tomorrow. It's got to be now," she said urgently.

He opened his sleep-heavy eyes. "What's the matter, Vaidehi?" he asked.

"You have always been completely honest with me, even when the reality has been difficult for me to accept. I have admired you for that, and now I want to be as honest and truthful with you."

"Vaidehi, get to the point," Mahesh mumbled, barely able to keep his eyes open.

"First, promise me that you'll understand me in the same way you have expected me to understand you," she said.

"I promise, Vaidehi. Now go on," Mahesh said, by now a trifle anxious.

This is going to be fun, thought Vaidehi.

"I wasn't a virgin when I married you," she blurted out. "No, I promise you I had never been in love, it was only lust. And like you I was very clear that when love struck, lust would not be allowed to lead it. I was right, wasn't I, for I found true love in you," Vaidehi whispered, her eyes downcast for a moment and then staring, unable to stop herself from looking at his face for his reaction. "You don't love me any less for it, do you?" she asked. "You said you wouldn't, do you remember?"

Since there was no response from Mahesh, she went on. "Mahesh, are you listening? I just had to tell you someday, for you have been so completely honest with me. So I thought that I should be the same with you, shouldn't I? Mahesh? Are you listening? Mahesh?"

Now, Mahesh was saying something but Vaidehi could not make out what. Guttural sounds emanated from his throat as his Adam's apple bobbed up and down. His eyes were glazed. He drew his reddened face close to hers and held her face with both his hands in a pose that by now she had understood to be one prefacing a kiss on her lips. He looked strange and a little cockeyed as he brushed back the hair from the nape of her neck. *What is going on? Is this some new form of foreplay?* she wondered, a little overwhelmed at his raw passion at this most unexpected point of time.

"Mahesh, I love you," she whispered, as she shut her eyes, pleasantly reconciling herself to the lovemaking that she was sure was now going to follow a second time that night. She shut her eyes as she felt his kiss on her lips. Then she clasped his shoulders with her hands, and began making the circular movements on his back that he had taught her to make and which he loved so much. Her body throbbed, aching to be touched by him. Then suddenly, she felt his hands on both sides of her neck, pressing menacingly.

In a flash, her eyes opened, registering what this was all really about.

"Ma ... aa..." she tried to cry out desperately, but was unable to. She flayed her hands wildly as she felt herself choking and feeling a sharp piercing pain that shot upwards from her ears to her temples. The world swam around her.

Vaidehi attempted in vain to push Mahesh back. He pinioned her to the bed with the strength of a monster and sat on her chest, his knees pinning down her arms on either side as his fingers cut deeper and deeper into her neck.

A few rasps, a couple of gasps, and Vaidehi had no more questions to ask.

YOU FIRST

The fairer sex, superior, behold her
Her standards impossible to match
That chip on her shoulder
Of being the proverbial catch

Rupal tried hard to fight her tears, as she held on to her phone tightly. The reception from the other end of the line was terrible, and it was a real struggle for her to understand what her father was saying. She had one eye on the clock as it counted down the seconds.

"... beta, Mr Shashidhar said that we cannot use this ... please talk to him..."

"Papa! Listen to me, carefully! I can't hear you ... hello?" The disturbance on the phone was getting unbearable, and she knew that she was on the verge of revealing something that would change their lives.

"... evidence is not ... protect you..."

Rupal slammed her other fist on her knee in anger, while trying to keep her voice calm. How many times had she told her father to just give in to the offers of the guards, and bribe them and get a little pocket phone. How was she supposed to put together his defence if he did nothing to help her?

But their ever-patient lawyer, Shashidhar, who sat next to Rupal that afternoon, held out a note, and asked her to read it to him. He also sat and made strange gestures, trying to tell her to calm down, and that it would be all right if she took a deep breath. At any other time, his oiled hair and soda-bottle glasses would have made him look very funny. The way he wore his trousers up high didn't help; instead making him look like a cartoon character from at least two decades before.

But Rupal wasn't laughing as she read his note out.

"Papa! Listen to me carefully, I have an idea, to show that you have been framed, but it means that Yash would have to help us, by testifying that he got the evidence by himself, voluntarily. If he were to testify against his father..."

Suddenly, when it came to telling her off, his voice came through loud and clear.

"Beta, what have you done? How can you tell Yash about this? He will never go against his father, he will turn against you too!"

Rupal couldn't deny this. Yash had been the love of her life since he returned to India after his master's degree in the University of Texas. Idealistic and honest, he was always surprised at the lengths Rupal was prepared to go to, to do what she believed was the right thing. There was a new word she had introduced into his vocabulary, jugaadu.

The two had fallen for each other when Rupal had walked into his office as an intern, a job her father Vikram had recommended her for. Vikram had been a loyal assistant to Yash's father for nearly two decades now.

That was until two weeks ago, when headlines broke out that Vikram had siphoned funds from government contracts from Mehta Industries, and profited from them. Normally, this wouldn't have been seen as the worst crime, but this was money that had been given to Mehta Industries to supply packed lunches to children in government schools.

But those who knew Vikram well, knew that he was honest to a fault, refusing to even offer a bribe to a traffic policeman if he was caught jumping a red light, not that he ever would do that in the first place. Perhaps it was a growing impatience with his refusal to bend the rules, however slightly, for the sake of convenience that made Rupal such a rebel and street-smart person. She would never do anything wrong, but wouldn't be afraid to stray slightly off the right path for the greater good.

"Beta! Are you listening to me?"

The beeping at the other end of the line grew more frequent. The holding cell lines only allowed calls lasting three minutes and their time was nearly up.

"Papa, don't worry about me. We have to do what we have to do right now..."

But before Vikram could respond, the line went dead, and Rupal would've thrown the phone on the floor if it weren't for the fact that she had had to save up for a few months to buy it, and for Mr Shashidhar's sweaty face staring back intently at her...

*

The plush offices of Mehta Industries were buzzing with the day's waning activities. The hum of conversations, clatter of keyboards, shuffle of papers, everything faded into a background murmur, punctuated by the occasional ring of a phone. It was an orchestra of the corporate world that breathed life into the lavish premises.

Yash stood in his office, his heart pounding an equally frantic rhythm, as he held the printed images Rupal had sent to him that morning. She had told him that she wouldn't be coming in to work that day, and he knew something was amiss. She never skipped work for anything.

But the images were damning; pictures of emails that had been exchanged between his father and a bureaucrat detailing how they would siphon the funds and make Vikram the scapegoat in case they ever got found out.

Late the previous night, Rupal being the intern, was the last one to leave the office. Before she did that, though, she had broken her way into Hiren Mehta's cabin, spent half an hour trying to crack the password to his laptop, which turned out to be Yash's birthday, and taken pictures of his emails before security could get wind of what was happening. As she had suspected, her father had been framed.

Hours later, Yash found himself standing in the unyielding shadows of the massive oak doors that led to his father's personal office. The Mehta mansion, an architectural marvel that housed generations of their lineage, seemed like a haunting spectre under the harsh moonlight. Its cold marble pillars and antique archways that usually spoke of grandeur now echoed with secrets and betrayals. Yash walked past them, wondering how many of them could be attributed to ill-gotten gains of his father. For Yash, the mansion had always been a symbol of pride and success, a testament to their legacy. Tonight, it felt more like a house of cards, teetering on the brink of destruction.

Inside, Hiren Mehta sat ensconced behind his mahogany desk, his face partially illuminated by the soft desk lamp. His stern face, usually brimming with confidence, was etched with deep lines of age and worry, in sharp contrast to the silk kurta that had become something of a habit for the senior Mehta in the Mumbai winter.

As Yash stepped into the room, the heavy doors shut behind him with an ominous echo. His father looked up, his usual stern gaze meeting Yash's troubled eyes.

"Dad," Yash began, his voice faltering under the weight of the words he was about to utter. He put the papers down on the heavy table, and Hiren picked them up, glancing through the pages, trying hard to hide his surprise.

"Is it true, Dad?"

Hiren looked at him, his eyes softening at the sight of his son's turmoil. "Did you frame Vikram? Betray the trust he placed in you?" Yash continued, each word slicing through the thick silence of the room like a knife.

The confession, when it came, felt like a punch to Yash's gut. Hiren's voice, normally steady and sure, wavered as he spoke. "Yash," he admitted, his voice barely above a whisper, "I did what I had to. For the family, for you."

The world seemed to reel around Yash as his father's words sank in. His degree, his future, all that he had been so proud of, felt tainted.

"Your education, your future," Hiren continued, each word a painful reminder to Yash of the magnitude of the offence. "Everything was at stake. I had to make some hard decisions."

The reality of his father's actions hit Yash like a brick wall. He had been living in a castle of lies, built on the ruins of an innocent man's life. As he stepped out of his father's office, he felt the weight of the truth on his shoulders.

But this was his father, what was he going to do? Send him to prison?

As Yash walked out, the moon hung low in the sky, casting long, ominous shadows in the opulent corridor.

In his luxurious apartment overlooking the city, Yash found himself caught in the throes of the night's revelations. He couldn't sleep at night, instead tossing and turning.

I did what I had to. For the family, for you.

Was this his fault? Was wanting to study in an expensive university his fault? Was it his recently deceased mother's fault, wanting to have and give her son a good lifestyle and upbringing?

No, he thought, no, it wasn't! Had he known where the money was coming from, would he have ever asked his father for more?

The morning sun streamed in through the full-length windows, casting a warm glow on his face, as his phone buzzed with a text from Rupal.

Can we meet?

Yes, I'm coming over now.

Shaking off the lingering remnants of sleep, he prepared to leave his apartment. He caught a glimpse of himself in the mirror. The face staring back at him was the same, yet it looked different. The naive belief in his father's integrity was replaced with a determined resolution.

Back at her apartment, Rupal readied a cardboard box, filling it with all the things that Yash had given her over the past two years. Of course he would end things with her, he wouldn't turn back on his family, and so she was trying to remove every sign of him from her life, even down to the University of Texas keychain that she had found amusing and shiny, and had been since gifted by him.

As she put together every one of his belongings that had been with her, she began to forge a path ahead, for she would have a lot of meetings with Mr Shashidhar if Vikram had to be acquitted. The trouble was, as he had explained to her in his extremely strong accent, they couldn't present the evidence that would acquit her father, because she had broken into Hiren's email to get it, which was going to be inadmissible. However, she was trying to think of a way that would perhaps enable her to cop it for the illegal way she got the evidence, but save her father from a life of shame.

Meanwhile, as Yash drove across Worli's Sea Face past the hordes of morning joggers wrapping up their run, the same thoughts from the previous night kept going on in his head. He had a long drive to the little house in Chuim village in Bandra where Rupal's family had lived for two generations; and being stuck in traffic had a way of clearing his mind and readying him for what lay ahead when he reached his destination.

As he parked his car precariously in the gully, the familiar smell of fish greeted his nostrils, as the breeze from the sea brought in the smells of the livelihood of the people who lived nearby on Carter Road. Yash made his way up the creaky stairs to Rupal's house, where she was waiting for him. Truth be told, she hadn't slept a wink at night either. As Yash looked around, he compared this house, two generations old, to his father's that reeked of opulence and new wealth.

"Do you want some water?" Rupal asked, tentatively. She had no idea how Yash would react. Yash saw the big cardboard box on the table behind where Rupal stood; it was a very small house, one of those where there was no real space to hide anything. Yash sat down on the sofa, and gestured for Rupal to come and join him.

"What's in the box?"

Rupal sighed as she picked it up and brought it to the sofa. As she put it down on the table, the little medals that Vikram had so lovingly sealed after she had won races in her school sports day rattled slightly. Yash peered inside. It really was everything, right down to the silly cat mask that they had both worn on Halloween, a tradition she had only discovered through Yash.

"What's the plan?" asked Yash.

"I'd rather not say," said Rupal, fighting the lump in her throat. Mr Shashidhar had warned her against revealing any information to Yash, if he was going to side with his father on the case. Yash's eyes widened, as he understood what Rupal had been thinking.

"So you don't have a plan then, do you?" asked Yash.

"How do you know?"

"Because that's what you always say when you don't have a plan or any clue what to do..."

The lump in Rupal's throat was becoming more and more difficult to fight. Of course Yash could see right through her words.

"I'll figure something out. Look, it's clear what has happened, and I can't be with someone whose father is the very reason that my father is in jail. How could your father do that to us, after twenty years?" she asked Yash, as a tear began to make its way down her face.

Yash instinctively reached out to her to embrace her, but she pushed him away.

"Yash, please, don't make this any harder than it is for me..."

"I don't need to do that, do I? You've made it as difficult as you possibly could."

Rupal looked at him, the tears drying up as anger rose within her. How dare he?

"Explain!"

"Did you ask me even once if I would help you before adding all these things up in your head?"

Rupal looked at him, confused. "What?"

"I'll get the information, Rupal. I want to help you."

"But..." *Against your father?* she wanted to ask.

Yash said nothing, and pulled her in for an embrace, looking around her house and saying, "I will probably need a place to stay for a while though, obviously."

Both of them laughed, and embraced each other, hoping that they would continue to do so in the face of the uphill battle that was inevitably coming their way…

YOUR GUILT OR MINE

Daughter, sister, lover, wife
What completes a woman in life?
If it lies in only being a mother
Does any lie towards that end matter?

Rashi's desk was clear of all papers at last. It hadn't been like this for many months now.

The last time that she had been able to go home having cleared all pending work had also been when Rajan had gone on an office tour. Like this time.

It was late, yet unlike most days she felt no compulsion to hurry back home and cook up a nice snack for him. She settled the contents of her bag leisurely and took one last sip of cold water before she stepped out of her cabin. How bare the same bustling corridors looked at this time of the day, she thought as she made her way out.

It was dark by the time she was walking towards her house. The air was thick with the sound of chirping sparrows. Birds made as much noise going home as men did, thought Rashi as she opened the gate of her house.

The house seemed so eerie without Rajan and the sounds typical of him in the evenings. The kicking off of his shoes, the TV blaring in the background, his voice over the telephone ... even the occasional clatter of his teacup against the saucer. And yet, Rashi felt a strange relief in the absence of all this.

It was a respite from the feelings of guilt that plagued her every evening as she observed him trying to distract and occupy himself … theirs was a common sorrow, yet it was not loneliness they shared. Not any more at least.

It was seven years now. Seven long years of waiting, hoping, praying. Rashi had often had herself medically examined and the doctors told her she was capable of bearing a child. But Rajan – no, of course not, there was nothing wrong with him either – the doctor too said so … she was probably just one of those jinxed, unfortunate women. Rajan never made it obvious to her, and yet it felt like their entire relationship had crumbled into a void of nothingness – all because of her inability to bear him a child.

Rashi was aware that she was better than so many women – much more talented, accomplished and more attractive than most. And yet with this one failure, even the most ordinary of women had triumphed over her. Many times over.

Rajan had never failed her in kindness. But in his own way he had withdrawn. A permanent sadness had crept into his eyes. His hurt expression tormented her soul.

She tried to atone as best as she could, knowing at heart that she would probably never be able to. Yet she went on – never once taking for granted his smallest want. She had seen so many of her friends doing that. But then, they could afford to – they were the mothers of their husband's kids. While she…

She ought to be grateful that Rajan hadn't left her for another woman, for she could not imagine life without him. If only she could give him a child!

Rashi closed her eyes as she relaxed on the rocking chair, exhausted with this now familiar tide of thoughts, unable to cope with wakefulness.

She was woken by the sound of the telephone ringing. It was Rajan's colleague and friend Mukul.

"Rashi, there's an important file that Rajan has left behind at home. It is needed for the company meeting tomorrow. Do you think I could come and collect it from your place?"

"That was rather careless of Rajan. Yes, of course, Mukul, come and collect it. I'm home," she replied.

Rashi tidied up the cushions that she had been lounging on. She had a quick wash and change of clothes. She then put some quiche in the oven and the kettle on the gas for coffee. She heard Mukul's car drawing up in the front yard.

"Hello, Mukul." She smiled. "You're just in time for hot coffee."

"Oh good, nothing better than hot coffee at the end of a long day at office. You must be tired too."

They sat for some time sipping coffee in the drawing room. Mukul was looking through the file that Rashi had given him.

"You know, the boss reminded Rajan to submit the file before he left on tour. He's becoming rather forgetful these days. Is there anything bothering him, Rashi? He looks rather tense even at work."

Rashi's cheeks felt hot and flushed as she heard Mukul. She thought of Rajan and how unhappy she had made him. Before she knew it, she was sobbing softly, shedding the mask of self-composure that was second nature to her.

Mukul looked up with surprise from the file he was reading. Surprise soon gave way to guilt at having precipitated this outburst. He felt like comforting her but didn't know how to do it.

"Please, Rashi, I didn't mean to upset you ... I'm sorry, very sorry," he said.

Rashi tried hard to regain her composure, but it seemed almost impossible. Mukul moved close to her and held her quivering hand. His touch coursed through her like a current. She placed her hand in his and lay her tired head on his shoulder. Somewhere inside she was aware that this was not the right thing to happen but her reflexes did not seem to heed the mind's commands, her body seemed weightless in helpless surrender. Her limbs succumbed, her mind went dead – only an arrow of anguish pierced the silence of the moments that followed as they made love to each other.

*

In the days immediately following this encounter, Rashi was wracked by guilt at what had transpired. Time and again she would berate herself. How could she have allowed this to happen? She had betrayed the man who had stood by her through all her incapabilities. A lustful monster, that's what she was – a barren woman, now fallen too.

Yet, as the days passed, the pangs of guilt that assailed Rashi slowly waned. For, like all good things that have an end, bad ones do too. How long could she hate herself, after all? Mukul was a bad dream and life had to go on. And with Rajan's return it did. Rashi slipped right back into her old routine – one for which she neither knew nor wanted an alternative and for which she was almost grateful these days.

All until that Saturday morning, when she came down with a dizzy spell. Rajan had left for work. Just as she was getting ready to leave for the office she felt her head spin. She sat down on the bed … maybe she needed to rest a bit and she would be able to haul herself up again, she thought. She rested her head on the pillow. Then suddenly, it was as though lightning struck her … it couldn't be … could it?

Later in the day as she walked out of Dr Srivastava's clinic, everything was crystal clear. She knew it was Mukul's child she was expecting. But the joy she had imagined she would feel were such a day to come was absent. All that came her way were endless moments of turmoil – anguish tinged with a macabre sense of triumph. It felt like a vindication to her. Wasn't this what she'd been waiting for all these days? It was the perfect chance to wreak revenge, on the world and on Rajan. Poor, unfortunate Rajan, carrying that perpetually wounded expression on his face. An expression which said that she had failed him. She felt a lot of scorn for him today – scorn at the manhood he was so cocky about.

Then, as the thought of her own indiscretion struck her, the anguish returned. Perhaps this strange twist of fate had been ordained for their future happiness, she thought. Did Rajan really need to know whose child she was carrying? It was a tempting thought, but one that implied inflicting a lifetime of deception on him. On the man who, despite his misconceptions, had stood by her through her apparent failure.

The battle in her mind finally called a painful truce. If the child was not Rajan's, it was not going to be hers either. It would be the most fitting self-inflicted retribution for her unfaithfulness to her husband. She would treat her foetus no better than an unwanted appendix that would have to be removed.

As she was clearing the dinner dishes that night, preoccupied in her own thoughts, Rashi felt Rajan's presence behind her – somewhat wary of his closeness.

"I have something to discuss with you, Rashi," he said gently.

For a moment Rashi froze in her tracks. Maybe Mukul had told him. But upon collecting her wits she realised that this was unlikely to have happened and so she composed herself and followed him to the bedroom.

There was nothing in the world that could have prepared Rashi for what Rajan had to say. He had found another love. He was sorry, but it was something he couldn't help. It was this dilemma that had been haunting him all these months and today he had made his decision. It wasn't her fault, Rajan told Rashi, but he had to face reality. The reality of having to leave her for another woman.

Shock and disbelief, enquiries and entreaties, tears and finally calm acceptance – emotions took the course usual under such circumstances. Except for the one realisation that made it different.

Rashi knew that if this had happened three weeks ago, she would have burdened herself with the guilt of her being barren that had failed to keep Rajan committed. But she was barren no more. Today she was not burdened by this guilt. An unsuspecting Rajan, however, mistook her immense calm in the face of trying circumstances as sheer strength. He came close to Rashi and attempted to caress her hand in a gesture of appreciation.

She looked deep into his eyes, smiled and said, "I'll release you from this bond. But I want that we should bid each other goodbye on a note of a celebration of the love we had. Let's make love for the last time today." She started unbuttoning his shirt.

Soon their bodies melted together in the raw and painful tenderness of the occasion. And even as his defences failed him Rajan was baffled by the bizarreness of it all. Yet, overtaken by the relief that Rashi had accepted his decision without much ado, he did not try to analyse her behaviour. For she laughed today like a woman possessed ... like the woman he had never seen earlier.

Rashi made no attempt to explain either. For it was only a matter of time before he would know.

Only a matter of nine months before her triumph over him would be crowned by a new life.

Section II

Reflections in Water

A CONNECTING DOOR

You loved my man
My man loves me
There is no way we can
Ever be friends you see

The warm forenoon breeze caressed her face as Vidya looked out of the train window. She had already zipped up her carry bag and prepared to get off at the next station, Igatpuri. As she took in the passing scenery and smells, she couldn't help thinking how different the feel of the countryside was compared with Bombay, much like the difference between childhood and adulthood. She was in the mood for indulging in nostalgia, because nearly everything about this trip was different for Vidya.

It was the first time in years that she was travelling without her husband and children. She had felt so strange saying goodbye to Anish. For a long time after that, she had had to combat the feeling that perhaps she had left something important behind. And it was only when she mentally went over her checklist a number of times that she was assured that everything was indeed in order.

Vidya and Anish were both journalists by profession. While Anish concerned himself with writing on political developments, Vidya covered social issues. It was their work that had brought them together. But marriage and the demands of conscientious motherhood had made Vidya decide to quit her full-time job in a prominent daily and switch over to becoming a freelancer, writing articles from home. She also chose to write on subjects that she could handle with only a little, convenient travelling within the city. In this way, their children Akash and Nisha had the privilege of having their mother around for their needs, while Vidya too kept herself mentally alert and active.

This time, however, the situation was different – it was a first of sorts for her. Vidya had learnt of a unique project that a team of fashion designers had embarked upon. They had chosen women of a village near Igatpuri to give them the opportunity to work for some of the best designers of Bombay. They were being taught to cut and tailor which would provide them with a source of income. It was an interesting subject for Vidya to write on, for the story would be a mix of glamour and social consciousness. The only hitch was that this assignment would entail a three-day separation from her family.

When she had discussed it with Anish, he had been ever so encouraging. "There's always got to be a first time. Let's try it out. It'll be a change for both you and the kids." He had offered to take three days off from work and manage the kids so they wouldn't have to be alone with the maid.

So it was decided that Vidya would take the work trip. The thought of leaving the children behind tugged at her heartstrings. Yet deep within her was also the excitement of perhaps reliving her days of independence before marriage – of feeling single and carefree.

Journalist Vidya was still known by her maiden name, and today, as she sat alone in the train, she felt like she was truly living the identity of that name; not Mrs Vidya Rao but Ms Vidya Thakur was taking this journey. It was not that she minded being known by her husband's name, but this new feeling was unusual and exciting.

Vidya realised that she had been smiling unwittingly to herself all this while, her stream of thoughts broken by the sound of the train screeching to a halt. She smoothed her hair and got down from the train. The platform was not crowded. A little further from where she was stood a charming young woman holding a placard with her name. Vidya walked up to her and introduced herself.

"Hello, Vidya, I'm Jaya," the lady said. "I'm coordinating this project on behalf of the Fashion for a Cause Foundation. The committee informed me that you've come here to document our project. I've been entrusted to look after you and take you around these next three days. I've read some of your articles and loved them. I am looking forward to us working together."

"I'm glad to be here too," Vidya said with a smile as they both walked towards the car that was to take them to the hotel.

Igatpuri was a small town surrounded by villages. And so, checking into the best hotel meant a room with clean bed linen, a wall cabinet, stool and the luxury of a television set. Jaya helped Vidya settle into her room. It was a room that adjoined her own and there was a door connecting the two. Vidya felt a strange familiarity and a great deal of comfort with Jaya around. She was ever so warm and helpful – she almost felt like an old friend. And Jaya more than reciprocated the feeling; she appreciated Vidya's easy nature and admired her intelligence.

Over the next two days, the two travelled together to the neighbouring villages. Vidya saw for herself how much this project had come to mean to the scores of women who were preparing to become self-sufficient, as they enthusiastically attended the tailoring classes.

On the eve of her departure, Vidya and Jaya decided to return to the hotel to spend a relaxed evening together. They put up their feet on their bed and Jaya ordered for coffee and snacks in her room.

"It's going to shape up into an interesting article," Vidya commented, as she leafed through her notepad. "We need trendsetting projects like this to make a difference in our country. And Jaya, do let me compliment you – I can see how much of yourself you've given to the success of this venture."

Jaya smiled. "I've been doing fashion designing for five years now. But I was beginning to feel a strange void in my work. I felt a strong need to reach out to people – real people – and make a difference. And so I hit upon this idea, which the top designers of the country took to with great enthusiasm. And today with the cooperation of voluntary agencies, I can see the dream becoming a reality."

"I'm so happy for you," said Vidya, holding Jaya's hand in a warm clasp. "But tell me, with full-time work and having taken on this project, how do you manage your family commitments? It's such a difficult thing for me..."

"I'm not married. I live with my parents," answered Jaya with a smile.

"Oh, I'm sorry to have been so presumptuous. I just assumed you were ... What a stupid thing to think."

"It's okay. At my age most women are married and have kids. I'm more the exception than the rule and I know it." Jaya laughed. "And I like to play up the mystery about my marital status by going only by my first name." She winked mischievously.

"What is your surname – and where are you from?" Vidya asked, her curiosity now piqued.

"Jaya Shroff," she replied, "and we're Gujaratis settled in Bombay. My parents stay at Carter Road. Now you tell me about yourself. You look every bit a glowing, happily married woman with kids."

But Vidya had stopped listening. She heard nothing beyond Jaya Shroff ... Carter Road. It was enough to stun her to silence.

How come she hadn't made the connection earlier? Jaya Shroff the fashion designer. Back then the fashion designing student. She was the one Anish had told her about.

No, they had certainly never met before. But the two were bound by a strange fate. A bond that Vidya became aware of only a minute ago and one that Jaya still did not realise existed. But a bond that perhaps no two women would be happy tied in.

"What's wrong, Vidya? Are you feeling sick?" Jaya asked, looking at Vidya's stricken face.

"Yes. I've got this sudden headache. If you'll excuse me I'd just like to retire for the day. For these headaches … they only disappear with sleep," muttered Vidya. She made her way to her room, refusing Jaya's offers of help. "I'll be alright. This happens sometimes," she managed to say convincingly.

Later on, in her room, Vidya wondered how convincing her excuse had been. It had been the only way she could extricate herself from a situation that had thrown her off-balance. Her feelings and reactions were in complete turmoil. She needed time to be alone to clear her mind.

Jaya was a part of Anish's past. Hers was the one proposal that had come to Anish a decade earlier. It was much before he had even met Vidya.

Those were the days when despite Anish's protestations, his parents were bride-hunting for their son, wanting to see him settle down with a wife of their choice. Anish had gone out for coffee with several of them for he had kept his mind open that this could be one way of meeting the "right one". But the spark, the magic, the energy were off with everyone – it just was not clicking. Eventually Anish had refused to cooperate with his parents.

Much later, of course, Vidya came into his life and all that he had almost given up on, happened. Several years of marriage later, their instincts about each other were still proving right.

But of all the girls he had been out with, Jaya's case had been a slight aberration. He had found her to be an interesting person, good enough to be a friend. She lacked the intellect Anish was looking for in his future wife. Her world of clothes and fashion had virtually nothing in common with Anish's. So, for all that it was worth, Anish had, with complete candour, told Jaya on third meeting that he didn't think they had a future together.

Unlike the other girls, however, Jaya had by this time unwittingly and completely lost her heart to him. Her mind told her that she must not think of him. But her heart ached for him and she dreamed of the day when he would love her back.

On one such day, when her heart overpowered her mind, she had invited Anish over to her flat. It was a day when her parents had gone out of Bombay for the weekend. She had expressed her love for him – and had also told him that she accepted his doubts and did not expect any commitment from him.

She had embraced him and begged, "Please, just pretend for today that you love me. I'll live by this memory and it'll mean so much to me."

Anish had later confessed to Vidya that he had given in – and given in, not hesitatingly, but with passionate desire. It was only when his ardour had cooled that Anish had wondered whether Jaya had planned the seduction all along. He did not quite know what to make of it. Especially since neither of them made an attempt to contact each other after that day.

Anish had told Vidya of this bizarre episode in his life a short while after they were married. She had been repulsed by the thought of it then, but the years had blurred the memory of the incident. Especially since she had never met Jaya and more so because Anish himself had been so sheepish about the whole affair.

But today, she had encountered Jaya in flesh, blood and body. Body that had been caressed and fondled with desire by her man. Vidya felt a wave of anger and hatred towards Jaya. She felt as if she could not breathe the same air as this woman, who stood separated from her right now only by a small connecting door.

Vidya tried to stave off the images that flooded her mind. Anish and Jaya holding each other, desiring each other. She felt her whole body convulse with hot flushes. She drank a glass of cold water and shut her eyes, breathing slowly in an attempt to control the images flashing past her mind.

How was she going to react to seeing Jaya for the remaining hours of her stay in Igatpuri? As of this moment, Jaya did not suspect anything. She probably thought of her as Vidya Thakur and had not yet asked about her husband. Should she tell her?

No, of course not. There was no need to do that and risk rekindling feelings dormant on her side. Vidya realised that somehow she would have to cover up her feelings and endure Jaya normally until the next day when she would leave for Bombay.

Her stream of thoughts was broken by a soft knock on the connecting door. Every muscle in Vidya's body became tense at the thought of encountering Jaya again. She would have given anything to not have to open the door. But open she must. And open she did.

Jaya's face bore a worried, hesitant look. "I couldn't help worrying about you. Are you alright, Vidya?"

Vidya looked at the contours of Jaya's body rather shamelessly. She couldn't help visualising that long-ago afternoon when Anish and Jaya had partaken the pleasures of each other's bodies. Then, as she realised that Jaya had caught her looking at her, she checked herself. Jaya had just the hint of a smile on her lips, a twinkle in her eyes that Vidya found disconcerting.

"Oh! I'm feeling much better now. I was looking at that nightgown you're wearing. I have one exactly like that," she muttered, trying to explain her wandering eyes.

"We have similar tastes," said Jaya. "I always knew that, Vidya Anish Rao."

BROKEN NEWS

A roller-coaster of lies
A litany of shame
Breaking news, where truth dies
Chasing fleeting moments of fame

Maithili gazed at the people seated around her at the cafe. They were varying degrees of good looking, some more than others, but all interested in looking at the door every time someone walked in. Never before had she seen people ogle at themselves on every reflective surface around them or stop to check their hair while showing energetic enthusiasm for the conversation they were pretending to have.

'Ugh, stop with the cynicism…' Maithili had to remind herself. A conversation with her mother the previous week had made her realise that life in Mumbai had hardened her and turned her into a grumpy old woman she thought she was incapable of ever becoming.

Chai Shots was tucked away amidst "day-hire" studios in Aaram Nagar, a quaint part of Mumbai frequented by actors and models for auditions. She felt extremely underdressed; her loosely fitted cotton salwar and hair tied messily in a bun were a sharp contrast to the blow-dried hair and body-hugging clothes that the men and the women were wearing.

The café itself was nothing remarkable, a simple establishment with rickety wooden chairs, peeling plaster, and sun-bleached posters of yesteryear's stars. The aroma of cardamom-infused chai mingled with the salty Mumbai sea breeze. Yet, it was an oasis in the chaotic dreamscape of Mumbai's entertainment world. Maithili was getting impatient, Suhani was supposed to be there nearly fifteen minutes ago.

Just then, right on cue, Suhani walked through the door, bringing in with her a gust of the warm Mumbai summer wind. A dozen heads turned her way, judged from her looks that she was no casting director on a lookout for "fresh faces", and turned back. Suhani spotted Maithili with ease, and joined her. Her leopard-print top was perhaps a bit too tight, just like her jeans. Maybe the poor sixteen-year-old girl needed someone to guide her on tasteful dressing.

But that wasn't the reason they had decided to meet that day. Suhani took a moment to catch her breath. She still hadn't taken off the oversized sunglasses that did little to mask the redness of her nose.

"Hi, I am sorry I am late," said Suhani in slightly accented English.

"It's okay," said Maithili. "Don't worry, I have time. Can I get you something to drink or eat?"

"Only water please, thank you..."

Maithili signalled the waiter for the same.

"He called me to the office for a script reading..." Suhani began to speak, catching Maithili off guard.

"Oh, do you want to start right away?" she asked, taking out her recorder. Suhani nodded but stared at it suspiciously. "Don't worry, this is only for myself, no one else will have access to this, not even people in my agency..."

"Okay." Suhani brought her chair in a little closer and spoke in a hushed tone.

"He called me to his office for a script reading," she started, her voice barely a whisper. "I thought it was strange when he asked his assistant to leave and began to record it himself. He asked if I was comfortable. What do I do? Was I going to say no to the biggest director in Bollywood?"

Suhani's voice began to shake, as the waiter brought them water and a refill of black coffee for Maithili.

The story that unfolded was a sickening tale of abuse and power play. She described how Kabir had made her rehearse a romantic scene, how he'd come too close, his hand resting uncomfortably on her waist. She recounted how his grip tightened, and he moved in to kiss her, which was neither part of the script nor discussed earlier.

"He said I should learn to improvise and follow the cues that my co-actor would give me, and then suggested we try again..."

Every word she had heard made Maithili's blood boil. As Suhani spoke, she thought of every single male figure of authority who had exerted control over her and her life, and of all the men who also continued to do that to the women in their lives. Fuck them all.

"And then what did you do, Suhani?"

Suhani took a tissue and dabbed her eyes from under her glasses. Maithili caught a glance at her eyes. They were swollen and red. She extended her hand and held Suhani's.

"I ran. I screamed..."

There was an uncomfortable moment of silence in the air, as Maithili gave Suhani time to compose herself. She looked around at the starlets around her, desperate for the attention and validation of their powerful overlords, who would unsurprisingly exploit them. The sad part was, most of them would give in and never look back.

"Suhani, I want you to listen to me carefully. I am going to do everything I can to tell your story and to bring you justice, but I'm also going to do my best to try and make sure that this never happens again to you or to anyone else. But for that, you need to do as I say and stay in constant touch. Are you ready?"

Suhani looked at Maithili's hand firmly gripping her own and nodded nervously.

*

"Ladies and Gentlemen," Arvind began, his voice echoing through the studio. "Tonight, for our main story, we take you behind the curtain of glitz and glamour, to give you a real picture of exploitation, power play and ruthless entitlement from the world of Bollywood."

Behind the camera, everyone was watching with bated breath. When Arvind Desai spoke about the biggest stories, his voice always became louder. The camera and sound technicians sat up and listened carefully; they knew that this was going to be a big story. Across the country, several thousand more did just the same.

"Kabir Mittal!" he said, as pictures of Kabir flashed on screen. "Director, producer, writer, and ... child molester?" said Arvind, as a pair of handcuffs the graphics team had hurriedly put together flashed across the collage of Kabir.

As Arvind delved into the story, Maithili's heart pounded in her chest. Arvind went on to eloquently and passionately deliver the news story like only he could. In a trial by media, Kabir would have been declared guilty before the show was over. The narrative was compelling, the evidence substantial, and yet, there was a gnawing discomfort in the pit of her stomach. Kabir Mittal's side of the story was yet to come.

Her attempts at reaching Kabir had been met with silence. His PR had sent a curt message about respecting his privacy, before she could even tell them what this was about. The arrogance of it all, she thought. Kabir's silence, Maithili knew, would prove to be both his defence and his downfall. Speculation and rumour would fill the void; it would fuel the narrative against him.

She remembered the time she showed Arvind the transcript of the interview with Suhani, along with the written reports of interviews from witnesses who confirmed that Suhani had left the building agitated and in tears. Days had blended into nights as Maithili pored over details of Suhani's case, gathering every piece of evidence, cross-verifying each detail, barring the voice of the accused. Suhani had been carefully briefed that she must not talk to anyone about the case till Kabir had been found guilty. Maithili had even offered to help with the cost of hiring a lawyer.

As the broadcast concluded, Arvind met Maithili's gaze across the room. His eyes sparkled with satisfaction, oblivious to her unrest. They had broken a big story, and the office buzzed with a sense of accomplishment. Maithili's phone hadn't stopped ringing.

In her quest for justice, she had unflinchingly exposed a man without hearing his side. The bitter irony of it wasn't lost on Maithili, but Arvind had given her the go-ahead. She remembered his exact words after he had gone through all the evidence she had collected.

"Has the case been filed?" he asked.

"Anonymously," answered Maithili.

"Will do," said Arvind, as he handed all the paperwork back to Maithili. "Let's screw them all..." he had said, before asking her to prepare the script for the night's broadcast.

In the hush of the evening, the office was a stark contrast to its daytime chaos. Maithili sat alone, the skeletal staff working the night shift huddled in the distant corner, their muted conversations a mere whisper in the cavernous newsroom filled with endless cubicles.

The scotch in her glass was fragrant. "Top-shelf shit" as Arvind called it. He had given her the keys to his cabinet and asked her to take whatever she wanted, before heading off home. She swirled the golden liquid in her glass, the soft glow from the solitary desk lamp playing with the amber hues. It had been a very long day, but the excitement of the morning had been replaced by anticipation and then relief as the night wore on. Sometime through the day, they had even received word that Kabir's assistant Naina had quit her job.

Bingo, thought Maithili.

Her eyes strayed to the muted television screens that lined one wall of the newsroom. By now everywhere the main story was Kabir, and several failed actresses came out, relating stories of Kabir and how some of them had always felt there was a disturbing side to his creative genius.

One half of the wall was always showing their own shows, and two televisions ran their competitors' programmes. Maithili was tired and felt that what she was seeing could have been part of a dream, but when she nearly spilled her drink from tiredness, she shook herself awake. It was no dream.

There, under the garish studio lights, sat Suhani. Her face was covered with layers of makeup. The oversized sunglasses were replaced by kohl-rimmed eyes that danced with newfound confidence. She was unrecognisable.

With a sinking feeling, Maithili ran out of her cubicle and reached for the remote to turn the volume up.

"And now," Geetika, the interviewer (and a thorn in Arvind's side) was saying, "we have with us the brave young girl who dared to expose Kabir Mittal. The nation is with you, Suhani."

Suhani. She'd revealed her identity. The anonymous complainant was anonymous no more. She had disregarded their strategy, stepping into the limelight without a second thought for repercussions.

And then it had dawned on Maithili. This was no coincidence. The girl had known this all along, getting the story in through one news channel, knowing that the others would want to one-up them. Maithili had been played.

As Suhani continued to narrate her ordeal, her voice no longer trembling but poised, Maithili felt a strange unease creep over her. It wasn't just the revelation of her identity; it was Suhani's demeanour. She seemed to be revelling in the attention, almost exploiting her own tragedy.

The celebratory drink in Maithili's hand suddenly felt too heavy. Dread slowly pooled in her stomach. Something was not adding up. She had an anonymous victim using her story to catapult herself to instant fame. It felt manipulative. It felt wrong.

The quiet hum of the office faded as Maithili's mind whirred. The one thing she had sought to prevent had come to pass – Suhani's victimhood was being commercialised. And in the process, she wondered if the truth had been the casualty.

*

"What the hell is wrong with you!" Arvind's voice bellowed through the office. All of Maithili's pride from the day before had come crashing down.

"How could I have known this would happen, Arvind? Please calm down," said Maithili.

"Come on, Maithili. Five years I've known you now ... I didn't think I'd have to double check still. She's a bloody actress ... she will do anything for fame, you can't not have seen this coming! We look like a bunch of idiots now while Geetika bloody Mehrotra looks like she's broken the real story."

Arvind was right. Maithili's hard work had all been largely for nothing. She had spent the entirety of last night at the office, sleepless and waiting for an appropriate time to call Suhani.

Of course, she hadn't answered.

Maithili found herself grappling with a disconcerting silence from Suhani. The girl who had once unflinchingly trusted her with her deepest secret was suddenly unreachable, her phone perpetually switched off. All of Maithili's messages went unresponded.

But as the day wore on, Suhani's name now reverberated everywhere, through all newsrooms and social media. The quiet, timid girl from Kanpur was suddenly at the centre of a whirlwind, her account of exploitation fuelling prime-time debates, op-eds, and sensational headlines. It seemed like the rest of the news world was cashing in on Maithili's hard work, and now she just wanted to shut this chapter and forget it ever happened. Kabir's

PR team still wouldn't take her calls and weren't commenting on the story anywhere.

But with every passing moment, Maithili's journalistic instincts screamed louder, urging her to dig deeper, to find the other side of this narrative that had gone out of hand. Frustrated, Maithili was about to call it a day when she received an anonymous phone call.

"Hello?" she said on the phone.

"This is Naina. Please check your mail," said the quiet voice from the other end.

Maithili scrambled to open her laptop.

"These are Kabir's audition tapes," Naina continued, her voice quivering. "He always records them for future reference. I think ... it's the proof you need."

Sensing that Naina was about to hang up, Maithili quickly asked, "Wait! Naina! I just need to know, for myself ... Why did you call me and not the other news channels blowing this up?"

Naina sighed. "Because you were the only guys keeping Suhani's name under wraps. I could trust you to do the same with mine. Please..." And with that, she hung up.

As Maithili watched the footage for what could have been the tenth time in the solitude of her home, she felt as though the ground beneath her was shifting. Suhani was the worst actress she had ever seen. It was disastrous, almost like asking an actor to purposefully act badly and ruin a scene. Kabir tried to step into the frame and speak to her directly instead of cueing her off camera, which she took as an invitation to flirt with him. It was painfully awkward though, and while Kabir seemed visibly taken aback, he handled the situation with nothing but professionalism and led her out of the frame.

This piece of damning evidence stood in stark contrast to Suhani's tearful account of her encounter. Maithili found herself staring at the horrifying truth; Suhani's claim was a lie, a smokescreen to cover her lack of talent and fuel her desperate thirst for fame. She couldn't decide what was worse – that Suhani had known her audition was bad, and decided to create this elaborate web of lies before she even left the building, or that this sixteen-year-old girl had successfully manipulated the media.

Armed with the truth, Maithili marched into Arvind's office the next morning. Her heart pounded in her chest as she mentally prepared herself for a heated confrontation.

"Are you sure about this?"

"Yes. I've watched it over and over again. All the way till the time she exits the door. This whole complaint is fabricated and the girl is lying."

"Fine, but if there's any backlash on this, I can't vouch for you any longer. It'll have to be an 'unpaid leave' if this doesn't check out," warned Arvind.

Maithili knew exactly what that meant, but she had other ideas.

"That won't be a problem, Arvind. Regardless of what happens, I'm done for a while. I need a break," she said, putting down her name tag on the table, and walked straight out of the office, leaving him stunned.

*

That night, ratings of the "News at 8" were at an all-time high, as footage showed Suhani's story and her allegations to be baseless. Somewhere in the city that never slept, a very angry Geetika was watching this and probably losing her cool. Arvind had no doubt though that other agencies would pick up the story from where he had left off, but tonight, the big story was his to own.

Maithili wasn't concerned about any of this. For the first time in as long as she could remember, she was watching the main story from the comfort of her home. Maybe tonight, finally, she would sleep well. Tomorrow, she would think about what lay ahead...

As she went to bed, drifting off to sleep while late-night infomercials on television lent a glow to the otherwise dark room, her phone buzzed, and she sat up straight.

It was an unknown number. Instinctively, she answered the phone, expecting it to be Naina.

"Hey, I want to thank you for that, I hope you're happy with the way it was all done. We didn't give any hint that it was you..." Maithili began to rattle off.

"Oh, but you did..." said a deep and husky voice at the other end. Maithili recognised it instantly.

Kabir Mittal.

"H-Hello, Kabir?" Great, thought Maithili, what a time to stutter.

"Finally, we speak..."

"I'm sorry, I guess. I did try to reach out to you several times..."

"Just like every other actor and actress who has messaged me and asked me to cast them in my next movie?"

He did have a point.

"I'm sorry, still. I didn't intend to destroy your reputation," she said, sheepishly.

"That's alright, you had your reasons, as I have mine for making this phone call."

Maithili was curious, if a little bit nervous.

"I heard you quit your job..." he continued. How did he know? It hadn't even been a whole day.

"Yes. I needed a break."

"Good, because I'm looking for a writer for my next film, and I wanted someone who really understands journalism to tell the story as true to life as possible. Maybe you'd be interested?"

"Writer? But what's the story?"

"Oh, funny you should ask. Have you heard of this actress called Suhani?"

FACE-TO-FACE

You travel across an era
To render me free of pain
Are you a dream, a chimera?
Come to make me whole again

"For reference only" said the familiar purple ink stamp on the first page of the book that Aparna had found with such difficulty. The letters faded but legible enough to put an end to her hopes of leaving the library early that afternoon with the book and spending the extra time with Amod. Now there was absolutely no chance of her being able to take the book home to make notes for Friday's tutorial. She was lucky to find this book to study all to herself in this library, for the two copies of *Slavic Wars* in the college library had been in circulation and had been difficult to lay her hands on these past two weeks.

Aparna carried the book and walked to the corner of the second table, ready with her foolscap sheets and ballpoint pen. She opened the chapter on "Roses", languorously slicing the pages that had stuck together with disuse. It made a delicious crackling sound. The book had obviously not been opened! She then mentally calculated that she would definitely be able to finish making notes in the next two to three hours, considering her reference chapter was only about forty pages long.

It was then that Aparna's eyes first met the "muffler" woman's. She came to sit across diagonally from Aparna soon after she had settled into her chair. A distinguished fifty-year-old, she had a cropped, no-nonsense cut for her salt-and-pepper hair. More salt than pepper actually.

That day she had worn a sari, but Aparna was to see her later in many attires; sometimes in salwar-kurtas, sometimes in trousers and once even in a long Tibetan chupa. She was certainly well preserved – the sort of woman who could easily look ten to fifteen years younger if she dyed her hair. But whatever it was that she chose to wear, the muffler was always covering her neck as protectively as though it were guarding a secret. Hence the sobriquet.

The muffler-woman had in her hand a hardcover that looked so much like the reference book that Aparna was working with. It was strange, she had thought at that time; these kinds of reference books were hardly leisure reading.

That day Aparna had gone on to make long copious notes. About half an hour after she had started, she lifted her tired eyes from the page she had been writing on. The muffler-woman, she noticed, was staring at her. But the moment their eyes met, she immediately looked away. Aparna also noticed that the woman was still on the same page as an hour ago. A highly distracted reader she was, Aparna had then thought!

The woman closed her book with a bored look and coughed softly. It was surprising how one sniffle or cough in the pin-drop silence of a library becomes a clarion call for others to follow suit. For a few minutes after that there was a virtual cacophony of such pent-up releases and then a gradual petering out. The familiar sound of silence descended once again, and Aparna saw the woman leave soon after.

The second time Aparna saw the woman was at the local supermarket. She was walking through the aisle, browsing the goods on the shelves. The muffler-woman would occasionally pick up a jar or packet, examine it distractedly and then put it right back in its place. Aparna meanwhile was busy, dutifully ticking items off the list her mother had given to her, as she put them one by one in the trolley. Each time she looked up from across the shelf, she would catch the muffler-woman looking at her. It felt like an eerie coincidence, to end up at the same place as she was – it seemed almost as if the woman had been following her. But then, as Aparna rationalized, the woman could be justified in feeling exactly the same way about her – she noticed that the woman, nervous and distracted, checking out the same packets of soup and noodles time and again.

Aparna caught her staring at her once again. She fought a sinking feeling in the pit of her stomach and gave the muffler-woman a broad smile. She was determined to humour this for now. After all, sometimes coincidences can leave one with an unnerving feeling; yet they are possibly nothing more than mere chance.

She was sure that the woman would smile back at her. And smile she did – a frightened and forced smile, like a child smiling in an act of bravery to mask the pain of an injection.

The muffler-woman proceeded to shuffle away, leaving a distinct distaste in Aparna's mouth. For the first time in their chance encounters a shiver went down Aparna's spine. She had to acknowledge an uncomfortable feeling that perhaps she was indeed being followed, and that this was not all too coincidental.

Over the next few days such encounters repeated ever so often. At Bandra railway station, at Jogger's Park where she jogged with Amod, at the Santacruz market where she shopped, at Fashion Street, even at Eros where she went to see a film with Amod – the muffler-woman always seemed to be watching her – yet she never seemed interested in befriending her.

Who was she? Why was she following Aparna? Could she be a private detective? Aparna did briefly consider it, but she ruled it out soon enough, for a detective would have surely followed her a little more discreetly. In any case, there really wasn't anyone in the world who would possibly want to put a detective on her.

After about a dozen such silent encounters, the whole thing was now getting a little too perplexing for Aparna. Suspense of this kind was exciting so long as it happened in the pages of a book, where all the answers lay just a couple of more pages away. And if, like Amod, one was too impatient to wait even for that, one could always dive straight into the last chapter and crack the mystery in advance. But this was happening in real life, and taking Aparna's mind in the most bizarre directions. If she did not get to the bottom of this soon, she would surely go mad.

Was the muffler-woman a serial killer? Or maybe someone secretly connected with the family? Her father's secret mistress? Now that Aparna thought about it, there had been more-frequent-than-normal episodes of mom-sobbing-behind-shut-bedroom-door and dinner-getting-cold-on-the-table these last few weeks at home.

But like always, Mom and Dad did seem to get over whatever problems they had had. Surely the muffler-woman could not in any way be related to such family problems. In spite of this, Aparna thought it wise not to share her anxiety about the woman with anyone in the family just yet. She was feeling too suffocated in dealing with it all on her own, however, and had to tell it to someone. That someone could only be Amod. This would also be a nice way of testing really how much he cared for her, thought Aparna.

Amod laughed his guts out when she first mentioned the muffler-woman. Aparna was offended and she got up in a huff from her chair in the college canteen. As she was about to walk away, he caught her hand and found it was so very cold. At that moment Amod's expression changed and he became serious. He made her sit down and pour out all her worries to him. Amod put his arms protectively around Aparna's shoulders. "Don't worry, we will get to the bottom of this," he reassured her. "Come on now, I'll drop you to the station. You're in time for the 4:25 local. Let's hurry. It's 4 o'clock already. You don't want to get caught in the rush hours."

They walked silently, hand-in-hand, each preoccupied with their own thoughts, making their way to the southern end of

Platform 1. The huge clock on the concourse read 4:07 p.m. and the indicator for Platform 1 showed that the train would depart at 4:25 p.m. Suddenly, Aparna noticed the indicator for Platform 3 reading "4:09 Andheri Fast". Now, catching that would be a good idea, she thought.

Aparna told Amod that she was going to go over the tracks to Platform 3, so she could catch the faster train. She had done this many times earlier too, so she bid Amod a quick goodbye and he watched her scurry away, concerned.

Aparna hurried down the slope of Platform 1 to go onto Platform 2. Suddenly she felt herself being rudely pushed. She fell to the ground with a thud. She was about to protest indignantly when, at that very moment, a train passed her by on the very track she had intended to cross.

In a flash it dawned upon her – someone had just saved her life!

A crowd had gathered there by now. Amod was by her side in seconds and helped her to her feet. Aparna was about to turn to walk back onto the platform, when she saw the face of the muffler-woman lying on the ground. There she was, staring at her as always, but this time with still eyes. Her torso had just been ripped apart by the train that had passed by. It was her familiar chilling gaze that now stood frozen forever.

Amod tried to pull Aparna away but she clutched his hand firmly and whispered hoarsely into his ear.

"It's she … the muffler-woman … the one I was telling you about."

A stunned Amod inched towards the body. He noticed faint bruise marks on either side of her neck. At close sight she looked sad and vulnerable, like a scared prey hunted for too long. In her lifeless hand the muffler-woman still clutched an envelope that now fluttered in the breeze, held precariously in a grip between her thumb and forefinger. Amod bent down, picked up the envelope and led Aparna away. By now he could see the station authorities walking towards the spot.

Amod and Aparna sat down on a bench on the platform. He opened the envelope and began to read softly.

My dear Aparna,

In these last few weeks I may have inspired many worrisome moments for you, with my horribly strange behaviour. I write this letter to you now, so that these worries can finally be put to rest. Believe me, to bother you or have you worried was the last of my intentions. In fact I pray that the Almighty puts all your burdens on my shoulders to bear and that he makes me of some use to your life.

You wonder why a stranger should feel such love for you. You are not a stranger to me. You are ... you were my daughter.

My daughter, my only child, died a slow and painful death due to cancer twenty years ago. She passed away in my arms when she was only four. I tried everything that a mother can to get over her loss. But the truth is, the grief of losing a child is not the kind you can ever come to terms with. The years went slowly by, somehow. Last year, my husband left me too, and I was left all alone in this world.

I wanted to die. I tried to hang myself but was saved by a neighbour. It is the marks of that attempt that are hidden by the muffler I always wear around my neck.

Then, last summer, I met Vespi. Vespi communicates with the dead. And he helps tormented souls like mine to know that their loved ones are indeed there – that they are still alive though in another body. He even tells us where and how they live. Vespi promised to let me know where my daughter had been reborn. It is he who told me that you were she, reborn in another home eighteen years ago! He warned me that I must not disturb you in your present life and that the knowledge of your past birth must be kept a secret between the two of us.

I tried very hard to do that. I tried to leave you alone. But try as I might I could not resist wanting to watch you, my beautiful angel. That was all the joy that I had left in my empty life. Yet, whenever your eyes would catch my glance I would wince. I was afraid that if you approached me at a weak moment, I would break my promise to Vespi and tell you what you were to me. And that would destroy your peace of mind. I loved you too much to want that to happen to you because of me.

I write this letter only to end the torment that my mysterious behaviour has caused you. I am sad that I have had to break my promise to Vespi and also to disturb you with my truth, so the best way to atone for my wrongdoing is to promise you that I will never see you again. It will kill me to do so, but it would be for the best.

I will finally learn to be alone. Thank you, my daughter, you have made me whole again, and with your beautiful memories, I will be able to live – live alone and die alone.

Yours lovingly
Mother

FRIENDS INDEED

A friend is a mirror true
Reflecting the passing years
Seen afresh, seen anew
Through the laughter and the tears

I

The air was fresh with the fragrance of marigolds and jasmines, and the arrangements had been made to perfection.

At one end of the Gymkhana Club lawn stood rows of tables lined with food warmers, their flames gently flickering in the fading light of dusk. At the other end was the flower-bedecked marriage pandal. Waiters in spotless red-and-white uniforms walked around offering drinks to the first few guests at the wedding of Prerna and Vimal.

In the cloakroom, Prerna's dresser was putting the final touches to her make-up. She looked radiant as only a bride could. She watched with sparkling eyes as parents, cousins, relatives and friends darted in and out looking ever so busy.

Almost all the faces familiar to her for twenty-two years were here today. Only for her. No wonder they called it the big day, she thought.

But where was Shreya, she wondered. Her face broke into a smile as she thought of her rebellious, spunky friend and neighbour of all these years.

To say that Prerna and Shreya were as unlike as chalk and cheese would be an understatement. People often wondered how the two were friends at all. Prerna was the shy, studious and obedient daughter while Shreya had always been an adventurous, daring nonconformist.

Prerna remembered with amusement the tiffs they had in school when Shreya ragged her in front of their friends. Shreya used to call her Little Miss Goody when Prerna refused to be party to their pranks. On a few occasions, Prerna joined Shreya's gang in a bid to conform. And if ever her parents would get to hear of these one-off instances, aghast, they'd force her to call off her friendship with Shreya. But time had passed, and everyone had simply come around their bizarre partnership.

Today, moving forward with so many childhood memories, their friendship had come full circle. They loved each other for their wholly different ideas and ways of living – both ever fascinated and supportive of how the other's life was shaping up.

As if in tune with Prerna's thoughts, Shreya appeared at the door. As always, she was standing out with her casual T-shirt, jeans and a ponytail on an evening when everyone else was revelling in finery.

Shreya embraced Prerna and winked wickedly. "Haven't you forgotten to wear your golden sandals?"

"I managed to put my foot down on that one," Prerna replied.

"Some rebel, you. It's a good beginning anyway." Shreya laughed.

Soon the ceremonies were under way. Prerna was too busy with being the perfect bride to notice the twinge of sadness on Shreya's face as the latter watched the proceedings, her mind wandering.

Shreya thought of Prerna whose life lay chalked out for her. While hers in contrast stood jumbled, chaotic, uncertain ... and challenging. But isn't that how she'd wanted it to be? Nevertheless, she was sad today. And that was because of a little setback in the otherwise perfect plan that she had worked out for herself.

In two days, she was to leave Delhi to join an advertising agency in Bombay. She would be living by herself in a paying guest accommodation, discovering life on her own terms; with the reassuring presence of her boyfriend Pradeep who would be living with her. That was until today.

Pradeep and Shreya had been going steady for two years. The job in Bombay was going to be Shreya's first. Pradeep too was in marketing and had worked for a year in Delhi. He liked the prospect of a different working experience in Bombay and was willing to move cities with Shreya. They both looked forward to freedom and togetherness, of which they could never have their fill in Delhi.

Shreya's parents, as always, had to give in to their daughter's wishes. For they knew that she would go ahead with her plans even if they did not give their consent. And that, they agreed, could be worse. Things, however, were not so hunky-dory at Pradeep's end.

Today he had met Shreya in the morning to tell her that he was sorry. He had finally succumbed to his parents' disapproval of his plans and had decided to stay back in Delhi. He suggested Shreya reconsider her own plans, too.

Shreya did not protest at his change of mind. But neither did she change her own. She was too independent in spirit to chicken out at the prospect of doing it all alone. Yet the happiness and excitement of leaving her home had definitely dulled a little.

II

"Seven years gone by and still as beautiful as the day we were married," Vimal said to Prerna.

"Just a few extra rolls around my waist, courtesy of our children," retorted Prerna as she looked at his face in the dim light across the restaurant table. For seven years they had made all kinds of adjustments with each other – some easy, some bitter. Homemaking, dealing with in-laws, teething and tantrum problems, job hops and transfers, they had braved it all together.

Theirs had been a fairly happy marriage with its normal share of ups and downs. Today, as they held hands across the table, they thought with satisfaction about the past and contentedly envisioned the future – now that they had just shifted to the mother of all cities, Bombay. Vimal had recently been appointed public relations manager at a reputed private firm in Bombay. He had been provided a furnished company flat and a car and was looking forward to his new job. Their two boys, Suhail and Nikhil, had secured admission in a good school.

After the first few days of settling down in Bombay, the first thing on Prerna's mind was to surprise Shreya with her presence in the city.

In these seven years, the two of them had kept in touch but inconsistently. Prerna knew that Shreya had made a mark for herself in the advertising world and was second in command in the creative department at Bombay's premier advertising agency, enjoying near-celebrity status. But she had remained single and her parents, though proud of her achievements, were concerned on that score.

It took a minute for Shreya to register the name. "Prerna, who … Oh Prerna … you horrible girl! Why didn't you reply to my last two letters … But where are you calling from?" Shreya shrieked with excitement.

"BO-M-BAY, and I'm here to stay," replied Prerna. "Sorry about your letters, Shreya. Life got in the way, with the kids, family, moving through cities and everything else going. Anyway, here I am to make up for lost time."

"Always good at excuses. Look, I'm dropping in this evening right after work. I'm dying to see you and the kids," Shreya said excitedly as she took down the directions to Prerna's house.

It was certainly an evening to remember. Shreya and Prerna felt seven years younger, back to the time of girlish chatter and giggles. And both threw well-meaning barbs at each other.

"Boring, contented housewife, don't you want to find yourself in life, Prerna?" asked Shreya.

"And you – bindaas Bombay babe! No time for marriage and kids. There's a limit to living it up in life. Aren't you ever going to sober down?" Prerna retorted.

And yet, each bared her soul to the other, as perhaps only two childhood friends can.

"Yes, it is lonesome and tough living alone in Bombay, with no family to come home to. I do wish I had a man to lean on – to take care of me. Sometimes I wonder what use is the money and status I have, when I've no one to share it with. I've had my share of relationships. But in the end, I always feel that I'm better off alone, for the men I've met are all in some ways like Pradeep was – no guts, no spine..." Shreya trailed off. "Don't you think men are all alike?"

"Hey, hey, don't include my Vimal in that category," replied Prerna. Then she became a trifle thoughtful. "He's really a good husband and a good father to the kids. I'm content with my lot. But to be honest with you, we do take each other for granted after all these years. Life is so boring and mechanical sometimes – it's as if all the romance of the early days was merely a short dream. Now as the kids are growing up, they're going to need me less and less – everyone will have their own life to lead except me. I will not have much significance left then," she added wistfully.

"Two lonely middle-aged women – that's what we both are. I think we should move in together and grow old, hand-in-hand," said Shreya with a twinkle in her eye as Prerna joined in with a hearty laugh.

III

Years went by. Prerna's boys grew up, Shreya's career graph climbed to even higher planes. Strangely, so did the loneliness of the two friends. And a score or two of black hair quietly turned grey on their heads.

With all this, however, there came new dimensions too. Prerna took up pottery as a hobby. She started selling some of her pieces and that gave her a feeling of satisfaction. But in spite of all this, somehow, she still did not feel complete.

In Shreya's case, it started as a passing fancy – listening to Osho's discourses on tape. This fancy gradually fuelled itself to become an option for an alternative way of life.

She often spent days and weeks away from her job at the Pune ashram. Later, back in Bombay, she would regale Prerna with the thoughts and systems that she discovered there. She often contemplated a complete initiation into the ashram as a sanyasin. But at other times she had her doubts. Looking back on life, she felt that she had missed out on the joys of marriage and motherhood, having shown contempt for it in her youth. But it was probably too late for a change now.

Then there was Prerna. She often felt like breaking free. Free from the compulsion of having to be good, right and responsible all the time. But should she? Could she? And if she did, wouldn't that imply that she had been frustrated all along and leading a life of pretence all these years.

Decisions, more decisions. Decisions that should be and yet need not ever be made.

IV

It had been more than a month since Shreya wrote to her from the ashram. Prerna was a bit worried.

In her last letter, Shreya had written very briefly about Shantanu – a middle-aged man whom she had met at the ashram. She told Prerna that for the first time she had come across a man who thought and felt like a woman. And who, like her, stood at the crossroads of life trying to make a decision about his future.

They must probably have both taken sanyas together, thought Prerna, as she managed a weak smile to herself.

Smiling had otherwise become impossible these days. The last few weeks had not been kind to her. Vimal had been having problems at the office and had been edgy because of it. It had all happened earlier too – an attempt to survive the rat race. It was a familiar pattern. Yet this time Vimal had not been able to take it in his stride. Nothing that Prerna tried to say or do helped him come out of his shell of bitterness.

Prerna knew that like all previous crises this too would pass. But this time she found it difficult to hold out. She often felt like running away to live only for herself and nobody else. It was a selfish thought and she recognised it for what it was.

V

It was a beautiful serene morning in Pune. There was a nip in the air – so characteristic of Pune weather. Prerna stood at the gate of the ashram, her suitcase in hand, feeling as though she'd finally come home. Halfway through the walkway she saw a familiar figure. Shreya was coming towards her, arm in arm with a man.

As Shreya's eyes met Prerna, she ran towards her. "I should have written to you. Actually, I wanted to surprise you. Shantanu and I are getting married tomorrow in Bombay," Shreya said, glowing with happiness.

"I am happy for you, Shreya. But I'm not here for you. I'm here to stay and discover myself." Prerna smiled back.

HAPPILY EVER AFTER

A liberated woman
Helped a lesser one
A lesson is learnt
A campaign is done

What a fantastic start to the last working day of the week. Sreela read the letter that had been lying on top of the mail pile for the sixth time in the last ten minutes.

The Morning Post
The Post Building,
Fifth Avenue
New York – 100 017
USA

Dear Ms Dixit,

Congratulations! You have been unanimously chosen by our jury for one of our annual journalistic awards. We are pleased to announce you have won this year's Best Asian Social Journalist award for your coverage of the Kundabai story last year.

We shall be informing you about the details of the awards ceremony next month along with your travel and lodging arrangements. But to proceed any further on this matter, we would require from you as early as possible the following: A formal letter of acceptance of this award, a copy of your resume with some of your recent pictures and, most importantly, 2-3 recent "happily ever after" photos of Kundabai to whose life you made all the difference.

Awaiting your response,

Yours sincerely,

Whitney Brown

Associate Editor, *The Morning Post*

*

Sreela's little cabin was soon teeming with people – her effusive colleagues, some smiling genuinely, others pretending to do so, shiny-eyed secretaries and even a couple of genuflecting juniors. All morning long Sreela smiled until her jaws ached. Then, her editor Pranay Bose, who had just flown in from Calcutta at noon, called her straightaway into his cabin.

Pranay Bose was beaming with pride on hearing the news, especially since he had given her the job in the first place. He had chosen her over and above several of the better qualified mass communication postgraduates nearly five years ago. The reason, as he had told her before, had been her fiery spirit, her strong, assertive opinions on everything and her zeal to change the world. She was told she lacked objectivity, but she made up for it by being strong on rhetoric and was therefore a refreshing change from the "trained to write well" graduates of journalism schools.

"I can afford only one Sreela in an editorial staff of ten. But one Sreela is certainly more interesting than all the nine put together," Pranay had often chuckled and admitted to his colleagues after a couple of drinks at the Press Club. He had also been completely unreserved in his compliments to her, only in private to begin with. In the course of time however he had started to express his admiration for Sreela much more openly.

"Sreela, you have really done me proud," he had said after one of her early stories had been publicly applauded. "Thanks to you, maybe we shall see the return of activist journalism that had been such a vital part of our lives in the eighties."

Sreela had certainly risen above the ranks of regular journalists who only reported competently or wrote about socio-political developments. And she had done this without having to join the ranks of pontificating editorial writers who had strong opinions to express without actually going out into the field. She consistently wrote stories that inspired change in her subjects' lives. Her first such story had been published four years ago. It had been a dramatic exposé on the case of a poor twelve-year-old girl, Salma, who had been "married" to an Arab in exchange for a little money for her poor parents. Thanks to the hue and cry and enquiries that had followed, the Arab had been forced to go underground. Salma was now in an English-medium girl's hostel, her educational expenses taken care of by a public fund set up by Pranay Bose's newspaper.

Pranay Bose had been proud of all of Sreela's seven-odd stories that had followed. Today, when a prestigious international magazine like *The Morning Post* had chosen to confer an award on Sreela, his pride knew no bounds. Pranay Bose couldn't stop shaking her hand today as she faced him in his cabin. "I'm so proud of you," he said again and again, his eyes transfixed on the letter lying under the paperweight on his table. "You must send them your acceptance letter and the documents right away."

"There's a problem there, sir," said Sreela, disengaging her hand from his with some relief to pick up the letter and read it out to him when she could well have described it instead. "It says here that they require from me a recent 'happily ever after' kind of picture of Kundabai, and I don't have one with me right now. For that I'll have to travel to Manmad again."

"So go, Sreela, go today itself. Tomorrow's a weekend. You can easily get the pictures and come back in time to post your stuff to the US by Monday morning. Consider your leave sanctioned and the office car at your disposal, and all your travel expenses are granted. You can fill up your vouchers later, take an advance right away. Anything for you, my dear girl. After all, you have done our newspaper very proud," said Bose breathlessly.

Sreela was an expert at travelling on a short notice. She slung her camera around her neck then satisfactorily examined the pair of keds she always kept at the office. They'd always stood by her in good stead when she had to traverse the unfriendly roads surrounding Mumbai.

She thought a little about her clothes. It seemed more convenient to buy a set of undergarments and a T-shirt to go with her jeans from the department store below the office, than waste a couple of hours going back home to pick them up! That decided it.

Before she knew it, Sreela was sitting in the backseat of the office car and out on the road. Organised and practical, Sreela usually used her time on the way to an assignment in mentally preparing for it. It was important to frame the right questions, arguments and counterarguments in possibly changing scenarios. But this time was refreshingly different. She could afford to empty her mind of all such burdens and instead bask in the pride of the award announcement that had arrived that morning. She could afford to revel in a sense of achievement at the positive change that she had brought about in someone else's life, and one for which she was about to be given her biggest bit of public acclaim.

Sreela took out the picture of Kundabai that she had clicked a year ago. Emaciated but beautiful, Kundabai sat cross-legged and determined outside the hut of her lover Vilas Kondke, staring with large sunken eyes at the tiny bundle of a baby in her lap.

"I really loved him. I really believed him when he said he loved me ... that is the only reason why I gave in to him. But now he refuses to marry me. Tell me, memsahib, is this not his child and am I not his child's mother, so why should he shirk taking responsibility. But, memsahib, I will not accept my fate like other women. I will sit here on dharna until he takes us both into his home," she had said resolutely. "Till then my house is here on a bamboo mat under the open sky."

What a poignant picture it had made for! And the way Sreela had captured and projected it, along with the four articles she wrote on it one after another, had resulted in a wave of national and then international sympathy for Kundabai.

Hundreds of people had sent Kundabai financial aid which she had proudly returned. Several villagers had been shamed enough by her story to even offer to rehabilitate her. Rajaram, the old moneylender of Manmad village, had even offered to marry her, promising to keep her well all his life. He had said that he wanted to give her so much happiness that she'd forget Vilas Kondke had ever happened. But the righteous Kundabai had scornfully refused. "My happiness lies in my acceptance by the father of my child, the man I loved," Kundabai had said, with steely determination.

Kundabai's story became a cause célèbre and had in the course of time made the village elders impress upon Vilas to make amends. A shamefaced Vilas Kondke had taken Kundabai and their daughter in.

"I think this is the house of that husband of hers," said her driver Kader.

"No, Kundabai does not stay in this house now," a voice muttered.

"Kundabai lives there in that pukka house," said a little girl wearing a muddied grey school uniform, the large red ribbons on her two tightly tied plaits bouncing as she played hopscotch. She pointed to a single-storeyed house at the corner of the lane, painted a bright pink.

Sreela asked Kader to park the car there. "Nice house," he commented. "Looks like Kundabai and Vilas are doing well for themselves."

Sreela walked across the road to the pink house and savoured its surroundings. It would surely make a pretty picture for the foreign papers. All the signs of a happy Indian home in the country – one that *she* had helped make happy.

Sreela focused her camera and adjusted it to include the rangoli design in front of the blue wooden door in the frame. The plastic toran leaves at the top of the door, each of which had an image of a different Hindu god painted in gold on it, flapped in the warm dry breeze of the early evening. Satisfied with the picture she'd taken, Sreela proceeded to knock on the door.

The door opened – only as much as the safety chain would allow it to – enough however to make clearly visible the smiling face of Kundabai. Her face lit up the moment she saw Sreela. She removed the safety chain quickly and opened the door to hug her. Sreela felt Kundabai sweating profusely beneath the heavy silk sari she was wearing. She had filled out everywhere and was almost unrecognisable – her belly clearly heavy with child. Her face was oily and shining, her maang filled with orange sindoor from her forehead to the back of her head. Kundabai was resplendent in the glow of a happy marriage and an impending second motherhood. The haunted look that Sreela associated her with had gone forever.

Kundabai plied Sreela with country goodies – puran poli, modak, chakli and much more – simply refusing to accept her protests. Eventually, Sreela begged her to understand that more than food, what she really needed was to click a happy picture of Kundabai and her family.

Kundabai finally did understand. She smiled and called out to a maidservant. The maidservant brought in Kundabai's one-year-old to sit on her lap, cautioning the child not to kick Amma, for it would hurt her little sibling in Amma's stomach.

"But I need Vilas to pose with all of you," Sreela explained. "Where's he?"

Kundabai's face fell. "He's not my husband anymore," she said. "I was wrong, memsahib, absolutely wrong. You all helped me. You made him take us back and fulfil his responsibilities. He did … he gave us a roof over our head, food, water, money, status everything that he could afford. But he couldn't love us, and I couldn't live without his love."

"So did he leave you and..." Sreela whispered hoarsely.

"No, memsahib ... I left him. I was the one who had chained him. And it was I who set him free too ... And then I set myself free too."

"But this house? And the child that you're expecting..."

"Rajaram's ... I married Rajaram."

"The old moneylender who had said that he loved you," Sreela cried out in horror, biting her tongue to avoid using the word "ugly" to describe him in these changed circumstances.

"At least he's not a liar. He doesn't just say it ... he really does love me. I've experienced true love, comfort and enough happiness to last me a lifetime in this one year, memsahib. You take your picture, memsahib ... a happy family photo you require, isn't it?"

Sreela stood up slowly from her seat and walked away from Kundabai. She turned around and stopped at an optimum distance of about twelve feet, and then aimed and clicked. *A happily-ever-after picture...*

JUST FOR MY SON

Your lover, my son
Of my womb born
How does our love compare
Between what I feel, and what you share

Ratt-a-tat, ratt-a-tat, ratt-a-tat; the wheels rolled and clicked over the track, as the train chugged along, gaining speed. Its rhythmic beat played musically on Veena's ears and she smiled to herself.

If Arjun hadn't been so naïve, she would probably have never found out for a long time, she thought. But then, Arjun *was* naïve. The budding liaison between him and Aarohi had been quite evident, thank god for that. It couldn't have escaped *her* eyes. Good that she had nipped it in the bud! And in the process saved her son from potential disaster, something his blind and desperate young age didn't allow him to see. That shameless woman! Trying to take advantage of her age! Veena shook her head. Fifteen years older to my innocent Arjun and leading him down the garden path.

But she had set her straight. Now Aarohi would never dream of fluttering near Arjun. Not anymore, thought Veena pleased with herself.

The young woman sitting opposite Veena had been lulling her baby to sleep. She now put him down carefully on the berth. A lone mosquito which had somehow entered the AC coach buzzed near the child's ear, then flitted in and out of sight, hovering over him. The young woman's eyes followed its aerial path suspiciously and focused themselves as the mosquito landed on the baby's tender arm. Veena watched as the woman slowly brought her hand near the creature and in a sudden movement squashed it against the child's skin. Mercifully, the child did not wake up to the mother's touch. As the young mother proceeded to wipe the red dot of mess with a napkin, the woman caught Veena's eye and smiled at her. Veena smiled back.

Aarohi will never forget my words, Veena thought victoriously. I have squashed *her* wayward intentions, she congratulated herself silently. All's well that ends well, she sighed. And especially if a *mother* has ended it well, she smirked inwardly. Feeling a sense of contentment, she began looking outside the window idly.

The trees lining the yellow-brown arid stretches of land ran as fast as they could. The sun raced alongside the train above the trees, now behind them, now out. The strong summer rays filtered through the thick glass of the big rectangular window and fell on Veena's face. She exulted in the warmth that added to her glowing heart.

"Going to Delhi?" asked the young woman.

Veena turned towards her and replied, "No. To Simla."

"Visited relatives in Mumbai?" the woman enquired.

Veena smiled. "My son. He studies there."

The woman waited as if expecting Veena to say more.

"He's preparing for competitive exams."

"He must have been very happy to see you," the woman said pleasantly.

"Oh yes!" Veena perked up. "You see, his father and I decided that if he intended to stay in Mumbai, we would provide him with a small flat there with basic necessities and all … but then he is alone and away from us for the first time. He is just twenty. He wanted to come to Mumbai and study in one of those fancy institutes. So we let him. But then I am not there to look after him every day. Naturally, he was thrilled to have me around for some days!" Veena sounded very pleased with herself.

She paused as the baby stirred.

"He is a very sensible boy," she continued. "He is young but not foolish like others his age, does not squander any money we give him for studies." A light frown appeared on her forehead as Aarohi's face suddenly flashed through her mind. "But even well-brought-up children can go awry these days. One needs to keep a tab always," she said worriedly.

The woman nodded in agreement.

"You must miss him."

"Yes, of course! More than that, I am worried about him all the time. His health has suffered, and his appetite too. He says it's the pressure of academics but I know it is because his life is suddenly so stressful. He is still getting used to being without us."

The frown dissolved into a satisfied smile. "But I set everything right during my visit..." added Veena smugly, remembering all the jars she had lined in Arjun's kitchen and the numerous other things she had tended to during her stay.

"That's what mothers are for!" the woman said and they both laughed.

*

Arjun stepped out of the one-room flat, his satchel slung across his broad shoulder. Aarohi was bent outside her door, picking up the milk packets kept near the doormat. As she straightened up to stand, their eyes met briefly. Lowering her gaze immediately, Aarohi turned and went back inside. Before she closed the door fully, Arjun caught a glimpse of her thick black hair open against her back. He pulled his own door and stood there for a second watching hers, as if hoping it'd come open again. Then he slowly walked towards the elevator.

As the elevator went down the ten floors, Arjun's skin tingled with a sudden flush. The memory of Aarohi's hair falling over her brown shoulders that peeped from the wide neck of her night gown stoked smouldering embers in his heart. He curled his fingers into a fist.

Aarohi leaned against the closed door, listening to Arjun's fading footsteps in the corridor. When the hissing of the closing elevator had died out, she widened her eyes and drank in the moistness which had crept in.

"Mom, what are you doing here?" Aarohi was startled by her voice. It was her seven-year-old daughter, Radhika. She stood there in the passage way, rubbing her sleepy eyes with one hand and clutching her teddy bear in the other.

"Oh nothing, dear!" said Aarohi, regaining her composure. "I just got the milk and was trying to remember what all I have to do in office today."

Radhika looked at her mother with sleepy eyes.

"Come on, hurry up! You don't want to be late for school, do you?" added Aarohi, and keeping the milk in the kitchen, rushed her towards the bathroom.

When Prema bai had taken away Radhika to school, Aarohi showered and wrapped herself in a robe. She sat before the dressing table, trimming her nails to the desired shape. Glancing at the mirror, she captured her reflection for a while. What she saw was a woman in her early thirties, with smooth skin, almond eyes and thick dark hair of medium length which lent a sensuous appeal to the contours of her face. Her long neck rested on well-shaped shoulders which cascaded down to an attractive figure. Aarohi was proud that she had conscientiously managed her curvaceous slimness even after Radhika's birth and the vagaries of life. When her husband had left her two years ago for another woman, she had grown to hate herself for a very long time. It was only at her mother's behest that she gradually let go of painful self-loathing and began to breathe life afresh again.

She thought of Arjun and of that morning two months ago.

*

It was Radhika who had informed her, along with Prema bai, that they had a new neighbour. The candy in Radhika's hand had displeased her immensely, and within minutes, she was outside the opposite flat.

"May I please request something?" Aarohi said sternly.

"Yes ... yes, please," Arjun said, baffled at her tone.

Aarohi stretched out her hand, holding the candy. "Please don't offer any sweets to my daughter ... especially without my permission."

"But I..."

"Please," she said.

"Okay..." Arjun relented, taking back the candy. Radhika was watching him from behind the door.

"Thank you."

As she made her way back to her flat, Arjun called out to her. "By the way..." he said, hesitantly, "...I'm Arjun."

Aarohi turned towards him.

"I'm Aarohi." She closed the door after gently pushing Radhika inside.

A week later, Aarohi had just entered home when Prema bai informed her that the boy next door had come to borrow a lemon.

"...a lemon?" Aarohi asked suspiciously.

Prema bai offered a possible explanation. "Yes. Maybe he cooked something today. Or maybe he's not well ... He wasn't *looking* very well in the morning."

Sensing her employer's discomfort, Prema bai paused. "Madam, he seems to be an okay guy, don't worry," she added.

"Okay, okay ... that's enough," said Aarohi brusquely and dismissed Prema bai for the day. Switching on the TV for Radhika, she went to the kitchen to prepare herself a cup of tea.

Next morning, as Aarohi was leaving for office, she noticed a pack of milk and a bundle of newspapers lying outside Arjun's door. On her return in the evening, the things were still lying there untouched. Strange, she thought. According to Prema bai, nobody had come out of the flat the whole day. While she made herself tea, Aarohi's thoughts strayed to the new neighbour and she began getting worried. *Is he ill, like Prema had suggested?*

Should I check? The boy seems to be living alone. What if he's in some trouble?

She knocked gently on his door. And then knocked again, feeling afraid by now.

A very pale Arjun opened the door. One look at him and Aarohi knew he needed help.

When her family doctor had checked Arjun, he told Aarohi, "He has very high fever. It's a viral relapse. He'll have to take loads of rest and the right kind of food … the usual, you know what."

Aarohi paid his fees and when he had gone, stared at the prescription replete with medicine names and doses.

Over the next week, Aarohi instructed Prema bai to take two meals a day to him. For dinner, she made the arrangements herself.

Seven days passed. Aarohi visited Arjun one morning before proceeding to work.

"How are you feeling now?"

"Much better, thank you." Arjun grinned. "Thank you a million times for all the help."

Aarohi smiled and moved to the door.

"I can give Radhika some candy now, can't I?" Arjun called out behind her.

Aarohi spun around and stared at him for a minute. Arjun cursed himself for his cheekiness.

Suddenly, Aarohi smiled.

"Yes," she said. "Yes, you may, but not as a matter of habit. Bye now."

When she had gone, Arjun smiled to himself and settled with a book in bed.

The evenings were suddenly full. Aarohi returned from work each day with an unknown anticipation gnawing at her. It was as if a fresh whiff of air had enveloped her drab routine existence. She often had Arjun over for dinner. The conversations flowed easily. Arjun often relied on Aarohi for small things and she reciprocated with that occasional cup of tea or that intermittent aspirin he required.

Arjun's boyish charm and sense of mischief drew out the laughter in her easily, as much as her deft handling of life, which he secretly admired, provided him a warm connection. As their formalities withered away, Arjun often complimented Aarohi, playfully flirting with her. In the days that unfurled under their nameless bond, Aarohi felt liked and desired. She had been lonely for so long that it almost came to her as a feeling she couldn't initially recognize. The newness of it all left her happy.

It was a Saturday and Aarohi's day off. She slept till late while Prema bai took Radhika out to the park for a morning round of play. When it was ten, Aarohi dragged herself out of bed reluctantly. After freshening up, she went straight to Arjun's door. The milk and newspaper were still lying outside. A twinge of worry touched her and she rang the bell long and hard.

After what seemed like ages, Arjun unlocked the door. He stood there smiling at her sleepily, hair tousled and eyes barely open. He went back and sprawled himself over his sofa-cum-bed. Aarohi felt a trifle conscious when she noticed he was wearing only a pair of neat boxer shorts. Arjun pulled over the white sheet over his bare back. For an indefinable reason she felt her heart skip a beat.

"You bunch of lazybones," she chided him.

"Don't be mean. I was up studying for half the night," mumbled Arjun, his face dug into the pillow.

Aarohi's expression softened.

"Shall I make you some tea?" she asked affectionately.

"Hmm, that would be nice."

Arjun's lazy gruff voice accelerated her heartbeat. Aarohi felt a shiver going down her spine. Soon, she came back with a steaming cup of tea and placed it carefully on the side table. As she stepped towards the nearby armchair, Arjun grabbed her hand.

Aarohi felt the mysterious moment drawing nearer. Years of repressed desire flooded her senses. She raised her eyes to meet his. Not letting go of her hand, Arjun sat up, looking at her with want which was as bare as it was enchanting. Without a word, he pulled her down to him. Moving his hand swiftly behind her neck, he clasped her open hair in a firm grip. She gazed at him with intense yearning. Arjun took her face in his warm hands and brought his lips close to hers.

"Mamma! Mamma!" It was Radhika in the corridor outside. Aarohi hastily detached herself from Arjun and ran to the door. Through the eyehole she saw Prema bai opening her flat and usher Radhika inside. At once nervous and limp, Aarohi waited for the door to close, then casting a long look at Arjun, who was watching her with longing in his eyes, she slipped out.

The days that followed the spark of intimacy were marked by a restraint which both tried to exercise mindfully. The intense attraction that Arjun felt for Aarohi was in need of a private moment, away from imagined fears and the humdrum duties to be performed in either's life. Often in a moment of blazing eye contact, Arjun felt his desire course through which he held back. The conversations still flowed but were illuminated by an awareness of the subterranean desire.

When Veena arrived a fortnight later, Arjun introduced her proudly to Aarohi and Radhika. After Aarohi had left, Veena accosted Arjun.

"You are not taking care of yourself dear. Just look at those sunken cheeks!" she lamented in quintessential maternal fashion.

Arjun laughed. "Ma, I've shed the remnants of baby fat which had clung to me, that's all. Besides, now if I need anything, Aarohi is always there like a good neighbour." He paused thoughtfully. "She is a dear friend," he added, and told Veena about how Aarohi had helped him when he was unwell.

"You need to have a check-up. A viral relapse is not a good sign," Veena persisted.

Arjun clicked his tongue. "I'm okay, Ma. It's a new life here, tougher than Simla. I've had this cough too which troubles me at night. Aarohi gave me a herb concoction which did make it better. So don't worry."

Veena felt an indescribable irritation. "Why don't you come back to Simla?" she suggested.

"No way! I love it here. And now..." Arjun broke off midway.

"Now what?"

"Nothing, I forgot," Arjun answered absent-mindedly.

Veena watched her son and wondered if he had changed in the past two months.

With each passing day, doubt wove itself around Veena's maternal instinct. Every time Aarohi was near Arjun, an invisible discomfort engulfed her. She began searching hard for tell-tale signs of hidden proximity between them. Though she couldn't really see any, Veena sensed an undercurrent of emotions running between Arjun and Aarohi now and then. At times, it was the odd glance Arjun threw her way; at others it was Aarohi's coy ease with him which she found unusual. Each day, Veena grew more and more restless. Slowly, a sure and firm dislike towards Aarohi lodged itself in her heart.

"Everyone should learn from Aarohi," Arjun said one day. "With all the troubles life has thrown her way she could have been a really bitter person. But look at her; she is still so kind and gentle."

A trail of jealousy slithered over Veena's heart. Aarohi's name was becoming irksome, to say the least.

It was the week before Veena had to leave. Arjun had left for his classes, promising her he'd return early evening. As she sat alone, the storm in Veena raised its ugly head, manifesting her maternal fears. Images of a provocative Aarohi seducing Arjun thundered in her mind. She imagined havoc in her innocent son's life. The more she tried to dismiss her thoughts, the more vehemently they raked themselves up.

In the evening, Veena heard footsteps outside. Aarohi was home. She waited for five minutes and then went and knocked on her door.

"I want to talk to you about Arjun," she said stiffly.

*

On reaching Simla, Veena was satisfied while recounting to her maid, her sole companion in the house, how she had settled everything in Mumbai. She had already begun missing Arjun but took consolation in the promise he had made – that he would sever all ties with Aarohi. Her motherly pride revelled in the knowledge that her offspring was dutifully obedient, unlike so many ungrateful people of his generation. The only thing that nagged her now was his health.

One night, Veena awoke with a start.

The phone was ringing. It was four in the morning and the shrillness of the ring was hauntingly ominous. Heart palpitating, Veena rushed to the phone.

"Arjun is very ill. Please come here as soon as possible." It was Aarohi. The discomfort of hearing her voice was overshadowed instantly by the urgency Veena noticed in it.

"What happened?" she asked, terrified.

"I don't know. The doctors want to speak to you. Please come as quickly as you can." Aarohi hung up.

When Veena arrived at the hospital, Aarohi was not around. Even through her cutting anxiety, Veena found Aarohi's absence reassuring. Veena entered the doctor's room and sat down fearfully, waiting for him to tell her things she didn't want to know.

The trip back home was quiet and dull. Veena's head was reeling from all that she had heard. Words uttered by the doctor, by Arjun, by her husband. She looked at Arjun, who was reclining against the seat, eyes closed in all-consuming fatigue. His twenty-year-old body was so youthful and vibrantly strong. Could it be true that he had a short time to live? Or was this all a nightmare her worrying senses were unleashing on her?

Arjun remained withdrawn at home. Much to Veena's surprise, he had taken the news with exemplary calm; as if he was convinced his stoic stand was the only way to contain the sinking sensation brewing inside him. Day after day, Arjun sat in the armchair with a book open in his lap, not a single page turned till evening.

On the fifth day after his return from hospital, Veena awoke in the morning to see Arjun getting dressed.

"Where are you going?" she asked gently.

"Classes..." muttered Arjun.

Veena couldn't muster enough words to refrain him. Neither did she wish to. She got up quietly from bed and served him breakfast.

When Arjun had gone, Veena sat on his armchair and stared into space. Her thoughts were blank at first. Slowly, from the vacuum emerged memories; clean, sharp images of Arjun since his birth. No tear could wash her pain. She got up and retrieved the album which Arjun had prepared for her while leaving home. Veena always carried it with her when travelling.

Arjun had pulled out all his photographs and chosen the best ones at each age, arranging them in sequence for her. There he was, his glorious babyhood shining through the plastic film of the first page. Further down, his cherubic smile dissolved into a mischievous grin at five years. In fact, smiled Veena, that grin had not transformed at all till this day. Those self-conscious looks in his teens stared back at her and then young adulthood came up where he appeared disarmingly confident and full of life.

As she flipped through the photographs, a familiar feeling crept upon her subversively. It was the same sentiment which she had encountered when she had sensed the physical wavelengths between Arjun and Aarohi. Except that this time, there was no anger. She looked at his baby photo once more and then at the last and most recent one. Yes, it was there in front of her, yet it was not. Arjun was an adult now, she told herself; an adult who had barely begun experiencing life and was about to lose it all too soon.

The vague impression of Arjun in the throes of passion disconcerted her. The dissonance with her attempts at acceptance was alien, and disturbing.

Sure, he had grown up, but not enough to handle deeper desires. Veena recollected how she had caught him ogling at the girl next door in Simla once, and how she had ignored the flush of his cheeks. In her plans for his life, she had not gambled with time. How cruel time was! It had snatched away all details and rushed up to an incomplete end.

A severe guilt overwhelmed her and Veena burst into tears. It was a race against time now. How could she squeeze in the milestones and make him a happier person before he died? She stared into space as the memories faded and what remained was a blank slate on which she had to painfully rewrite Arjun's remaining life.

It was almost six p.m. Veena rose and went to Aarohi's door and rang the bell. There were footsteps approaching the door, then a long pause. She rang the bell again. The door opened.

Aarohi stood there, her face freshly washed and her golden-yellow salwar kameez adding a divine glow to her smooth brown skin. Her hair was tied up in a high bun, revealing her slender neck gracefully.

"May I come in?" asked Veena.

Aarohi hesitated. "Yes," she replied.

Veena came in and stood in the living room unsure, looking around idly. Aarohi closed the door and stood at a distance from her. Radhika and Prema bai were not around. Veena opened her mouth to speak but Aarohi interrupted her.

"I'm sorry that I was the one who called up suddenly that night. But I didn't have an option. Arjun was very ill and he had rung my bell in the middle of the night. Another neighbour and I together rushed him to hospital..." She paused. "I would have done the same for anyone ... I have no other interest in your son whatsoever." Aarohi's voice quivered even as her eyes glistened.

Veena listened silently. Aarohi noticed her eyes were welling up. She stepped closer and asked with genuine concern.

"What is it, Veena-ji?"

"I've come to tell you something," Veena said. "Arjun is terminally ill..."

Aarohi was shocked. Her hands went cold. She fixed her eyes on the floor, trying to digest what she had just heard. When she looked up, her eyes carried a strange blankness.

Veena watched Aarohi. In an instant, she could see into this woman's soul. Something about that woman came through to her, something she had not seen before.

"I need your help."

"Yes?"

"Can you start again with him from where you left off?"

Aarohi stared at her, stunned.

"I always thought I knew everything about Arjun," Veena carried on. "That I could set right his life and guide him to each moment at the right time. But today, time itself has belittled me. It has raced ahead and given me a few moments to see my child live. And I want to see him live them with as much fulfilment as possible. For his sake, will you help me?"

"Are you saying that I…?"

"Yes, that is what I mean. I have seen what Arjun and you hold between yourselves. I don't know if it is love, or fondness or plain desire … I don't wish to question. Whatever it is, it's a shade of life I want him to experience, to live and lessen the pain of his race against time."

Aarohi stood statue-like, her tears the only movement on her chiselled face.

"He will go away soon, no matter how hard I try … my Arjun … he will…" Veena began to sob.

Aarohi came forward and put her arms around Veena.

"I understand your loss. I know your pain," she said. "Arjun will live as many moments as he wants with me. It will be beautiful, I promise."

MOTHER COMES BACK

Those sandals are difficult to get into
But they will have to do
I have walked miles in them
And you have to too

Suchitra ran the brush through her hair for the last time. She twirled and then gathered it up into a neat bun deftly. She smoothened the folds of her sari and, giving herself one last look in the mirror, proceeded towards the kitchen.

The main course was all prepared, for she had been cooking for this lunch since early morning. The rest – salad, rice and chapatis – the house help Bahadur would surely be able to manage on his own. She checked the trifle pudding in the refrigerator. It had set perfectly. Then she surveyed the dining table with satisfaction. How nice the new set of tablemats looked! And those lovely red roses in the vase, plucked from her own garden – everything was perfect.

There was not much else to do now except wait for Aditya and Sujata to arrive, thought Suchitra, as she relaxed on an armchair and flipped through the pages of a magazine.

Aditya was the son of her next-door neighbour, Mrs Chowdhry. Although Mrs Chowdhry was much older than her, Suchitra and she were more like friends. Mrs Chowdhry confided all her thoughts and worries in Suchitra, who in turn had always been generous with her kindness and sympathy.

Aditya Chowdhry had married Sujata about a month ago and they had just returned from their honeymoon. This was, however, not his first marriage. His first wife, Geetanjali, had succumbed to meningitis about six years ago, leaving behind their two-year-old son, Abhishek.

Since then, it had seemed as though sunshine had never touched their house. A thick pall of melancholy and gloom had hung over every inch of that once cheerful household. It had been very difficult for Mrs Chowdhry to cope and she had often wept in front of Suchitra.

Aditya had really loved Geetanjali and, after her death, he had drawn into himself an entire world of sorrow. For a long time he had refused to share his feelings with anyone. He continued to grieve silently, and there was little his mother could do about it, her hands full with little Abhishek and his growing needs.

"How long am I going to live, Suchitra?" Mrs Chowdhry had once wept to her. "What will happen after I am no longer here? What will happen to Aditya and Abhishek? You know, I used to chide him about his boisterous behaviour and now ... He seems so distanced and detached from everything. I often feel he has aged more than me..."

Over the last few months, Suchitra had tried to help Mrs Chowdhry in her efforts at drawing Aditya out of his shell and making him consider a second marriage. He had eventually softened a little to the idea. But though he wanted to ease his mother's worries, he still had some apprehensions. He was not ready to erase the memory of Geetanjali yet and that wouldn't be fair to another woman.

"Give me time," he had pleaded. "I will settle down again when I am more in control of my feelings, when I'm confident I can make my second wife feel secure in our marriage, given the rival claimant to her husband's love – even if it is a dead former wife. And above all, Mummy, I have to think of Abhishek's feelings and his future. He will be getting a mother, so the girl has to be very nurturing and loving towards him. These would be difficult conditions for any woman to accept. And it won't be easy for us to start life afresh now."

Suchitra had later consoled Mrs Chowdhry, "He's right," she had said, "especially about Abhishek. I know from personal experience how miserable I felt when my father married again. I was never happy in that house. Aditya is being sensible. Let him take his time. If God is willing, happiness will return to your home one day."

Sujata was a lovely girl – innocent and loving, and very sensible, for she had seen some rough times growing up. She was the eldest among four in an ordinary middle-class family. Her parents could ill afford the kind of status and lifestyle that Aditya had, nor could they give any dowry. For them, it was the best that their daughter could get under the circumstances. Mrs Chowdhry liked Sujata. She didn't want anything but Aditya and Abhishek's happiness. Aditya also felt he had found the right person. And so the match was sealed.

They had a small wedding and a week's honeymoon in Mahabaleshwar. Today, a month and a half later, Suchitra had called the couple over for lunch. Aditya would be going back to his office after, but Suchitra looked forward to chatting with Sujata after that. She was curious to know more about the new bride and how she was feeling...

Suchitra heard the sound of the gate opening then the tinkle of Sujata's bangles. She opened the door and welcomed them inside.

A hearty meal later, Aditya left for office and the two women were left in each other's company. They settled down comfortably against the sofa cushions in the drawing room, sipping their coffee.

"You're happy, aren't you, Sujata?" asked Suchitra.

"Yes, Aunty, very happy. Aditya is so caring and understanding and Mummy is simply wonderful. She often tells me how helpful you've been to her," she replied.

"She herself is such a kind and good soul," said Suchitra. After a moment she continued, "What about Abhishek? How is he taking this new situation?"

Sujata became quiet for a moment, as if to ascertain whether she should really confide in Suchitra or not. Then, as though she had assured herself that she could, she started, "To tell you the truth, Aunty, it's a very strange situation. He ... he does seem to resent me. I suppose it's natural. Whenever I call him to have his breakfast or lunch, he tells me he's big enough to have it himself or that I needn't take the trouble. Or he takes it from his grandmother. He doesn't let me sit next to him or serve him, and if his father is not at home, he just carries his plate into his room and bolts the door. He's my child too now, and I want to care for him, but at times I feel helpless and guilty. Perhaps he feels I've deprived him of his father's love. You know how children have this set image of a stepmother. Oh! How I hate the word..." Sujata made a futile attempt to fight back the tears that were streaming down her cheeks.

"Oh my dear, I am sorry to have upset you," said Suchitra.

"No, Aunty, I feel so much lighter having told you this. I don't want to trouble Mummy now that she is finally finding some peace. In any case, this is my battle and I have to fight it myself. But believe me, Aunty, I am trying to win over Abhishek and he's really a lovely child except that he just doesn't seem to have accepted me. But of course, everybody is only going to think that I must be cruel to him and that is why he's like this. Oh! What shall I do, Aunty?"

Suchitra held her hand for a moment. "Don't worry, darling," she said. "Give it a little time. Everything will be all right."

The words uttered for the lack of better alternatives could only help Sujata so much, for when she sat by herself later that evening she wondered whether that would really ever be. Suchitra looked back on her own childhood. Her father too had remarried when she had been Aditya's age.

She had hated her stepmother. Ever since she had entered the house and their lives her father had very little time for

Suchitra. He no longer told Suchitra stories about her beautiful mother like before. In fact, everyone had slowly begun to forget all about her mother ever since her stepmother had come. Suchitra had felt she was the only one who remembered and missed her and that hurt her till the very last day she spent in her father's home.

Today, however, she could understand the predicament her father had been in. He was trying to start his new life away from the shadows of the past while his heart ached as he made himself part from it. He had loved Suchitra and had watched in pained helplessness as she often spurned her stepmother's overtures. Time, unlike what she had told Sujata so reassuringly, had not by itself healed anything.

Suchitra thought sadly of all the pain that she had unwittingly caused her father and more so her stepmother. But she had been too young and confused then, and no one had explained anything to her. And it was too late for her to make amends.

Too late?

Suchitra walked to the storeroom. She wiped the dust off her stepmother's framed photograph where it had lain for years now in a corner. She placed it beside her parents' picture on the mantelpiece.

There was nothing more she could do, she realised with a heavy heart.

Then she thought of Sujata for whom there was still time. All that was needed there was a helping hand.

Sujata was surprised when Suchitra called on her the next morning. She held her hand and whispered, "I have understood something, Sujata. I know you are doing your best in these circumstances. But what I have to say today has more to do with Aditya. I think he never lets the past catch up on you out of fear of hurting you. And I'm sure Abhishek feels very insecure and left out. He unconsciously sees himself as a part of that very past that his father seems keen on forgetting, in an effort to make space for this new life and for you."

Suchitra paused and then continued. "Tell me, does Aditya ever behave with you as though he … he's kind of guilty for Abhishek?"

"Yes. Maybe you're right, Aunty. At the same time he also behaves as though he's embarrassed and guilty for what he's done to Abhishek…" replied Sujata.

"Poor Aditya," said Suchitra. "Sujata, he is the link between you and his son, his role is crucial. He must spend lots of time with Abhishek. Also none of you should make his mother's name taboo at home. I know you're sensitive enough to understand this. Don't take it the wrong way, my dear. I'm saying all this because I was once in little Abhishek's position. There was nobody who explained to me what was happening then. I was confused and unhappy, though my father and my stepmother always wanted the best for me. I realise that now … but it's too late." Sujata had a faraway look in her eyes.

Now it was Sujata's turn to hold her hand.

Later that evening when Suchitra's husband Ranjeev returned home from his tour, she poured out the happenings of the past two days to him. He held her hand protectively and comforted her.

"Do you know, Suchi, this Thursday is the first day of the shraadh fortnight when we feed the poor at the temple in memory of our parents. Let's make an offering for your stepmother this time. Let us do it every year."

As they returned from the temple that Thursday, Suchitra noticed Sujata playing a game of carrom with Abhishek in their garden. She waved to them. And as Sujata and Abhishek, playfully laughing, waved back at her, she knew that her offering at the temple had been accepted.

NOT WITHOUT MY SISTER

You my sister, my daughter
You are both to me
My tears, my laughter
You will set me free

The flashbulbs went on and off as the cameras clicked away impatiently, documenting every possible nuance expressed by her face and features.

Debut star at seventeen, Anita Fakhri sat surrounded by a motley group of hungry reporters and answered their rapid questions with astounding élan which belied her age. She smiled, tilted her pretty head and replied earnestly to what they wanted to know. Her auburn hair, styled into glossy waves, fell to her shoulders languorously, and her deep eyes strayed from one journalist to another in trained movement.

Her mother Ibu Nora Fakhri, mesmerised, watched her daughter from a little away. A satisfied glow illuminated her thirty-nine-year-old face which didn't look a day older than thirty. It was a fresh kind of contentment which hid beneath its folds, wishes satiated, destiny fulfilled.

Fifteen minutes later, Nora barged into the arena and announced, "Anita has an appointment elsewhere now. So, if you'll please excuse us..."

Anita rose and thanked the reporters and followed her mother to the Mercedes sent by the producer, waiting outside the studio. Her willowy figure and elegantly cultivated gait elicited admiring glances from onlookers. She sat beside her mother in the back seat and directed a final wave to the hovering journalists as the car slid away. When the scribes had receded from sight, Anita rested her head back and closed her eyes.

"Tired?" asked Nora with concern.

"Yes, Ammi."

Nora let her be as they drove home.

When they reached the small corner house in their lane, Nora thanked the driver. As soon as Anita stepped out, a bunch of neighbourhood kids ran up to her.

"Anita didi! I saw your movie with Ma-Papa yesterday! You are so beautiful in it!" exclaimed a six-year-old. It was Chandu, the son of the family next door.

Anita's face lit up.

"Didi, I saw you on television! You were looking so fantastic!" said another, tugging at her shirt.

Nora ignored the children and went inside. Anita patted the eager kids one by one on the head. "Thank you," she said lovingly and followed Nora in.

Once inside, she kicked off her high heels and curled up on the old creaky couch in the hall.

"This is just the beginning," said Nora proudly, pouring herself a glass of water. "Wait till the other offers pour in!"

As if on cue, the phone rang just then.

Nora took the call and moved to another room. Finding a minute alone, Anita switched on the television and surfed through the channels mindlessly. She stopped at an entertainment news channel airing one of her recent interviews. She listened to herself for a few seconds, and then bored, moved on to another programme.

"Anita! Anita!" called out Nora as she entered the hall again, smiling broadly. "It was producer Devnani's call ... He saw your work ... he wants to meet you sometime next week!"

"That's great!" Anita responded, her eyes glued to the television.

Nora sat near her and opened the diary in her hand. She ran her finger down a scribbled list.

"There! We'll keep it for next Wednesday." She turned to Anita and said, "If you finish with the four appointments lined up in the coming week, I'm sure something big will come your way soon."

"Yes, Ammi." Anita was preoccupied with the TV.

Nora continued, "All we need to do is be careful and a little choosy about meeting the right people. I think you should…"

Suddenly Anita rose and switched off the TV.

"Ammi, can I go to bed early today?" she interrupted Nora with a big yawn.

Nora was displeased with her lack of attention. But Anita's droopy eyes restrained her from taking the conversation ahead.

"Of course, darling. Go, get some rest," she said, trying her best to conceal her disappointment.

Anita bolted the door of her bedroom and went and stood in front of the mirror. She stared at herself for a few seconds and then suddenly froze into a pose. The next minute, she was preening, watching the reflection, posing playfully and pouting at the glass. Five minutes into her game with the mirror she was back to her usual seventeen-year-old self.

Under the warm blanket, Anita nudged herself towards a deep, much-needed slumber. After a while, as if from a distance, some voices in argument floated to her ears hazily but she was too weary to strain and pay attention. She pulled the blanket tightly over her head to shut the noise out.

*

In the morning, Anita found Anwar sleeping on the living-room divan. The muffled sound of her footsteps on the carpet made him stir.

"Good morning, Abbu," Anita called out to him as she walked towards the kitchen.

"Good morning, Annie." Anwar sat up lazily. Anita came back sipping a glass of water and sat beside him. He patted her on the head.

"I saw your interviews ... it seems you are doing well for yourself," Anwar said with a smile.

"Yes, Abbu, the initial response has been good."

"Allah bless you ... you have attained success at a young age." A shadow of worry crossed his face and Anita noticed it immediately.

"What is it, Abbu?" she asked him.

"Just don't let it go to your head, beta," said Anwar, lowering his voice.

Anita smiled.

"Yes, Abbu, I understand," she said.

Anwar looked at his daughter with immense affection. "I know you do, Annie, I know you do." Then throwing away his blanket, he said, "Go, child, run and get your old man a cup of tea now."

"Right away, Abbu!" Anita laughed.

*

College was nice after a long time of being away. Nothing had changed much except the appreciative glances Anita received from those she didn't know and the congratulatory greetings from those she did. Lina caught up with her on the stairs.

"Hey! You're back!" she said, brimming with excitement.

"Yes, and am I glad! I was really missing college."

Lina was in splits. "You are crazy! The whole country is talking about you, and all you want to do is come to college?"

Anita frowned at her best friend. Lina stopped laughing.

"Okay, I'll not pull your leg. But come on, let's ditch the history class today. I have so many things to ask you," Lina pleaded.

Anita raised her arms in protest but saw Lina's childishly wrinkled-up nose and mouth and couldn't help smiling. Lina was ecstatic.

"Done! History period phut!" And they ran down the stairs.

The backyard behind the old chemistry lab was deserted as usual. The high wall on one side and the rundown empty building on the other hid them from the buzzing college campus a little away. Nobody came here and that is why, every time Lina and Anita needed to escape from the gang of canteen friends, they chose this hideout.

They lay on their backs on the uneven brown grass, the thick branches of the nearby tree forming a canopy over them. Sunlight streamed through in between the leaves and fell on the two girls. Anita spread her dupatta over her face to dampen the glare. Lina turned onto her side and pinched her lightly on the arm.

"Ouch!" cried Anita.

"So, you're still dreaming," said Lina naughtily. "Tell me, Annie, how is it to be famous?"

Anita had shut her eyes and was enjoying the diffused warmth offered by the sun playing peekaboo.

"It's weird, Lina," she said sleepily. "It's nice when everyone is paying you so much attention. And I do love acting. It's a different high. But when I'm not there, when I'm with you, or at home, I forget all that so easily."

Anita paused. She removed the dupatta from her face and turned her slender neck to face Lina.

"Maybe I'm still getting used to it," she added, smiling.

Lina let out a deep sigh.

"You're so lucky. You're doing so much so early in life. I'll probably rot in this college for another two years and then Papa will either ask me what I want to study further or..."

"Or what?"

"He'll marry me off to some half-cooked recipe called a husband. Three years later, and I'll be visiting you on the movie sets with two kids in my lap." Lina laughed that hearty laugh of hers.

Anita laughed too. A faint faraway look clouded her face.

"That must be so lovely, isn't it, Lina?"

"What? The movie sets?"

"No, silly! Marriage and kids!"

"Ugh! Are you nuts?"

Anita covered her face again.

"I think it's nice to be in love and marry and have kids," she went on dreamily.

Lina smiled at her friend and thought she was a nutcase.

*

Anwar walked into the hall and stopped. Nora was talking to a man seated on the couch. He was in his early thirties, semi-bald and lean. His eyes hid behind the thick lenses of his spectacles. Seeing Anwar, Nora got up and smiled at him.

"This is Anita's father ... Anwar Fakhri," she said to the man. The man rose and greeted Anwar. Then turning to Nora, he said, "I'll take your leave, Mrs Fakhri. Good evening." He nodded at Anwar as he walked out of the door.

Anwar's eyes met Nora's briefly before he proceeded to keep his laptop on the table. While he sat down on the couch and took off his shoes, he noticed a white envelope kept on the table. Just as he reached out for it, Nora came forward swiftly and picked it up.

"This is Anita's cheque," she said proudly.

Anwar didn't answer as he resumed taking his socks off. Nora became a trifle restless.

"Won't you ask how much it is?" she asked sharply.

Anwar looked up at her in mock surprise and replied with an equal edge to his voice. "Nora, have I ever?"

Nora watched him in disdain. "I don't really blame you, Anwar. Money has never been your forte I guess."

Anwar glared at her. Nora stared back at him defiantly. He lowered his gaze, and gathering his laptop and shoes went inside.

*

Time flew. For two months after the release of her first movie, Anita juggled stardom with academics, incipient fame with a routine student life, salon visits with gymnasium sessions, and parties against moments of quiet privacy. Nora kept track of how her daughter groomed herself to maintain the identity she had recently acquired.

Towards the end of those two months, one evening Nora walked into Anita's room. Anita was studying at her desk. She looked up from her books.

"Hi Ammi."

"Hi Annie." Nora sat down on the bed.

"I think you should quit," Nora said. Anita turned from her desk to look at Nora in amazement.

"What? Films?" she asked incredulously.

Nora burst into laughter.

"No, dear! I would never suggest something like that. I meant … college."

Anita pursed her lips. A hesitation crept over her.

"But, Ammi, I promised Abbu I'll complete this year at least," she said.

"And do what, Anita!" Nora got up, exasperated. "Do *what*? It won't help you. Your path is decided. You're not going to teach at a substandard college like your father and earn peanuts! Besides, you have three commercials and one potential project lined up. Where do you think you're going to find the time to take your exams?" Nora was wringing her hands restlessly.

Anita was quiet.

"Look, baby. If Devnani finalises you, there's no looking back. It's an opportunity of a lifetime…"

"Okay, Ammi," interrupted Anita. "But…"

"Abbu? Oh please! Leave that to me."

Anita nodded and smiled at Nora, who hugged her.

*

When Anita woke up in the morning, her heart felt heavy. She dragged herself to the hall and saw Anwar sleeping at his usual place, the divan. Anita stopped by his side and stared at him. A child-like innocence marked his face; a child with a golden heart, honest lines of age on his tired face. Anita felt her eyes smarting. As if he could feel her pain too, just then Anwar opened his eyes. When he saw her standing there, he got up and sat against the wall, like he always did. He looked at her with silent understanding. Anita sat next to him and hugged him.

"I'm sorry, Abbu. I'm really sorry," she whispered.

Anwar hugged her back and caressing her hair, replied softly, "It's okay, Annie. You'll do fine, just fine."

A tear rolled down Anita's face.

*

Anita's big day arrived. Mr Devnani's secretary had called and requested Nora to bring her for a screen test. Devnani's next project was huge and he had chosen Anita Fakhri from amongst hundreds of other starlets.

"The screen test is just a formality," informed Nora, as she ferried Anita to the studio in an air-conditioned cab. "Just concentrate on your lines, everything else will fall in place."

Devnani was a stout man of medium build who wore a thick gold chain around his neck, and like they said, he had a sharp eye for new talent. He sat talking to the director while Anita rehearsed her lines for the last time.

The lights came on. The camera whirred to life. She looked at it, donned the required expression effortlessly and began to speak.

The words floated in her head and the lights broke into a hundred fragments, blinding her. The equipment and Ammi and the producer's face swam in front of her eyes and blended into one large throbbing image, the sounds around her fading instantly.

Anita wavered on her feet and slumped to the floor of the studio. There was commotion all around as Nora rushed to her side and, with the help of some unit members, carried her to the green room.

The screen test was cancelled for the day as Devnani had to attend to another urgent matter. When Anita regained consciousness a few minutes later, Nora took her home and propped her up in bed. She appeared pale and sickly. Nora was worried.

"I told you; don't burn your energy with all those books. If you had paid heed to my advice earlier, this golden opportunity could have materialized today. Tch! Tch! What a waste!" she lamented. Moving towards the door, she announced, "I'll call the doctor."

"No, Ammi! Please don't call the doctor!" Anita was almost desperate.

Nora turned to her. "But why? You're sick, Anita!"

Anita insisted, "I'm already feeling better, Ammi. It's just the heat, I'll be okay … You know I hate medicines."

Nora shook her head in helpless surprise. Half an hour later, she brought Anita her favourite chicken soup.

"Thanks, Ammi," she said, eyes half shut. "Keep it here. I'll have it in some time."

Nora kept the bowl on the side table and left.

It was around midnight. Nora passed by Anita's door and felt she had heard something. She waited and listened. It seemed Anita was not asleep yet. She knocked gently on the door.

"Anita? … Anita?"

There was no answer.

Nora opened the door and looked around the room. Not finding her there, she was about to leave when she heard the trickle of the tap in the bathroom. Curious, she walked up to the door. It was slightly ajar. Her brow wrinkled with worry, Nora pushed it open.

Anita, dressed in her gown and standing near the sink, spun around startled. Nora's sharp eyes caught her moving her right hand behind herself reflexively.

"What are you doing, Anita?" she asked. She was haunted by a strange premonition. "And what is that in your hands? What are you hiding?"

"Nothing, Ammi." Anita's colourless pallor was accentuated by wide fearful eyes. "Nothing at all."

"Anita, what do you have in your hand?"

As she spoke, Nora stepped ahead and grabbed Anita's wrist. Anita winced but not before Nora had jerked her arm to find a small object in Anita's fingers.

It was a pregnancy test kit.

Nora gasped in horror. She snatched it from Anita's grip and stared at it. There were two lines on its tiny screen, indicating a positive test. Horrified, she glared at Anita.

Anita began weeping. A sudden surge of rage hit Nora. She raised her hand and slapped Anita hard across her face.

Anita let out a cry.

"Ammi, please don't hit me! Please don't Ammi. I didn't mean to..." she begged.

"Who is he?" asked Nora icily.

Anita stared back at her through the blinding curtain of tears, fear lurking in her eyes.

"Who is he?" Nora screamed.

Anwar had entered Anita's room. He stood watching them both, confused horror playing on his face.

"T-Toni..." Anita stammered.

"*Who* is he? And where did you meet him?" Nora slapped Anita again.

"At Shauna's party ... I had a few drinks that day ... and..." Anita burst into loud choking sobs.

Nora smiled sarcastically at her. "Here I am ... like a fool trying to fix your wretched life ... a life your father gave us ... a life without any comfort ... and there you go sleeping with someone you don't even know, putting all my efforts at stake!" she yelled.

"No, Ammi, I know him! Toni is not a stranger ... I-I love him!" Her voice trailed off. "We love each other."

Nora laughed. It was a hollow laugh of mockery. Anita stared at her, afraid. Nora brought her face very close to Anita's.

"Love? Do you even know the meaning of love?" she hissed.

Anita stepped back and lowered herself on her haunches. She sat huddled on the cold bathroom floor, crying incessantly. Nora turned away in disgust and looked at Anwar who was standing near the bedroom door. Without another word, she walked out of the room.

Anwar went to the bathroom and lifted the sobbing Anita by the arm firmly. He walked her to the bed and made her lie down, pulling the blanket over her neatly. As he began moving away, Anita grabbed his hand and pressed it against her cheeks. He sat down on the bed by her side, not looking at her.

"I'm sorry, Abbu … I'm sorry again," she mumbled over and over again.

Anwar remained there till her sobs died out and her eyes shut themselves to sleep.

*

Nora occupied the rocking chair in her room, staring at the blank wall in front of her. The night was a dark monster which threatened to consume her and the life she had planned. Her mind was a cauldron of snakes raising their ugly heads, sneering at her predicament. Panic surged through her suppressed aspirations; those ambitions which had fed on a gaping vacuum for years, which had blamed Anwar for their unfulfilled status and which she had carefully grown like a creeper and entwined heavily with Anita's destiny.

And Anita's destiny? That was her own creation, wasn't it, she thought. How dare Anita tamper with that? Nora rocked the chair back and forth furiously till the motion calmed her senses to a dull peace.

She woke up with a start at the break of dawn and rushed to Anita's room. Anita stood by the window, looking out at the grey-blue skies melting away to a clearer shade. Hearing Nora's footfall, she turned around. The previous night's tears had left their marks on her young supple cheeks. Nora went and stood before her.

"Get rid of it. Today itself," she said grimly.

Anita's swollen eyes were strangely serene.

"No," she said, a newfound spirit in her voice.

"What does that mean?"

Anita looked into her mother's dark eyes.

"He will come and take me with him. I know he will. We'll decide together. Everything will be okay. He promised me he'll never desert me."

Nora felt the panic cutting through her.

"And your career?" she asked angrily.

"What about it?"

"Don't be ridiculous! I've spent my whole life constructing yours. You can't be so reckless with it. You can't throw it all away on a foolish whim!" She was suddenly very fidgety as she caught Anita's hand. "Come with me!"

"Ammi! Leave my hand." Anita freed herself roughly and pierced Nora with smouldering eyes.

"If you force me to kill my baby, I'll also kill myself. And that's a promise," she said.

Nora was stunned. She turned around and retreated.

In the days that followed, the eerie silence that pervaded the Fakhri house was like that of a graveyard. Nora withdrew like a wounded animal. Anwar stopped coming home on time. Anita did not find him on the divan on any of the mornings thereafter. Anita called Toni's number many times but in vain. All she could find out was that he was in Australia for a course his father wanted him to pursue.

When she couldn't trace him, Anita called up Lina. "Help me find Toni," she said.

Lina helped like a true friend, but all mails and calls remained unanswered.

"I don't think he'll come back, Annie. Stop being foolish. Don't hurt yourself more," she told Anita in an effort to make her see some sense.

But Anita knew he wouldn't forsake her. Days passed and then a full month. Anita was two months into her pregnancy. Most of the time, she remained cocooned inside her room, breathing moments of waiting. Any movement outside was watched over by a silent but hawkish Nora. Devnani's office was told that Anita was on temporary bedrest for some health issues. Yet with each passing day, Nora got more and more bitter.

"When? Where is he? How long will you wait?" she asked Anita every few days, overcome with anxiety. And Anita looked at the skies and always replied hopefully, "He'll come … he said he will."

Nora was distraught. She started spending most of her daytime out on the verandah in her rocking chair. She sat there watching the day go by, hoping fervently each moment that Anita would agree to abort the baby before it was too late.

*

One day, late afternoon, Nora sat in her chair, her eyes transfixed on the distant patch of grass dying to a dull brown.

Anita came through the gate and smiled at her. Behind her, descending from a car was a young, handsome man.

"Toni, come and meet Ammi. Ammi, this is Toni," said Anita.

Toni came up the stairs leading to the porch and greeted Nora warmly. Anita's big full-term belly lent her a mature persona.

Nora looked down at the ground. It was covered with cloudy mist and she couldn't see anything beyond their feet. When she looked up in panic, Toni and Anita were walking through the gate again. Toni was carrying a small bundle in his arms. He came up to her and placed it in Nora's lap.

Anita's baby opened its eyes and gurgled at Nora endearingly. Toni and Anita stood watching Nora with the baby, arm in arm, glowing in their togetherness. Toni glanced at his watch and decided it was time to go. Anita took the baby carefully from Nora's lap and started walking towards the gate with him. From a distance, Nora heard them laughing. Once outside the gate, Anita turned and waved at Nora.

"Bye, Ammi! Take care of yourself," she said and receded into the fog that had thickened without warning.

Nora shivered. She got up and trudged into the dim, lonely house. She glanced at Anwar's photo, a dry garland draped around it. Suddenly, someone came up and hugged her from behind.

"Nani! What are you doing here? Come on, let's go to the garden and talk. I have so much to tell you about my first shoot."

Nora turned and looked at the young girl. She had the same auburn hair, the same creamy complexion. She was a shadow of Anita but much younger and very, very beautiful.

The loneliness of the house withered away in the girl's sunny smile. Nora knew she was safe. Another star had lit up her path.

*

A chilly breeze nipped at her and broke Nora's reverie. The sun was sliding down fast and the dusky sky appeared malevolent in its changing colours. A young thought began seeding itself in Nora's head. Before she could grab it, a voice called out.

"Ammi?" Nora turned and saw Anita standing at the door of the living room opening onto the verandah.

She remained seated. Anita came and stood in front of her. She was wearing a pale blue dress which fell till her calves. Anita went down on her knees.

"Yes, Annie?" asked Nora coldly.

Anita shifted forward on her knees to come closer and threw her arms around Nora, crying softly.

"What happened?" she asked.

"He is ... not coming back, Ammi! He doesn't want to take responsibility of the child ... he wrote to me ... he will not..."

Anita hid her face in Nora's lap, her sobs rendering themselves in short, sharp gasps. "Ammi, what will happen now?" she said, her voice drenched in despair. Her hands touched her belly, afraid to hear what she was sure her mother would suggest.

Nora's eyes shone. She pushed up Anita's face by the chin.

"You intend to have this child, don't you?" she asked calmly.

Anita nodded.

"But, child, you do understand that you will be an unwed mother? The stigma that comes with this decision can ruin your career ... and what about us?" For a second, she looked away and sighed. "What about Abbu?"

Anita was expressionless. The only movement on her face were the tears welling up in her eyes. She kept her head in Nora's lap again. Her body shook with sobs.

Nora let her tears subside to a calm trickle. She took a deep breath and said, "Annie, you can have this child."

Anita was motionless.

"Listen to me carefully, Annie. I said you may have your baby. No one will take it away from you," said Nora.

Anita stopped crying and looked up at her mother in gratitude. Her eyes shone with new hope and her lips quivered but she couldn't utter anything. She just stared at Nora.

"Yes, you heard it right, Anita. You may keep the baby. But that's about it," said Nora.

Anita scanned Nora's face for more. Nora continued.

"I will speak to Abbu and probably take you someplace where no one knows us. You can deliver the child there. But when we come back, the child will be in my arms, not yours."

Anita gazed at Nora, disoriented but just about beginning to understand what her mother meant.

"Yes, Annie, you will have to call your child your sibling. I will raise it, not you. That way, you can resume your career, avoid the stigma of being an unwed mother and have your child near you too. That is the only way you and all of us can..."

Anita found her voice.

"You'll do all this for me, Ammi?" she whispered, her eyes fixed on Nora's face in amazement.

"Yes, I will, Annie. You are my baby. And I don't want to hurt you anymore. I think this is what will keep us happy and together."

Anita's tears of gratitude overwhelmed her.

"I was so wrong about you, Ammi! So wrong! I thought you hated me for what I did, but you ... you..." she sputtered. "I will never, can never, forget this kindness. My life is yours, Ammi, only yours," she cried.

Anita threw her arms around Nora in desperate relief. She smiled for the first time in two months.

Nora smiled too. The gamble had paid off. The sun had gone down on the day but a new day was round the corner. A new life had found its way.

SCREAMING SILENCE

We stand by each other
Game for a good fight
Take on the world together
Fight with all our might

The meeting was about to begin when Mrs Sharma, late and out of breath, burst into a roomful of people at Mrs Mehta's house.

"I'm sorry … very sorry," she apologised to all the women present, and yet to no one in particular, as her eyes darted from one end of the room to another.

Mrs Mehta and Mrs Patil moved to create some space for Mrs Sharma to sit among them.

Mrs Mehta smiled at her. "Overslept the afternoon nap, did you?" she asked as she looked at her watch. "I guess five o'clock is a bit early in the evening. But I insisted you should all be here by this time so you could hear for yourself the goings-on in the neighbouring house. You cannot imagine how disturbing and upsetting it is for us," she explained.

"Of course we can imagine," asserted Mrs Patil.

"We live in the flat below that horrible man's and we too hear his abuses and assaults every evening, day after day. It's worse if we come out into the balcony. I tell you I haven't heard such abuses ever," she continued.

"Deva, Deva, Mahadeva. What is the world coming to," said Mrs Narayan, touching her ears with the fingertips of both her hands as if to drive away the sounds that had assailed them over the last few days.

"Such a nice, peaceful atmosphere we had in this building before this rascal came here," said Mrs Das. "It's all that Deshpande's fault. He should have checked out that swine's background before renting the flat to him."

"It's not his fault, Mrs Das. How could Deshpande have ever imagined that this Mr Adhikari would turn out to be such a scoundrel? He seemed like a normal man even to me when I visited him on the first day he arrived next door. I went to meet him and offered him any help he might need, just as any good neighbour would do," said Mrs Mehta.

"Yes, but you did mention to me that he didn't even invite you inside the house that evening," piped in Mrs Das.

"Yes, that's true. But I didn't make much of it at that time. He came to the door still dripping from his bath, wrapped only in a towel. I didn't expect him to call me inside in that state. He was polite in thanking me and said he'd get back to me soon. He seemed like a normal, regular sort of chap. But in these last fifteen days that he's been here, he has neither visited nor have I seen him anywhere else in the building."

Everyone nodded their heads as if to affirm the truth of Mrs Mehta's statement. None of them had seen Mr Adhikari.

"It would have been all right if he wasn't the mixing type – we don't mind that, do we?" said Mrs Das. "The point is we all live in a civilised society. How can we just hear him abuse and beat someone evening after evening and pretend that we haven't heard anything?"

"Someone? What do you mean by someone? It's probably a woman – his wife – who else could it be? Who else but a wife would tolerate such nonsense from a man?" said Mrs Patil, as all the other women in the room nodded in agreement.

"That poor dear. I've not even seen her once – answering the door, or going shopping – you know ... doing the normal things women do."

"It's almost as if she doesn't exist," said Mrs Mehta.

"Who would want an existence like that anyway? It'd be better to die than to have to live that way," said Mrs Patil indignantly. "I think it's time we women went to help the lady suffering alone. It's us women who have to take the lead in helping out one of our own." Mrs Patil rose to her feet, ready to act that very moment.

"Yes, yes, we have to help her. But we'd have to wait for the opportune moment if we are to catch him red-handed. I know people like that; they're skilled at covering up their dirty deeds. Let's wait a bit and then catch him in the act," Mrs Sharma proposed. "No more of this nonsense, not for another day!" she continued righteously.

"Wait!" Mrs Mehta exclaimed. "I just had an idea. You remember old Mr Percy who used to stay in the flat before Adhikari? He had given us a spare set of keys to his flat for safe keeping. I still have the key to the main door with me. I don't think the rascal has changed the lock – so we can all enter the flat. That way he'll have no chance at all to cover his tracks."

Mrs Mehta excused herself and came back with the all-important key.

"Shh-Shh. I think if we all remain silent we can actually hear the thumping start. Every day it starts around half past five. It's like a ritual for the beast. Hear..." Mrs Mehta implored with a finger on her lips.

And sure enough, in the hushed silence of the room, the unmistakable sounds began to build up.

"You f*#%*&g bitch. You swine ... here, take this." *Thump thump*. "What do you take me for ... I'm a bloody man ... Take this ... and this ... I'll teach you a thing or two about dealing with me," Adhikari raged and ranted.

Mrs Sharma sprang to her feet. "That's it. We can't wait anymore. Let's go in right now," she implored, as everyone rose to their feet.

The women all lined up quietly one behind another and made their way down the staircase to Mr Adhikari's flat. Mrs Mehta turned the key to his door. It opened noiselessly, and they entered.

The sounds were loud and clear now and the ladies were repulsed by their vitriolic content.

"You whore ... you want me to respect you, you f*#%*&g bitch. You think I don't know your true colours. Just because you sleep around with a rich guy you think you've become a decent woman and you can order me around? He's a parasite of the first order. He's had hundreds before you and will probably have hundreds after you in this suite. You dare throw your weight around with me? Who do you think you are? Now I'm not going to take any more of your nonsense." *Thump ... smack ...* "Here, take this ... that'll teach you how to behave," he went on.

The women looked somewhat quizzically at each other. His words did not make much sense. Besides, it sounded more like a monologue from up close. Surely the woman he was beating would at least groan in pain.

Has she become immune to the beatings by now? Was she already dead? thought a stumped Mrs Mehta to herself as she led the group inching forward. It was a chilling thought. Mrs Mehta gave the door a push and took the lead in making their collective presence felt to Mr Adhikari.

"Stop, you bastard. Stop at once. Stop!" she started as the others joined in.

Mr Adhikari was speechless upon spotting the crowd. He stood there gaping at first, and then made a hurried attempt to cover his naked upper body with his hands on which he wore a pair of boxing gloves. Rivulets of sweat from his body had rendered his boxing shorts completely wet. The women's eyes now caught the punching bags above Adhikari's head that were still swinging.

"Boxing … is that what you're up to every evening?" asked Mrs Mehta hesitatingly.

"Yes? But what are you all doing here? Is this how respectable neighbours enter another man's home in this building?" asked Mr Adhikari even as he removed his boxing gloves and wrapped a king-size Turkish towel around his torso like a shawl.

There was only stunned silence that answered him.

"Will someone please explain what's going on?" Mr Adhikari asked again as he led the women through the passage into the hall.

As the group stood awkwardly around, he signalled them to sit down on the sofas. "Don't tell me you need my permission to sit down when you didn't need it to enter my house," he remarked caustically.

"We're sorry, Mr Adhikari. We hadn't the foggiest idea that you were only boxing," said Mrs Mehta.

"We thought you were beating some poor soul black and blue every single evening. We assumed it would be your wife. What we did today was only out of a sense of concern…" stuttered Mrs Das.

Mrs Sharma pitched in hesitantly. "Sir, you cannot blame us. You must admit that your abuses … your colourful language as you … er … box … would make anyone suspicious. We didn't want to be heartless to the fate of someone innocent being assaulted every day right next door. Of course it's a relief to know that nothing of the sort was going on here. We're really sorry, Mr Adhikari."

Mr Adhikari's disconcerted expression had somewhat softened by now. He sat down cross-legged on the floor, probably not wanting to soil the sofas with his still sweaty shorts.

"I will not leave your mystery half-solved. Now that you are here, I'd like to explain everything," he said. "I'm not fond of beating anyone – which you have already ascertained. I hate abusing too. But it's part of my therapy," he said.

"Therapy?" asked everyone in chorus.

"You see. I work as the lobby manager in a five-star hotel. All day long I've got to keep a straight, plastic smile across my face. Every other minute I've got to mutter 'yes sir, no sir, yes madam, you're right madam, certainly sir, in a minute madam'... It's so sickening, this 'customer is always right' nonsense. I can never be myself, never answer back, no matter how wrong or stupid the person I'm dealing with is. It's unfair and unjust, and after a few months at the job I had known that I wouldn't be able to cope.

"Then I tried therapy. I gave myself a chance to see if I could cope with my job that way. My therapist suggested seeking a means to catharsis, which involves the release of pent-up emotions. He suggested that since I couldn't afford to open up to my feelings at work, I should release my frustrations by doing all that I could possibly not do at work – in the privacy of my bedroom. Perhaps I overdid the abuses but let me tell you that the therapy has really worked for me! Today, for example, I was punching the bags pretending to beat and abuse this arrogant mistress of a filthy rich old man – who orders me around all day. Do you think it's easy for me to go back to be kicked around tomorrow if I don't punch these bags today? This therapy really works ... it does! Well, since it has worked so well for me, and now that you all also know what it's all about, I'd like your permission to keep at it every evening! Is that fine by you all?" he asked.

"Yes, yes, by all means, it's fine. We'll all find some way of coping with the noise," said Mrs Das with a chuckle. "If it is all right, we have just one request. Can you make the abuses gender neutral?"

Mr Adhikari gaped at this unusual request.

"You see," Mrs Das continued, "it is really rather sickening to hear abuses aimed at women. I understand, it is a cultural thing ... We are brought up that way. Most abuses tend to be directed at women ... bitch, whore ... it's always a woman ... But I am sure you are not a misogynist. That, it's just a case of picking up what one hears around us. If we can be mindful of that..."

Mr Adhikari nodded his head and muttered, almost to himself, "Yes, of course, I mean ... I did not realise ... yes, of course, I could keep the abuses gender neutral ... maybe even keep it to the boxing..."

A couple of handshakes and namastes later the troop left and Mr Adhikari went back to punching his bags.

And the residents of the building did indeed find a perfect way of coping with the noise from that very evening. Even as Mr Adhikari went silent on the abuses, limiting himself to thumping the punching bags, the women discovered therapeutic effects of their own catharsis within the safe confines of their bedrooms.

THE GURU

Practise what you preach
Follow what you teach
What's a guru worth at all
If he does not heed his own call

Indu looked at the contents of her carry bag again. Two saris, one nightgown, undergarments, three frocks for Aditi and lots of nappies. And right at the bottom of the bag her beloved pair of ghungroos.

Would the clothes suffice? She was not sure. For unlike travellers who pack their bags keeping in mind the destination and the duration of the journey, she wasn't certain of either. The bag with its contents was only an evidence of her decision to leave.

Indu picked up a sleeping Aditi, clutched her handbag with one hand while she held the carry bag in the other. She looked around the bedroom she had shared with Amitabh these last two years. For a few brief seconds a wave of nostalgia washed over her, as her eyes fell upon the double-framed picture kept on the bedside table. On its left was a picture of their wedding day. Amitabh was looking at her with an amused expression on his face through the flowers of his sehra, trying to comfort her – "grin and bear it for just a little while more".

Amitabh had really loved her. She knew that he still did. But it was time he learnt that she had been grinning and bearing it for far too long now. Her leaving the house today was an ultimatum for him. He should either stand up to his parents or lose her altogether. Reminded afresh of the reason that had forced her to take this hard step today, Indu tried to turn away from the photograph, but her eyes were stuck to the picture on the right.

It was a photograph that Amitabh had taken of a tired-looking Indu cradling a day-old Aditi at the hospital. Indu put down her bag for a moment, removed the photograph from the frame and put it in her handbag. This was a statement she was making to Amitabh, who would hopefully understand how she was feeling when he would see it missing that evening.

Indu looked at the clock. It was 11 o'clock and her mother-in-law would soon return from the market. She had to leave now.

Indu walked out of the house, and as its familiar grey front gate shut with a clank, her heart sank. She was doing this to teach Amitabh a lesson but what if her plan backfired? What if instead of changing for good, Amitabh simply gave up on her and the promise of the independent home that he had been making for so long?

Indu steeled herself once again. If that was what was going to happen, so be it. It was better for her to face the harsh reality than harbour any more illusions.

She hailed a taxi. "Kalanagri," she told the cabbie as she first kept her bag on the backseat and then settled into it.

Kalanagri was the housing complex where her guru lived. She had been there only once earlier for a short while, when he had invited them all for the grihapravesh of his house. That was four years ago. At that time, she had been introduced to all those present as Guruji's "star-pupil" – one for whom he said he had great dreams and hopes. That had been such a happy and auspicious occasion, so different from today.

But where else could she possibly go in this big city in this condition. Apart from her marital home, the only place Indu knew fairly well in the entire city of Delhi was the hostel of the Odissi Kendra where she had spent five beautiful years of her life. She had come there after fighting a minor battle with her parents in their Moradabad home and had finally been allowed to come to Delhi to pursue her training in Odissi dance. And it was for this reason itself that there was no question of going back to her parents. Too many years and too much distance now rested between them.

But today she had no links with the Odissi Kendra either. The only link left with the place and with dance itself – which had once been her lifeline – was Guruji.

Guru Manna Lal was a temperamental guru. A senior teacher at the Kendra, his name was always taken in reverent tones by critics and students of Odissi alike.

Guruji himself had learnt dance under the most pristine and strict codes of the guru-shishya parampara. But as a concession to modern times and urban living, he had chosen to teach just a handful of students at the Odissi Kendra, run with the patronage of the illustrious industrial group of the Lalji's.

Indu had been lucky that Guruji had chosen to teach her. It was not a question of him sensing potential in a candidate alone – theories abounded that he turned away many, extremely talented candidates who came with hope to the Odissi Kendra year after year for admission. It was said that he looked for a certain combination of shraddha (devotion) and dhairya (patience) in a student that was sometimes inconsistent with talent itself. And he had obviously found that in Indu.

Indu's eyes brimmed with tears at the thought of the fatherly love that she had so often seen in Guruji's eyes. She remembered his hand on her head as he had blessed her when she had taken Amitabh to meet him, and introduced him as the man she wanted to marry, nearly three years ago.

A few days later Guruji had sat her down after class. "Beti, I have taught you like my own daughter. And you have also done the kind of sadhana that I would expect from a good daughter of mine," he had said.

That evening, in the pale shaft of the setting rays of the sun in the dance room, he had looked old and tired. "I have many hopes from you, and I wish you marital happiness as I would for my own daughter. But through the decades of my experience I have observed that once a girl gets married, she no longer pursues her passion with the same devotion as before. There is never enough time in her hands or never enough encouragement from her family," he had said with a sigh.

"That is a very frustrating situation for both the guru and the shishya. For if you have really felt that dance is a part of your life, it is not something that you'll be happy giving up. I'm concerned for you, beti. How are you going to balance dance with your domestic life? You're a woman after all," Guruji had asked with concern.

Indu remembered how she had proceeded to reassure Guruji about his concerns for her at that time. She had been sure about it. And that was because Amitabh, who had been attracted to her in no small measure due to her dance, had promised her all his support for her to continue to pursue dance. She had often told him that dance was both her dharma and her karma in this life, even more than being a wife and mother was, and he had always assured her that it would remain so.

How naïve she had been! Dance and art, sadhana and riyaz – they simply meant nothing to Amitabh's parents, and it was now getting apparent, to Amitabh too. Amitabh felt guilty at having gone against his parents' wishes to marry a girl of his choice. He was therefore ever ready to give her dreams a backseat, just to not upset them any more than they already were.

Indu was therefore requested to first ingratiate herself with them before she could get her way. Sooner or later they would "melt" and then all would be well again, Amitabh had told her reassuringly. Till then she had to try to be a good and "traditional" sort of bahu. This involved doing everyday chores and participating in all the rites that were part and parcel of an Indian joint family. But now, even two years down the line, Indu's mother-in-law showed no signs of softening.

In fact after Aditi's birth, even Indu's attendance at the dance practice sessions at the Kendra, which had been coldly accepted earlier, were frowned upon. "*Bachchi ko chhod, ma nachne jati hai,*" her mother-in-law had complained to Amitabh and as always he had requested Indu to toe the line. Little did he understand that by asking her to stop dancing, he was crushing her very spirit.

It was a mistake to have married Amitabh. How right Guruji had been in his concerns, she thought. And therefore, it was only at his feet that Indu could hope to start her life afresh – with or without Amitabh but certainly with dance. For these last few months were enough to make her realise what was more central to her existence.

*

But now as Gururani – whose feet she reverentially touched when she entered their home – led her inside, Indu was suddenly afraid. Bereft of the festivities that she had earlier witnessed in this house, there was a strange stillness in the air. It made her feel alone and dwarfed.

Guruji sat on a divan in his riyaz room. On the wall right behind him was a mammoth black-and-white picture of him in a meditative dance mudra, so huge that it minimised his actual presence. Guruji looked surprised to see her. Then, as his eyes fell upon the bag that she was holding, he sensed something was wrong.

Indu put the bag down and, still holding Aditi, bent down gingerly to touch his feet.

"*Jeeti raho,*" he muttered. Indu felt a trifle embarrassed looking directly at Guruji in his lungi and vest, so different from his usual attire of the kurta-pyjama that he always wore to class.

Indu sat a few yards away on the cold marble floor and cradled the still sleeping Aditi on her crossed legs. She began to search for the right words to explain her predicament. But Guruji lifted his hand in a gesture to stop her from doing so.

"I have had years of experience not only in dance, but also in life and people. *Ye baal dhoop mein safed nahin hue,*" he said. "I can see that you have reached the crossroads in your life and have to decide which direction to take. This house is yours until you have made your decision," he assured her. "Only, you must abide by all its rules as long as you're here."

Just then Gururani entered the room, her head covered with the pallu of her starched pale blue cotton sari. The soft tinkle of the bunch of keys that hung at her waist accompanied her as she walked towards him with his thali of food. She placed the thali onto the floor and then began to search the room for the stool on which to place it in front of him. She found it a few moments later and placed it in front of Guruji. Then she placed his thali on it.

Guruji thundered angrily, "In all these twenty-five years you have still not learnt to place the stool before me before you get the thali from the rasoi. You know this ruins my mood even before I start my meal and yet you never improve your ways." He glared at Gururani.

Gururani cringed with embarrassment and muttered softly, "*Bhool ho gayee.*" Then, avoiding Indu's eyes she made an exit.

As he saw her leave, Guruji shook his head from side to side. "*Aurat zaat ko bhagwan ne chun kar dheeth banaya hai.* They will just never learn," he muttered to himself.

Gururani entered the room again with a freshly baked puffed phulka on the plate and offered it to Guruji.

"Why are you dancing on my head like this? Can you not see that it will take me some time to finish the one on my thali? Is it such a chore feeding me that you want it over and done with as soon as possible?"

"I thought you might have finished the first one, sometimes you do eat it fast … I'll take it back," Gururani muttered apologetically as she walked out of the room.

Indu watched the scene, trying not to react as she observed Gururani make a dozen entries and exits through the meal. At last he finished eating, and as Guruji burped when Gururani took the thali away, Indu caught a look of relief on Gururani's face.

"It's time for my afternoon nap now," he declared to Gururani and Indu. "Take care of this girl and see that she is comfortable in every way," he instructed her.

Gururani dutifully settled Indu and Aditi into the room that actually belonged to their son Rahul. Rahul was in college and was spending a week at his maternal grandparents'. Gururani told Indu that for the next two days the room was hers to use, after which Rahul would be back. She would make some other arrangement for her if it was needed, she added.

Indu nodded. She soon realised that Gururani was ever so gracious and maternal. She marked with marvel the fact that Gururani's face never registered any look of hurt brought about by Guruji's insults. As the latter served Indu her lunch and fed Aditi with the same affection as her real grandmother would have, she couldn't help broaching the subject.

"Guruji is worshipped by the whole world. But it is I who have the privilege of keeping his home and hearth. His insults are a small price I have to pay for this privilege," she explained to Indu softly.

Indu looked up from the food that she was eating. Though it was Guruji who was her link to Gururani, at the moment she felt closer to Gururani than to him.

"He depends on me for all his needs. He's like a child," Gururani said, smiling proudly.

"But even a woman has needs of her own. Don't you think a man should appreciate and fulfil them in the same manner that he expects her to fulfil his wishes?" Indu questioned, thinking of her own life.

"A woman has to forget her needs and aspirations when she gets married. They can never ever be fulfilled the way a man's can be." Gururani sighed as she cajoled Aditi into eating the last morsel of the dal-bhaat mix that she had made especially for her. "It is better to come to terms with the situation and at least enjoy keeping a beautiful and happy home," said Gururani. Then she wiped with the back of her hand the few specks of food that remained on the table, before she proceeded to the kitchen to wash up.

Gururani had insisted on serving Indu and feeding Aditi first, before eating herself. "It is the dharma of the woman of the house to eat last," she had said righteously.

It was now Indu's turn to serve Gururani and in the best of Indian tradition, to cajole her into taking more generous helpings. She did it with a sense of belonging even though she knew that this was not her own home.

Gururani smiled at her. "It feels nice to be served," she said. "All I ever remember of my marriage is just cooking and serving." Then almost as if she were afraid that Indu might get a wrong impression, she added hastily, "But of course, *yehi to ek suhagan ka dharam hai*."

"Has Guruji never eaten with you?" Indu could not help asking, though she knew it was too personal a question.

"No, never," Gururani replied. "But I don't mind that. He doesn't have to eat with me or express his affection for me to show that he cares for me. I know that he does. He has always cared for me. And so have I. I have always loved him, ever since I can remember," she said shyly.

Indu stared at Gururani's bright red tika, and the saffron-coloured sindoor marking the beginning of the parting on her forehead. She thought to herself that Gururani must still be completely awestruck by Guruji. She was so grateful for being married to Guruji. And Guruji, she assumed, could have been only tolerating her to make the best of the situation he must have forcibly been placed in.

Indu could certainly not imagine Gururani being a soulmate to Guruji's creative spirit. No wonder he treated her the way he did – he must have found it difficult to connect with her. Perhaps, in small measure, the same way that she found it difficult to relate to Amitabh anymore. Gururani and Amitabh – they were both made of a similar mettle – with no passion for art and creativity despite being married to people for whom these were the life forces.

Gururani stared at Indu almost as if she had read her thoughts. "I'd like to tell you something, beti, *bura mat maanna*. It's not as if I resent giving you shelter here – but I would like to give you a piece of advice. You're a married woman and a mother now – don't stretch your luck too far. If your husband treats you and your child well, don't leave him merely for some vague artistic pursuit. Ultimately a home is much more important for a woman's life and security than any artistic merit," she advised.

Indu nodded her head in agreement. She did not want to argue with or hurt Gururani. After all, what Gururani had said was probably right from her narrow point of view. The point of view of a woman, who, though married to an artist, had probably never experienced magical moments of aesthetic thrill or creative flight.

Gururani had finished eating and urged Indu to take Aditi with her to Rahul's room and make sure to keep her quiet for the next two hours. "Guruji likes complete silence in the afternoon while he is taking a nap. I take care even to remove my footwear when I walk around at this time, lest the sound of my footsteps disturb him," she explained. "He gets very irritable otherwise."

Indu nodded, amused at Gururani's constant reference to her husband as "Guruji", as she led Aditi to Rahul's room. She noticed Guruji's trophies and pictures all along the walls of the house. It seemed as if no one else but Guruji lived there.

The next two hours passed uneventfully. At five o'clock, Guruji emerged, dressed in his kurta-pyjama. He was fresh from his evening bath and looked more the picture of dignity that Indu had always associated him with. He was soon joined by two of his disciples and prepared to leave to inaugurate the Hiralal Natya Sammelan that was to start that day in the suburbs.

Indu watched as Gururani fussed over him, choosing the appropriate attar for him to wear for the occasion, handing him his kerchief and wiping his Jaipuri jootis to gleaming perfection. She saw Gururani watch with satisfaction as he slid his feet into the jootis and bid them both goodbyes.

Gururani shut the door after him. Then in that instant, like a caged bird suddenly set free, Indu saw Gururani transform. She beckoned Indu to join her as she stretched her legs out on the divan and blissfully chewed on the paan from Guruji's paan daan.

"You don't usually go out with Guruji?" asked Indu.

"He doesn't ask me to go with him, and frankly that's all right with me. I can enjoy some time of relaxation when he is away. Besides I have to get his meal ready to be served the way he likes it when he returns, and if I go with him that won't be possible," she reasoned. Then suddenly Gururani sprang up from the divan.

"I've never seen you dance, Indu. Guruji says you are a very good dancer. Why don't you dance for me? I have about an hour before I start my work in the kitchen," she said.

Indu looked at Gururani with confusion. In a sense, the thought was tempting. She would be more comfortable initially practising her steps in front of the non-judgemental Gururani, than Guruji, who she was scared might judge her out-of-practice performance too strictly. And she was sure that if she stayed on in their house any longer, he would very soon want her to dance in order to assess her skill.

"I'd love to, Gururani, but without Guruji's accompaniment or the tape of his singing..." said Indu hesitantly.

"Why, what am I here for? I'll sing for you. *Chalo jugalbandi ho jaaye*." Gururani smiled.

"*Aap*?" stuttered Indu. Surely Gururani knew nothing about dance, leave alone accompaniment, which was the forte of veteran gurus of dance. A non-creative, non-artistic woman. Was Gururani playing a joke on her?

But Gururani would have none of it. She rushed into her room and brought out a pair of ghungroos for Indu.

"Mine," she said, "from the days I used to learn dance from Guruji at Natyakshetra," she continued, as she handed them over to Indu.

A bewildered Indu began to tie the ghungroos on her ankles as Gururani continued reminiscing. "How much I fought with my family to go there. They did not speak to me for the five years that I was there. It was only after I was married and Rahul was born that..." she trailed off. "I don't really blame my family, what would they understand of art and my creative needs?" she sighed.

"Maybe they would not. But what about Guruji?" asked a shocked Indu.

Gururani gave Indu a piercing stare. Then, in the next instant, as though embarrassed at doing so she looked away.

A perplexed Indu muttered, "I'm sorry. I didn't mean to..."

But Gururani had not heard her. For even before Indu could complete her sentence she saw Gururani shut her eyes in deep concentration as she dwelled on the "samaa".

"Sa..." she sang, perfectly on note, and it seemed at that moment, as if all the elements in the atmosphere concentrated only upon her. Then Gururani began singing. The strains of her voice floated effortlessly – oblivious of the occasional protests of her throat at being taken through long uncharted territory.

Indu's feet moved and her face registered the different mudras of the abhinaya. Gururani delightfully kept taal by clapping her hands and on one occasion even got carried away to shyly twirl in perfect sync with Indu.

It was certainly not a perfect performance, interspersed as it was by much giggling, and frequent stopping and starting but it was one that its participants enjoyed. At last a huffing and puffing Gururani plunked herself on the divan and somewhat sheepishly began to wipe the sweat from her brow with the end of her sari.

Indu walked up to her. "You have shown me the way, Gururani. But now I can't stay here any longer," she said. And then Indu turned to make her way to Rahul's room to pack her bag.

A bewildered Gururani followed her there. "No, don't go. What will I tell Guruji?"

"Gururani, you will tell him that he's not my guru anymore. I have found my true guru ... someone I look up to and who has done all that I don't know if I can or will ever be able to do," she answered.

Then Indu removed the ghungroos from her feet and placed them beside Gururani's feet, as her forehead now bent to touch them in reverence.

THE PERFECTIONIST

She wanted everything just so
Never a thing out of place
By perfection she always swore
But the imperfect too has a grace

I

As she finished instructing the maid about the day's menu, Tanuja glanced at the clock on the wall. It was past 10 o'clock.

There was no way she would be able to make it for the 10:30 appointment at Brigade Road. It would be better if she telephoned her income tax consultant and postponed her meeting by at least an hour.

However much Tanuja tried, she usually ran about an hour behind schedule every day. It had nothing to do with her efficiency, there was simply too much to do.

Tanuja believed in doing everything to exacting standards. It gave her an immense sense of satisfaction to see even the most mundane of tasks done to perfection.

Perfection. It was the keyword of her life. Alas! It was also the one aspiration that played truant when she sought it in some of her more difficult relationships. Primarily her relationship with her elder sister, Manna.

Manna – how must she be? What must she be eating for breakfast this morning? Thought Tanuja, as she cut the mushroom and cheese omelette on her plate at the table.

She always thought of Manna at mealtimes, for Manna was the one who had taught her to cook. Now, Tanuja hardly ever felt like cooking for her own family. Without Manna to share what she had cooked made her so much more aware of her absence.

It had been four months since she had made the extremely painful decision that Manna could no longer live with their family. For Manna's weird behaviour resulting from her schizophrenic condition had begun to affect her two young children, Siddharth and Sneha. And so she and her husband Anup had decided that it was best to leave Manna in the care of a mental institution.

Though the decision was logical, it was a difficult one for Tanuja to reconcile with. For her, it signified in many ways the end of a symbiotic relationship. Of shared secrets and close confidences. Of times spent together, spanning almost a quarter century. It encompassed all of Tanuja's formative years; from birth, through school and later, till the early years of adulthood.

But scores of justifications later, Tanuja still pondered at the irony of not being there for a sister who had always been there when she had needed her.

On an impulse she decided to visit Manna; to hell with the taxman's appointment. He could wait for the day.

II

Is this what ESP was all about? Tanuja thought, as she looked back at her impulsive action of coming to see Manna. She usually didn't do impulsive, unplanned things but today she had. Perhaps because an inner voice had led her to Manna, who she realised had needed her.

Tanuja had arrived in the asylum to the horrifying spectacle of a screaming nurse who had just discovered that Manna had burnt her arm in an accident in the kitchen. But Manna herself was quiet, somewhat bemused at the panic around her.

Tanuja turned her face away as the doctor proceeded to dress her blisters. She tried to hold Manna's other hand supportively, but Manna threw off her hand, looking at her as if she were a stranger.

Manna felt no pain. She smiled, amused at the serious look on the doctor's face as he continued dressing her wounds.

Then suddenly, she became restless and the doctor finished his job with great difficulty as she squirmed. Then she ran off, as if reminded of an important task to be done.

Tanuja followed her to her room and watched Manna through the window. Manna was singing to herself. She tied a turban around her head, pretending to be a queen, commanding imaginary subjects around. The next moment she pretended to be a little child, chasing a butterfly in her imaginary garden with joyful abandon.

Tanuja felt sad watching Manna in this state. But she wondered whether Manna was feeling sad for herself.

No, Manna looked anything but sad. Engrossed in a universe of her own creation – of which she was the master. She was able to change circumstances according to the dictates of her own mind. She could become anybody, go anywhere, do anything, free from the shackles of the sane mind. She was beyond pain and hunger, heat and cold, human needs and even feelings.

Manna had achieved a state of mind that millions of people aspired to, a state of transcendence. Tragically, she was unaware of it.

Tanuja smiled as she started to make her way home. Today, a great weight had been lifted off her. She had achieved perfection in her relationship with Manna at last.

THE THORNY PATH

She thought she was the one
The other woman an imposter
But when truth dawned
She saw she was the other

"There is good and there is evil. In goodness can reside a drop of evil, and in evil can surface a ray of good. Strive we must, to purify our good and lessen the evil in us. When our goodness does not the crutch of evil hold, our souls ripens to true love..."

The words of the priest floated lightly on the air, reaching Raagini's ears. She sat on one side of the marble steps leading to the temple, half facing the porch where a thirty-odd audience, comprising mostly elderly and some young Indians, sat around the priest and devoured his discourse on the non-absolute nature of mankind with single-minded devotion. Interspersed between the dark Indian heads were a few blonde and brunette ones; American disciples in pursuit of the "Hindoo" way of life as they called it.

It was a huge temple, standing grandly on the outskirts of New Jersey, surrounded by sparse human settlement and stretches of foliage. This temple held fond memories for Raagini because it was here, a year ago, that Shayan wed Raagini, eight years after she had handed over her heart to him. Shayan's struggle for a Green

Card since his arrival in the US had led to an interminable wait of two years before their dream finally took shape. Raagini had flown down from India and herself chosen this particular temple to stand testimony to her and Shayan's precious bond, which, she proudly felt, had withstood the rigours of time and distance.

Raagini glanced at her watch. It showed half past five. Shayan should be here any time now, she thought, bracing herself for the moment when she would break the news to him. She hoped secretly, and with a tinge of sadness, that he would be thrilled with what she had to share, remembering how very self-involved he had been recently with his work and ambitious goals. Despite Shayan's obvious love for her, Raagini had often felt sidelined and lonely when she would find him obsessively preoccupied with his, and only *his* plans, forgetting that she was as much a reality in his life. She hoped all that would change now, after this wonderful moment.

A strong waft of incense from the interiors of the temple reached her with the breeze. An American girl, wearing a beautiful Rajasthani skirt-and-kurti ensemble and loads of bangles, walked up the stairs. Her attire reminded Raagini of her own simple yet bright bridal dress she had so fondly chosen over endless options. The chants that had been uttered at the simple wedding ceremony resounded in her ears pleasantly till today.

The American girl was standing on her toes now. Reaching upwards, she rang the overhead temple bell thrice. Raagini shut her eyes and murmured a small prayer, smiling involuntarily.

"Ahem!" someone cleared his throat. Raagini opened her eyes. Shayan stood before her, smiling.

"Lost?" he said with a hint of tease.

"Hmm ... lost," she answered, a warm blush flooding her cheeks at being caught unawares in lovelorn thought.

Shayan sat himself beside her, facing the stairs and nudged at her playfully.

"So! Why are we here today?" he asked her.

Raagini smiled. "Patience, dear, patience!" she said, getting up and taking his hand in hers. "Let's pray first."

Shayan rose and they walked the last couple of steps to the temple porch together. He slipped his arm around Raagini's waist and pulled her mischievously closer to him as they reached the landing.

Suddenly, with a jerk, he withdrew his arm. Raagini felt him stiffening. She looked at him. Shayan was a bit flustered it seemed and he was looking towards his right. Following his gaze, Raagini's sight rested on the American girl she had noticed previously for her prominent Indian dress. The young woman was watching them, and Raagini couldn't help noticing that there was something queer in the way she was looking. Shayan continued walking towards the main precinct, now looking ahead.

"What happened?" Raagini was curious.

"Er ... nothing ... just got a little conscious ... you know ... people around..." Shayan explained hesitantly.

Raagini let out a laugh.

"Conscious? You? Since when?"

Shayan smiled weakly at her and reminded her, "Let's go and pray. We'll get late."

Raagini had barely moved forward with him when she heard some commotion behind her. She spun around to see a small crowd gathered near the stairs. Before Shayan could say anything, she returned there to see what the matter was. Making her way through the flock of people, she saw the American girl in colourful attire slumped on the floor, unconscious.

Someone had fetched water. Raagini knelt beside the girl and slapped her cheek gently in attempt to revive her but the girl didn't respond. When water was sprinkled on her, she stirred but didn't open her eyes. Slightly worried, Raagini said to the nearest person, "She needs to be taken to the hospital."

She looked around for Shayan and saw him standing at a distance, watching her passively, which she thought was queer, but in her concern for the girl pushed the thought to the back of her mind.

"I'll check her bag for any contact details," said Raagini as a lady helped the girl to a sitting position and another rubbed her palms. She went to where Shayan stood.

"Raagini, let's not waste time," he said to her when he saw her sitting on a nearby marble platform. "The others will take care of her."

"Oh come on, Shayan, don't be so selfish. That girl needs help," said Raagini, without looking up, and emptied the contents of the bag onto her lap in haste.

She sifted through the jumble that came out from the bag. There was a lipstick, some keys, a comb, a small calculator and some photos held together by a band. There was no card, no name anywhere. Raagini took the small bundle of photos and released them from the band. The first was a snap of the girl herself. As Raagini removed it to check the reverse for any number, her sight fell on the second photo.

She froze.

It was a frame of the young American girl, in complete Indian bridal finery, with Shayan. Raagini stared in disbelief as if she had seen a ghost. Her heart beating wildly, she strained to have a closer look. Yes, it was definitely Shayan. She quickly went to the third, and fourth and then the rest of the photos. All held images of Shayan, with the girl, in what seemed to be their wedding. Was God playing some kind of joke on her? Raagini looked up at Shayan who stood a little away from her, watching her intently. In the moment that their eyes met, Raagini's disbelief was answered.

A young Indian boy came running to Raagini.

"Any contact?" he asked.

"No … none at all." stuttered Raagini, trying to shake off her stupor.

"The ambulance is on its way," informed the boy and left quickly.

Raagini rose without a word. She gave Shayan a long vacuous stare and returned to the spot where the girl was. He followed her.

Within minutes, an ambulance had arrived.

"Let's go," Raagini told Shayan.

"Where?" he asked, surprised.

"We're going *with* the ambulance," she informed him.

There was protest in Shayan's eyes but he didn't manifest it. As the girl was carried to the ambulance, Raagini followed like a robot, numb with a thousand questions hammering her senses all at once.

"I'll drive," she said bluntly as they reached their car.

The people who had helped were still around, so Shayan sat inside without arguing. As it drove away, he turned to her and said gently, "Raagini, I can explain."

"Later," Raagini cut him short icily.

Shayan threw up his hands.

"Why did you need to volunteer?" he asked, exasperated.

Raagini braked hard. Without offering him as much as a glance, she uttered in a hardened tone, "I think I should be the one here asking the 'whys.'"

Half an hour later, they had reached the nearest hospital.

*

As the doctor examined the American girl, Raagini waited in the lobby. Shayan came up to her. Sitting beside her, he sighed.

"Sabrina. Her name is Sabrina."

Raagini was quiet.

"I met her at a friend's party. She was drawn to me. She began falling for me. And I…"

"And you two-timed me?" whispered Raagini sadly.

"No!" Shayan came down on his knees in front of her. "Listen Raagini … I married her … but it was … was all a hoax…" He stopped as Raagini turned her gaze on him sharply. "I did so because it helped me to…"

Shayan watched as Raagini's eyes welled up with tears.

"Raagini, don't cry … listen to me. You remember when I called you up in India and was very frustrated about my Green

Card? I married Sabrina because that solved my problem and it brought us, you and me, together faster ... that's why, honey!"

"You married her for the Green Card?" Raagini asked, tears streaming down her face.

"Yes, Raagini, for the Green Card! For you! That is why I divorced her soon after. I had to. There was no other way ... please believe me," pleaded Shayan.

Raagini looked away from him. Shayan scanned her face desperately for a reaction. She turned to him a moment later.

"Does she know why you dumped her?"

"Of course not. I gave her other reasons," replied Shayan.

"Shayan, do you know why I called you to the temple today?" she whispered fiercely.

"No, honey," said Shayan, subdued and miserable.

"I'm pregnant," Raagini blurted it out, her voice broken and terse. She hid her face in her hands and cried.

Shayan was overcome by pain and happiness, thrill and helplessness, all at once. He bent forward, wanting to hug her but just then, the doctor arrived.

"Ms Raagini?" the doctor asked.

Raagini wiped her tears and stood up.

"Your friend is quite okay now. She's a bit weak, but should be able to go home tomorrow morning. My assistant will brief you about the rest," said the doctor and went away.

Shayan held Raagini by the shoulders and turned her around. "Now let's go home and talk it out. You need to trust me, honey, I'm telling you the truth. We can see ourselves through this!" he said.

Raagini was suddenly bereft of emotion.

"I need time, Shayan."

"Okay, but let's go home now," insisted Shayan.

"No," said Raagini adamantly.

Shayan was nonplussed. "But why? You've brought her here; you've done your bit. *We* need to talk. Let's go."

"*You* go," Raagini said.

"What's wrong with you? Haven't I explained everything to you? I know you'll take time to forgive me, but why are you being so stubborn?"

"This is not only about *us*, Shayan. This is about *her* too. I don't know why, but right now I want to stay here."

Shayan shook his head. He paced up and down the lobby, hands in his pockets, contemplating how to convince his wife to give up the idea. Once again, he stopped beside her. "You're coming with me?"

Raagini said nothing.

"Done!" Shayan said caustically and with extreme irritation. "I guess you need to explore various truths yourself, like a typical woman. Suit yourself! But I'm going." He walked away, adding as he did so, "You give me a call when you're through. I'll come and pick you."

Raagini didn't answer. After Shayan had gone, she walked to the room Sabrina had been given. Before going in, she waited at the door a few minutes, trying to make sense of the situation in her mind. Here she was, about to step into a room where she knew she would discover bitter new truths, into a chapter of her life where the unknown and the painful would be encountered; something which might even twist her life in another direction forever. She opened the door and stepped in.

Sabrina heard her footsteps and opened her eyes. She saw the Indian woman from the temple standing before her. She noticed Raagini's elegant brick-orange kurta lined with gold, and her straight, very long hair, plaited till her waist. She also noticed Raagini's almond-shaped eyes lined by kohl which was now smudged at the edges. Sabrina could make out she had been crying.

Raagini looked at the frail figure lying on the hospital bed. Medium height, blonde shiny hair, not very thick, tied in a loose pony, white slender neck, slightly freckled nose and blue-grey eyes. Sabrina's lips were beautiful, full and pink. Sabrina smiled at her without inhibition, without hesitation. Raagini returned the smile, albeit unsurely. She pulled up a chair and sat next to the hospital bed.

"Hi," she said. "I'm Shayan's wife."

"I know," Sabrina replied simply. Raagini thought she saw a curtain of hidden fear in her eyes.

There was an awkward silence. Neither knew what to say.

"Don't be afraid to ask anything," said Sabrina.

Raagini looked up. Though unwell, Sabrina's face was radiant. The light in her eyes was soft and kind and the vibes reaching Raagini were positive. She relaxed.

"I'm sorry about Shayan and you," began Raagini.

"Don't be. It's not your fault."

The matter-of-fact manner with which Sabrina said that left Raagini at a loss for words. "Which part of America do you belong to?" Raagini asked Sabrina, trying to make conversation.

"Illinois. I came to New Jersey because it's closer to New York where I'm studying Indian art at the university."

"Indian art?"

"Yes. Some years ago, I had visited India with my parents. When I came back, I decided I wanted to study Indian art," Sabrina explained. She lifted her head from the pillow suddenly. "Hey! That thing around your neck, it's called a mangalsutra, isn't it?"

Raagini nodded. She couldn't help smiling too.

"I used to wear one when Shayan married me, but took it off when we got divorced."

There was a strained silence.

Sabrina smiled her honest smile. It reached her eyes effortlessly. "Thank you for your help. I'm sorry for being such a pain at the temple," she said.

"No. You're welcome. It was the least I could do."

Another pause.

"Can I ask you something?" Sabrina broke the silence. Raagini nodded again.

"Shayan didn't stop you from coming here to the hospital?"

Raagini's lips curled into a helpless grimace. "He did. But I wanted to stay. I wanted to talk to you. And I guess you'll understand why."

Sabrina understood. Her eyes said so.

"I'm glad that Shayan found somebody to love so much. I noticed how happy you two were at the temple," she said.

"Yes," said Raagini, looking down at the floor. "We are." At that moment itself, she felt like she had lied.

A nurse came in. She handed Sabrina her clothes in a neat bundle, which the latter kept beside her on the bed. The nurse proceeded to check her pulse. Before going out, she informed Raagini that she would have to leave in an hour.

An hour and so much to ask, thought Raagini. The shock that had snatched her happiness had mellowed to remorse, riding on intense compassion she felt for this woman. Sabrina's genuineness struck her as unique. She seemed to be a simple, non-threatening woman who had loved and lost terribly and unfairly at that.

Glancing at her watch, Raagini turned to Sabrina.

"I need to know something," she said, lowering her gaze.

"Anything. Tell me please." Sabrina's response was prompt, as she sat up in bed. Raagini observed she was a little out of breath now. Probably the fatigue was overwhelming her.

"Were you and Shayan … happy…?"

"No, we weren't," Sabrina answered. "In fact, that was the premise he used to divorce me; that I was incompatible with him and…" She couldn't speak further, suddenly overcome. Concerned, Raagini went and sat on the bed near her. She watched Sabrina sobbing, even as her own eyes began smarting again.

Sabrina looked up at her. Spontaneously and silently, Raagini held out her arms towards her.

Sabrina threw herself into Raagini's embrace. She clutched her tightly, her body shaking with sobs. Raagini held her firmly.

"Do you still love him?" she asked Sabrina, when the tears subsided. Her hoarse voice caught Sabrina's attention. She freed herself and looked at Raagini.

"Why do you ask?"

Raagini rose and walked up to the door. The small round window carved in the door allowed her to view the corridor.

"I don't want Shayan to feel that I'm hounding him, because I'm not. Please tell him I don't need anything from him now," Sabrina said.

Just then, Raagini saw Shayan walking down the corridor towards the room. She excused herself and went out. He came up to her.

"You're still here. You didn't call either. Raagini, what is wrong with you?"

"Sabrina told me everything."

Shayan smirked. "What did she tell you that I didn't?"

"Of course, you told me plenty, Shayan; even all that you didn't ever see or feel."

Shayan raised his eyebrows. "What's that supposed to mean?"

Raagini faced him squarely. She pulled in her breath and waited. Weighing her thought for a burdensome second, she told Shayan in plain measured words, "I've decided not to be with you anymore."

Shayan was astonished.

"Are you out of your mind? What has this woman told you which you have believed so easily? Don't you trust me? Damn!"

In a fit of rage, Shayan barged into the room. Sabrina froze on seeing him, her face suddenly pale.

"What is all this, Sabrina? I told you it's over between us. We're divorced, damn it! Don't you want me to be happy with Raagini? Why are you poisoning her mind?" he shouted at her.

Sabrina stared at him. Raagini rushed in behind Shayan.

"Don't! Don't speak to her like that!" she retorted.

Shayan spun around.

"You're siding with her? Raagini, are you insane?

Raagini sighed. "This is a hospital, Shayan. Keep your voice down. I don't want to live with you anymore. It's my decision. Don't blame Sabrina."

"You love me, Raagini. We love each other. You can't throw away what we have just like that. I left her because I had to be with you ...can't you see that?"

Raagini's heart skipped a beat. This was the man she had waited for, for eight years. He had not cheated on her, yet had deceived her. She looked at Sabrina who was watching them silently. The storm of conflicting emotions ravaged her mercilessly.

Getting a hold on herself, she said calmly to Shayan, "Sabrina also loved you, Shayan. People come and go, but the reasons have to be right."

Shayan looked into her eyes and knew what she was hinting at. He looked at Sabrina helplessly. Sabrina came down from the bed and stood before Raagini.

"Raagini, you don't need to do this. You can be happy with Shayan."

Raagini raised her hand.

"The need is mine, Sabrina. It's not about you."

Sabrina withdrew quietly, unable to say anything further.

Shayan broke into panic. "This is madness, Raagini. Yes, the reasons have to be right. Look at ours, Raagini. Look at what we are going to have. Think about our baby."

Sabrina was startled. She looked at Raagini, astonished. Raagini looked away.

"I *am* thinking about our baby, Shayan. I'm thinking what kind of foundation I'll be giving the baby if I compromised on my values. We can never be happy now. Never."

"Okay, enough is enough. Now listen to me very carefully. I've tried my best to explain, and you know my heart is in the right place. If you are not going to come with me, I'll have a lot to tell the immigration authorities."

Raagini's eyes grew wide with amazement as Shayan continued.

"You married me for easy access to the Green Card, right, Mrs Raagini Shah?"

Raagini's amazement turned to horror as the meaning of his words dawned on her. No, this was not Shayan, not her Shayan. She struggled to fathom what could have possibly brought about these evil shades in her lover and husband. Eight long, very long years of companionship and where had they led her? Did she really know this man? The words of the priest in the temple reverberated in her ears.

There is good and there is evil. In goodness can reside a drop of evil, and in evil can surface a ray of good. Strive we must, to purify our good and lessen the evil in us. When our goodness does not the crutch of evil hold, our souls ripens to true love.

A fresh spate of tears overwhelmed her.

"You, Shayan? *You* will report me to the immigration authorities? You will humiliate me?" she whispered in utter disbelief. Breaking into sobs, she sat on the nearby chair and looked up at him, lost and insulted.

"Raagini, are you coming with me? I'm asking you for the last time."

Sabrina had been watching passively all this while. Shayan threw one last look at Raagini and began moving towards the door.

"Wait!" shouted Sabrina.

She walked up to Shayan. Shayan stopped in his tracks.

"It's me who will be calling in the immigration authorities now, Shayan," Sabrina said, fire in her eyes.

"And why is that?" asked Shayan.

"It is *you* who married me for a Green Card, Shayan. And it's time, I think, I opened my mouth," continued Sabrina.

Bewildered, Shayan looked at Raagini, then back at Sabrina.

"Yes, I've known all along, Shayan, but I chose to remain quiet. I loved you, though now, I feel you were not worthy of my love. In fact, I'm grateful that you dumped me, and I'm happy that Raagini, such a wonderful person that she is, has the sense to drive away from you. Take your pick, Shayan," she warned him. "Set Raagini free or lose your freedom in the US of A."

Shayan looked at both women, shell-shocked. Raagini couldn't remove her eyes from Sabrina's new avatar.

Shayan gave Raagini one long, hard look and went away without another word.

Sad relief engulfed Raagini. She smiled at Sabrina gratefully. Sabrina hugged Raagini warmly.

"Thank you, Sabrina, I'll never forget the gesture," said Raagini.

Her one hour was over. Raagini kissed Sabrina on the forehead and with a promise to see her again, took to the new path time had chosen for her to walk on.

TWO GOLD GUINEAS

Girls love, girls hate
Girls often don't know why
But whatever is their fate
Girls do not cry

I

The critical forty-eight hours were almost up. Biji would surely pull through. As in the past she had once again proved to be a survivor, thought Achala as she looked at Biji's frail body slumped against the pillow on the impersonal hospital bed. Biji's dark lips looked so parched, for she had been breathing with her mouth slightly ajar. The black peppercorn-sized mole at the edge of her lip now shone even more prominently and centimetre-long twin white hair sprouted from its peak.

Achala touched the moistened cotton swab to her lips and Biji opened her eyes for a moment. Rolling her pupils as though she was peeping into her own eyelids, she looked like one possessed, before she shut them again.

Biji was fair, slim and short. Ever since Achala could remember, she had been dressed in a white salwar-kameez that was always clean but never bright. At this moment too, everything about her was the same as it had always been. Her dull white salwar-kameez, her silver-turning-to-yellow hair neatly plaited. Only the familiar aroma of "desi ghee" that enveloped her at home had been punctured by the antiseptic and iodine smell so typical of a hospital. And the white chunni she covered her head with and then wrapped like a scarf around her neck had now slipped under her back as she lay supine on the bed.

Suddenly Achala noticed the two gold guineas that Biji always kept guarded in the knot of her chunni. To outsiders they appeared like the petty coins that old women often kept, either to give beggars or offer to deities at temples.

It was just as well, thought Achala, for if they knew the value of those two gold guineas, many would not hesitate to conclude that the old woman's life was infinitely less worthy than the guineas. But though she always agreed that times were bad, Biji refused to see reason whenever Achala suggested that she remove the guineas and keep them somewhere safer.

Every morning when Biji prepared to go for her bath she would undo the knot of the chunni she had been wearing, remove the guineas and then knot them into the edge of the fresh chunni which she was to wear soon after her bath.

The guineas were all that Bauji had been able to give her. He had told her that they were his only family heirloom and were to be passed on to the first two members who joined the family tree by marriage – whether they were sons or daughters-in-law.

Biji often recounted how Bauji had himself knotted the guineas into her chunni as they prepared to leave their home in Lahore during the partition riots of 1947. Biji had then been pregnant almost full-term with Achala. A bewildered Bauji had held their four-year-old son Achal Kumar's hand in one hand, and supported Biji with another, as they tried to wend their way through the crowds approaching Lahore station to get onto the train going to Delhi. In the melee, Achal Kumar, who had somehow failed to hold on to Bauji's hand, had got lost. A stunned Bauji had had to make the critical choice of clambering on to join his remaining family onto the train or stay behind to search for his son. And when he clearly couldn't decide, the crowd made the decision for him and he got swept along. Everyone around convinced him that the child had probably already been crushed under the feet of the waves of humanity that surged towards the train. So it was decided that it was better to escape with his wife and unborn child.

Achala had been born in a refugee camp and named in memory of, or as compensation for the lost Achal Kumar. In a short passage of time Bauji virtually willed himself to death, unable to live with the feeling of responsibility for Achal Kumar's loss. A stoic Biji plodded on, living as women manage to do for the sake of their children. Biji brought up Achala alone, taking as much care of her as she did of the two gold guineas knotted in her chunni. Biji, Achala and the guineas – there were the same three of them in 1947 as there were today in this hospital room, thought Achala, glancing at the knotted guineas. Biji, Achala, and the guineas. Fifty years later as fifty years earlier.

Amala, it seemed, had come and gone from their lives like a teasing, fragrant breeze that they would both do anything to woo back into their arid lives.

Achala checked the drip of the intravenous tube that fed Biji's arm as the clock struck 12.00. She sat on the stiff wooden chair next to Biji's bed and opened her diary to its first page. It was time she kept the promise that she had made to herself. It was a momentous moment to begin her diary – the striking clock had just heralded the completion of fifty years of her existence. If nothing, she must write to commemorate that there was yet nothing to commemorate. She began to write.

II

It is a moment to celebrate but I have no one to celebrate it with, except frail, unconscious Biji with the two gold guineas knotted in her chunni and perhaps no one who will claim those.

Jatin should logically have been the first claimant. Jatin, my lawfully wedded husband who left me nearly twenty years ago, consumed by an inexplicable spiritual wanderlust when our daughter, whom he had named Amala, was just a few months old. Amala, which he explained meant the pure one. For once he had done right – in naming her, that is.

Jatin had, in the true tradition of the Buddha, set out to discover the true meaning of life. He had left me without any warning, just disappeared one morning. For he had probably believed that if he didn't do it that way, he wouldn't ever be able to shake off the desires and bonds that tied him to this world of "maya". I had sensed that even on the few occasions that he had been romantic with me, he seemed to hate, even while loving, me for being the object of his desire. His eyes never met mine when he made love and the act itself was more akin to the desperation of a man easing himself. And so after it was over he always looked a mixture of relief and shame and half expected me to look guilty for having tempted him. I knew that for him I was symbolic of Manu's philosophy that woman is a necessary curse for mankind.

To be frank I was actually relieved when he finally left – at least he had made a decision. Never mind if I had to fend for myself, my daughter and my mother. At least he'd given me this lovely, beautiful child. Caring for her became the sole focus of both Biji's and my life from then onwards.

It did not particularly bother me what the world thought of my marital status, or whether I qualified as widow or divorcee. At that time I didn't miss physical and emotional intimacy either – for I had never known it until Ravi came into my life. Till then, I was comfortable playing daughter, mother, and man of my home, for after Jatin left I had also had to start earning a living to support Biji and Amala.

It was while playing this man's role that I met the man who would make me feel like a woman again – in fact more than I had ever felt in my life before. I joined Ravi's office as a secretarial assistant and ended up as what the world – if it had known about us – would call his mistress.

Ravi was my boss at the office. Away from there, he was my pillar of support. He had always been there for me when I needed him. He was there when Amala needed to be admitted to a good school, when Biji had to undergo an emergency bypass surgery and on several other occasions. He enjoyed caring for me and often confessed that it was only when he was with me that he felt like a real man. Frankly I could never understand what he saw in me, for his wife Ketaki was stunning to look at. She was also a competent businesswoman, and would have been an asset to any modern man.

When I mentioned this to Ravi he had said that the difference between Ketaki and me was like the difference between synthetic and natural fabric. (After all, he was the son-in-law of the founder of the famous Alliance Textile Mills!) Synthetic fibre always falls well but feels dead. The natural fabric – alive to the ravages of time and treatment – often does not look as good but it breathes and allows to breathe and is therefore alive…

"You are my earth," Ravi would often say after we became lovers. I remember how much he hated it when I once dyed my greying hair. "Never do that again. You remind me of Ketaki," he had said in a distinctly wounded voice.

Strange are the ways of life. Here was a man who wanted to give and care but whose wife did not want it. In fact her complaint was that he was just not dynamic enough. For she on her part was already a minor celebrity and was always working towards a higher profile for the textiles company that she had inherited from her father.

Ravi and Ketaki had a modern marriage, an arrangement where each was left free to do their own thing, bound only by the slender thread of common concern for their son Vikram. The only problem was that deep in his heart Ravi did not believe in the concept of a modern marriage, while Ketaki happily seemed to have made the most of the arrangement.

It was for this reason (though I hate to think of myself as Ravi's mistress) that I probably appealed to Ravi. I was actually so much like a wife. And the fact that I didn't expect much from Ravi made him want to give and care all that much more. And so he cared and I bloomed in our memorable years of togetherness.

Yes I did so often question myself. I questioned our love. I felt guilty about the immorality of what I was doing, but Ravi always reassured me. He explained that except in the eyes of the world, he really had had no marriage going with Ketaki. So I was no "other woman". I was the only real woman for him.

Both of us were committed to our roles as providers to our families, and as parents. Neither Ravi nor I were prepared to disturb the status quo, but surely as we often justified to ourselves, we deserved the personal happiness that we gave each other. It was a fulfilment that actually made us happier and more compassionate providers in our respective families. It made sense to our lives and yet did not harm those we cared for.

Ravi and I met at our secret home about thrice a week and shared moments of pure ecstasy with each other on the six-by-four-foot bed. That was real lovemaking, not the helpless and guilt-ridden experience I had earlier thought it was all about. To tell the truth it was only these moments of our secret lives that had made the grind of the last twenty years so much easier to bear.

Ravi's wife knew about us but she probably didn't care less. Ravi hadn't told their son about us. Just as I did not dare tell Biji or Amala. I often had a feeling that Biji suspected something (a mother's instinct?). But soon enough the feeling would always pass. And Amala? I would die a thousand deaths at the very thought of telling her. Though I knew that one day I would have to.

She was pure, fragile, and so very innocent. She thought the world of me and Biji and for her we could do no wrong. She knew of all the hardships I'd been through but knew nothing of my joys. As a child, Amala often told me that she would look after us and make us so happy that we'd forget all the hardships we had ever faced. I must confess that I enjoyed wearing the mantle of martyr that the world had put like an ornament on me. I revelled in the "sacrificing all for your happiness" role that I played for Amala. Many a time I thought of telling her about my true relationship with Ravi, but the fear that my image would crumble in her eyes if I did that prevented me from doing so.

At other times, the fear of her getting to know elsehow and rejecting me because of it was so overwhelming that I would decide to call it quits with Ravi. I would come to the entrance of our love-nest, mentally prepared to bid it goodbye forever. But having crossed that threshold it would become impossible to turn back. I would look at Ravi's smiling visage, and sit beside him. The lines I had rehearsed in my head would all go missing. Ravi had an uncanny way of finding out exactly what was going on in my mind, without me having to explain too much. And he always succeeded in making me change my mind.

I remember the last time I was feeling this way. Ravi sat me down on the mattress. He removed my glasses and put them aside. He cradled my head against his chest and stroked my head – as if he were consoling a child. I was feeling so mixed up at that time. One moment I was like a child, soaking in the comfort of a parent's bosom and then in the very next moment I transformed from child to woman. A woman whose every nerve was alive, throbbing and pulsating to the touch of her man.

I had never been able to figure out why I always turned to putty in Ravi's hands. Maybe he was an exceptionally good lover. Maybe I was too ready, and too vulnerable to the only man that I had ever loved. Ultimately I gave up trying to give up my feelings for him.

I was finally learning to enjoy the best of both worlds. I told myself that since Amala was by now a most understanding and mature girl I should soon be able to tell her all about Ravi. Little did I know at that time that my dreams of a friendship with my daughter were never to be.

Then Amala fell in love. Nitish was ten years older than her and worked in the same office that Amala took up her summer job with. I remember the day. It was, as I later learnt, the first date and she had agreed to go out with him for dinner without telling Biji or me. It seemed so innocent when I think of it now – so right for her to be doing such a thing at her age. But so horribly wrong to discover that her own parent had been up to much worse.

There she was looking into Nitish's eyes, talking perhaps of love, dreams and a future. And in the next moment she suddenly saw me clasping Ravi's hand. For me too it was unusual to concede to such a public display of affection, but it was this rare occasion when Ravi had insisted that we celebrate our fifteen years of togetherness at that restaurant.

Amala's world crashed and so did mine. Once she knew what Ravi meant to me, I had to give her all the details. The hypocrisy of my stand crushed her. There was just no way she could accept my double standards. She did not believe that I had not wronged his family, or mine.

"I was prepared to fight my natural urges and dreams of marriage only so that I need never have to leave you, and that's what I'd been telling Nitish. I wanted to spend my life taking care of you. But now I see that you have other people who do that and also give you what I can never give. You do not need me," was all that she had said tersely. And her words were indeed a portent of the future course of our relationship.

A few days later, Amala came home with Nitish, informing Biji and me that they had just been through a court marriage. They were leaving within the week for Bombay where Nitish had found a challenging job.

Biji and I were stunned. There had been no reason for her to do it this way, for we would have accepted anyone she wished to marry. In any case Nitish did seem like a nice person and was also genuinely in love with her. But Amala did this just to spite me and I could not defend myself in front of Biji who was completely unaware of what had transpired between us.

In spite of that, Biji held me to blame. In the true tradition of the partial grandmother, she felt that I had gone wrong somewhere for my daughter to have done this.

"You have failed to be her friend," Biji had said accusingly.

I accepted her verdict. Yes, of course I had gone wrong – only much more wrong than Biji could ever imagine. So very wrong that I had lost the right as a parent to point out my child's mistake or even to voice my protest. I suspect that Amala knew this and was enjoying hurting me, even as she herself was hurting.

It's been a year since Amala left. Gradually I stopped meeting Ravi and even left my job with his company. It was not because I stopped loving him – if anything, I love and miss him more than ever before. But soon after Amala's departure, even though she was no longer in the same city, each time I'd meet him I'd feel as if I was somehow hurting her all over again.

Ravi was hurt but he accepted my decision. The women in his life, he had remarked sadly that day, had always taken the decisions about their relationship and he had always had to go along. First Ketaki had done it and now I had.

Amala was a married woman now. My little girl who had never known a man before she wed – not a father, not even a brother – was now a woman. I'd often worried on that count and hoped that our similar backgrounds wouldn't lead to similar fates. But there had been no other option but to let go. There was no use worrying.

I wrote to Amala several times after she left. She would reply but did not tell me much about how she was doing. Every reply from her was evidence of the battle waging within her. A few lines that she would write to me would sound like the Amala of old, as if nothing had gone wrong between us. Reading these, my heart would skip a beat as I would imagine that she had finally forgiven me and was going to give me a peep into her life.

But in the very next paragraph she would be on guard and terse again. Could I hope that the first Amala would one day break free of the shackles that the second Amala had bound her with? I could only hope that time would heal. Dare I hope?

III

Achala put down her pen. It was past 5 o'clock in the morning.

Fifty years, five hours. Or fifty years in five hours that she had just penned. The long and short of time and of life itself. She looked at Biji stirring with the new lease of life that she had got. Soon Biji would regain consciousness. Her eyes would most certainly search for Amala.

Achala had called up Bombay soon after Biji had been admitted to hospital. In the dead of night Nitish had picked up the phone. He had sounded a bit strained when he had told Achala that he would "pass on the message to Amala", instead of calling Amala to the phone. Perhaps Amala may not have wanted to come to the phone or maybe he was just being protective.

Achala had been expecting Amala to come. Despite all that had happened with her, she must most certainly have been concerned about Biji even if she had stopped caring about her. For this was Biji's second attack after her bypass surgery and Amala was well aware of the threat to Biji's life during her earlier hospitalisation. There was certainly something mysterious and worrisome about Amala not having come to see Biji so far.

With the first chirping and twittering of the birds came the sounds of life stirring in the hospital corridor. The swish-swoosh sound of huge thread mops, the faint but comforting smell of tea brewing in the pantry, the sounds of buckets filling up with water in the adjoining bathrooms – all heralding the beginning of another day of healing.

Suddenly there was a sharp knock on the door of Biji's room and Achala rushed to open it. The plump matron walked inside. Surely it was premature for Biji to be given a sponge bath today, thought Achala as she let her in. The matron entered and shut the door behind her.

"Madam, there is something strange going on," she told Achala. "Since last night a young girl has been sitting on the bench outside this room. She said she was related to the patient in this room. So we allowed her to come in even when the visiting hours were nearly over last night. But this morning as I passed through the corridor I found that she is still sitting crouched on the bench. She looks ill and very scared. Please tell us whether you know her or else I'll have to inform security."

Achala was rushing out even before the matron could complete her sentence. There, crouched on the bench, she saw the huddled figure of Amala. She looked pale as a ghost, and as haunted as an animal in captivity. She had lost a lot of weight and her usually kohl-rimmed eyes now looked so sunken. As she saw Achala rush towards her, Amala started to weep, her body racked and heaved as she sobbed.

Achala hugged her. Amala buried her face in the pleats of her mother's sari, feeling its warmth as she used to when she was a little girl. Achala led her inside Biji's room as the matron who had followed Achala outside stared bewildered at the scene. Achala wanted to hold Amala tight but the arrangement inside prevented her from doing so. Achala forced her to sit on the lone chair in the room, as she sat facing Amala on the stool.

"What's the matter, Amala? Why did you not come in earlier? Do you still hate me or were you afraid that Biji...?"

"I don't know why I did not come in. But I know that I love you, ma, and I need you," she whispered, extending her hand to stroke Biji's emaciated feet. "I love you both," she said in a hoarse whisper.

"What's wrong, my child?" said Achala.

"I have sinned, ma. I think it is god's way of punishing me for having judged you. I don't know why I did it," she cried.

"What have you done?" asked Achala, concerned, but afraid of being betrayed by the sound of her own voice, actually wondering and hoping that her sympathy was truly warranted.

"I left Nitish a month ago. Ma, I thought I didn't get the love I was looking for from him, and I found it in Rahul ... or so I had thought at that time. I have been living with Rahul this past month. But even with Rahul things are not what I thought they would be. I wronged Nitish. I've made a mess of my life and now I have nowhere to go." Her words poured out disjointed and scattered as her thoughts.

"How did you get to know about Biji?" Achala asked, strangely relieved at Amala's explanation.

"Nitish rang me up the day before yesterday at Rahul's house and told me about Biji. I left Bombay yesterday. Rahul did not even care to drop me to the airport. His look was almost a message to me that I was not really welcome to return. I guess my emotional needs were too much for him to bear – he was looking for something else. I have been a fool, an utter fool. Rahul didn't want my emotions, he only wanted me. And once he got me, it was all over. Ma, I really wronged Nitish. I found him too boring and staid but the truth is that when I was with him I always felt that there was someone to take care of me. I have hurt him and therefore god has punished me..."

"I am there for you, Amala. I have been waiting so long to be able to take care of you," said Achala.

"But I have no right to expect that now. I have hurt you two, haven't I? I've hurt you so much."

"One hurts those whom one loves. But tell me, Amala, do you still love Nitish?"

"More than ever before. I know that I sound most selfish, but the truth is that I love and value him more than ever before. But now I know that it's too late," she admitted.

"You will not lose him. I will try my best to see that you don't."

Achala was determined not to let that happen. For, if you lose someone who loves you and whom you love, you lose bits of yourself. Like grains of sand flying about in the desert, unable to recognise your shattered self. Arid, and unwelcome to the world. As she had been since she had lost Ravi. And the same grains of sand that lie beside the sea get their form from it. Every woman is like sand. It is fate that gives her a desert or the sea as her companion. So her man is either as restless as the wind or as stable as water. She was destined to be in the desert, but would take her daughter to her sea.

There was a knock on the door. This time it woke up Biji who stared sideways at the entrance as if expecting someone there, completely missing looking at Achala and Amala standing close by.

Achala opened the door and stared in surprise at Nitish. The disbelief writ large on Amala's face slowly turned into belief as he walked with serene steps towards her.

"How are you, Amala?" he asked and the lines on her overwrought face melted away.

"I'm all right, Nitish … I've learnt so much about life and love recently. But I know that it's too late now to make amends for what I've done."

"It's not late – it's never too late to understand and forgive in love," said Nitish.

"You mean it's possible for you to accept me after all that…?"

"It's not that I can't accept you again. But even if I do, what happened to you some time ago will happen again unless…" said Nitish, looking her in the eye. "Unless you accept and face up to something you are avoiding…"

Nitish held Amala's hand and led her towards the door as Biji's soft moans reached their ears. Nitish paused and turned to look at Biji. For the sake of her weak ears he reassured her in a particularly loud voice, "Don't worry, Biji, I'm coming back. I'm just going to get someone who should have been here right through. Just coming back, Biji."

Biji stopped moaning immediately.

"There is someone whom you have to accept, before you expect me to accept you," Nitish explained. "A person who is as important to your family as I am … and today I've brought him here with me." Nitish opened the door of Biji's room and led Amala to the long corridor.

There at the far end, seated on the same bench on which Amala had crouched all night, sat Ravi.

"Go, Amala, go and accept him with all your heart. If you can do that you will be able to love yourself … and only then will my love be able to reach you. Only then will you truly be able to love me, Amala. Me or anyone else. Believe me, for once believe me," said Nitish.

"I do," whispered Amala.

Ravi stood up and looked at Amala, in a strange way able and yet unable to meet her stare. Amala walked towards him with clouded eyes. She folded her hands and cried, "I'm sorry, Ravi uncle, really sorry."

Ravi held her drooping shoulders and then put her head on his chest, patting her head as she wept, so drained and comforted that she didn't want anything to stop or change this moment. But change it still did, as Nitish reminded them of Biji who had actually connived with her illness to make all this happen today.

They walked back towards Biji's room where Achala met them, her eyes dry and lips unable to stop smiling. They went past her and close to Biji's bed. Biji's eyes were now wide open.

Biji's face looked beatific, her wrinkles showing up on her skin as she attempted to smile. Her eyes were twinkling, seeming to speak a thousand words. She signalled to Achala who walked towards her from the far end of the room.

Achala put her ears close to Biji's mouth. "Guineas," Biji whispered hoarsely.

"They are there, Biji. They are still tied in your chunni knot. No one has taken them," said Achala, sounding exasperated as she reassured Biji as if she were talking to a child.

"I want to hold the guineas," said Biji, her hoarse voice cracking but firm.

Achala was surprised at Biji's instructions but proceeded to fulfil her wish. She opened Biji's chunni knot and placed the two guineas in her left palm. Biji shut her eyes and closed her palm to feel the familiar and comforting presence of the guineas one last time. Then, as though satiated, she opened her eyes again.

"Ravi beta," she whispered. Ravi bent forward to come closer to her. She placed one guinea in his hand. Ravi looked nonplussed as Achala looked on amazed.

"Nitish puttar," said Biji. He stared bewildered, and then hesitantly walked towards Biji. She placed the second guinea in his palm.

"God bless you all. Now I can finally sleep in peace and talk to Bauji in my dreams," she said as she sighed and shut her tired eyes.

WAXWORKS

Do you feel sorry for me?
Do you think I am mad?
Can it be that you dare pity
The life I have had?

They were seated on adjacent chairs at the beauty parlour. For want of much else to do while waiting for the bleaching cream on her face to dry, Bulbul looked at the woman's image in the mirror in front of her.

Her closely set and thin, arched eyebrows reminded her of the bunny hops that her four-year-old daughter practised in her handwriting book. The very thought made Bulbul smile. The white dust of talcum powder was clearly discernible on the woman's brown skin. She seemed so small, as she sat there on the large parlour chair. A gaunt shrivelled-up scarecrow-like creature. Who would ever find such a woman appealing, thought Bulbul, even as she realised in the next instant what a mean thought that was.

The woman moved forward to the edge of her seat as she peered into the mirror in front, checking the colour of the roots of her hair. She caught Bulbul's eye looking at her image in the mirror and proceeded to give Bulbul's image in her mirror a wide smile in return. Then, all of a sudden, her face stiffened.

"Suzy," she called out in a shrill voice that had suddenly turned angry. "I'll teach you a lesson, Suzy! How dare you treat me like this! I've been waiting here ten minutes and no one is attending to me. What's going on in here?" she shrieked, much to the surprise of Bulbul. It was at this point that Bulbul noticed that the woman's front teeth protruded and that there were also scores of wrinkles on her neck. Too much skin and no meat, thought Bulbul, and for once she felt less despairing of her own plumpness.

Suzy entered the room from the anteroom with a puzzled look. She took one look at the woman and realised that she was the one who had shouted out her name. She sighed with exasperation as she made her way to Bulbul.

Showing her back to the gaunt woman defiantly, Suzy started to touch the white cream bleach on Bulbul's face and found its foam come off easily. "You can wash it off now, madam," she told Bulbul gently.

By now the woman had left her chair and was standing just behind Bulbul. "Suzy!" she shouted, "you have time for everyone else but me." The next moment she toned her voice down. "Don't I pay for all my treatments and ... and don't you remember the big tip I gave you the last time?" she continued with indignation.

Bulbul found it difficult to understand what was going on. Suzy never ever behaved like this with anyone. She could not help but stare at the stone-faced Suzy who was now putting away an assortment of combs and scissors into a holder, oblivious of the woman's remonstrations.

Bulbul made her way to the washbasin near the entrance to the anteroom. She splashed water on her face and rubbed off the bleach from it. Before she could reach for a tissue on the adjoining rack, Suzy was already dabbing her face for her. Bulbul was surprised that Suzy was so completely unaffected by the utterances of the gaunt woman as she proceeded to examine Bulbul's face for the effect of the bleach.

Bulbul was uncomfortable with the strange vibes in the room. Suzy held Bulbul's chin up. She arched her face, then turned it to the right and then the left, looking at it from various angles, satisfied at the soft golden glow that shone in the light. She declared with pleasure, "Your face is glowing, madam."

Suzy beckoned to Bulbul. "Come on, madam, we'll go to the anteroom for the facial."

"Suzy, what about that client outside? What's the matter? Why aren't you attending to her?" asked Bulbul. She knew it was none of her business and yet she could not hold her curiosity any longer.

"Oh I am sure that one of the others will attend to her sooner or later if she keeps at her whining and complaining. You need stamina to deal with her, and today I just don't have that kind of energy," Suzy said matter-of-factly.

"Is she a difficult customer?" asked Bulbul.

"Not in the way that difficult customers are usually difficult. Difficult customers are exacting, they want perfection, which is tiring but understandable. This one is a weirdo."

Bulbul smiled to herself at Suzy confiding in her. She knew that she herself was a really easy customer. It came naturally to her, for she was an easy person. Also, despite knowing that she was paying for being attended to, there was something so utterly feudal about being in a beauty parlour that Bulbul couldn't bear to be anymore vain than the situation naturally made her be. She guiltily enjoyed her monthly makeover here, but could never bring herself to demand more than was regularly given to her. And to give Suzy her due, she always did a good job of transforming Bulbul.

"I don't understand," Bulbul said. "In what way is she weird?" she asked as he lay down on the bunk in the anteroom. The room was full of the smell of boiling wax that bubbled in a saucepan on the hotplate near the entrance. It was just like the aroma of caramelising sugar ... an unusual smell but one that Bulbul loved, just the way some people inexplicably loved the aroma of petrol. She inhaled it deeply.

"You lie down and take your face massage, madam," said Suzy. "I will tell you why I'm behaving like that with her."

Suzy started to work on Bulbul's face. She made gentle, circular moments with her fingertips on both her cheeks, working from behind Bulbul's head.

"Mrs Nair. Her name is Mrs Nair," said Suzy. "She stays just down the road. She has been coming here for thirty-odd years and I have watched her from the time my mother used to attend to her and I used to merely watch her. Mummy told me that her husband had taken one look at her on their wedding night and had been devastated. They hadn't let him see her before that. You know how Hindus had these strict arranged marriages even about a generation ago," Suzy declared with an air of superiority.

"He simply couldn't bear to think that he would have to spend his whole life with her. So at the first available opportunity, he left for the Gulf, leaving her here in his flat down the road, pretending he'd call her once his job scene settled down," Suzy continued. "Everyone knows that he has married again in the Gulf and even has his own family. He hasn't returned in all these years but the man can't bear to tell this woman the truth. He continues to send her money for her upkeep every month. Though people have tried to hint to her about the truth, she doesn't believe them. She doesn't want to believe them. She feels that since he sends her money every month, he still cares for her and will surely return one day."

"That's rather sad," said Bulbul.

"She has a comfortable amount of money to spend and nowhere really to spend it. Over the years she is getting mentally affected. Alzheimer's disease, some people say, and I too agree that there's something really wrong with her. She comes to the parlour every two to three days, for she wants to be in perfect shape for him when he returns. She sees imaginary unwanted hair on her arms just two days after we have waxed it and pesters us to repeat the entire procedure all over again. And if we protest she simply insists that we do, just because she is willing and able to pay for it."

Suzy sighed. "In the last couple of years she's been coming to us to dye her hair even when there is just half a millimetre growth of white hair at the roots. She is paranoid about greying. For a long time now she has lost her sense of time and imagines that her husband left for the Gulf only a couple of weeks ago. It has been thirty years but she thinks that he will send for her soon. Madness, sheer madness." Suzy shook her head.

"Do you know, madam, she keeps asking us why she is greying even though she is only in her twenties? Once, she even accused one of my girls of tampering with the hair dye and permanently damaging her hair. Imagine!"

Suzy's usually gentle movements on Bulbul's face were turning more vigorous in tandem with her animated monologue.

"I simply don't know how to deal with a woman like that. I can't drive her away and I cannot reason with her either. I feel sorry for her and at the same time angry too. Angry with her and angry with her husband too. Angry, also, with our own hypocrisy. Why doesn't someone dare to tell her the truth? Why can't she understand and accept it?" she continued.

"I wonder if it will ever happen but I hope at least for our sake, that it happens soon. I'm at my wit's end handling this woman and her crazy demands. But the only thing is, how are we to tell her? And how will she take it when she is told?" said Suzy despairingly as she began to wipe out the excess cream from Bulbul's face with a cotton swab.

"This is how she will take it," said a voice behind them.

A shocked Bulbul opened her eyes. A horrified Suzy turned around. Mrs Nair stood behind, glaring at them.

She had heard all that Suzy had been saying all this while, and now stood there holding the saucepan that had been boiling with wax.

"Here's to both you beautiful women!" she said, as she hurled the hot molten wax at their faces. And her banshee-like laughter melded with their screams of burning horror.

Section III

The Mirror Does Not Lie

A CURE FOR ALL ILLS

Life can seem all sorted
Yet be rather a mess
Till you come to be pitted
Against a woman who is no less

Everything in this world appeared beautiful to Surili today. She was in seventh heaven as she hopped into the auto waiting outside her office. As the three-wheeler spurred on, Surili basked in the sunshine of appreciation poured on her throughout the workday by peers and seniors alike. The toil of working on those two stories for months had paid off finally. And to top it, her boss had promoted her to the post of senior correspondent.

There was one thing that daunted her though. Attached to the promotion came a story commissioned to her, which would require her to be stationed away from home in a remote village. She had been chosen to study the habits and social trends of the tribal community inhabiting that village. Surili wasn't sure whether she wanted to take up this assignment, since it would mean a rough-and-tumble existence, disconnected from the outer world, and a mammoth adjustment to an environment far removed from what she was used to. She was a tough girl and used to the rigours of her profession, but after a long year of hard work, she had planned to take some time off with Anish and relax. Though this assignment was significant for her career, she wanted to strike a balance right now.

The auto had moved into the road leading to her locality. Excited at the thought of meeting Anish, Surili reached inside her bag and touched the small gift she had got him. She had so much to say. She wanted to thank him for the patience he had shown whilst she had been working long hours of late.

Paying the fare, she entered the society building and, instead of taking the lift, walked up hurriedly. Mrs Kripalani, her sixty-five-year-old neighbour, smiled at her from her door. Smiling back, Surili entered home as quietly as possible. Anish was in the kitchen making tea for both of them. She tiptoed up to him and hugged him hard from behind. Anish turned around smiling and returned her hug generously.

"Anish," she said excitedly, "this is for you." Her eyes sparkled as she pulled out the gift and gave it to him.

Anish's face lit up. "Hey, thanks. That's so sweet. Hmm ... Surili Rai is famous, huh?"

"Kind of. You see, I have been the chosen one in office. Nobody ain't beatin' me at this game darlin'." Surili was mock arrogant as she swirled the words in her mouth, posed and then laughed aloud at her own antics. "Anish, you should have seen the flowers at my desk today. And you know what? The visiting editor-in-chief himself shook hands with me."

"Great!" Anish was thrilled at his wife's accomplishment. He kept the gift on the kitchen platform and opened it. It was a miniature lamp.

"Hey, this is beautiful. Thanks, Shirley." Surili smiled at Anish's nickname for her as she walked towards the bathroom.

When she came back to the living room after a quick shower, Anish was waiting with tea. She chatted away as she dried her hair. "Hope your presentation went..." She stopped suddenly as her eye caught Anish's expression. He seemed to be a bit lost. "What happened, Ani? Had a bad day?"

Anish pursed his lips and shook his head to say no, but his eyes were preoccupied. Surili knew that look.

"Okay, out with it. What is it?"

Anish looked at her doubtfully. His words were measured. "Ma and Papa called this morning." Surili raised her eyebrows as her eyes grew wide. Anish carried on. "Yes, I was also surprised. They want to come and stay with us for some time."

"Stay with us?" Surili threw up her hands in amazement. "But they can't stand me for a second. How are they going to live with me?"

Anish explained, "Well, it seems they are on their way to accepting our relationship. And as a mark of their willingness, they want to come and spend some time with us."

Surili fell quiet for a few seconds. Anish too. They sipped their tea together in strained silence.

Theirs had been a bumpy relationship. Anish came from a pretty orthodox background. His parents were the quintessential simple, doting lot but with rigid notions about being the sole possessor of their son's life. When Anish had told them he wanted to marry the very urban, assertive and self-dictated Surili, they both had hit the roof. For days they lamented about how much he had hurt them even as Anish tried in vain to convince them. Eventually, Surili and he had taken legal recourse to wed, and his parents had refused to even acknowledge that reality.

And now this. Just as Surili had adjusted to the fact that her in-laws couldn't see eye to eye with her, time was throwing this bombshell at her all over again.

Surili and Anish spoke little the rest of the evening. A simple dinner and a couple of TV programmes later, they retired for the night. Anish fell asleep after some time, but Surili tossed and turned the whole night.

Next morning, Surili dressed casually in her new Levi's jeans and khadi kurti and prepared breakfast. She smiled at Anish when he joined her at the table.

"You're going early today?" Anish asked her between yawns.

"Yes, have loads of work to finish," she said lightly.

Anish looked at her lovingly. She was everything he had wanted in his woman. He liked everything about her, even her strong-headedness. He engulfed her in his arms and said, "Can I say something before you leave?"

"Yup. Sure."

"Shirley, when Ma and Papa are around, can you just observe a couple of things, please?"

Surili had been expecting this. "What?"

"Generally, you know what ... like..."

Surili pushed him away. "Like overdone sindoor in my hair? Like ... let me think ... as in wearing saris like a uniform? Ugh!" She screwed up her nose in disgust and then added sarcastically, "Or ... yes! Like cooking four-course meals three times a day?" Surili got up and went inside the kitchen. She began packing her lunch and banging the tiffin box on the granite platform noisily. Anish followed her.

"Shirls, it's a temporary thing! You can be the way you want to be after they leave!" Anish's voice was raised with exasperation.

Surili turned around and stared at him in disbelief for a long moment. When she spoke again, her tone was low. And fuming.

"Anish, my job doesn't allow me to be dressed very elegantly most of the time. That's one thing. Secondly, what's this about it being temporary? All the more reason that I'm against any unreasonable adjustment. Why ... why should I be somebody I'm not, even for a short while? That's pretence, right? And since when have you started endorsing pretence so much?"

It was Anish who stared at her now. "I can't believe I have to justify a simple request to you so much! I don't want any confrontation during their stay, that's all. I admit they are a bit conservative..."

"A *bit*?" said Surili mockingly.

"Don't use that tone with me," said Anish. "Okay, they are quite orthodox. So? But let's also acknowledge that by calling on their own, they've made a start. It will be wrong if we don't do our part."

"You mean *my* part. Ani, give me a break. All the adjustments have to come from me only, right?" Surili walked out of the kitchen.

"It's always about you, isn't it? Your life, your job! We have a life here in Mumbai for us which is ours, the way we want it. If my parents come and share it for a short while, why can't you be practical and adjust? Didn't you do so the first time we met them after our wedding?"

"Precisely, Anish. When I did go their way temporarily, did it make them happy?"

Anish sighed. "No, it didn't. But this time it's different. They have mellowed."

Anish remembered how Surili had draped herself in saris and ornate jewellery lent to her by Ma. She had acted the part of the perfect bahu to the hilt. At that time, Ma had found fault with every attempt of hers. But he knew this time things would be better. If only Surili would cooperate.

Anish missed being able to do something for his parents. He did not agree with their rules, but the distance between them made him sad about not being able to discharge his duties towards them. He tried again.

"Shirls, please, let's not make a mountain out of a molehill."

"No, Anish! Not this time. If things are so different, let them accept me the way I am. I cannot pretend and be untrue to myself anymore."

"How self-centred can you be? What is the matter? Can't you see that your adjusting to some of their ways can pave the way for better relations tomorrow? Or doesn't it matter to you anymore whether my parents reconcile with us or not?"

Anish threw up his hands in despair and shouted, "Fine! Suit yourself! They will probably turn up after a month. If you want to change your mind, you can try."

"I don't think so. Bye, Anish. See you later." Surili walked out in a huff.

*

Once outside, the air nipped at her and fuelled her anger. *How can Anish be so insensitive towards my needs? How long can one maintain a farce to make others happy?* she thought.

Surili reached the office and sat at her desk idly for some time. Answering some greetings absent-mindedly, she stared at the computer screen.

"Ahem." A polite intervention brought her back. She saw Mr Goenka, her editor, standing next to her.

"Busy?" He smiled at her and Surili rose to her feet.

"No, sir. Tell me please."

"In my cabin. I need to speak to you."

Surili followed Mr Goenka. Once inside, he said, "Surili, I need to commission that tribal story fast. Will you be able to decide about going today itself?"

Surili thought for a moment. She could still feel anger gnawing at her. She looked up at Mr Goenka.

"I'll take it up. I'll go," she heard herself saying.

Mr Goenka's face lit up. "Wonderful. When can you leave?"

"Tomorrow, sir?"

Mr Goenka was mighty pleased.

*

Back at home, Anish was quiet as he watched Surili pack her things. They hugged each other before she entered the lift. Surili looked at him.

"You'll come back on time, won't you, Shirls? Please?"

"I don't know, Anish. Please give me some time. I need to sort this out." Surili's eyes moistened for a second.

Later, when she looked up at the flat from the taxi, Surili saw Anish standing at the window. Neither of them waved.

The train journey and the following bumpy bus ride were punctuated merely by her stray thoughts about life, Anish, career and her seething ire at his unrealistic expectations.

The NGO representative, who had arranged to mediate between Surili and the village administration, was there to receive her. He introduced her to the village head, a semi-educated man of seventy with sharp eyes. He was kind enough as he deputed Nanda, a middle-aged widow, to be Surili's escort throughout her stay. The NGO representative left after some time.

For most of the next few days, Surili roamed the nearby area with Nanda, trying to understand the village's geography and demographics. She took some pictures of groups of women. Curious onlookers stared at her – sometimes suspiciously, at other times, curiously. A bunch of half-naked children looked at her camera wistfully, and when she attempted to talk to them, they only grinned in return. Nanda spoke some Hindi and explained everything about the ways and mannerisms of the village as clearly and passionately as she could.

Surili noted that most of the women pounded grain and masala in the scorching sun, while the men loitered under the numerous shady trees. The couple of wells were the only source of drinking water. The straw products the women made were beautiful and simple. Surili couldn't resist buying some from them.

When Surili got up one morning, she had a splitting headache. Surili opened her bag and searched but there was no aspirin. *I must have forgotten to pack it,* she thought to herself. She tried to relax but the pain was excruciating and Surili knew that she was on her way to a migraine attack. She cursed herself for not carrying the requisite medicine.

By afternoon, the pain had ballooned. Surili sat on the cot, pulling her hair with her fingers and trying to ease her scalp, but the monster was closing in on her. Nausea was beginning to surge inside her. After she threw up the first time and slumped to the floor drained, Nanda called for a tonga. When it arrived, she helped Surili to her feet and brought her outside.

"Where are we going?" Surili asked, barely able to speak.

"Madam, I am taking you to the witch doctor."

"Witch doctor? What is that? I mean, who is that?" Surili was alert despite the killing pain. "Look, I'm not into all this mumbo-jumbo. I need medicines, not mantras."

"It is sacrilege to doubt the witch doctor. She can cure anything. Madam, last year, when Rekha's son became unconscious, she cured him with some magic potion in a day and the lad was up and running by evening."

Surili was intrigued. Nanda continued as she helped Surili onto the tonga. "She has powers. How else can she cure somebody so fast? But she is a good witch. If nobody disturbs her, she is kind. People say if you irritate her, she may turn you into a cabbage."

Surili smiled at Nanda's fairy-tale horror as much as the blinding pain allowed her to. Nanda was offended. She told the tongawala where to go and turned to Surili.

"You don't believe me, do you?"

Surili stopped smiling. "No, no, I do. Fine, we'll go. Let's see what she can do for me." Surili was in so much pain that she just wanted some relief from anywhere.

It was past two when they reached the outskirts of the village. The tonga stopped at the base of a small hillock that rose from above the undulating stretch of brown arid land.

"There," said Nanda. She pointed at the top of the hill. Surili squinted in the sun and trudged along. Her headache was thumping monstrously by now and she began hoping that this visit would work. The small climb uphill took five minutes. At the top, the land was flattened out like a plateau. The witch doctor's hut sat there. Nanda shook the bell hanging outside the thatched door.

A few seconds later, the door opened. A face appeared.

"Maiji," Nanda said, her hands folded in respect, "this is Surili madam from Mumbai. She is staying in our village for some work. Today, she has a terrible headache. Please do something."

Maiji looked at Surili, who was a bit taken aback by her appearance. Maiji was not a very old, shrivelled-up woman as she had imagined. She looked just about in her early thirties. Surili couldn't guess clearly as her skin was painted with vibrant reds and yellows. Her eyes were heavily kohled and her long oily hair were split into numerous thin plaits. Her bright yellow sari was tucked under her legs in the lavani style. She was wearing a lot of bangles on her wrists, and her neck was full of beads of all shapes and colours. The white of her eyes stared back starkly at Surili. She held a rosary in her fingers and mumbled something constantly as she sized up her new visitor.

Nanda sat at the door, waiting for Maiji to respond. The woman gestured to them to come in.

The interiors of the hut were cool and soothing. It was quite dark inside. Once her eyes got used to the dimness, Surili noticed that there was a cot in one corner and a mud stove in another. Some huge copper utensils were properly stacked near the stove and jars of eatables were placed on the shelves nearby. A faint aroma of incense sticks lingered in the air. Surili held her head, wincing in pain.

Maiji gave her a stiff, assessing look and came closer. She touched her chin and pushed her face up slightly, reading something only she knew. A few seconds later, she disappeared behind a curtain which led to an adjoining room. After about ten minutes, she reappeared. She held a glass of water that she offered to the patient. Surili looked at the contents sceptically. The water was chalky. She looked at Nanda who gestured to her to drink it without questioning. Surili hesitated. She kept the glass down. *How can I do this,* thought she. The pain notwithstanding, Surili was reluctant to be led into what she considered a humbug treatment.

Surili was shaken out of her thoughts by Maiji's mumbling. The witch doctor had picked up a small broom and was chanting intensely as she sat on her knees in the centre of the room and swayed her head from side to side. As her performance scaled up, so did Surili's pain. Maiji had now inched closer to Surili. When she was at arm's length, she placed the broom on Surili's head and became quiet. A moment later, she got up and stood at a distance, staring at Surili.

Nanda was asking her to pick up the drink. Surili didn't know what to do. Her headache was making her faint now. Desperate for relief she was blind to all logic and rationale, and in a split second of confusion, she raised the glass and drank the concoction. It was quite sour. Moreover, the taste was familiar. Before she could register anything beyond that, the bell outside rang.

Maiji hurried to the door. As soon as she opened it, a young girl, barely in her teens, rushed in with a one-year-old child in her arms. The child was on a shrieking spree and the more he yelled, the more his mother panicked. The more she panicked, the more he screamed.

The girl was talking to Maiji animatedly, tears in her eyes. Surili couldn't understand what she was saying but knew that it was the local dialect. Maiji kept chanting seriously as she nodded.

Maiji took the child in her arms and moved behind the curtain. The child kept howling for a few minutes more, after which his cries waned. Another five minutes later, Maiji came out with the child sleeping peacefully in her arms. The mother fell at her feet and kept mumbling something weird. Maiji handed over the child and blessed him with her outstretched hands.

Surili watched the proceedings with fascination. This was such a different world, so unreal. She couldn't believe that this was the same twenty-first-century world she inhabited.

Then, all of a sudden, Surili realised that her headache had subsided considerably. Only a numb throbbing remained and the relief made her aware of how tired she felt. She got up lazily and thanked Maiji in Hindi. Maiji only raised both her hands in blessing.

Surili went away with Nanda.

At night, she made notes on her laptop about Maiji. The fact that she had cured her headache bothered her sceptic self. Surili felt she had to get to the bottom of this. She dozed off soon after.

*

One week had passed since her arrival in the village. The next few days were a rerun of the same routine. Surili would wander around the village with Nanda and stop where her curiosity got the better of her. She made notes, took pictures, observed and internalised. Often, they would pass by the base of Maiji's hill and Surili could feel a strong desire to go up again and unearth what she felt didn't meet the eye. Seconds later, she would discard the thought and move on.

There were moments when she missed Anish terribly. But her mobile was not within network range here. The only connection she had was with Mr Goenka through the sole phone in the village head's house and she was uncomfortable calling Anish from there. In any case, something stopped her from within. She didn't want to rake up that issue between them again.

Surili had called up the NGO representative, requesting her migraine medicine from the nearest town. He had got it delivered in two days. Keeping them in her bag, Surili couldn't help thinking about Maiji. She wanted to discover more about this bizarre character but knew she had to be careful.

During one of her journeys through the village, Surili came to the bottom of the hill once again. Nanda wasn't with her that day. Her monthly curse, as she called it, disallowed her to see the sun. Surili gazed at the hut for a few minutes. Surili could not get the curtain behind which Maiji had disappeared twice out of her mind. Something told her that the room behind that curtain was the key to her mystery. She began climbing.

When she was near the hut, she noticed a huge boulder at its side, under a big shady tree. Surili went up and sat on the rock. She knew she would have to wait for the woman to go out before she could venture in. Surili sat there for about an hour before she heard a rustling. Somebody was opening the door. Surili ducked behind the rock and waited. She heard footsteps. They sounded as though they were going downhill as they faded. When they had died down completely, Surili came out of hiding and rushed to the hut.

Once her eyes had got used to the semi-darkness inside, Surili's attention went to the curtain. It was a bright red cloth, as if asking her to stop right there. Surili took a deep breath and stepped straight towards the room behind the curtain. Her heart was thumping loud. There was a window in the room but right now it was covered by thatched panes. Sunlight was creeping in from the edges and that helped her move towards it. Surili opened it slightly. In the light that crept in, she turned and looked around.

It was a much smaller room than the outer one. It appeared busier, with various pieces of old furniture lined up against two walls. Most of this furniture comprised chests of drawers, with the exception of a wooden bench and a pot of water sitting in one corner. The bench was wide enough to hold one person, with a pillow at one end. There were spoons and pieces of cloth neatly wrapped on a small table near the pot.

Surili moved towards one of the drawer sets and opened one gingerly. Inside were a couple of yellowed catalogues and an old pharmacy book. The catalogue listed various drugs, their common names and their uses. She felt vindicated. *I knew something was wrong,* she thought. Egged on by her small discovery, Surili opened another drawer, and to her amazement, she found bottles stacked inside in neat rows. There were hordes of them, in various shapes and sizes.

Surili looked behind her. She would have to hurry. Maiji could be back any minute. She picked up one bottle and another and then another. She scanned the labels. Each bottle was filled with tablets and pills and capsules and the labels were nothing but names of common allopathic drugs. A mixed feeling of anger and fear swept over Surili. This woman was a fraud, making a fool of these innocent villagers.

Surili spun around at the sound behind her. She saw Maiji standing inside the room, glaring at her.

"I'm sorry ... I-I had just stopped by to thank you for the other day ... I just got..." Surili fumbled for words.

"Curious?"

Surili attempted a smile. "Yes ... a little bit. You see I'm here..."

"You are a reporter. I know. Rajju told me."

"Rajju?"

"The shopkeeper down the road."

"Oh."

Surili began moving towards the curtain separating the rooms.

As she crossed the door and cut across to the main room, Maiji stopped her. Her eyes were raging.

"Wait."

Surili stopped. Maiji's voice was menacing. Images of cabbages floated through her mind.

"What brings you here like a thief? Tell me. You have no right to intrude in my home like this. Tell me or I will call the villagers here. Then they will decide your fate."

Surili knew she couldn't escape. She decided it was best to be honest. "I want to know why you are making a fool out of these simple people. It's not right."

Maiji looked at her sternly. Her nostrils were puffed with anger. Suddenly, her face softened a bit.

"Sit. I'll get you some tea."

It was a command. Surili did as she was told. Maiji made tea and brought it in earthen cups.

"I do not make a fool out of anyone. I only do so to live my life."

Surili was about to protest when Maiji raised her hand, stopping her from speaking further. She went on.

"My husband died five years ago. My in-laws tortured me day in and out. I suffered for three years till one day..." She stopped for a moment and then proceeded to recount, "One day, Tarabai's husband had high fever. I gave him this antibiotic for three days and he recovered. My in-laws ostracised me, saying I was a witch, but the miracle helped me earn the respect of the villagers. They gave me this space just outside the village and, since then, they have come to me for their health woes."

Surili couldn't help admire the pluck of the woman sitting in front of her. "How do you know what to give which person?"

"I have studied till Class 10. My husband was a medicine supplier. I know some basics. I use that knowledge to survive. I am alive because people here are in awe of me."

Maiji went on to tell her that her real name was Ruma and that she had two brothers in a nearby village who had deserted her after her parents died. She was practically alone.

"Can I ask you something?" Surili asked.

"Yes, you may."

"What did you give me that day?"

Ruma laughed. She took Surili's hand and took her to the other room. Her beads rattled as she opened a drawer and took out a box. She produced a leaf of the most common migraine medicine from inside it.

"This is what I gave you that day. Crushed and dissolved in water, with lime juice squeezed in." Before Surili could respond, Ruma picked up a bottle from the shelves and said, "I gave this to the little child. It's a paediatric sleep inducer. Very mild and very safe. That child was suffering from colic."

"Doesn't anyone know that you are educated and…?"

"No. My husband never told them. We thought my in-laws would be more agreeable to me that way. But it never worked. Later, this very secret became my weapon."

She added, staring at Surili. "You tell me, if this small pretence helps me survive and keep myself happy, what's wrong with that?"

*

Later that night, Surili was awake for a long time, thinking of Ruma, of her instinct to survive and her practical thinking. She was fascinated by her tenacity.

Days went by. Now that Maiji had told her everything, Surili was no longer an unwanted stranger to her. In fact, she would often spend her afternoons at Ruma's, and their camaraderie gradually developed into an empathetic understanding of each other. Surili discovered a soft-hearted woman beneath all the garish attire and found it incredible that such a sensitive heart could disguise itself in such pretence, merely to live life smoothly. One day, Maiji even removed her thick paints and revealed her real face to Surili, who thought she had rather nice features.

Surili also told Maiji about her situation and how she had refused to cooperate with Anish. Ruma just said, "To each his own."

One evening, Surili met Ruma at her hut. Ruma eye's had a glint of sadness. A quiet despondency dwelled on both of them.

"Surili-ji, I have one request."

"Yes, Ruma?"

"Please do not expose me in your story when you go back. If you tell my truth, I'll be ruined. Please. You may ask me for anything in return."

Surili smiled. "I've already promised you. Have faith in me. And you don't have to give me anything in return. I've already gained a lot."

*

It had been a month that Surili had been away. Anish was on tenterhooks. His parents were arriving in an hour. As he paced up and down the station, he thought of Surili. If only Shirley would understand. What would he tell his parents about why she wasn't there? What if they ridiculed him? Why was she doing this to him?

His parents alighted from the train. Ma had tears in her eyes. It had been long.

All the way back home, Anish's mind was racing for excuses. By the time he had reached the flat, he had made up his mind to tell his parents the truth.

He opened the door to the flat. The pressure cooker was whistling in the kitchen.

Surili was waiting in the living room. She greeted her in-laws by touching their feet dutifully. "You must be tired. I'll make some tea for you."

Anish was dumbstruck. There she was, resplendent in a pink silk sari. A thick line of red vermillion adorned her pretty forehead. He was stupefied to see her like this.

Surili proceeded towards the kitchen. At the door, she stopped and turned to look at Anish. He looked at her, grateful and relieved.

Surili put on her naughtiest smile and winked at him. He smiled back.

A HEROINE

What makes one a hero?
The willingness to carry on
When all hope for tomorrow
Seems bleak and life appears undone

Forty-five-year-old Meghna Bhatt watched closely as the nurse tidied her room diligently. She kept each item back in its place dutifully, changed the stale bedsheets and pillow cases and arranged the numerous sheaves and bottles of medicines in an order which only she understood. Her crisp white tunic rustled with each movement, and her hands worked deftly with a precision which was truly professional.

Although her name was beautiful, Noori was not pretty, at least not in the conventional sense, thought Meghna. She was short and slightly plump, with dark but even-toned skin. Her black, naturally permed hair, which was typical of the women from her native state, Kerala, was tied in a tight bun held by tiny pins. But despite her average looks, it was her eyes which stood out. Meghna thought her eyes were mesmerising simply because they held her soul so clearly that it was impossible to ignore their sincerity.

Noori was a kind woman and a very efficient nurse. When Meghna suffered a stroke six months back, she had lost hope completely. That was till Noori came along. Her business-like demeanour and empathy inspired Meghna. Notwithstanding her limp, lifeless legs, Meghna became convinced she could revive herself, thanks to Noori's encouragement. In six months, Meghna had traversed a journey from discomfort to baby-like ease, wherein she gradually surrendered to Noori's supervision of all her needs.

Noori bent to pick a piece of dirty napkin from under the bed. Meghna, seated in her wheelchair just behind her, smiled at her well-endowed hips, covered but prominent under her skirt.

"That's a bountiful butt you have there," she teased her.

Noori straightened up and turned towards her.

"You are naughty," she answered coyly.

Meghna laughed aloud.

"Yup! As naughty as I can be on this damn wheelchair!"

Noori laughed and exclaimed, "I shudder to imagine how much naughtier you would be if you weren't in this damn wheelchair!"

"Oh well!" Meghna sighed.

Noori sensed from her voice that she was beginning to feel low.

She went inside the bathroom to wash her hands. When she emerged from there a few moments later, she took Meghna's hand gently.

"Come, it's time to rest now."

Meghna let her wheel the chair closer to the bed and support her as she slid onto it carefully. Noori lifted Meghna's legs and placed them comfortably and then propped her up with pillows.

"Seriously, Mrs Bhatt, you will be fine in another six months."

Meghna sighed again. "You can call me Meghna, sweetheart!" she said, her eyes twinkling with innocent mischief.

At this point, Meghna's husband entered the room bustling with energy and smiling broadly at her.

"Hi dear," she responded cheerfully. "How did the meeting go?"

"Oh, it was fantastic!" Arjun responded with excitement as he plonked himself next to her and took her hand. Noori left the room quietly.

"The board has decided to promote me to executive vice-president!" Arjun's eyes shone with satisfaction. "Boy, was I waiting for this day!" he added.

Meghna held out her arms. Arjun snuggled up to her. "I am so happy for you," she said to him. "You deserve every bit of this success. Congratulations."

"Thanks, Meghna."

Arjun fell quiet for a moment.

"Arjun?" said Meghna.

Her voice sounded hoarse. He looked at her. Meghna had tears in her eyes. She started to say something, but he put a finger to her lips.

"Let me ... Arjun. It's been hard on you. I mean, managing everything alone ... the house, the children at boarding, your work, everything. I am rendered so useless. I can't lift a finger to help you."

Arjun clicked his tongue. "It's not your fault, Meghna. You were such an active person. Maybe too active. Maybe it's god's way of telling you to slow down, for your own good." Arjun became pensive. "And then, He also knows He can't keep a person like you down for long." He picked the newspaper kept nearby. "I read your column today; fantastic piece. Look at them. They still devour your pieces. They still want you."

"Yup, they sure do, but it's not like before. I mean ... I'm not their *heroine* anymore. I am not the centre of attraction at their parties."

"That's not fair! Hey! You'll be fine, you know that," Arjun remonstrated.

All at once, Meghna switched back to her usual cheer. "Of course, I'll be fine! What do you think?"

Arjun laughed. "That's better." Rising, he added, "I'll look into the dinner scene now."

*

The physiotherapist Sanjay Mane arrived punctually in the morning. The ordeal of exercises was gruelling, but Meghna, the fighter that she was, had begun looking forward to these sessions. The belief that her discipline and commitment towards improvement would pay off eventually was enough to get her involved sincerely.

"Good morning, Mrs Bhatt. All set for today?" Sanjay greeted her as he came in.

"Good morning, buddy!" replied Meghna with forced enthusiasm. "Can't wait to begin!"

Noori shut the door of the bedroom and joined Sanjay in assisting Meghna. Together, they lifted and shifted her, stretched her legs, wriggled her toes, raised her thighs and bent her knees. With every second of effort, Meghna concentrated her strength towards each motion, her valiant attempts underlined silently by fervent prayers. Half an hour later, Sanjay gave her a break of ten minutes.

Noori fetched Meghna a glass of water. As she gulped it down gratefully, she wiped the perspiration off her forehead with a towel. Suddenly, she pushed Noori's hand away.

She looked down at her feet and then at Noori. Then back at Sanjay. And then again at her feet.

"Sanjay! Something happened!" she exclaimed.

Sanjay came to her and knelt down.

"Where?" he asked Meghna.

"This ... this second toe from the thumb, there ... again ... it's ... it's like a pin pricking me."

"Are you sure, Mrs Bhatt?"

"Yup, man! Sure as hell!" Meghna's eyes sparkled.

Sanjay broke into a grin. "That's a good sign then, Mrs Bhatt. That's a good one. You'll have to visit the hospital tomorrow for some tests. And now, let's get back to work fast."

For the remaining half hour, they toiled again, except that this time, Meghna carried a higher flame of new-found hope in her heart.

That night, when Arjun heard the news, kissed her goodnight and was gone, Meghna lay back in bed and lived a moment of victory after days of defeat. The exhilaration was cautious but nevertheless she felt a lightness of spirit after many a burdensome day.

The hospital visit confirmed what Meghna had felt. Sensation was returning partially in some nerves, though progress was anticipated to be slow and unsure. The news served to enhance Arjun and Meghna's happiness.

The days and nights that followed were lit with a nascent spark in Meghna's life. The driving motivation to get better inspired her to write more than she ever had in the previous six months. The thoughts for her column were fed voraciously by the burning fire to reach out and grab life with both hands. Meghna practised her exercises several times a day like an enthusiastic child. With each session of therapy, the strength in her revived.

The life in her toes surfaced first. Her legs were still listless but like Sanjay said, the benefit would slowly percolate upward to other muscles.

A month later, Meghna was walking a couple of steps with support. Arjun often arrived home early and found that Noori had helped Meghna walk to the terrace. She sat on the cane chair reading the newspaper, her wheelchair abandoned a little away from the sitting area. Arjun and Meghna then sipped their tea together, watching the sun go down, just like old days.

One evening, Meghna was particularly tired. Arjun was going to be late from work, so Noori served her an early dinner and settled her in bed. Meghna slipped into a drowsy wakefulness. After a while, Noori arrived with her evening sponge. She proceeded to take off her shirt and pyjamas and then peeled off her inner wear. In her sleepiness, Meghna watched her passively. As she moved the wet sponge in circular motion on her skin, a tingle waved over her, making her self-conscious. Meghna realised just how much she had come to rely on this woman. She lay there before her, naked, vulnerable, being cleaned and wiped thoroughly like a helpless child. Noori assisted her in getting dressed and took away the water and sponge. When she came back, she had her night medicines on a tray.

"You never leave my side, do you?" Meghna laughed. "You're like my shadow."

"You should get well fast and move on with life. That is my wish," she said.

Meghna gave her an affectionate look.

"Thank you, Noori. Thank you very much."

She slept like a baby that night.

The following morning was beautiful. The air was crisp and clear, the sun was at its vibrant best and the birds outside Meghna's window were chattering with unusual energy. Meghna opened her eyes and looked around. Noori was already up and dressed in her tunic, her hair tucked neatly at her neck. She turned to face her.

"Good morning, Mrs Bhatt."

Meghna mumbled a greeting in return. She lifted her upper body and sat on the bed.

"Noori, today, I'll try and walk to the bathroom on my own. Please give me the walker."

Noori brought the walker close to her and spontaneously extended her hand to help, but Meghna shook her head. "No, let me. I can do that much now."

Noori stood at a distance and watched. Meghna strained to bring her legs to the bed's edge and push them down. A few seconds of struggle later, she had managed to slip down, hands on the walker, and stood with her weight on the device.

"I'm like a car which has stood all night. In the morning, the engine needs to idle a bit before warming up," she said, grinning.

For a second, she ascertained how to make the first move. A weird sense of numbness made her feel odd. Slowly shifting her weight onto the right leg, she took a step shakily. A tiny pain shot up her thigh. Gritting her teeth in stubborn determination, Meghna shifted the load to the other foot and moved forward. Noori walked beside her, smiling encouragingly.

The very next moment, as Meghna moved her right foot forward again, the fragmented, painful life she carried in her legs disappeared and she stumbled. Everything around her spun wildly and she fell to the ground, her rubber-like legs giving way.

Noori rushed to her. Holding her under the arms, she helped

her up and half-pulled, half-dragged her listless frame to the bed. She raised her limp legs carefully and made her lie down. Meghna was panting for breath.

"Are you okay? Do you feel anything?" asked Noori, worried.

"Nothing. Noori, I feel nothing." Meghna was in panic.

Noori consoled her. "It's okay, Mrs Bhatt. The sudden strain must have taken a toll on you. Don't worry … don't worry, the strength will come back."

Meghna stared at her, eyes glazed in disappointment.

The next week was fraught with trepidation. Though she tried hard to ward it off, a sinking hopelessness began gripping her. Her will to fight back her debilitating condition waned with each fruitless session of therapy despite Sanjay's encouraging words.

"It's just a question of time," reassured Sanjay.

But all that time did was flow past Meghna, offering her nothing. The days grew into weeks and the weeks into months. Meghna was surrounded perpetually with Noori's devotion, Arjun's undiluted love and Sanjay's professional passion, and to keep up with their unflinching support, she continued her attempts at betterment. But soon, her heroic spirit became but a façade, a mask only she knew she was wearing. Within herself, Meghna was slipping into a tornado which whirled mercilessly, sucking her willpower and persistence. With each passing day, her hope wilted more and more.

During one particular session of physiotherapy, Meghna went through a very tough and demanding schedule. It was as if she was nearing a cliff's edge, and that particular day, she felt closer to the edge than usual. When the mask of bravery became a bit too heavy, Meghna quit the exercise half-heartedly.

"I'm done for today," she said to Sanjay. "I'm tired."

He relented and ended the day's schedule.

What is the point? There won't be any improvement, thought Meghna.

*

The news that Meghna Bhatt had relapsed into her previous condition after a graph of recovery spread to her fraternity of journalists. There were calls, some offering words of hope and others sympathy, some potential help and others just plain enquiries. Meghna took a few calls and avoided the rest. To the ones she responded, her boisterous cheer still sounded the same – undying and stable. But inside, Meghna had this nagging feeling that everyone was waiting to forget her. At this rate, her bylines, quotes and presence in the media would soon cease to exist and she would be a nobody. And anonymity, which she had abhorred all her life, was just waiting around the corner.

"Things will be better in another six months. I'll hang in there; I know I will," she told her editor-in-chief over the phone just the other day. But sometimes, she didn't believe it herself.

December crept in, bringing with it the gentle coolness of morning and evening. It was a Sunday and Arjun had called over some friends for an early dinner. The camaraderie of known, trusted people would make her feel good, he told Meghna.

The evening went off as smoothly as planned. Meghna was at her cheery best and Arjun was thrilled that she was more relaxed than on other days. After the guests departed, he, with Noori's help, tucked Meghna in bed. Noori was instructed to retire early as she was also tired after the evening activity. Arjun gave Meghna her daily sedative and kissed her goodnight before leaving.

Despite the pill, Meghna couldn't sleep. The restlessness she was experiencing tonight was far more disturbing than what she had been through on previous nights. She looked at Noori, who had dozed off on the couch at one end of the room. Her faint snore indicated that she was sufficiently deep in slumber. Meghna pulled herself up with effort and sat, watching the moonlight streaming inside from the window blinds and making beautiful patterns on the floor. The ethereal radiance of the smoky designs stirred pathos in her, which ballooned into a queer depression gripping her badly and threatening to tear her apart. She rested her head back on the pillows and let loose the pain she had contained for so many days and nights.

When the tears were exhausted, Meghna shifted position for comfort. As she did so, her eyes fell on the bottle Arjun had given her a pill from. Noori always kept the sedative in the drawer above the side table, at a height, where she generally stocked her night medicines. Tonight, Arjun had left the pills on the table itself. Meghna picked up the bottle mindlessly and began reading the label. As she read, a thought invaded her fatigue with sudden force.

Yes, thought Meghna, there was no point living this life of sheer helplessness. Hope had dwindled to depression which, in turn, was pushing her towards an easy and inviting option – freedom.

The thought was attractive, luring her like a temptress. The ray of hope it offered blinded any remnant of rationale and sense in the tired Meghna. She tarried as her thoughts momentarily flew to Arjun. She smiled wryly. Arjun would be better off without her.

A new determination set in. Meghna glanced at Noori who had turned over, now facing the wall. She tucked the bottle of pills under her pillow and slipped down to a lying position. Damn! She couldn't reach the water bottle. She lay there for a long time, just savouring being alive for some time.

Dawn broke and Meghna sat up and counted the first rays of the sun which had replaced the moonlight. These would be her last sighting of the rays. The more she thought about ending her life, the more the thought endeared itself to her. The excruciating helplessness would be gone, and she would finally be free.

"Mrs Bhatt, you're awake?" Noori enquired as soon as she rose.

"Yes, Noori. I woke early today. I have been thirsty for water … could you…"

"Oh! Of course. You should have woken me up. Shall I take…" she muttered, handing her the glass.

She took a sip and then tactfully kept the glass close by on the bed. Thankfully, Noori did not notice it.

"No!" interrupted Meghna. "Actually, I don't feel like going to the bathroom right now. Just please bring my basin here. I'll wash my face."

As Noori was filling the basin with water, Meghna took the bottle of pills out from under the pillow and slipped it between her legs, covering them with the blanket adequately.

After the basin went back, Noori began propping up her pillows. For the first time in so many months, Meghna felt irritated with Noori. She was always with her – too much, she thought – and never left her alone even for a second, just as Arjun had instructed her to. For the first time, Meghna found Noori's presence a hindrance rather than a comfort.

"Noori, I don't feel like sponging just now. I want to rest. Why don't you go and attend to your personal chores first and then come back later today to attend to mine?"

"Okay," said Noori and, gathering her towel, she proceeded to the bathroom.

Twenty minutes. That was precisely the time she would be gone, calculated Meghna. Fifteen minutes was what she had to set herself free.

Meghna glanced around quickly. With one hand, she grabbed the day's newspaper Noori had left on the bed for her to read, and with the other, she retrieved the bottle from under the blanket. Quickly, she spread the newspaper so as to give the impression that she was reading. As she unscrewed the bottle's cap, her eyes fell on the glossy supplement that had slipped out from the main folds. Meghna stopped.

There was a photograph of her from last night's dinner as she sat in her wheelchair smiling and talking to her friends. It was a happy photo, or appeared so at least, thought Meghna. The photo was placed in the centre of an article. Meghna kept the bottle down and opened the supplement broadsheet to its full.

It was an article on her, Meghna Bhatt, the esteemed journalist, columnist and lifestyle writer. It was captioned 'A HEROINE OF OUR TIMES'. With trembling hands, Meghna lifted the paper and scanned through the content hungrily. Excitement seeped in and made it impossible for her weary faculties to maintain coherence. The words kept slipping from her sight and concentration. But as she grappled with bits of words here and there, the grey clouds in her head began breaking up.

The article was an account of Meghna's struggle with personal adversity. It was written by a close journalist friend who had been part of the previous night's dinner. It spoke of her tremendous courage, willpower and perseverance in the face of insurmountable odds. Meghna skimmed through the last part that read, "And thus goes the story of our own hero, Meghna Bhatt. Her story is an inspiration to numerous men and women suffering a tragic twist of fate but who have chosen to accept and make the best of god's wonderful gift called life."

Meghna slumped back. A ray of sunshine had crept over the edge of the bed and was barely caressing her feet jutting out from under the blanket. Her skin and flesh refused to feel the warmth, but Meghna was suffused with the invisible surge of hope revisiting her at that moment. Tears of relief flooded over her. Here it was – eight hundred square centimetres of heroism generated by her and acknowledged by the press, recognizing her nameless life. Her quest for new confidence had reached its first milestone.

The tap had stopped running in the bathroom. Meghna could guess Noori would be out at any moment. Quickly, she replaced the cap of the bottle of pills and kept it back on the side table.

Noori emerged from the bathroom. She saw Meghna engrossed in the newspaper.

"Are you okay, Mrs Bhatt?" she asked.

"Yup! Sure am, Noori!" answered Meghna, suddenly peppy. Noori noticed a twinkle in her eye. She smiled.

"You look happy today," she commented.

"So I am!" replied Meghna. Keeping the newspaper down, she added, "Could you please pass me my notebook and pen? I just remembered I need to finish what I was writing last week."

A PERFORMANCE AT LAST

Of course everything is fine
There are no real complaints
For what then does the heart pine?
Do desires still throb ever so faint?

"We're both right here, Appa. Bay number 3, as you said!"

"Yes, beta. I don't see either of you … Let me ask…"

Aashna grabbed the phone from Aditya, who gave her an angry look. He hated when his sister did that.

"Appa, are you at Terminal 1 or Terminal 2?"

Silence.

"Okay, yes, beta," said Rajender, his tone decidedly softer. "Give me five minutes."

Aditya and Aashna rushed back towards the entrance of the terminal to get away from the gentle drizzle that the end of May sometimes brings to Mumbai. An earthy smell filled the air, and they felt a sadness come over them as they were hit with the same thought.

"Should we pick up bhutta on the way?"

Ma loved bhutta in the monsoons. It was the one thing that she had always loved. No doubt Appa had had the same thought as they sat in the car and drove out of the airport.

"Do you want to go home to freshen up?" he asked, adjusting his rear-view mirror to get a good look at Aditya.

"Let's go straight to Ma. We are late enough as it is thanks to the whole parking fiasco."

"There was no fiasco. It just took a few minutes longer. That's all," said Appa.

Aashna knew exactly when the tension in the air was rising and interjected, "Let's just go, Appa, and stop at a bhuttawaala on the way there."

"Was the flight okay?" asked Rajender, addressing his question more to the air than to either of them in particular.

"As good as can be," said Aashna, stretching her legs. She turned up the radio, which was playing the latest Bollywood hit single, '*Ishq Sunehra*'.

"Appa! It's Shanta-di's song!"

A woman's beautiful voice broke through the synthesised rhythm which was interlaced with MC Karim's rap about love flying through the streets and taking over. Of course, the children remembered the woman's voice distinctly. It had echoed through their home several times in the past. Shanta Dandekar had been a student of Rajender's before making her way into commercial music.

Rajender reached out towards the radio and turned it off.

"That girl used to have a golden voice ... until she became a salesgirl," he said, shaking his head in disappointment.

They enjoyed the rest of the ride in silence, with Aditya gazing out of the window, determined to not engage in conversation with his father.

Normally, the drive to Lilavati hospital from Mumbai airport is a rather lovely one in the rain, kissing the coastline before it swings back into reclaimed land. But the spot of beauty in the concrete jungle of Mumbai was lost on them today as they entered the parking lot of the hospital. Even the pitter-patter of the raindrops on the roof of the car had stopped as they neared the entrance. Aditya and Aashna went through the mandatory temperature checks like zombies, and before they knew it, they were in room 627, with their mother looking pale and tired in the bed in front of them. They rushed forward and embraced Rukmini one by one.

Appa waited around, not knowing what to say, but then decided to throw away some of the flowers in the room that had begun to rot.

"Are you starting a florist shop or something, Ma?" asked Aditya jokingly.

"Funny," said Rukmini. Aashna, afraid that she would tear up, said she was going to use the washroom.

"It's okay, beta. I know how it looks."

As Aashna left the room, Aditya instinctively went to his mother's feet and began to press them. It was a ritual every time he visited. After a massive meal of home-cooked biryani, she would oil his hair and he would press her feet. Mother and son would then proceed to sleep like babies. But that wasn't going to be – not this time.

"We brought you fresh bhuttas, Ma." Aditya began to take out the thin blue plastic bag that they had snuck past the guards at the hospital.

"No, beta! Please keep them. The smell of food makes me sick."

"Ma, but..."

"Beta, please," said Rukmini.

"Aditya," Rajender said from behind him, sternly. Every time he heard his name in that tone, Aditya felt something simmer within him. But before he could react, Aashna stepped into the room, as if on cue.

Aditya gave her a glare, an age-old signal between brother and sister. Things were not good. Aashna struggled hard to swallow the lump in her throat. Both of them had known that the chemotherapy wasn't going to be easy, but seeing Rukmini looking so pale hit hard. Appa left the room to give them some time alone with Rukmini.

Waiting a few seconds to make sure that he was out of earshot, Aashna held her mother's hand with some urgency.

"Ma, quickly, we both have to tell you something," she said and gestured to Aditya.

He looked at his sister bewildered. They had barely come in, but despite being younger, she had led the way as she so often did.

Aditya cleared his throat. "Ma, I've quit my job. I haven't come just for the week. I've come back for good."

Rukmini looked at Aditya, almost angrily. Aashna chimed in before she could react.

"Appa doesn't know about this yet. We will tell him after the event tomorrow, and by the way, I'm also here for a while. Rakesh is taking care of the candle business and everything else in the meantime."

Rukmini looked at her children, tears in her eyes. With great effort, she sat up straight in her bed.

"What is wrong with you, bachhas?"

The children looked confused.

"For good? What do you mean for good?" she demanded.

"You know what we mean, Ma," said a confused Aditya.

"Six months; a year at the most! That's what the doctor said. And when I'm gone, what then? You'll go back to Rakesh." She gestured towards Aashna. "And you?" she demanded of Aditya. "Will you be sitting here with Appa? You, with no job, around Dad all day? Is that what you really want?"

"Ma, please, we'll see about it later. I wasn't happy anyway, but I don't want to hear Appa's 'I told you so' right now."

"I don't know what to say to you."

"Ma, we'll figure it out. Let's just get through tomorrow without any drama, but in the meantime, I have a surprise for you."

"What?"

"You'll see."

As Rajender watched from outside the room through the slits of the blinds, his heart felt heavy and a solitary tear flowed down his face.

*

The Rangasharada auditorium in Mumbai's Bandra Reclamation was adorned with modest decorations. To Aditya and Aashna, the faded maroon seats and their elderly occupants appeared like a vista from a world steeped in sepia.

On the stage, the picture that had hung on the walls of their first home in Juhu occupied a solitary table, with a garland around it. Below the table on which it sat was a solitary and rather ancient tanpura. The smell of incense filled the air as one by one, people from the audience came to pay their respects to the framed image of Pandit Ranjit Bedekar and thank his foremost student Pandit Rajender Prabhakar.

An audiovisual film was projected onto a white screen in the middle of the stage. Aditya knew this one all too well. He had put it together, and it had played on every single death anniversary of his father's guruji for the last five years. And then Rajender proceeded to tell everyone that he would be gathering resources and funds to open a school of music in ten years' time, a school where underprivileged students would be able to learn Hindustani classical music without having to pay for it.

The speech was short by design. Rajender knew that his wife Rukmini wouldn't be very comfortable and would need a rest after the harrowing chemotherapy of the day before.

But it wasn't short enough.

Rukmini began to feel queasy halfway through the speech and tried to steady herself and focus on not feeling sick. Aashna was quick to gauge the situation and took her mother outside the auditorium. Aditya watched as Rajender barely reacted and continued to wrap up his speech quicker than he had planned. Aashna came back into the auditorium to give him a thumbs-up, and Rajender proceeded with the rest of the ceremonies as planned.

Wow, as if nothing happened, thought Aditya.

*

Back home, Aashna fetched Rukmini her anti-nausea medication. The bag of food from the hospital still had the bhutta in it, and with a sad heart, she threw it away.

Rajender began to take Rukmini's shoes off before Aditya stopped him and took over.

"It's alright, we will manage."

"There's no need to be rude. We are all trying to help," said Rajender.

Despite Rukmini's own discomfort, she knew exactly when things were about to boil over between father and son.

"Beta, please."

"Please what, Ma? What happened when you had to leave in the middle like that? I don't think he even noticed from the stage."

"Adi, come on. Not cool," said Aashna.

"No, no, it's fine. It's completely 'cool', Aashu," said Appa. He took off his Nehru jacket and kept it on the hanger. "It's been two days ... and you have not lashed out at me, so might as well come out with it."

"Yeah, Dad, sure. Like I'm the one who starts it."

"What do you want me to say or do? You think life just stops here when you go back to your job and your city?"

"What do you care, Appa? What the hell have you ever cared about? It's just your music, your students, your riyaz, your recording. You don't give a damn about my job or anything. You're the only thing in your life you respect."

"That's not true, Aditya, and you know it," said Rukmini.

"Really, Ma? Really? When was the last time you sang freely in the house? Does Appa even know about your secret compositions?"

Rajender stared at the two of them blankly. Aashna looked clueless, while Rukmini let out a sigh. It was going to come out sooner or later, and she lay back in the bed, resigning herself to it.

Appa sat down slowly. This was a can of worms they hadn't opened in a long time. Aashna was too young to remember; Aditya had grown up waking up to the sounds of Rukmini's voice stealthily singing the lyrics of Abba and the Bee Gees, while sounds from the living room wafted in of Rajender and his students. For years, the sound of the tanpura had been a constant in the house, mixed with the bold Western vocals that Rukmini seemed to belt out only for her son's ears.

Slowly, the metronome and Appa's heavy vocals had taken over her voice completely. By the time Aashna had come around, Rukmini's voice was confined to humming to her in her sleep.

But it wasn't always like that. Once upon a lifetime ago, she had been the voice behind radio jingles, biscuit commercials and many other advertisements. Television commercials were booming in the 1980s and Rukmini had been at the right place the right time.

And that's when she met Rajender. At a recording session where she was hosting the morning radio talk show, she introduced a shy young man who had come in with his tanpura for a short singing performance in honour of his Guruji's tenth death anniversary.

That was exactly thirty years ago.

It had been a match of chalk and cheese. She was westernised, outspoken and confident, while he was a quiet and diligent practitioner of his craft. And she respected him immensely because she had always dreamt of being a singer.

But love has a funny way of expressing itself for an artist, for Rukmini discovered slowly that the ones the guru cares about the most are often the receivers of the harshest of criticism. The love of a guru is not for the faint of heart.

And so, slowly, she stopped learning from him. Love him immensely, she did, but be his pupil, she never could. It was one or the other, and before she could decide, life had made a decision for her.

She had become pregnant with Aditya. The rest of it seemed a blur. A beautiful blur for the most part but often outlined with mysterious pangs of what might have been if . . . she didn't know what.

*

"You have been writing poems? Why did you feel the need to hide this from me?" asked Rajender.

"How could I not, Rajender? You were always critical of everything I did – my voice, the way I don't wake up at five a.m. and practise like you or pray to my instruments. If music or art had a place in the house, it was always your way and on your terms, else it wasn't worth respecting."

"Yeah, why would you anyway? Your students worship you because they don't know how you treat us," interjected Aditya.

"Adi, will you just shut up?" said Aashna, pinching her brother.

"And what is wrong with the way I treat you? Have I stopped you from doing anything you want?" Rajender said.

"So what? You have always been clear about how little you respect it or me?" Aditya shot back.

"How does it matter how I feel about it? Of course, I wanted you to pursue music and learn from me. How do you think I will feel if tomorrow I hear a recording of one of my students and my son is doing a sound check for them? Cueing them with a one ... two..."

"Well, maybe I would have pursued it if you hadn't been such a hard ass about it."

Aashna interjected, "Adi, dude no, enough."

"It doesn't matter now anyway."

"Why?"

Aditya pulled out his phone and opened his email, showing it to all of them. It was a confirmation of a recording session booked at the studio for the very next day. Rajender looked at them bewildered.

"How? I mean, how are you going to do all this?" asked Rajender, turning towards his wife. He looked concerned, staring at Rukmini closing her eyes for relief. "Why, Roxy, why? We're counting days and weeks here, and you want to spend your time with this?"

It had been years since he had called her by the name she was known as an RJ.

"That is exactly why, Rajender. It's been my lifelong dream to record something, and if it's six months, I don't have much time before my strength starts failing me."

"I'm going to record Mom's poems tomorrow, dad. Whether you like it or not," said Aditya before storming off.

*

These days, there were good days and bad days for Rukmini.

Today wasn't a good one. Barely retaining any of her food from the previous day, she felt particularly weak. Aashna and Aditya took out the wheelchair from the storage section.

"Dad said it was needed just once a week ago ... it needed to be dusted before it was used. But not now. It's almost every other day."

"Hmmm," said Aditya.

"Do we really have to do this, bro? I mean, if it's just a recording, can't we do it at home?"

"It isn't about what is sensible, Aashu, all of us have already given up hope. Mom needs this to happen in the way it would have if it were a professional thing – totally legit. We can't half-arse it."

"Yeah, but..."

"Dude, she needs this, trust me."

*

Studio Shankh in Bandra is a real overload for the senses. The front door is adorned by a massive painting divided into nine equal frames, one for each of the rasas. The whole door is lined with a gold film to give it an ornate look. It's a feast for the senses as one enters through it, like it is a realm of performance, and nothing short of perfection will do.

This was, of course, in stark contrast to the hoodie and trainers that Aditya and Aashna rocked up in. Rukmini sat in her wheelchair as her two children wheeled her in. It had been a long, long time since she had seen the inside of a studio.

Held close to her was a bag of her notebooks. She hadn't been able to sleep all night out of excitement, carefully going over and choosing from years of scrambled rhymes and poems and wondering which ones she would choose to record first. She didn't know how long she could last.

"Warm water, Mom?" said Aditya as he got her a glass.

"What's that smell?" asked Aashna.

The room they were seated in reeked of something that Aditya had almost grown too accustomed to, to notice.

"Pepper, for the warm water, and sweat. Still can't have the air conditioner on while recording, so there's a lot built up here."

"Yuck. How is Mom?"

"Mom will be fine. This is what she did all her life before you two decided to show up, remember?" chimed in Rukmini over the monitors.

She had already settled into position and moved the microphone down to her level as she rested her wheelchair against the soundproof padding on the walls.

As Aditya settled into the chair on the other side of the glass, he gave her a cue.

"Awake, beat the drums of my heart with the dreams in your mind … Be the shadow to my light, the anger to my kind … watch me burn like a fire that shines through the night … but it will never be as bright, never once survive the fight…"

Aditya listened intently as Rukmini hummed and tried, but there was simply no energy behind her powerful words.

She tried again and again, and yet it seemed like a simple reading. It was sad for him to watch … he had heard so many of her recordings. This was not the voice that the whole city used to look forward to starting their day with. Aashna watched through the glass, smiling at her mother and egging her on.

And then they were interrupted by a knock – a rather loud one. It was completely against etiquette.

"Bloody noobs," muttered Aditya.

But it wasn't a noob. It was Appa.

Rajender stood at the door along with a large black case. It was his tanpura.

"Dad?" said a confused Aashna.

Rajender didn't respond. He simply proceeded to open the door to the recording booth and arranged his cushions on the floor, unpacking his tanpura and bringing it inside with him.

But he wasn't done yet.

He unpacked his little leather briefcase, and in it were photos, memories.

Their wedding, 1994.

Aditya's birth, 1998.

Aashna's first steps, 2002.

Carefully, he proceeded to place them in the small recording booth, all in Rukmini's direct eye line.

He still hadn't said a word. He dragged his cushions and his tanpura closer to her and held her hand. Aditya and Aashna almost felt like they were witnessing something alien. Rukmini paused, not knowing what to say or do.

"You can do this, my love. Just listen to the notes and breathe."

There was something majestic about the sound of the tanpura as it filled the room with every note. Aditya and Aashna sat up just a little bit straighter in reverence to the instrument they had heard all through their childhood.

"Awake..."

Rajender changed his key to match with the note of her voice.

"Beat the drums of my heart with the dreams in your mind..."

With every loud syllable, Rajender plucked the tanpura with increasing volume.

Even Aditya, who had earlier been dispassionate and focusing on capturing all the sound correctly, stopped to take notice. The air was thick with a tension that Rukmini's unassisted vocals just couldn't match.

And there she was, as if transported thirty years back in time – the last time that they were in a studio together.

Husband and wife, in perfect harmony.

"Watch me burn like a fire that shines through the night ... but it will never be as bright, never once survive the fight..."

An hour later, Rukmini was exhausted, but gone was the pale skin. She was glowing. Rajender packed up the photographs and his tanpura, and removed one last item from his bag for Rukmini, her shoes.

The wheelchair was left behind in the car as an exhausted Rukmini walked out of the studio. Aditya was speechless. He had never seen his parents perform together.

"Where to now, Ma?"

"Well, it's raining and we're outside. Bhutta, of course!" she said.

A PRAYER IS ANSWERED

She hated uncertainty
And loved to plan
So she chose to be certain
As only the certain can

The formalities of checking in at the airport were finally complete. Shikha handed over her boarding card to Uday and walked towards her aunt, Radha. Her eyes met Radha's, only to well up one more time.

Yes, tears were certainly in order. After all, she was a week-old bride leaving her mother's home in Bombay to go and live with her husband, Uday, in Calcutta. Yet these were not ordinary tears of separation. They were tears of the pain of a heavy and real loss – one that was impossible to compensate.

Radha held Shikha in a tight embrace as they both sobbed in unspoken sorrow. Seeing this, Uday walked towards them. Putting his shoulder over Shikha's, he led her away. Radha too tried to regain her composure as she waved them goodbye.

If everything were normal, Shikha would be seen off by her parents, Shoma and Nikhil. And Radha maasi, her mother's sister, would have long been back at her own home after the wedding.

But Shikha's mother was still in shock and in no position to see off her daughter and new son-in-law. So the task had fallen on the aunt's shoulders.

As Radha drove out of the airport and onto the highway, she thought for the umpteenth time of the recent bizarre events in her sister's family.

The month had started on a note of celebration. Shoma's daughter was to wed Uday, while her son, Anmol, had come down to Bombay after his final exams, bringing along a Welsh girl named Casia. The two had been living together for the past two years, and now Anmol wished to seek his parents' approval to marry her. His family had all heard so much about her in his letters and looked forward to meeting her.

One conversation with the girl and Anmol's liberal parents had approved, for they knew that with her lay their son's happiness. In fact, they wanted to formally bring Casia into the family fold by getting the two of them engaged on the day of Shikha and Uday's wedding. After this, Anmol and Casia planned to return to Canada.

And so the first fortnight of the month had been very happy and eventful. It was a family reunion with two welcome additions. What more could Shoma and Nikhil ask for?

The days flew by – shopping in the mornings, snacking and chatting in the afternoons and partying in the evenings. Each night, after the parents finally retired to their room, the thought dominant in their minds would be that the house would soon be empty of cheerful clatter and banter and that they would be alone again. Shoma would sometimes sigh wistfully at the possibility. At such times, Nikhil would reassure her with a hug. "We'll celebrate our second honeymoon – this time without any worries about the future. After all, having brought up the children to be self-sufficient, we've earned the right to indulge ourselves."

Sometimes it would work the other way round. Nikhil would sigh about their impending loneliness. Then Shoma would cheer him up. She would remind him of their plans to finally do all the adventurous things they had both wanted to do together through the years but hadn't been able to because of the constraints of domesticity. Reading, birdwatching, photography – oh, there was plenty to look forward to. Thus reassured, Nikhil and Shoma would sleep content and awake enthusiastic the next morning to make the most of the happiness-filled day ahead.

Finally, the day of the wedding dawned. The house was filled with relatives and friends who had come to participate in the rituals involved in Uday and Shikha's wedding and Anmol and Casia's engagement.

As Nikhil and Shoma held hands amidst the chanting of mantras that sanctified the two unions, their thoughts went back to their own wedding day. To them, it seemed only yesterday that they had been thus united and yet they had come so far together. It was a humbling thought that they had traversed such a long path without having encountered any major hurdles...

A happy week passed by in the euphoria that followed this day. On the seventh night, Anmol and Casia were to leave for Canada. They had an early-morning flight to catch and were all packed and ready at 11 p.m. Everyone had stayed awake to wish them goodbye and Nikhil and Shoma were to drive them to the airport.

And then it happened.

Just as Nikhil revved up the car, he grimaced. He clutched his chest as beads of sweat appeared from nowhere on his temples and his right hand pulled out the key from the ignition, only to fall back limp on his thigh.

Uday and Anmol lost no time in rushing him to the hospital. But it was too late. Nikhil had succumbed to his first, and only, heart attack.

Dying of excitement and happiness? Yes, it was a strange but real probability, the doctors had explained to the stunned relatives.

Days followed that were as long as years. What does one make of life when a fortnight of great joy and ecstasy gives way to one of deep pain and mourning? Shoma did not know and did not want to know either. For nothing, absolutely nothing, mattered to her any more. She was going to be the worst affected by the tragedy, for the children were on the threshold of new lives and would be able to get on, with perhaps a dull ache remaining in their hearts at the loss of their dear father. But Shoma would be haunted forever by the month that had just concluded. Especially by the one moment that had changed her life and her future irrevocably.

The children had been very concerned. Both Shikha and Anmol had pleaded with her to stay over with either of them and not be left behind alone in Bombay. But Shoma had refused their offers and tried to put up a brave front by assuring them that she would be able to manage.

And so, albeit with heavy hearts, the two young couples prepared to leave. Yesterday, Anmol and Casia departed, and today, Shikha and Uday too had left. Only Shoma remained in that once-full house, with just her memories for company.

Thinking of her sister, Radha felt her heart ache as she drove on. Soon, she too would have to go back to her husband and children in Bangalore, leaving Shoma behind. The latter had turned down her suggestion to come to Bangalore for a while, let alone consider settling there for good.

Radha slowed down and parked the car at the kerb close to the beach, gathering her thoughts while still strapped in the driving seat. She couldn't even begin to find a solution to Shoma's predicament. How would she cope with this blow of fate ... this every person's nightmare, a life alone, come true? It would be a life awaiting death, especially after having imagined that life as a second honeymoon. She was scared for Shoma. What if ... what if Shoma tried to kill herself?

Indeed, her sister turning suicidal was a very real and tangible fear. Radha felt faint with these dark thoughts swirling in her mind. She got out of the car to get some fresh air and started walking towards the beach. Radha imagined Shoma spending the future in the throes of utter loneliness and shuddered. She too would be thinking of suicide if she were abandoned this way, she realised.

Radha tried to control the course her mind was taking but felt powerless against the tide of thoughts. Ravi dead, the children settled elsewhere and she, all by herself... The food in her stomach now surged up her gullet, with her clammy hands limp by the sides as she walked on. Her eyes shut themselves tight in fervent prayer.

"No, God, no! Don't ever make me have to go through this, please. I want to go from this world knowing that all my loved ones are alive, healthy and happy. Please, God, don't let me have to see what Shoma has had to. You can call me to your abode anytime and I will be ready. Anytime, God. I promise. I will. Anytime..." She uttered the prayer again and again as she walked further and further into the rushing waters of the sea, not realising just how far her anxious and racing mind had taken her.

By now, she was soaking wet, with the water having come up to her waist. The swirling currents pulled her into them with an indomitable ferocity. Her feet swiftly lost their ground in the abyss, and the waves rushed above her head. Water, water everywhere ... She struggled to breathe. A few gasps, bubbles and splashes later, the waters were calm again.

God had answered her prayer.

A RACE AGAINST TIME

She died a little every day
But before death came as an end
She wanted it her way
She would neither break nor bend

Sunlight streamed into the room through the small window high up in the wall, holding in its shaft countless dust particles in an exquisite display of energetic dancing. Kantaben, all of eighty-one and with double the number of wrinkles, sat huddled on the worn-out antique resting chair, at the base of that golden warmth. Her diminutive figure peered over the newspaper in her shaky hands, keeping it close to her bespectacled face, as if she would devour what she couldn't read.

"Chanda, where is that public advertisement you were reading to me yesterday? I can't find it," she raised her voice as much as her aged chords allowed her to.

Chanda, her housekeeper and companion of sorts, entered the room with a grey duster and began wiping the furniture and several knick-knacks adorning the shelves there. She hummed a nondescript tune.

Kantaben was impatient. "Tell me quickly, baba, I want to read it again."

Chanda continued dusting but deigned to respond. "You mean you want *me* to read it again for you. Amma, I've read it ten times since yesterday. Please, what is so special about that announcement? Why don't you let me finish the housework on time? You don't want a late lunch, do you?"

This namesake conversation, like everything else in Kantaben's life, was a routine. Every morning, Chanda would help the old lady with her morning rituals, bring her a cup of tea and attend to her like a robot. Then she would proceed to her daily chores, punctuated by her mistress' demands and stories of yesteryears. Today was no different.

"If my eyes were better, I wouldn't ask you to read for me. Arre, I had such wonderful eyesight even till about five years ago. But god curse them, they ditched me ever since that cataract operation went wrong," said she.

Chanda was back in the room by now. Her face had softened a bit.

"Why only my eyes. Even my back was as straight as a young girl's till I was sixty-five. Age has not weakened my bones so badly, uh? Oh yes, I was always a strong woman. And all because I was such a good athlete at school. You know, Chanda, my teachers always praised me for running so well. Nobody could beat me. I could fly with the wind."

Chanda looked at her mistress intently. She saw the customary moistness in those old eyes which appeared every time memory lane was traversed. Now, she moved closer and sat at her feet. Kantaben couldn't stop lamenting.

"If Pappa had not insisted on me marrying Jaikishen at seventeen, I would probably have gone on to be an Olympic champion." She sighed wearily. "If only..."

Chanda knew this history by heart. She had heard it a million times. Every time Kantaben began delving into this golden part of her life, her voice had a faraway quality to it.

Kantaben was back to being a young girl of seventeen. "First the district level, then the state and then at the nationals. It was a clean sweep. Chanda, then one day I ran to Ba with the newspaper in my hands. Ba was so proud of me when she saw my photograph in it." Her eyes sparkled as she spoke. "Being selected for the pre-Olympics was such a dream … especially for a girl. But look at me today, would anyone even believe that this was true. Would anyone care for an old woman like this?" Kantaben raised her sagging arms half up in the air with emphasis.

Chanda, who always listened well for the first part of this story, often snapped out of her patience when Amma came to this momentous memory, more because she somehow couldn't relate to Kantaben and the Olympics in the same breath.

"Amma, I know you could have done wonders. I'm sure. But now, it is time for you to rest. Come on, go and lie down. I'll get your medicines," she said, as she extended her hand to help Kantaben rise from the chair.

Kantaben mumbled something as she walked slowly towards the huge four-poster bed, the only grand thing in the ancient room. Chanda brought her water and her daily pills. After gulping them down, Kantaben lay down on the brown flower-printed sheet. As she rested her weary head on the thin pillow, she continued muttering.

"I'm telling you, I was the best. You don't believe me, do you? I'll show you that photo one day. I *have* the paper clipping kept somewhere. Let me get my hands on it someday … if only Pappa would have listened to me." Her voice gradually trailed off as Chanda left, and slowly drowned in the clanging sound of dishes coming from the kitchen.

The rest of the day was spent in the usual chores and Chanda reading out the "Mumbai Marathon" advertisement to a fascinated Kantaben another ten times.

The next morning, Chanda prepared Kantaben's tea. *Amma is so naïve,* she thought. *Yet so very gutsy, just like a child.* She had felt a twinge of remorse at having been blunt with her the previous day. To make up, she had woken up ten minutes earlier than usual, to make Amma her special cinnamon tea this morning as soon as she awoke, and without her having to sit up and wait for it.

Cup balanced gingerly in one hand and a plate of Parle-G biscuits in the other, she made her way towards Kantaben's room. As she crossed the old wooden threshold of the bedroom, she stopped. A feeling of panic swept over her.

Amma's bed was empty.

Half an hour later, Mihir Mehta was asking Chanda repeatedly where Kantaben could have gone. Chanda kept sobbing, scared that Mihir sa'ab would blame her and hand her over to the police.

Mihir was Kantaben's younger son. Though he lived a few kilometres away, Kantaben had refused to live with him because she couldn't stand the condescendingly polite attitude of his wife Sumana. Since her elder son was settled in the US, that practically meant that Kantaben would have to be on her own. On Mihir's insistence, Kantaben had agreed to keep domestic help and so Chanda had been brought in for his mother. Mihir was an affectionate son, but quite helplessly caught between his stubborn Ma and manipulative wife. Right now, he was worried. After Chanda had revealed all that she could, Mihir grabbed his car keys and stepped out, his mind racing.

Just then his cellphone rang.

"Switch on the TV and go to Daily News. You won't believe your eyes." Sumana's voice was dripping with sarcastic sweetness.

Now what could that be, thought Mihir, as he went back in and did as he was told. Chanda stopped crying and stared at what he was doing. As soon as Daily News came up on the screen, Mihir stood there, still as a statue.

There, framed by a moving TV camera, was his dear mother Kantaben, walking the Mumbai Marathon at Nariman Point. As the camera focused on her eighty-one-year-old frame, a reporter stopped her and asked animatedly, "And what is *your* name?"

Kantaben was now panting a bit. The reporter helped her sit down on a nearby bench and waited for a response. Kantaben looked straight into the camera like an experienced artist and smiled weakly.

"Kantaben. Kantaben Mehta."

"How old are you?"

"Eighty-one," came the proud reply.

By now, Chanda had forgotten her tears as she watched the TV screen, dumbstruck.

The reporter raised her eyebrows. "Awesome! Eighty-one years and participating in a marathon? What makes you join in at this age?"

Kantaben beamed.

"So what if I'm eighty-one? My spirit is still intact. I was an athlete when in school. I have run for my country as a teenager, and won too. I was going to the Olympics that year ... but my father married me off!"

Kantaben chuckled, shaking her head. "I want all senior citizens to know that we are not as useless as we think we are. We may have ripened in age, but we still have it in us."

It was the reporter's turn to smile. She thanked Kantaben and gave her a hand. She then turned to the camera and as Kantaben walked away, she concluded, "This is probably the best example of the spirit of the never-say-die Mumbaikar. And of just how much aamchi Mumbai is caught up in the marathon fever. This is Sunehri Singh, reporting from Daily News, Mumbai."

Mihir switched off the TV and rushed out.

The sun had climbed the sky and was playing hide and seek with a few grey clouds. Kantaben was having the time of her life. Her sari pallu was tucked neatly at her shrivelled waist. Her feet, housed in her old black pump shoes, were aching, but her heart was full with the exhilaration of the adulation she had just received. Her white hair was soaked in perspiration, beads of sweat trickling down her furrowed wrinkles. She walked on along the side of the road, aware that TV cameras were hovering near her all the time. Every five minutes, she would stop and breathe hard, then resume with renewed gusto. She had walked two kilometres so far, sipping the water provided by volunteers only once. She waved at the cameras now and then.

News of this eighty-one-year-old spirited lady participating in the marathon spread like wildfire. Her claim to the near-Olympics past added fuel to the fire. Residents from nearby chawls and slum colonies streamed towards the main running route to catch a glimpse of this new sporting hero. More TV crew covered her courage on camera, relaying her arduous, yet unusually brave, journey nationally.

Kantaben was famous at last.

Meanwhile, the organizers at Nariman Point were busy tallying some data, handling the press and checking on the arrangements. Jostling his way through a group of people, Mihir rushed up to them and spluttered, "Where is your manager?" He looked at his watch. It was almost noon. The manager promised him that they would locate her on the route and bring her back. He wanted his mother to give up this show. She was too old for all this. As he made a mental note of how he would give her a piece of his mind, his reverie was broken by loud shouts.

A small group of middle-aged women from a feminist NGO were chanting, "Kantaben ki jai! Bharat maata ki jai!"

Just as he was about to approach them and ask them to shut up, a volunteer hurried to him, saying that they had located Kantaben. She was about 7 kilometres away from the starting point. So would Mihir like to come with them? Mihir joined the volunteer on a bike and ambled along the pavement, his eyes searching for his mother desperately.

Kantaben sat on the bench and sipped a little of the glucose water. The kind young girl, clearly a volunteer, was looking at her, concern writ large on her face.

"Mataji, are you okay? You look very tired."

"Of course I'm tired. But it's so much fun, can't you see? Here, take this."

Kantaben handed the paper cup to the girl. With the support of her hands on the bench, she pushed herself up and wiped her face with a disposable tissue offered by the girl. Kantaben pulled herself together to walk on again. The girl wasn't very convinced, but she let her go. Suddenly, two camera crew descended on Kantaben from nowhere and began walking with her. Kantaben was, however, in no mood to pause.

The sun had by now emerged from behind the clouds and was beating down relentlessly. As determined as Kantaben who looked up to the heavens and moved on.

Mihir was just half a kilometre away now. He spotted her white sari and jumped off the bike. He ran towards her with the TV crew which was practically clinging to her every movement.

For a second, Mihir lost sight of her. The crew had blocked his view. He rushed towards her. Pushing his way through the group of people around her, he almost tripped. When he regained balance, he could see her again, a few steps ahead of him. He quickened his steps and reached out to touch her shoulder, calling out sharply and with urgency, "Ma!"

At precisely the same moment, even before she could turn and acknowledge her son, Kantaben swayed dizzily for a second and slumped to the ground, her head hitting the pavement.

She lay still. Completely still.

Mihir froze with horror. He saw several hands picking his mother up. There was commotion and too much noise. He stood there and stared uncomprehending for a moment, before reality dawned.

At the city hospital, Mihir continued staring. Sometimes at the floor, sometimes at the ceiling, as he stood outside the ICU. Chanda sat nearby, tears rolling down her face. Outside the hospital, all the local news channels had their crew stationed to cover this most poignant act of courage by a senior citizen.

"Mihir." A hand on his shoulder made him look up mechanically. It was Dr Dalvi, Kantaben's physician and their family friend, stood next to him. "Are you okay?"

Mihir could only gulp down a lump which had been forming in his throat for long now. He tried and opened his mouth to speak, but the words were lost in a sudden gush of tears. Mihir clutched Dr Dalvi's hand and sobbed like a baby.

"Why didn't you tell her not to? You could have stopped her. She was not fit for such activity. Why didn't you warn her, Dr Dalvi? After all, she saw you every week for a consultation and must have taken your advice as she always did."

"But I did, Mihir. I did warn her."

Mihir looked at him stupefied, but before he could say anything, the attending doctor exited the ICU. Immediately, Mihir's focus shifted to him.

"How is she now, doctor?"

The doctor, a greying man in his late forties shook hands with Dr Dalvi and then turned to Mihir.

"Hmm. She is just about okay. Currently under observation. We will watch her for the next forty-eight hours. And yes, you can meet her briefly. But one by one please." He paused for a second and then turned to Dr Dalvi. "I'd like to discuss a few things with you, doctor. Would you?" He gestured towards his cabin.

As Mihir watched both doctors walk away, Chanda asked him gently, "May I go in first, sa'ab? I am very anxious about Amma, please."

Mihir nodded blankly.

Kantaben looked frail and helpless on the white hospital bed, her hand punctured with a drip needle and her forehead bandaged at one side. Chanda walked to her, taking in the cold, clinical ambience of the quiet ICU. Once near, she placed her hand calmly on Kantaben's shoulder. Kantaben's eyelids opened. Her pale lips stretched out in an equally pale smile.

"You gave me the shock of my life, Amma. For heaven's sake, don't do such a thing again," said Chanda hoarsely, her eyes welling up with tears again.

Kantaben could barely speak. She moved her lips, wincing slightly, but words betrayed her. Chanda told her not to make the effort and sat there holding her hand as she slipped back into a semi-conscious state. A few minutes later, Mihir was beside his mother. Chanda disengaged her hand to leave. But Kantaben, now alerted by this movement, opened her eyes and whispered to her. Chanda bent and brought her ears closer to her.

That evening, Chanda sat on the floor, surrounded by all the books in the house. It was past midnight and her eyes were drooping as she dozed off intermittently between sifting through each book. And then suddenly, she was awake with a jerk. Once she had read the yellowed, brittle newspaper clipping about a young girl of seventeen who was going to the Olympics, she didn't go back to sleep. She took an auto and went to the Daily News office instead.

Next day, at the break of dawn, Mihir met Dr Dalvi in the hospital lobby and together they proceeded to the ICU. Just outside the entrance, they paused.

"So Ma visited you alone that day. I guess she didn't even tell Chanda about it. Neither did she give me the slightest hint," said Mihir.

"Yes, and despite my telling her about her latest reports, she continued demanding permission to participate in the marathon. And I kept saying no, of course. Was there any option? You know what her condition was. I must have told her at least ten times that if she participated, it could prove fatal for her. But how could I imagine that she wouldn't listen to me?"

"But it beats me why she would want to do something so drastic to herself. I mean, I know she always spoke of her unfinished dream … but a marathon? At this age? What is she trying to prove? What does she want?"

"Maybe this, sa'ab," said a voice from behind them.

Mihir and Dr Dalvi turned around to see Chanda standing there, a copy of that day's *Daily News* in her hands, now extended towards them. Mihir took the newspaper from her hand and scanned the first page. His face was a map of awe, as he handed over the paper to Dr Dalvi.

Chanda had never felt such gratification as she experienced when Kantaben looked at the newspaper report carrying her Olympic photo and her marathon story. As her blurred vision rove over the print and deciphered her reprinted Olympic photograph in the day's newspaper, Chanda quietly put Kantaben's glasses back on her eyes. Never before had she seen such a placid expression on her mistress's face. Amma's eyes shone dimly, the hunger in them satiated. As she smiled at Chanda, a lone tear crawled down her cheek onto the pillow. Chanda took her hand and whispered, "You have done it, Amma."

Kantaben smiled and closed her eyes.

Chanda held Amma's hand for five minutes. Then she took her glasses off and called the nurse.

Mihir stood dumfounded at the foot of the ICU bed, watching the nurse pull the sheet over his Ma's eyes. For once, Chanda was not crying. She went up to Mihir and said, "Don't cry, sa'ab. Your mother was brave and she had a glorious end."

Dr Dalvi took Mihir to the hospital canteen and got him a cup of coffee to comfort him. Mihir stared at his coffee, as if it was the genie for all his wishes, and an answer to all his questions. All of a sudden, Mihir, till now lost in thought, looked up at Dalvi.

"Oh my god! Oh my god, Dr Dalvi!" he exclaimed.

Dr Dalvi was startled. "What is it, Mihir?"

Mihir looked at him fearfully, as if some horrid secret had just been unravelled to him.

"How many times did you say Ma asked you what will happen to her if she participated in the marathon?"

"About ten times, Mihir, I could swear, but why do you ask?"

"And you clearly told her that she could collapse and die with the strain if she tried?" Mihir put the newspaper on the table, the feature on Kantaben screaming from it.

"Yes, I did. But…"

Then it dawned on him as it had on Mihir just a few moments ago.

"Yes, Mihir … yes. You are right," he whispered. "She knew well and that was her plan. It would give her release and it would give her the glory that had eluded her ever since she was seventeen."

Both of them stared at the newspaper.

DAWN TO DAWN

Few can resist the pull strong
Of the green grass on the other side
It didn't take her too long
To learn to swim with the tide

I

The pale light of daybreak played upon the stream as she felt the water's gentle ripple tease her hands. The earthen pitcher that Zavia held against the flowing stream was full at last. Droplets of water glowed on the flawless skin of her hands like numerous shining pearls.

She was a beautiful woman. Even more beautiful today with the fullness of youth.

It was the enthusiasm characteristic of the start of a new life. A happiness that came out of performing the most mundane of chores in this new home that she and Jishu had chosen to set up. One that she had prayed for and dreamed of through years of uncertainty. Zavia balanced the pitcher on her waist and, with long strides, wound her way to her haven.

Jishu and she had been in love for nearly five years. But it was only a week ago that they had publicly taken their vows in the temple of Lord Tagamo. She had almost lost hope that their love would ever come to fruition. Maybe Lord Tagamo had at last been moved by her prayers. How else could one explain the sudden turn of events that had made their union possible?

Jishu had been living underground all these years. He was one of the most devoted corporals of Shoonzol, whose name struck terror throughout the length and breadth of their Sinapuri country. But to Jishu and hundreds of people of their Chidlia community, he was no less than a messiah – a man fighting for the rights of the Chidlia minority against the Sinapurians.

The Chidlians had, for generations, sweated and toiled for Sinapuri. They felt no ties with their original homeland – the neighbouring Himastaan. And yet the haughty Sinapurians treated them as second-class citizens.

When Shoonzol visited the Chidlian settlements, it was as though a prophet had decided to walk the earth. Young men paid obeisance at his feet; little children kissed the ground on which he trod. Shoonzol spoke simple words. He spoke of how the Chidlians would have to fight for a life of dignity and equality. They would have to be prepared to sacrifice everything for the sake of the rights of their coming generations.

The Chidlian crowd would listen to him mesmerised. At the end of every such address, dozens of young men would follow Shoonzol to his next halt, as though hypnotised. Zavia had often heard Shoonzol speak. His lofty speeches left her feeling ashamed of her own petty turmoil. Her anguish arose from seeing Jishu so spellbound by him that he would willingly lay down his life for the movement without any thought of her. He would not hear a word against his leader.

It was five years ago that Jishu had formally enrolled himself as a volunteer with Shoonzol's CPLP, the Chidlia People's Liberation Front. And his fervour had not dulled for a moment since then. But a lot had happened otherwise. The Sinapurians had begun to feel the heat of the movement and had started addressing the activists' grievances.

The movement had grown from strength to strength. Now Shoonzol did not mix around with his people as before. He had a battery of volunteers, whom he supervised from within his fort on the Gicha hilltop. He was heavily guarded and rarely seen. But no sooner had he issued the smallest commands than his faithful guerrillas had already carried it out. Jishu had successfully accomplished many missions for his leader, with a single-mindedness that had endeared him to Shoonzol as few others had been.

But about a fortnight ago, there had been a sudden turn of events. Maybe it was the culmination of the prayers of Zavia and those of hundreds like her…

The Himastaani government that had for long been covertly sympathetic to their movement was negotiating with the Sinapurians for the cause of their Childlian brethren. This time, Shoonzol had responded to their overtures. The president of Himastaan had persuaded the Sinapuri government to concede many of the demands of the CPLF.

Shoonzol too probably realised that it would be more practical to compromise. The CPLF had suffered great losses in the last few months. However, a few disgruntled Chidlians, most of whom were influenced by Corporal Huria, started to hint that Shoonzol had compromised their cause. Huria soon fell out with Shoonzol and began building up his own small following among the Chidlians.

Then Shoonzol signed the agreement with the Sinapuri government. Following this, Jishu, like so many of his followers, surrendered his arms and went back to his village. And to Zavia, whom he married a week ago.

II

Jishu had long been awake. But he continued to lie in bed waiting for Zavia to come and wean him away from this delicious stupor. Or join him in it. After all these years of a regimented existence, it was as though a permanent languor had seeped into his system. He wanted to lie like this forever.

"Chikamer," called out a voice. Jishu jumped out of bed. That was the call from Shoonzol's camp. What could have happened?

"The chief wants to see you," said Paru, Shoonzol's messenger.

As Jishu put on his khaki uniform, he looked around the house that they had just started to set up. How bare it was. There was a lot to be done. God alone knew what was going to happen now.

Zavia entered the house with the pitcher on her waist. She was surprised at seeing him dress. Pangs of fear assailed her.

"I have to go, Zavia," he said simply.

Their eyes met. She looked long, hard and hurtfully at him. There were no tears to reflect the storm that was raging within her. She had thought her wounds were healing. Oh Lord Tagamo, was happiness never to be hers.

It was as though this one week had been nothing more than a mirage in the desert. Zavia was soon back to carrying on the business of living. There was her small vegetable garden that had to be looked after, pitchers of water to be filled, and cooking, sweeping and washing to be done … so much work to maintain one tormented soul.

*

It had been a fortnight since Jishu had left. She heard from the villagers that the struggle had been revived. Shoonzol had fallen out with the Sinapuri president who had retaliated by striking with vengeance at their camps.

Paru came to the village every few days with news of Jishu's whereabouts. There he was again today. Zavia looked up from the patch of soil she had been weeding. One look at him and she knew that it was all over for her. The army had surrounded Jishu and his companions who had swallowed cyanide to evade capture.

Zavia stared out of the window into the dark night, as black and silent as her future. There was a sharp knock on the door. In this village stalked by the silence of death, it was as though the sound came from the netherworld. Zavia was afraid for a moment. But then there was nothing to be afraid of anymore, there was nothing more to lose. She dragged her feet to the door.

It was Shoonzol, the chief himself.

The man for whom her beloved had left her. Jishu had probably thought more of him than of her when he decided to end it all, thought Zavia. Shoonzol had won over her.

What did it matter to him, sitting in his safe, remote fort while innocent fools like Jishu died like dogs? She never did trust Shoonzol much. At this moment, she hated his very sight. A wave of repulsion swept over her. The bile in her empty stomach surged up and went down her throat again.

And now? Was she to feel touched that he had personally come to pay her his condolences after having sent Jishu to his death?

Zavia looked away. If it had been any other of the village widows, they would have wept at his feet.

"Jishu was one of the most loyal soldiers our cause ever had. His name will go down in Chidlian history. I'm sorry for you, his young widow. But his loss is as much ours as it is yours," said Shoonzol.

Zavia stood rooted like a statue as he went on.

"I'm making you an offer, Zavia. Think about it," he said. "You could take his place in the CPLF. Because of Jishu and what he meant to us, we know you'll be as loyal as he was if you join us in this struggle. You really loved him, Zavia, so wouldn't it be fitting that you finish the task he left incomplete? Paru will come to see you in a few days for your answer."

III

Zavia looked around cautiously. Shoonzol was deep in sleep. His loud snores reminded her of the grunting pig in her backyard in the village. How hateful he looked!

She stealthily moved the sheet that covered her naked body and stepped out. Dressing as quietly as she could, she looked at Shoonzol's face for any signs of wakefulness. But he slept without care. He trusted her completely.

She rummaged through the pockets of his khaki trouser. There it was. The third receipt of the money he had surreptitiously been accepting from the Sinapurians all these months. This was the last piece of evidence she needed against Shoonzol. Evidence for which she had tormented both body and soul in this past year since she had joined the CPLF. At first, as Shoonzol's corporal, then his trusted aide, and then as his mistress. She was not going to allow Shoonzol to do to other innocent Chidlians what he had done to Jishu. It wasn't for nothing that she had borne the humiliation and depravity of these last few months. It was not for nothing that Jishu had died.

Today she was to meet Huria. He had been in league with her all these months. They had scheduled a secret meeting of CPLF volunteers tonight.

Zavia buttoned up her shirt to the neck and tightened her waist belt. She looked at her watch. It was midnight. The CPLF rebels would have assembled at the Tagamo temple by this time.

If everything went right, the CPLF rebels would surround Gicha fort a little after midnight. Shoonzol would be dead, Huria would have taken his place and the Chidlian struggle would be rid of the traitor. Zavia would then go back to her village and her vegetable garden, and Jishu's soul would rest in peace.

IV

Everything went as per plan. Down to the smallest detail. Shoonzol was taken by surprise by the ambush at Gicha. Snoring like a pig one moment, lying cold in a pool of blood the next.

As the fascinating story of the happenings of the past months spread among the Chidlian populace, mobs gathered outside Gicha fort. There was not an inch of vacant space below when

Huria appeared in the balcony to address the swarming crowds. The CPLF had elected him as their new leader.

He could not speak as well as Shoonzol could. But everyone listened in rapt attention as he spoke about Shoonzol's betrayal and Zavia's sacrifice. Zavia stood by his side. She could see the women in the crowd looking at her with proud, shining eyes. Many wept, overwhelmed with emotion. The garlands thrown at her were collected in a heap on the parapet below.

"Long live Zavia. Lead us, Zavia. Long live Zavia." The cries rent the air loud and clear.

An exhausted Zavia stretched back in the armchair. This was going to be her last night at Gicha. The next morning she would be returning to her village. To a simple and lonely life.

These last few months had changed her so much. Would things ever be the same again? Could they?

Zavia looked around the room that had been her home these last eleven months and observed her khaki uniform, the stiff whipcord, the polished epaulettes, and the bright shining metal of the rifles in their cases. She looked at the stuffed head of the man-eating tigress that Shoonzol had shot a few months ago.

She too had tasted blood. It was as though the tigress was still alive, its eyes beseeching and beckoning her. It had never seemed like this before. And in the eyes of the tigress, she saw hundreds of pairs of proud, shining, brimming eyes. Eyes that said, "Long live Zavia. Lead us, Zavia."

She was not going to lose all this. She would never get it back again. Did she really want to leave it all? For whom and to what end?

Zavia pictured herself on Shoonzol's chair. Surrounded by armed corporals, waited on by hundreds at her beck and call, wooed by leaders, worshipped by Chidlians. A life of glory and romance, power and adventure awaited her, all for the asking. It was now or never.

The early rays of the sun played upon her window. Zavia had finished dressing and Huria's men waited outside the room to escort her downstairs. They wanted to give her a warm send-off after a ceremonial breakfast.

She saw respect and admiration for her on every face in that room. They would never suspect her. Zavia clutched the cyanide pill in her left hand. She started passing around plates of the soft maize bread to the men in the room. It was full of so many nuts that the cyanide pill would not be noticed on Huria's plate. Everyone was busy talking with each other about the happenings of the night that had just passed. It needed only a gentle push for the cyanide pill to get embedded in the slice of bread kept on Huria's plate.

Zavia busied herself pouring water into glasses for everyone to drink. She did not want to look at Huria when it happened. Soon there was commotion all around.

"Huria ... He's collapsed."

V

Zavia stood on the balcony, staring down at the swarming crowds. A perfect picture of the reluctant new leader – the stoic figure's halo resplendent in the early rays of the sun.

"Zavia is our chief. Long live Zavia ... It is the will of God ... Lead us, Zavia ... Zavia is our chief."

FAMILY TIES

The need to belong
Was really too strong
A shortcut echoed in her head
Her happy choice she made

Only Vijayalakshmi Nair knew exactly how difficult this journey had been. She was a hundred per cent certain that none of her twenty-nine graduating batch-mates at Kerala's first business school could ever dream of where she really came from. To them, she was the urbane and cute "Lux" she had so successfully projected herself as in these last two years.

It was all very well to read and admire rags-to-riches stories in the newspapers. But Vijayalakshmi firmly believed that as long as she was a student here, her friends would be both embarrassed and disdainful, and wouldn't accept her as easily if they found out about her background. But yes, one day in the future, Vijayalakshmi would definitely tell her story. Then, she was sure, there would be only admiration for both her and her family, not only from people at large but also from her peers. For it would only be then that they would look at the situation from the right perspective that would come with the passage of time.

Vijayalakshmi knew that such a day was not very far away now. After her graduation ceremony today, she would be leaving for Mumbai right away to take up a job in a multinational company. Then, in a short span of time, she would send for her parents from their village in Thekkady to live with her. She would groom them to presentable levels and then share their story with the world outside.

Vijayalakshmi straightened the collar of her shirt and smoothened the non-existent creases of her jacket. Ten minutes more to go for the ceremony. She took out the photograph of her parents from an envelope kept in the jacket of her diary and looked at it. She had not informed them of the ceremony. She knew they would have come if she had. She would have been happy to see them, but it would also have embarrassed her. She knew everyone would have sniggered at the sight of her father in his dhoti and turban, and her mother in her coarse sari and plastic chappals, her chapped heels in plain sight. The smell of coconut oil from Amma's hair and the sour odour of sweat from Appa's armpits were fragrances that meant the world to her. But here, in a hall full of three-piece-suit-clad fathers and chiffon-sari-clad mothers sporting pearls, they would have been the object of ridicule.

Appa and Amma had always taught her never to judge anyone by his or her outward appearances. She had initially tried not to do so, but they had no idea how much the world today really did. And if, god forbid, it had to judge her parents, she knew that they were too innocent even to understand. She pledged to herself that she would make it up to them – for all their toil and sweat, for the nights they starved, the reaping and harvesting that her father had to do to send her to this school, the tonnes of spices her mother pounded after all the housework was done, just to be able to send her some pocket money. Her eyes brimming over, she stroked the black-and-white picture of her stiffly posing parents and put it back in the envelope.

She made her way to her marked seat in the first row. In the row behind sat the staff and behind them were the twenty-odd parents of the proud graduates. The speeches began in earnest but were disturbed only a few minutes later by some confusion near the entrance.

Vijayalakshmi turned to look. Her heart sank. There stood Appa and Amma, just as she had visualised them only a few minutes earlier as she had stared at their picture in her room. They were convincing the security guard in their native dialect, Tulu, that they had the principal's invitation to be here. The uncomprehending guard looked them up and down and then examined the invitation. He reluctantly signalled them to join the audience, not wanting to disturb the proceedings any further.

All this while, Vijayalakshmi had sat in her seat, frozen. The principal called out her name as the recipient of the best student award for the year. Vijayalakshmi walked with heavy steps to the stage, looking at the audience from the corner of her worrying eyes. Appa and Amma were clapping loudly, their smiles stretching from ear to ear. Vijayalakshmi accepted the award but did not go back to her earlier seat, choosing instead a seat from where she could keep an eye on Appa and Amma.

She settled down carefully, putting her medal into its case and the case into her trouser pocket. Then she discreetly glanced at her parents. Appa and Amma looked uncomfortable as they sensed so many eyes upon them. It also appeared that they had realised that some of the sniggering around had something to do with them. Vijayalakshmi saw Appa whispering something into Amma's ears. She silently prayed that they wouldn't do anything to embarrass her any further.

Vijayalakshmi saw Amma and Appa get up and walk to the entrance. The principal, who had by now come off the podium, went towards them. He looked confused as he said, "You must be Vijayalakshmi's parents?" The forced warmth in his voice was unable to hide the look of slight contempt in his eyes as he appraised them from head to toe. "I had sent a special invitation to Vijayalakshmi's home since she was to receive the best student award," he added.

Vijayalakshmi could sit no more. She almost jumped out of her seat and walked quickly towards the trio. She opened her mouth to explain but the voice of Appa beat her to it.

"No, saar, merely workers in Vijayalakshmi's parents' farm, we are. Vijayalakshmi's Appa and Amma? They are in foreign land. We only came to see her. Now we've seen, very nice, saar, all very nice ... Thank you very much, saar."

Appa folded his hands and led Amma away quickly.

The muffled laughter and squeals of "how cute" and "how touching" in the hall caused Vijayalakshmi's eyes to well up. She was afraid the tears would fall and was too conscious of the many eyes upon her.

"Vijayalakshmi, I think you ought to see them out to the gate. They are such sweet village folk. Just imagine, you're nothing to them and yet they came so far to see you," said the principal, secretly relieved though he was that they were not Vijayalakshmi's parents. "We city folk must learn from them ... These rural people are so large-hearted." He continued shaking his head from side to side. "But you, Vijayalakshmi, where are your manners, my girl? Off you go behind them. Go on, see them off to the gate."

"Yes, sir," said Vijayalakshmi as she followed, with great relief, Appa and Amma.

MOVING ON

You are ready to fly the nest
And I must find a way to deal
With my memories and loss best
And know that time never stands still

I

Rachna stepped into the small living room and lowered her suitcase onto the floor. The air inside felt musty as she took a deep breath and sat herself on the sofa covered with a white sheet. The dust-coated furniture and curtains drawn over closed windows whispered testimony to bygone years. Rachna sat immobilised, her head resting wearily on the sofa back. She found her thoughts wandering towards her children. As if taking a hint, her eyes moved to the framed photograph kept on the corner table. She lunged sideways to pick it up. Bringing it close, she clutched it hard. Gently, she wiped off a thin layer of dust from the glass with her bare hands. It was something for which she always hollered at her maids.

Rahul and Mihika smiled back at her from the frame. *My two angels*, thought Rachna, as her eyes became moist. Today her children had flown the nest. Yesterday, they were all hers. As memories surged, Rachna remained seated on the sofa and shut her eyes.

It had been a splendid morning ten years ago. She had hustled into the bedroom with a bundle of ironed clothes and glanced swiftly at the gift-wrapped object kept on the edge of the bed. Heart fluttering with excitement, she opened the box and cried with joy. "Rohit! Oh Rohit! Thank you so much! This is so very beautiful." Rachna ran out of the room and straight into Rohit's arms, who hugged her as she excitedly continued, "So thoughtful of you, Rohit! Look, Rahul and Mihika are looking so angelic in this. And you've got the framing done superbly. Mmm ... I love you!"

Rohit smiled at her affectionately. "If I had not got this photo framed for one more day, I'm sure you would have kicked me out by evening!" he teased her. They had both burst into a hearty laugh.

That laughter had melted away all the tensions of the previous week, which they had spent bickering with each other. Their quarrels were frequent in those days and often, the children would watch as both got at each other over various issues. As she had clutched at the photo frame, Rachna had felt a sense of comfort, that had been lacking for a while in their relationship, crawling back, leaving her very, very light that day.

Little did she know that the calm was a lull before the storm. Two days later, a tense Rohit had told her that he had to go.

"I'm leaving, Rachna. I need to go."

Rachna was sure she wasn't awake. After the initial shock had seeped in, hysteria took over.

"But why, Rohit? Everything is just so fine ... now!"

"No, Rachna. Everything is *not* okay."

Rachna stared at him. "It's ... it's because of that Priyanka, isn't it? Tell me, Rohit, isn't it?"

Rohit looked at her sadly and said, "No, it's not about Priyanka." And then, after a long pause, he said, "Rachna, believe me, it's about you."

Before leaving the next week, Rohit had said, "I love you, Rachna. I'll always be there for you and the kids. But I can't live with you anymore. Let me go."

Letting go was not easy. Rachna had fought, squirmed, cried and even blackmailed Rohit to bring him back, but he had been adamant. Her world had crashed. A world she had created twenty years ago when she had left her hometown against her parents' wishes to be with Rohit. Life had been tumultuous for some time before things calmed. The children had brought infinite joy overcoming all opposition.

For Rohit, Rachna had been the ideal homemaker and mother. He had always loved her orderliness and penchant for perfection. She was a terrific home manager. His shirts were perennially creaseless, the house always shone like a gem and her hair was never out of place. The children, even when they were babies, were never untidy. Rachna took care of everything, all the time.

Sometimes, Rohit would want her to ease out a bit, but to no avail. Her guilt would kill all the fun and pleasure of taking it easy. A subtle distance crept in between them and before he realised it, her regimented life became too obsessive for the fun-loving Rohit. The next thing he knew, he was filling the nameless vacuum inside with the sunshine and spontaneity that Priyanka offered. He knew his marriage was in trouble when the fights began and he started making quiet comparisons between the two women in his life.

After Rohit left, Rachna was reduced to a potpourri of feelings. If it was love, jealousy, alienation and possessiveness one minute, it was hatred, disillusionment and grief at the loss the next. Rachna finally settled for bitter animosity. And she chose animosity only because it had found her. She kept it alive because it kept her breathing. The more she hated Rohit, the more she managed the strength to survive.

The bitterness she carried only reinforced what Rohit had left her for in the first place. Rachna recoiled and pulled in the children tightly. Her preoccupation with a meticulous life enlarged multifold and spilled over to her children more than before, as if she was trying to guard fiercely whatever was left. Rahul, then nine, and Mihika, five, were too young to protest. Besides, they didn't know any other way of relating to their mom. It was the way Mom had always been, and now, with Dad gone, Mom was their universe. Any attempts to request Dad's presence were met with stiff replies and complaints of how much he had hurt them all by leaving. Before the divorce came through, Rohit called once to speak to the children. Rachna had snatched the receiver from Rahul and slammed it down.

Now, in this dark, dusty room, big teardrops fell from Rachna's eyes and spattered on Rahul's face in the photo. Rachna smiled wryly. She remembered how Rahul had wiped her tears when she cried after the divorce and said, "Dad is so mean. He makes you cry so much. Mom, when I grow up, I'll fight with him and ask him why." Rahul's innocence warmed her heart. Mihika, toeing her brother's protectiveness for Mom, climbed onto Rachna's lap and joined in. "Yes, Mom. Daddy baddy."

Gradually, Rachna had brought her life back on track and had moved ahead with her bitter bag and baggage. She took up a teaching job and refused to take any help from Rohit. Her children blossomed under her surveillance, and she swore they would never see their father again.

*

That was till Ma fell ill. Rachna's father had passed away five years after her divorce and Ma had been living alone, refusing to move in with her daughter. When Sudha aunty, Ma's neighbour, informed Rachna about her illness, she did not know what to do. She had to leave and be with Ma. But where would she leave the children? In the last ten years, they had always been together, living in the city or travelling. This time, though, it was different. Rahul's pre-board exams were approaching, and Mihika was a member of the school basketball team for an upcoming match. Neither could miss school to live out of town.

Sarita, Rachna's colleague, suggested Rohit. Rachna was horrified.

"Talk some sense, Sarita! They detest him. How will they stay with him? And what makes you think I will let them?"

Sarita smiled. "That's what I'm saying, Rachna. *You* will not let them. You *never* let them. It's unfair."

"Unfair! And what *he* did was fair to them? Please, Sarita, let's not start this all over again," Rachna shot back.

"Yes, let us not," retorted Sarita. "Because you will never see what I am saying."

It was true. Rachna never saw reason when Sarita attempted to counsel her about this issue. The mere thought of Rohit gaining access to her children made her anxious.

But that night, Rachna did see something. She saw that life had cornered her once again. She had to leave within two days, and the children had to be left somewhere. Rohit lived in this very city, and despite whatever she felt for him, she knew that being their father, he would take care of them better than anyone else. She recollected the numerous instances that he had tried to reach out to them only to be rebuffed by her. Yet Rohit had refused to make it a custody issue. Probably he felt guilty about having walked out in the first place and wanted them to be with Rachna who might otherwise have been very lonely.

But Rachna could not help being gripped by her fears all night. What if Rohit takes it all out on her in one stroke and doesn't return her children? What if Priyanka ill-treats them and Rohit watches passively? What about the other two children, Gaurav and Smriti? What if they harm my babies? At the break of dawn, Rachna got up an hour earlier than usual and went into the kitchen to prepare herself a cup of tea.

The phone rang.

Rachna stood still, scared to pick it up. Who could be calling at this unearthly hour? Images of Ma in pain shot through her head. She ran to the phone. She was out of breath when she picked up the receiver.

"Hello?" she said hesitantly.

"Rachna?" It was Sarita. "Listen, I'm sorry, I'm calling at an odd hour. I'm going to Pune for a day. Will be back by late night. I wanted to tell you..."

Rachna interrupted her. "What? What happened?"

Sarita hesitated before saying, "I called Rohit. He will call you today."

Rachna's heart missed a beat. Before she could answer, Sarita said bye and disconnected.

The children were away at school when Rohit called. His voice was gentle and conciliatory.

"Rachna, Sarita told me about Ma. Listen, please leave the kids with me. It will be a pleasure, really."

"But..." Rachna was thinking about Priyanka. As if reading her mind, Rohit promptly added, "Priyanka is also looking forward to having them, trust me. Come on, let's bury the hatchet just this once. Ma needs you. Go in peace and let the children be with me."

"Okay." That was all Rachna could manage.

When the children were told about the decision, Rahul took it maturely. Mihika was visibly unhappy though. Rachna explained, "It's only for a few days. You don't have to interact with anybody much. Treat it like being at a hotel. I'll be back as soon as Nani is better. And I'll call you as often as possible."

When Rohit came to take the children away, Rachna felt herself breaking into a hundred pieces and being scattered all over by a sudden gust.

II

The first two days with Ma were a whirlwind. Doctors' visits, medicines, check-ups and managing Ma's house consumed Rachna. The hectic schedules were aggravated by the constant uneasiness plaguing her.

When Rachna called Rohit, a lady answered. There was a strained pause brought on by instant recognition. Without acknowledging Priyanka, Rachna spoke as cordially as she could manage. "This is Rachna. I..."

Before she could finish, the woman at the other end responded warmly, "Hi, Rachna. Rahul is in his room. Just a minute..." She called out to Rahul. "Rahul? Rahul! Mom on the phone!" A distant sound of hurrying footsteps was cut short by the same warm voice. "You can take it from the bedroom too, beta."

The footsteps faded away. *She's trying to be too nice to them,* thought Rachna dryly. A few seconds later, Rahul was on the line.

"Hi, Mom!" he said cheerily.

Rachna sensed an inexplicable relief flooding her.

"Hi, angel. How are you?"

"First, tell me, how is Nani?"

Rachna smiled. Her son was always well-behaved, as she had taught him to be. "She's better. Dr Mittal says she will regain full strength very soon."

"Great! And you, Mom? How are you?" Rahul sounded concerned.

Rachna felt a lump in her throat. "I'm okay. Missing you both. Where's Mihika? Call her."

"She's gone out with Dad and Smriti to shop for school shoes."

Rachna was not pleased. "School shoes? Why didn't you tell her to wait till I came back?"

"The sole of her old pair gave way. Dad insisted she should get a new one immediately." Rahul could sense his Mom's anxiety. He tried to change the topic.

"Mom, my maths paper went quite well."

Rachna was all attention. "Very good. Practise your physics well too. Last time, you made some very careless mistakes."

"Yes, Mom, I will. In fact, this time Dad is helping me out a lot. He says he used to love doing numericals in his days." Rachna was listening. "Mom?" Rahul said tentatively.

"Yes, beta?"

"I had a talk with Dad yesterday."

"About what?" Rachna's forehead wrinkled with worry.

"About us. I mean, I couldn't help it. I've always wanted to ask him why." Rahul waited for a reaction. Rachna was anxious but silent. He went on. "Mom, Dad is not a bad person. He cried and told me that he missed us all the time. It's just that ... just that he was scared you would get hurt if he tried too hard to meet us."

Rachna felt a fleeting anger. She had been fighting this battle with herself for ten years and Rohit and turned the tables so niftily. She made a mental note that she would speak to him about it later.

Rachna pondered for a second and then said, a trifle sadly, "Okay. Now I have to get back. Tell Mihika I miss her. I'll call again. You both take care of yourselves, Rahul. And concentrate on your pre-boards, beta. No distractions, please. Bye."

Rachna clutched her phone even after she had disconnected. A fresh burst of worry came over her. She could visualise Mihika buying shoes with Rohit. *He'll take her away from me by buying her things*, she thought.

*

Another week went by and then another. Ma was recovering quickly. Now that the pressure had eased off a bit, Rachna had a little more time with herself. Ma too was a little chattier. Often, both would sit on the porch, sipping tea and reminiscing about the old days. In one such instance, Ma said to Rachna, "Chhoti, you can leave now if you want to. I'm quite okay."

"No, Ma. Let bhai come down from the US first. Once I hand you over to bhabhi, I'll be relaxed. It will take another week. That's all, Ma."

"And till then, you'll worry yourself to death about the kids."

Rachna was pouring herself some tea. She looked up. Ma was looking back at her intently. She sighed, saying, "Ma, worrying about one's kids is very natural, isn't it?"

"Yes, it is. But not the way you do, Rachna. For god's sake, they are not babies anymore. And they are with Rohit. And if you have forgotten, he is their father."

Rachna's face clouded. "I *know* he is their father. That's why I'm scared. It's been years, Ma. It's been so many years."

Ma was quiet for a moment. Then she gently put her hand on her daughter's shoulder. "Rachna, why don't you go out with your old friends one day? You need a break, darling."

Rachna answered mechanically, "I'll think about it, Ma."

Something about the way Ma had spoken to her, the three weeks of separation from the kids, and the unplanned break from the routine propelled Rachna into thinking of things she had evaded for years.

That night, Rachna scanned her old albums. *How young and vibrant I look in these,* she thought as she flipped through the pages. When she had closed the last album, she stared at herself in the mirror for a long time. A strange weariness descended on her. She was suddenly very, very tired. The control she had built over her life all these years crumbled and fatigue overwhelmed her. Rachna didn't remember when she dozed off.

Two days later, Rachna met her childhood friend over an evening of tea and snacks. The conversation and laughter were refreshing. Later, as she walked back home, Rachna realised that she had almost forgotten about her children in the preceding three hours with her friend.

Guilt seized her and she stared at her phone. Before dialling, she paused. It was Mihika's birthday the next day and she had to call anyway. Should she call today too? The guilt of having lived a few free moments and the paranoia of losing her children to others pulled her in two different directions.

Rachna dialled. Her heart was pounding.

The minute the landline phone rang, somebody picked it up. It was Gaurav.

"Hello?" He was almost shouting into the phone. When Rachna asked for Mihika, she could hear music and laughter in the background. As she waited for her daughter to come to the phone, she listened for the sounds in the background.

"Mom! Hi!" It was Mihika. She was sounding very, very happy.

"Hi, darling. You okay?"

"Just okay? Mom, I'm having a blast! Priyanka aunty threw a birthday bash for me today – a surprise! All of Smriti and Gaurav's friends are here." Mihika was gushing with joy.

"Your birthday? But that's tomorrow, angel."

"Yes! But we're having a party today because tomorrow Dad is taking us out to the movies and dinner. Just family."

The last two words cut across her like a razor. Rachna's heart sank. She didn't know how to react. Trying her best to sound cheerful, she said, "Oh! That's nice. You go on, beta. Have fun. Give the phone to Rahul?"

Rahul was standing near Mihika, waiting for his turn to speak. Rachna enquired about how he had fared in his exams and finished the call. She walked back home in a daze.

When she hit the bed that night, Rachna broke down. She sobbed and sobbed till she couldn't cry anymore.

When she called and wished her daughter the next day, Rohit took the phone from Mihika.

"Hi, Rachna. How are you doing?"

"I'm fine. Thanks."

"I should be the one thanking you. Really."

"For what, Rohit?"

"For the children. It was because you agreed to let them be with me that I came to know them after such a long time. Rachna, they are beautiful. And all credit goes to you. They truly are angels."

Rachna stiffened. Rohit continued, "Priyanka was saying she has never seen a more well-mannered child than Rahul. In fact, she and Rahul discovered that they loved the same authors. And once they start talking about that, nobody gets a chance to say anything else." Rohit laughed heartily. "He has plans, I must say. Big plans. Wants to be an architect. For his age, he has pretty radical views about environmentally friendly urban structures." Rohit's voice was packed with pride. He paused. "Rachna, you there?"

"Yes, I'm listening."

Rachna was not listening. When Rohit had finished what he was saying, she told him of her plans to return.

"I'm coming back next week."

"Hey! That's great. Which means Ma is okay now."

"Yes, she is."

Rohit was quiet for a few seconds, which seemed like ages to Rachna. When he finally spoke, he was hesitant. "Rachna, can I request you for something?"

"Yes, Rohit? What is it?"

"You know that Rahul's exams are over. He has a few days before he settles down for the main board preparation. Mihika also has post-term holidays after a week. I was wondering if they could stay for some more time with us." He paused. "I mean, with your permission of course. I could help Rahul with his studies. It will take some load off you for more time ... but ... only if it's okay with you." Rohit said everything in a rush and then waited, almost expecting a strong reaction.

But Rachna didn't protest. She couldn't. All she could feel was a sense of loss that she couldn't put a finger to, together with relief at being free after so many years. She realized that even if she hadn't acknowledged it in as many words, she had resigned to this possibility over the last few weeks. It was no use. The children were his too. If they had chosen to be happy with him, she couldn't possibly object to that. Her nightmare had come true. But with it, came a freedom, from herself, her limitations and her boundaries. Her world had crashed again.

III

Rachna realised that it was almost dusk. She had been sitting on the sofa for hours now. She kept the photo frame back in its place and got up. She neither opened the windows, nor pulled back the curtains. Bolting the main door, she went straight to her room. After washing up, she made herself a simple meal and ate alone. It was the first time in ten years she was eating alone in this home.

There's always a first time for everything, she thought.

The next morning, Rachna noticed the white sheets still covering the furniture and the dust still on the floor. She ignored it and got ready to go to college. She couldn't bring herself to do anything.

At college, Sarita was pleased to see her. They had their regular break in the café, took their respective classes and attended a department meeting called by the head. All through the day's routine, Sarita noticed that Rachna was quiet and preoccupied. But there was a calmness on her face that Sarita had not seen before. Her normally taut face appeared relaxed.

Later, Sarita dropped Rachna back home in her car. On the way, she said, "You've changed."

"Have I?"

"Yes, but I hope you're okay."

"I've never been better."

Sarita glanced at her friend's face. "How are Rahul and Mihika?"

"Must be fine. They're still with Rohit. They love it there." Sarita thought she felt Rachna's voice filling up. Before she could say anything, Rachna added hurriedly, "But I'm okay with that. I'm feeling so free. And there's so much to do."

Sarita left Rachna at the gate and drove away. Rachna unlocked the main door and braced herself for another lonely evening. It was dark inside. She moved towards the switchboard.

"Surprise!" There was a chorus of yells. The lights came on and Rachna almost jumped out of her skin.

There, on the centre table of the living room, was a small cake lighted with a single candle. Rahul and Mihika stood nearby, grinning ear to ear. The minute Rachna saw them, they ran and hugged her. As she hugged them back, one in each arm, Rachna was still numb with surprise. She held them for a long moment. In that moment, the warmth of their proximity broke through her daze and she realised that her children were back at home. Hot tears of gratitude and pent-up love flowed freely as she kissed them each on the forehead. Rahul held her arm protectively and made her sit on the sofa. Rachna noticed the white sheets had gone. The room was sparkling clean. The windows were open and the curtains pulled back neatly. Not a speck of dust was visible. Everything was in place.

The candle on the cake shone on the words "Welcome Back" iced thickly on the cream. Rachna looked at Rahul and Mihika affectionately.

"You devils. That was the best surprise I ever had."

Rahul smiled and Mihika giggled.

"But ... but you were supposed to stay back longer at Dad's place, right? That's what Rohit told me. So ... what happened?"

Rahul sat down on his knees in front of her and took her hand in his. He looked up into her eyes.

"Mom, it was great at Dad's place. Awesome, in fact. Everybody is so damn good there. We had a rocking time. And we know we will go back some day again. But..." Rahul waited for a drop of tear lurking at the edge of Rachna's eye to roll down. "But that will be only for visits. Mom, we missed you. Badly. We can't live without you. When you were away, we realised how much you mean to us. It's you who is everything to us."

Mihika put her head in Rachna's lap. "We love you, Mom." Rahul came closer and hugged them both.

They sat there like that for ages.

Rachna's world had built itself afresh on a new foundation.

MISS SEPTEMBER

An image to conform to
A standard she had set
A deceit she bid adieu
When her true self she met

As Nisha tapped her perfectly manicured fingernails on the marble top, she made it clear to the bartender that she was getting impatient for that martini. She sensed someone a few feet away recognise her. It often happened this way; someone would recognise her from a billboard or an advertisement and spend a few minutes mustering up the courage to talk to her.

This gentleman took two.

"Erm, excuse me, sorry to bother you, ma'am, but aren't you the model from the Save the Animals Today ad?" he asked, a polite hesitation masking his charming voice, afraid he might look like he was hitting on her. Of course Nisha was used to this. She ran his eyes over the man from top to bottom; he was indeed charming. If she was in a better state of mind, she would have even entertained a conversation.

"Yes, I am," she said as the bartender brought her the martini. For years, it had been vodka that she had resorted to, the least unkind to the waist. She turned away from the man and focused on the drink.

The man grimaced awkwardly. "Well, it was good to see you, and I wish you good luck! Have a safe flight," he said and turned to exit the airport lounge.

Nisha smirked to herself rather cynically as she remembered the print ad that the man was talking about. STAT, as she abbreviated it, had wanted a "real" face to pose near a tiger, and it was one of the scariest yet most rewarding days of her modelling career. Of course, "real" only meant not conventionally good looking. Being a bit dusky, Nisha with her otherwise classical good looks had learned to tread that line with finesse over the ten years she had been active in her career.

Truth be told, Nisha was a warm and sociable person at most times, but today she was tense. She had reached the airport a whole three hours before her flight and wore thick sunglasses as she entered. She was going home but not with the good news that she had hoped for. As she gulped down the martini, she became aware of a buzzing in her pocket. She knew what the news would be.

The buzz in the media was that, for the first time, celebrity businessman Vinay Mehra's calendar was going to feature a dusky model with small-town roots. She would have been Miss September. Of course, it was very different work from what she had been used to, more of a publicity and PR stunt than anything else, but after Miss September, the doors to high-end modelling shows, fashion weeks, ramps around the world would be, well, if not open, within knocking distance.

But all those dreams would have to wait, she realised as she checked her email with dread. It was her agent. They were dropping her; it was done. "We lost it, Nisha. Whatever happened last night was totally wrong, but what you did may have just cost us a lot of work. Let's take a break, go home, recharge and come back and then let's see what's in store for the future. But for now we'd like to put a pause to our arrangement."

Nisha put her sunglasses back on and fought back the tears. She looked with disdain at all the people around her in the executive lounge, dressed sharply and behaving sophisticated. *What a bunch of disgustingly pretentious pigs*, she thought to herself.

That was it. People seldom came back from a break in their career. Out of sight was far out of mind. Flashes from the previous night hit her like the hard light bulbs of the camera, not pleasant.

Last night, she had gone over to Mr Mehra's penthouse in the fanciest tower in for what she thought was a celebratory dinner and contract signing.

Alas, it wasn't. Vinay had cornered her after dinner and a couple of drinks and tried to force himself on her. For a moment, she had even felt bad for pushing Vinay away, as she realised that no one in her position had ever said no to him before. Nisha, however, couldn't exit with grace, threatening instead to ruin Mr Mehra and bring down his reputation with him by revealing that he preyed on the women who wanted to pose for his calendar.

Screw it, she thought, as she called the bartender again.

"Two white Russian cocktails, with double whipped cream."

The barman looked confused, even a little bewildered.

"NOW!" she said.

*

Indore's Devi Ahilya Bai Holkar Airport wasn't particularly busy that day.

That is why the welcome that Nisha received was all the more conspicuous. Her little sister, Divya (well, not little, just a few years younger than Nisha), had teamed up with her oldest friend, Arvind (or Arvu, as she had always called him). They held up a big banner outside the airport: "WELCOME BACK NISHA (MISS. SEPTEMBER)!"

Wow, thought Nisha, *the one time I wanted them to be subtle and not make a scene.* This was not the celebration she was in the mood for, nor the reminder that she had wanted…

"Didi!" said Divya as she rushed forward to embrace her elder sister.

"Chup, pagli, is this your idea of subtlety?"

"No, it is mine." Arvind smiled. Of course, it had to be. Arvind had always been in love with her, and a few months before she had left for Mumbai to pursue her dreams, he had confessed his feelings by organising a surprise for her in the college canteen and making everyone sing for her as he went down on his knees and asked her out.

That was a very long time ago though. Arvind now had a family and a daughter, and he was a well-respected businessman in the city. His habits of indulging those he cared for, however, hadn't changed. As people gathered to see Nisha, Arvind obliged them by opening the sunroof of the car and encouraged her to stand up and say hello to them.

As she stood in the car and smiled at the people lining the side of the road, pointing and calling out her name, she muttered her breath to Divya and Arvind in the front seat, "How do they know I've come back?"

She got her answer a few moments later when they passed a vinyl billboard with her face on it, saying, "Welcome, Miss September!"

Yet none of this felt good. What Nisha really felt like doing was to crawl up in a little ball and disappear. She almost certainly knew that this whole toast-of-the-town business was not going to last. Her career was over after what had happened last night.

Poor Divya had been so excited for her to come back and was yapping away to glory, but Nisha just couldn't deal with it any more. Arvind sensed that something was wrong and took a different path back to their house, avoiding the main roads.

*

When after college Nisha had told her parents that she wanted to go to Mumbai to pursue a career in modelling, they had refused to speak to her for days. Her father, Bishen, was incensed. It was almost akin to her telling him that she wanted to pursue the career of a bar dancer.

There were the usual whys and hows and the concerns of what the neighbours, uncles, aunties and the street dogs would say about this. When Nisha had finally left, it wasn't on a good note. Her father refused to speak with her ever again. Divya used to tell Nisha that her father never mentioned her name after she left. It was almost like she had died, or worse still, never existed. But her mother, Girija, had been very supportive of her. Secretly saving some money to send her every month so that she could sustain herself. Nisha remembered the time that she had spoken to her mother to give her the news that she had been offered representation by her first agency. Girija had to pretend like she was talking to a friend of hers who was calling to share the news that her son had been admitted into an IIT.

But things had changed slowly. Soon Bishen couldn't ignore his elder daughter any more, mostly because people in the street would come up to him and say that they had recognised her in a magazine for a skincare commercial. The tipping point had been when her own school principal had asked if she would come down to judge their annual talent show.

Of course, rumours of link-ups had not helped and had caused some anguish for Bishen and Girija. But finally, when Bishen had come around, he had come around completely. The walls of their living room were now adorned with every ad campaign that Nisha had been a part of. Yet ten long years had passed before Nisha had decided to come home. She had never felt that she had quite earned the right to turn up with all her success and tell her family, I told you so…

At dinner that night, even though Girija had made Nisha's favourite khichdi herself, Nisha had no appetite. Of course, her mother had told her that she had become so thin and weak and loaded her plate with food, saying the usual, "*Bachhi toh khati hi nahin!*"

Normally, Nisha would have objected, but once again that day, she thought to herself, *screw it*.

"What's the matter, beta?" asked Bishen, concerned that his daughter looked very worried.

"Nothing, Pa … just tired."

"It's okay, beta, we can talk tomorrow. You just eat and sleep well today."

Divya smiled at her mother. She knew that Girija had told Bishen to be as nice and kind as possible since she did not want her daughter to be upset.

But Nisha couldn't get any sleep. Every time she closed her eyes, the events of the night before assailed her. She remembered the moment when she felt the most vulnerable, when she even considered for a second the possibility of giving in to his advances.

"This will change your life," he had told her. "You will never have to test for another part again, they'll all be yours…"

But even though she had worked so hard to come this far, having dealt with rejection after rejection and worked multiple odd jobs to make ends meet, she just couldn't bring herself to do it. Perhaps that was her fault. She was, after all, a small-town girl with small-town values. Maybe that was her undoing?

No! That wasn't fair, to her or to her upbringing. She picked up her phone and sneaked out of the house.

*

That night, Arvind was awakened by a buzzing on the bedside table. He didn't even move and continued to sleep like a log; his wife, Deepa, used to snore ever so lightly, and Arvind had got used to it…

But the phone kept buzzing till it fell off the table, and Arvind awoke with a start. He scrambled to pick it up and sighed when he saw who it was.

"Seriously, Nisha? It's 3.30 and I have work tomorrow…"

"Usual place. Get the lights!" Nisha disconnected, and Arvind half contemplated going back to sleep and forgetting the call had happened, but of course, he knew he couldn't.

"Lights" was the code for cigarettes. And the "usual place" was a little spot near the Saraswati River. It seemed somehow overlooked by the rest of the city, which was busy sprouting malls, restaurants and cafes in almost every other neighbourhood.

Arvind picked Nisha up outside her house, and they drove to the predetermined location. It was their favourite spot in college, where they would go to hang out, sometimes to sneakily have a drink away from prying eyes and sometime to just be.

"Can't sleep?"

Nisha nodded, lighting her cigarette.

"What's up, Nisha? This was supposed to be a break for you. Doesn't look like it..."

"Seriously, Arvu, I literally just landed today after ten years and you're going to comment on how frazzled I am?"

Arvind looked at her with apologetic eyes. "Tell me, am I wrong?" he asked.

Nisha broke down. She burst into tears and cried on his shoulder. Nisha held nothing back as Arvind did what he had always done – listened patiently.

"It's all gone, Arvu, it's all over!"

"What? What are you talking about, Nish?"

She proceeded to tell him about all the events of the previous night.

"I had wanted to be on that calendar for years. It was the gateway to everything that I had ever dreamed of. It would've opened the door to movies, ads, campaigns – everything that I left home for. I just didn't know that this is what it would take. I never would have agreed to meeting with that bastard ... They're all like that; it's work for us but they just pick and screw over whoever they want..."

"I'm so sorry, Nisha, I really don't know what to say."

"Yeah, you know, Pa was right. The world doesn't think of us as more than a piece of candy. Use us and when you are done, just throw us out and move on to the next one. What's the point of all the auditions and interviews and hard work if the gates to success are simply between my legs? Why the hell did I work hard anyway?"

Arvind took a deep breath. He had known something was wrong since her arrival. Nisha had never been the silent one. She had always been the life of any room she had walked into.

"And now what? Where do you go from here?" he asked.

"I don't know, Arvu. I haven't told my parents that I haven't got the calendar shoot, that I'm not Miss September. To be honest, I don't even know if there's any point in going back to Mumbai. My agent told me to 'take a break' and come back later, which means they're going to drop me, I'm sure. That bastard Mehra will see to it even if they don't want to. I'm back to square one. Being celebrated by a town for a reason that's no longer true."

In the distance, the sound and flickering headlights of trucks interrupted the darkness of the night. Nisha wiped her tears and threw her cigarette away.

"Come," said Arvind.

"Where?"

"Shut up and come. I've listened to you rant. Now come with me. I have to show you something..."

As they sat in the car in silence, Nisha contemplated everything she had shared with Arvind. Would he judge her and her world too harshly? She was quite embarrassed by it all, oddly enough, despite having done nothing wrong aside from standing up for herself. *My stupid complex,* she thought to herself.

"Where are we going?"

"My place."

"Arvu, relax, just drop me home. I'm fine."

"I will, but I want to show you something first..."

Arvind's house hadn't changed. The bungalow had been lived in by many generations of the family. She remembered when he had excitedly shared with her the time they had remodelled the verandah and made way for the large SUV that he had bought, the one they were seated in now. It was pretty much the highlight of his last decade. That and his daughter, Trishla, getting into a very prestigious school.

Nisha had always been very fond of her and concerned about the girl, particularly after Deepa had passed away a few years ago.

"Shhh…"

"What the hell, Arvu! Why are we sneaking around your house?"

"Shut up, Nish!" said Arvind, pointing at his empty wrist.

Yes, of course, it is nearly four thirty in the morning, thought Nisha. In the faint glimmer of the moonlight, she could see Deepa's garlanded portrait front and centre in the hallway.

As they crept up the staircase, Arvind whispered about his foresight in having it remade with marble instead of wood, else they would have been creaking away to glory.

They approached Trishla's room. Arvind held his breath and opened the door as silently as he could. His daughter was sleeping soundly, and Arvind lit the lighter in his pocket and held it above her head. Nisha was confused. What the hell was he up to? And then she saw it.

It was a life-sized poster of the first campaign Nisha had ever done. Although she had several copies of the poster, she had not been able to look at it for years. Too critical of herself and the way she posed, she had found her eyebrows unkempt, her posture all wrong and several other things embarrassing.

It felt like a lifetime ago.

Arvind led her by her hand out of the room, careful to not wake Trishla. That campaign had made Nisha a hero in Indore, and every girl looked up to her. It was for an organisation called We Women Work, an NGO fighting for equal rights and pay parity for women in workplaces all over the country. Seeing Nisha's picture there, a lot of organisations in Indore had pledged to work for women's rights.

"That's what I wanted you to see and remember."

When Nisha had done the campaign, it was a huge break for her, a breakthrough moment for her career. Always wanting to make her family proud, she looked for meaningful and impactful work that they would be proud to display in their own house ... Today, it was in Trishla's room while the young girl slept soundly nearby.

When Nisha watched the sun rise the next morning from the balcony of her home, she hadn't slept a wink and yet she felt fresh and energised. The city was waking up. She was home for now but she would go back to the big bad world she had come from and make her people proud once again, Miss September or not!

NOT MAN ENOUGH

There was once a little girl
For whom, her father was the world
A girl who would
Rather be a man if she could

I

Babuji had just returned home. Devi spotted him through the jali as he walked across the veranda and towards the last room, where Mai usually sat at this time in the afternoon on her charpoy with her knitting or crochet supplies.

He looked ever so kind and handsome in his dusty white kurta pyjama. His grey sideburns shone with droplets of sweat and the stubble on his cheeks made him look a trifle sad and weary.

Devi ran across the inner rooms to reach Mai just as she got up in response to his knock.

"You're back early," said Mai.

"Tell Shakuntala to get some water and tell Kaka to make tea to go with the matthis," Mai told Devi as she took the parcels that Babuji handed out.

Devi looked at Babuji's face. He smiled at her. She was relieved that he was not upset with her.

This was about the fourth time in the two years since her sister Vasanti's marriage that her in-laws had summoned Babuji. The now sickeningly familiar routine had been laid out the very first time that he had been summoned. "Get your daughter to improve, or else take her back," Vasanti's mother-in-law had warned Babuji.

Babuji had stood there, a small man made smaller listening to the litany of complaints against his daughter. For, as they all pointed out, her misdemeanours were a reflection of her bad upbringing.

Of course they had a right to say anything they liked, Babuji had thought bitterly, his head bowed, not daring to exchange but a fleeting look with Vasanti, who sobbed at this open humiliation of her father at her in-laws' hands.

A father of four daughters – what could he possibly do right anyway in this country? He had thought about this, biting his lips, as Vasanti's mother-in-law had gone on and on that first time. And from the solemn expression that Devi saw on Babuji's face at this moment, she knew that it had probably been the same scenario this time around too.

II

It was all because Vasanti, unlike her elder sisters Riti and Babli, who had had their marriages arranged, had dared to fall in love. It was something that good girls simply did not do.

Brijesh's parents were unhappy that they had had no control over this most vital aspect of their son's life. Their logic was simple – a daughter-in-law who already had their son's affection would not feel the need to be good to others in the joint family in order to win it. Brijesh and Vasanti had tried to dispel these misgivings, but Vasanti's mother-in-law was never convinced. No matter what Vasanti did and how. Brijesh chose to remain the silent spectator, for taking up for his wife would only mean adding fuel to the fire that already raged within his mother.

Poor Babuji had borne all this stoically – as stoically perhaps as he had borne the birth of one daughter after another, never failing in his love and duty towards them, even as Mai often openly cursed her faith. Riti, Babli, Vasanti – they were all married now, for better or for worse. Only Devi, all of fifteen years old, remained with them.

Somehow, Babuji's steadfast stoicism seemed to crumble only at the thought of this last one departing after marriage, just like her sisters. For although her birth was the final nail in the coffin of his hidden disappointment at not having a son, she had ironically brought him more joy than all the others put together. She had played cricket with him in the backyard, driven his tractor, kept his accounts and done all his banking errands ever since she was ten.

Devi had no time for trinkets and other girly things. She loved to dress in the beige or brown trousers picked up from the streets of Jaipur by Babuji, which she wore with the loose-checked T-shirts bought in the smallest adult male size from the same markets. She had snipped off her hair into a boy's haircut and the only pieces of jewellery she always wore were the two tiny gold studs in her ears.

Mai had always been irked by Devi's style of dressing and behaviour. She often commented that all this would be tolerable for only a little while more and that sooner rather than later Devi would have to become more feminine. Babuji, of course, would merely look on indulgently when Mai would start her tirade against Devi.

Devi thought nothing of rolling up her sleeves to fix a light bulb or of twisting an errant nut into submission. Once she had even amazed her friend Deepti by picking up a dead lizard with her bare hands. She had yanked it over the garden wall and Deepti had been so nauseous at the sight that she had thrown up soon after. When Deepti had regained her composure and appetite, she had of course been completely awed at her friend's courage and had related it to a proud Babuji.

Deepti always looked up to Devi. In Devi's presence, Deepti felt ever so safe and protected. And Devi simply loved Deepti's wide-eyed innocence. She felt ever so protective towards her. In these last few years, they were such a happy twosome that there was no place for a third person in their circle of friendship.

Until recently, Mai used to tease them as "Mr and Mrs" whenever she saw their interaction and their vastly different tastes in clothes. Of late, she had stopped joking in this manner. It was clear that she did not find it amusing anymore.

Devi knew exactly why Mai had stopped joking about them. It was since Deepti, four years younger than her, had started menstruating while Devi showed no such signs of impending womanhood. Even Devi's bust-line had refused to emerge from her chest, as though it was cooperating with her gender-defiant instincts.

"Just not sprouting," Mai would often comment as she poked Devi at her bust-line. "Your sisters were all fully developed by fifteen."

"Is it my fault?" Devi would retort. She refused to brood about it. In fact, in no way did she miss what Mai was missing on her behalf. From Deepti's descriptions of the discomfort that the monthlies entailed and her own memory of Babli's screams of pain when she was in labour last year, womanhood in all its physical manifestations was hardly anything to look forward to. The very thought of her ever getting her periods and "officially becoming a woman" would terrify Devi. She had almost taken it for granted that she was not meant to be a woman and was rather delighted living in that little bubble of hers.

She even recalled the piles of stained sheets that had been brought out of Babli's hospital room after she had delivered her baby. She remembered Babli walking groggily into her room when she returned to their house. It had been the peak of the summer season, but the fan in Babli's room had never been allowed to go beyond its minimum speed. Her room had always been filled with the smoke from the incense sticks constantly burning in one corner. Beside Babli's bed had been kept a jug full of warm black-coloured water. The water was bitter due to the juices of jeera and ajwain that had been boiled in it. Devi remembered Babli swathed in layers and layers of clothing, rivulets of sweat trickling down her neck.

She had been so tired and uncomfortable one particular day, but one look at her husband Madhav, who had come to visit her, and her eyes had shone. They were both so much in love with each other. Before she could talk to him, however, the womenfolk had led him away from the room, as though she was in danger of being impregnated by him all over again even if she merely had a conversation.

And in this stuffy room, she had remained with her child throughout the customary forty-day seclusion with minimal exposure to the outside world.

In those days, Babli often thirsted for a cool drink of plain water, but all she had been allowed was the black water with all its carminative properties that were to do mother and child a world of good. Babli had confessed to Devi that she craved for normal food, but she was only given the lightest of yellow washed lentils and jowari roti and a different variety of gourd each day, for it was believed that whatever the mother ate or drank entered the infant through the milk from her breast. And so keeping the infant's tender systems in view, the mother was to eat, drink and clothe herself to minimise any danger to these. It was a mother's first big lesson in the lifelong selflessness that being one involved.

Devi remembered how she had once offered Babli cool water smuggled from the refrigerator. Babli had given in to the temptation, confessing to Devi as she drank it that she had felt satiated for the first time in all those weeks. But all hell had broken loose the next day as the baby had come down with a cold. Their secret was found out and Mai had duly chastised Devi. For Babli, the guilt of seeing her child suffer because of her indulgence was punishment enough and was another lesson learnt for life.

After a few days, Babli had left for her husband's house. She had looked resplendent and was glowing at the prospect of finally being allowed to stand next to Madhav, contemplating the magic of love and happy parenthood.

Devi wondered if she could ever feel that way about any man as her sisters did. She hated looking at men's pictures. She even detested the posters of film heroes that Deepti, like the other girls in her class, put up in their rooms or pasted on the inner walls of their cupboards. In fact, what she did enjoy was looking at girls.

She loved staring at the beautiful curvatures of their bodies and their colourful clothes. This was, however, not a love of wanting to be like them. It was more, as Devi had started admitting to herself lately, wanting to love them. She wanted to hold, feel, caress and kiss them – feelings that only a man was supposed to have towards a woman. And it was this conflict between what she wanted and what she was supposed to want that would consume her often.

Devi had confessed her feelings to Deepti who had told her that irrespective of whether what she felt was right or wrong in the eyes of the world, she would always love her for who she was. Deepti had then held Devi's hands and driven them over her tender, budding breasts and then shut her eyes with mysterious pleasure. Devi too had felt a strange pleasure deep in her as she touched and caressed Deepti. She had ached to but resisted touching her more. Devi had shared these feelings with Deepti now, as she had shared everything else in the past with her – things both moral and immoral, named and unnamed.

And now she shared a brand-new secret with her. It was perhaps a really wild dream. But also one which had the potential of exploding into fantastic reality if the words of the story that Devi had read so many times in these last two days were indeed true.

It was Deepti who had read this story first. It was an article in *Today's Woman* magazine, published from Bombay, and profiled a sixteen-year-old girl whose story read just like Devi's. It was the story of a girl who had felt like a boy trapped in a girl's reluctant body and whose battle to come to terms with her strangeness had had a fairy-tale ending. The girl had undergone a series of sex-change operations to finally emerge as a boy. Lalita had turned into Lalit and was blissfully happy at last.

Devi's heart had pounded the first time that she read the story. And it continued to pound, with no less force, every single time she reread it. Thereafter, it almost burst out of her chest when Deepti goaded her to emulate Lalita and even promised that she would marry her "when" (not just if) she became a man. Her chances of being allowed the operations were high, as Deepti explained to her, for she had not started menstruating and, like Lalita, she would surely score full marks in the psychological tests that the doctors would conduct before they consented to do the operations. Devi was manly and most importantly for her believed that her body wasn't destined for womanhood.

For Devi, Deepti was proving to be a real soulmate. She was giving words to Devi's forbidden dreams and bringing them into the realm of the possible. She was daring her to dream. If Lalita could become Lalit, surely Devi could turn into Dev! For the first time in all these years, Deepti was taking the lead in their friendship as if there was truly as much in this for her as there was for Devi. Devi saw how Deepti suddenly seemed so mature and aware, so intelligent and practical. For if it hadn't been for Deepti and the words that she had used to tell Babuji about it, they would never have been able to even discuss such an issue with her father.

At first, Babuji had been incensed, but then he had turned a little amused. A little later, he had muttered, completely mesmerised in his own thoughts, "Dev ... Dev ... Dev?" He had smiled such a strange and beautiful smile. Yet it had taken many such rounds of convincing before Babuji had finally consented to give this fantastic idea serious thought. And think it over he certainly did, for deep in his heart he knew that he would not be able to take the eventual departure of Devi as stoically as he had been able to take those of his other daughters. Perhaps this was his last chance – in fact his only chance – of keeping her with him forever.

So many wonderful things were possible and were happening in the world, he thought. Perhaps this was one of them. But then again, Babuji would think of the ancestral wisdom which he had been brought up with and which simply advised that one must never tamper with nature. And playing with nature was exactly what this sex change was going to involve.

Devi and Deepti could sense that Babuji was wavering. They were emboldened by this wavering which was all too apparent on his transparent face and pestered him over and over again. In the end, Babuji had, somewhat in a serious-faced manner, admitted that he was finally feeling positive about the whole issue. He said that he would consider finding out a little more about the possibilities of Devi's transformation. It was, however, at this time that he had received the summons from Vasanti's in-laws, and this issue had taken a backseat. Of course they all decided that Mai was not to be told anything right now, knowing her propensity to beat her chest and overreact under stressful circumstances.

III

Babuji sipped his tea, lost in thought, not once looking at his favourite snack of matthis that Mai had put on the table in front of him. Deep furrows of thought had appeared on his forehead. Devi remembered her mother's favourite piece of advice that she had given to each of her sisters before they were married as she now looked at her father's face.

Mai had told each one of her daughters as they were leaving home an important thing: "There is a secret way in which to get your way with a man … any man. If you can judge the right moment to approach a man with a request and when to retreat in silence, you will have conquered the world."

The world! A woman's world, that is. The territory that lay enclosed within the perimeters of her home. Of course right now, Devi was going to heed this piece of sane advice, for she did not intend to disturb Babuji with anything controversial. And so she waited patiently and quietly in a corner of the room, not venturing to ask him whether he had made up his mind to take her to the doctor in Bombay that they had read about in the magazine.

But Mai knew that Babuji needed to talk as much as they needed to know what had happened today at Vasanti's house. He related it all wearily – the cold reception he had received from her father-in-law and sorrow at the fact that Brijesh's eyes had not met his even once. Vasanti's mother-in-law had beat her chest and wailed about the havoc his daughter had created in their family.

But what had affected Babuji more than all this, he said, was Vasanti sobbing and gritting her teeth as she heard it all silently.

"What else can a woman do but cry and bear it?" said Mai bitterly. "After all, she has to live there all her life. She is supposed to enter her in-laws' house in her doli and leave it only in her arthi."

"That's how our people, our society, have chosen to have it. It doesn't really have to be like that. I would like Vasanti and all my daughters to know that if they are ever in need or in trouble, they have their father's house to come back to," said Babuji softly.

Brave words indeed, they swelled Devi's heart with pride.

"It's all very well to say that but think of the long run. How long will her father and mother be around to look after her if a daughter were to return? In our household, there are no brothers to take care of them. Can a daughter eventually live alone here even if she were to return from her marital home?" asked Mai with a sigh. It was a familiar sigh, a burden-of-four-daughters sigh. "If only god had given me one, just one, son," she continued. Then, looking rather oddly at Babuji, she added, "If only you had given me one, just one, son."

How foolish of Mai to have said that and what bad timing, thought a shocked Devi as she watched Babuji's face stiffen. They all understood enough biology to grasp what Mai had known for some time but had spoken about only today.

Her words had hurt Babuji and it showed on his face. He looked at her with a glint in his eyes.

"Maybe I can still give you a son," said Babuji as Mai now looked at him with embarrassed disbelief. But only Devi, from her corner of the room, knew the exact import of what Babuji had just said.

Babuji got up and walked away. As he passed Devi and she looked up at him, he caressed her head and then held up her chin. "I will take you to Bombay. Get ready to leave tomorrow morning," he said smiling. "Now I will do all that I can to fulfil your fantasy – our fantasy."

Devi's elation knew no bounds, but she took care not to display it.

She spent all evening packing her suitcases with Deepti, sharing their future dreams. Mai had not the faintest idea of the mission of this trip, and neither Deepti nor Devi could bring themselves to tell her anything about it. Babuji promised them that he would tell her in due course, when he felt the time was right and when they themselves were sure of what was indeed possible.

The next morning, Babuji finished his bath and his prayers. He had thought that he would be nervous but was overwhelmed by his own sense of calm. He looked at his watch. It showed 7.30 a.m. Mai was praying in the aangan. He had not told her anything about the trip and had simply said that he and his favourite daughter Devi had planned a week's holiday in Bombay. Mai had found this odd but she did not suspect anything – at least nothing as bizarre as the truth.

Babuji came out of his room. He stood outside Devi's bedroom door, surprised that there were no sounds from inside. He had fixed her alarm last night for 6.30 a.m. and she was usually the one to be ready very promptly. He smiled at the thought that she had probably been too excited last night to have slept on time. She might have switched off the alarm and gone right back to sleep.

He knocked at her bedroom door once and then a second time. A little alarmed now, he knocked several times more. There was still no response. Babuji pushed the door gently.

A hoarse scream escaped his throat. There was Devi, hanging from the ceiling fan dressed most unlike herself in a ghagra choli. A thousand screams joined into a long wail as Babuji cried out. Devi! Why! Why Devi? Babuji screamed again and again, unable to comprehend what he was seeing.

And then Babuji's eyes fell on Devi's favourite pair of beige trousers, the one she had been wearing the previous evening. There they lay on the ground, the crotch still damp with a maroon stain of menstrual blood.

NOT NOW

To be loved a little
Despite the way you are
A desire so brittle
As distant as a shining star

As usual, the bus stop was teeming with students. Groups of boys and girls were engaged in animated talk, some serious, most not, but all exuding the energy of youth.

As she stood alone under the shelter, Niharika once again wondered whether she was really a part of this particular crowd of young kids. They were all students of her college, and yet no one was ever seen brooding in classroom corners or looking forlornly out of library windows.

If Malani had come to college today, the day might not have been so dull, for she was the gregarious sort. With a lot of friends and acquaintances, Malani had a way of including Niharika in the group and making her feel somewhat wanted.

Niharika's thoughts then turned to Anuraag, her classmate who lived close to her house and had once dropped her home on his motorbike – it was the day the riots had broken out in the city recently. Her heart still missed a beat whenever she saw him. But it was clear that he now deliberately avoided her. In any case, sighed Niharika, there was little with which she could hold anyone's interest. Who would care to look at a face with a pair of thick glasses and an oiled tight plait?

Yet she would often daydream about the man for whom she would be queen and who would love and cherish her. And he almost always ended up looking like Anuraag. She would often try to catch a glimpse of him during class. But if he ever caught her eye, he would immediately look away, leaving her feeling utterly small and ashamed of herself. Yet she never really succeeded in stopping herself from gazing at him again and again.

Today, Professor Ranjana had even made a caustic remark upon seeing her lost in her thoughts. "And who, may I ask, is fascinating you so much, young lady? You may please leave the class if you are not interested in the lecture."

Rudely jolted back to her surroundings, Niharika had wished that the earth would open up and swallow her but had managed to hang her head down and mutter, "Sorry, ma'am."

Cruel, mean Professor Ranjana and her acid tongue! Oh how she hated her for this humiliation... Niharika bit her lip, recalling the embarrassment of the morning as she climbed into the bus listlessly.

She was the only one who sat alone. As she looked at the high-rise buildings that the bus went past, she felt more and more small and insignificant. Her existence did not matter to the world, she was convinced.

She soon reached her house and unlocked the door. After a wash, she served herself lunch. It had been cooked by her mother many hours earlier. Usually, she never did bother to heat it up, though her mother would remind her to do so every morning as she left for the office. All of a sudden the silence enveloping her was broken by the sound of a movie playing on the video next door.

Niharika imagined the neighbourhood children returning from school and being fussed over and fed a hot, sumptuous meal by their mother. The entire family would now be settling down to an afternoon of enjoyment and leisure in each other's company. Alas, how much their cheerful life contrasted with hers! Niharika remembered her mother, who, as always, was against her attending tomorrow evening's farewell party in college. She had not said anything except, "The decision is up to you. You're old enough to know what's right and wrong." But the stern look on Mummy's face had been clearly disapproving.

Niharika now stopped halfway through her meal. The suffocation at having no control over the course of her life suddenly took on epic proportions in her mind, sucking her ability and even desire to breathe. Beads of cold sweat populated her forehead as she was struck with a daunting thought. Suicide.

Yes, by taking her own life, she would punish all those who had rejected her and been unkind to her – Mummy, Professor Ranjana, Anuraag and, in fact, everybody she knew. The thought of retribution was the only relief today for her tormented soul. It refused to go away and, in fact, seemed to have overpowered her entire being. Her mind continued to plan her impending end meticulously even as she resumed eating and went about her usual chores in the house.

She would not be violent. No burning or hanging herself. Instead, she would do the easiest thing. An overdose of sleeping tablets, enough not to misfire by any chance.

When? Not today, for she wanted to plan to the last detail. Yes, she would do it after the farewell party tomorrow. Indeed, Niharika had decided that she was going to attend.

She imagined her classmates and teachers looking shocked and regretting their callousness towards her upon later learning that she was dead. Professor Ranjana, Anuraag and Mummy would suffer the most. With sadistic pleasure, she visualised their horror-struck expressions. At long last, she would triumph and be the centre of attention in death as she had not been in life. Nobody had ever cared for her, so why should she care about them now? Even Mummy had never really understood her.

Niharika did realise that life must be difficult and sad for her mother as a widow and a working woman. But she was not all that lonely, was she? She had her daughter with her but had always neglected her. *So let her lose me to realise my true value,* Niharika thought bitterly.

Yes, this was the only solution to her predicament.

The decision was her faithful companion till the next day when she began preparations in the afternoon. She took out the thousand rupees that she had so painstakingly saved and set out to the market. She was able to get the required number of sleeping tablets from five different chemists.

Then, for the first time in her life, she stepped into that famous beauty parlour she had so often heard the college girls talk about. She tried her best to sit through all that was being done to her face and hair, hands and feet, arms and legs, with the air of one very familiar with the whole routine. She felt like a queen with three beauticians attending to her, and stepped out afterwards looking no less than one. Then she bought herself a beautiful new dress from a boutique and took an autorickshaw back home.

Why travel in a crowded bus today? After all, it was going to be her last day in this world and she might as well make the most of it!

Mother was still not back from the office. In any case, Niharika was not interested in meeting her disapproving eye. She laid out the sleeping pills on a piece of paper in her drawer. Then she wrote a note informing her mother about her attending the party and left it on the table.

Niharika gave herself a final look. She was surprised at what the mirror reflected – beautiful large kohl-lined eyes, clear and smooth skin, a pert nose, rosy lips shining with gloss. She pinned up her long shining hair on one side, just the way she'd seen the girls at college do, and wore the lovely oxidised silver jewellery set that Malani had given her on her last birthday. She folded her glasses and dabbed on the last of her old and almost evaporated perfume stashed away in the closet. She now stepped out daintily, feeling second to none.

As the party began she realised that she was very much in demand. So many people wanted to talk to her that day. She too had so much to talk about that she was surprised at herself.

As she spotted Professor Ranjana having a moment's respite between talking to students, she made a split-second decision to go up to her. She would greet her so politely that the lady would be miserable with remorse the next day when she would learn of her death. Niharika also wanted to shock Professor Ranjana with her new appearance.

"Good evening, ma'am. How are you?"

"Oh! It's you, Niharika. How nice to see you look so cheerful and fresh, my dear," said Professor Ranjana. She paused and then continued, "By the way, Niharika, something has been weighing on my mind since last evening. I'm sorry for having ticked you off in class yesterday. You see, my dear, the exams are so close, I get upset when I see any student dreaming in class. But I'm sorry if I hurt you. I'll always remember you as a lovely girl.'

"It's all right, ma'am. I understand. It was my fault," Niharika said. She had set out to conquer her teacher with her own magnanimity but stood utterly defeated by the humility she had just encountered from the other side. Professor Ranjana smiled again and departed, only to be back once more with a plate of ice-cream. "For you, my dear," she offered.

Niharika was certainly enjoying herself today. Everybody seemed so nice. Her friend Malani was simply thrilled about her transformation. But Anuraag ... she still hadn't seen him, and it was him that her eyes searched for.

She spotted him at last. There he was among a group of other boys. And he was coming towards her! She felt her heart thump as loud as a drum beat.

Niharika did not know how the rest of the evening flew by. She and Anuraag chatted about so many things. She laughed more than ever before in her life. If ever there was a seventh heaven, it was here and it was now, she thought.

When the party wound up, he offered to drop her home in his car. She was overjoyed and accepted his offer, chuckling to herself at this fitting finale to the memorable evening. Anuraag opened the car door for her and waited until she was seated next to him.

Soon they were on their way, whirring past the twinkling street lights as they speeded along the highway. The cool breeze that swept across her face complemented so well the warm presence of her companion. Niharika was certainly enjoying herself thoroughly. But ... did he take a wrong turn here?

Before she could speak, the car braked to halt in a deserted side-lane.

Anuraag pulled Niharika towards him. She felt his breath smelling strongly of liquor. His nails clawed into her waist. She gasped while his breathing seemed deafeningly loud. She felt his lips come closer to her face.

"No, never," she screamed as he pushed his hands away with all her might. "I thought you were different, and I loved you. But you love me today only because I'm looking attractive. I don't need you anymore."

Feeling more contemptuous than scared, she forced open the door of the car. She fell and grazed her knee, but she was up immediately, running into the dark street. As she ran, she kept looking behind. Thankfully, he was not following her.

Niharika ran on without stopping. She could hardly make out her way with the tears in her eyes blurring her already hazy vision.

Mercifully, she reached home in one piece. As she waited to catch her breath at the doorstep, she realised that her problems were not over yet. Mummy ... what in the world was she going to say to her mother? Blood was oozing from her knee, and the mascara had streaked her tear-stained face black.

Her mother's face was wrought with anguish too as she held her hand and let her in. Niharika looked cautiously at her for a familiar stern look, but she found only tears streaming down her cheeks.

As her mother bandaged her knee, Niharika asked, "Have you eaten?"

"No. I was so worried. I'm sorry, Nihar. I've really neglected you, haven't I? Will you forgive me," she cried.

"No, Mummy, please don't say that," said Niharika, sobbing into her mother's pallu.

"My poor Nihar," said her mother, wiping her daughter's tears and kissing her forehead. She asked no questions and expected no explanations.

Still in a daze, Niharika proceeded to take a bath. She opened the drawer for a rubber band to tie up her hair. It was then that she noticed the pile of sleeping tablets that she had laid out that afternoon.

Not now, thought Niharika, laughing aloud as she threw the pills out of the window as forcefully and as far as she could.

SISTERS-IN-ARMS

What am I without you
Where would my life be
Like a pod holding peas two
Like the mirror reflecting me

She was everything to me. Worker, assistant, companion, sometimes friend and at times foe too, except that her enmity was limited to innocuous sulking and mumbling. Her multifaceted role was the pivot on which my home functioned. She came to me from a woman who had worked at my friend's house for years. Before the septuagenarian lady expired, she extracted a promise from my friend that her seventeen-year-old motherless granddaughter be safely placed in a good home as she called it. My friend hired the young girl and later passed her on to me when she shifted to Delhi because she trusted me with possessing the prerequisites of a decent employer.

I, Naina Rathore, called the young girl my maid, but like I said, she was everything to me.

Rano was the reason I could leave home at eight in the morning and reach office by nine-thirty. She was the reason why my first-born got warm food after school. She was the reason why my small son could stay at home till age four and not be pushed prematurely into the rat race called playschool training. She was the support which heated dinner for my husband on the odd day when he reached home before me.

Sure, there were moments when she was hauled up for laziness; when she forgot to change the bathroom hand towel or didn't mop the wet kitchen floor. But she was terrific with the children and like any working mother I secretly knew the gospel truth that my professional ambitions leaned on her ability to maintain my children's lives in my absence.

So one fine day, when Rano's maternal aunt dropped in and announced that her niece had to be married off as promised to her mother, my world crashed. Five years had flown by and now suddenly a crisis of sorts loomed ahead. But being the Good Samaritan that I was, how could I possibly hold back a young girl's future? So I let go, albeit painfully, and not before telling Rano that if ever in life she needed shelter and support, our doors were always open for her.

As her aunt stood outside the door waiting for her, Rano hugged my two children who began weeping when they sensed she was going for good. As I shut the door, I noticed Rano wiping her eyes near the staircase.

Life came to a temporary halt after she had gone. For the daunting task of finding another maid, I took leave from office and so began the excruciating process of hiring one. Friends, relatives, agencies, other maids, everyone was in the loop of information regarding my need.

The first who came in was immensely focused.

"What will you pay me?" she asked straightaway.

I looked at her strangely, but answered nevertheless.

"What work I will have to do?"

I was already having doubts about her, but since the conversation had begun, it had to be taken to a logical conclusion. As I briefly summarized her duties, I noticed she was stealing glances at the four corners of my home, as if sizing us up on. I felt irritated but continued with the list. When I had finished, she looked at me without saying anything.

"So?" I asked her.

"No, won't be able to."

My heart sank. "Why?"

"I can't wash clothes. My knees don't allow me to sit in one position for long."

I thought fast.

"Okay, we'll manage the clothes. What about the rest? You know how to cook?"

"Only fish and rice."

I showed her the door and returned to the living room, my anxiety rising meteorically.

The next few days were replete with similar encounters. The more traumas I went through, the more I missed Rano. She was goddess compared to these interviewees. I cursed myself for letting her go so easily. I also felt regret for all those days when I had been a bit too demanding on her.

After a week of nightmare, I found a substitute who was the closest to what I needed. Life limped back to normal; almost.

Rano called after a month. Her voice was ringing with joy.

"Naina Didi, how are you? I'm calling from my village."

It was nice to hear from her. "I am fine, Rano. How are you? How is married life?"

She was bursting with enthusiasm. "My husband is very good to me. He takes care of me and never leaves my side. Yesterday, he brought me a huge bangle box. Didi, it is so beautiful. When I come to visit you, I will get you one like that."

"Oh thank you, Rano, but that's not really required."

"Didi, how are the children? Did you find someone to look after them?"

"Yes, I did. But the children miss you. They haven't adjusted to the new maid yet."

There was a sniffle at the other end, and a pause. I broke the silence with something that had been on my mind earlier.

"Can't your husband work in Mumbai, Rano? Then at least you can work from morning till evening here."

She was prompt in answering that. "No, Didi, he doesn't like the city. He says he is happy here."

I kept quiet.

"Okay, Didi, I have to go now. Give my love to the children. Bye."

"Bye, Rano."

The children were playing in the nearby room. The new maid was working in the kitchen. I looked at the calendar. Five more days of leave, and I was still feeling unsettled.

As I sipped my evening tea, I thought about Rano. She had sounded so happy and contented. As her voice echoed in my head, a strange thing happened. I realised I was feeling sad. I had asked Rano to call me when she was leaving and she had done so. I was the first one to bless her and tell her how glad I was for her. Then why was I feeling despondent? Rano had served me faithfully for five years. I owed it to her to be happy for her. Then what was this uneasiness about her laughter? Suddenly her ringing laughter was poison to my ears.

I shook the thought from my head. I was just missing her, I told myself, and went to the children.

When I told my husband that Rano had called, he smiled.

"So? Is she happy?" he asked casually.

"Yes."

He looked up from the newspaper.

"Why are you so glum?"

I sighed. It was a long, winding, coded sigh.

"Don't know. Maybe it's the recent stress."

My hubby dear smiled angelically. "Don't worry, Naina. This maid will manage well. Everything will be okay. Relax."

Amen, I prayed silently.

I resumed office the next week. It was maddening; the pace which sucked life once again. To top it, there were things at home that were irking me. One day, the little one's sauce-blemished face was not wiped properly. Another day, the vegetables were not cut in proper size. The irritation grew but I had to control it for the sake of pulling along. One month passed like this.

One Monday morning, I developed a headache which kept throbbing despite aspirin. When it became unbearable, I informed my boss and left early for home. I was looking forward to resting awhile and spending some time with the kids that evening. On reaching my building, I noticed the elevator was out of order, so I trudged up the stairs.

Opening my bag to pull out the keys, I froze as I heard a wail from inside. It was my son! Maternal instincts told me something was not okay with that cry. In panic, I entered home and was horrified to see the young fellow crying his lungs out, my daughter hovering over him in an attempt to pacify him. When they saw me, they ran and clung to me. I held my son till his sobs subsided and then asked the elder one, "Where is the maid?"

My daughter pointed her finger up towards the stairs. I couldn't understand. Son in arms, I went up quietly and called out her name.

"Sarika! Sarika!"

There was no answer. The door of the storeroom was shut tight. That was odd because it was generally kept open to enable easy retrieval of stuff. I stepped forward and pushed it open.

There was a shriek as somebody disentangled herself from the arms of a man. I was horrified and let out a scream. Before I knew it, the man gathered himself hurriedly and brushed past me, stumbling down the stairs. When I shouted to ask him who he was, he ignored me. The next second, he was out of the house. I turned towards the maid. She was shivering with embarrassment and shame, too tongue-tied to say anything. It took me a second to gather what was going on. She scurried down and I followed her.

"Who was he? And how dare you call somebody inside without my permission. Are you out of your mind?" I yelled at her. "You call your lover here and my kids are alone downstairs!" I was shaking with rage.

"He … he was…"

"Shut up! I don't want to know who he was. Get out of my house! Now!"

The maid took her things and walked out.

I slumped to the sofa and cried. The pressure, the anxiety, the strain, the workload and now this; I couldn't be more miserable.

When my husband came home, he heard everything and said kindly, "Let's go out for dinner. You don't need to cook after such a horrible day."

Despite his valiant efforts to calm me, I couldn't relax.

At bedtime I was equally tense. "I'll resign," I said, choking over tears.

"You want to?" he asked gently.

"I don't have an option."

"We'll see. Get some rest now."

It took me a while, but I fell asleep with exhaustion, both my children close to my side.

Morning came and brought a weird pent-up emotion with it. I felt anger surging inside me. For some unexplainable reason, I felt angry at Rano more than anybody else, even more than at Sarika.

"If she hadn't gone, nothing would have been wrong today."

"But, Naina, how can you expect her to not go? Rano would have married sooner or later."

"These people, they marry their girls off so early! What's the sense of it? She was just twenty-one. They could have waited," I fumed.

My husband shook his head.

I spent the day setting things right in the house and for the children. There was a silent prayer lurking in my heart which asked for Rano. If only she could return to Mumbai.

Two days later, the doorbell rang.

It was Rano.

I stared at her. Had god answered my prayers? Wait a minute, I chided myself. No, she must have come to visit me.

She came in and smiled at me. She sat on the floor and asked me how I was. My son was sleeping on the couch in the living room. She looked at him affectionately and smiled again. I noticed she wasn't as chirpy as she usually was. She looked around furtively.

"Where is your maid?" she asked.

"She is on leave today." I surprised myself with the lie. What was I trying to hide from her?

"She manages well?" asked Rano

"Yes, yes, quite well. How are you, Rano?"

"I'm fine." She looked the other way. Something was amiss.

"What's the matter, Rano?"

She started sobbing. I was stunned for a second, then rushed to her side and put my hand on her shoulder.

"What is it, Rano? Tell me please."

Rano was inconsolable. Through her tears, she managed to squeeze in a few words. "It's all over, Naina Didi. That horrible, horrible man, I've left him."

I was genuinely concerned. "But that day…"

"That day everything was fine. But … but…"

"But what, Rano?"

"He started showing his true colours after a month. Didi, you tell me, who will tolerate her husband coming home drunk each day. And then one day, he hit me. I forgave him when he promised he would never drink so much again. But he made it a habit and then he would hit me almost every day."

I listened intently, feeling sorry for her. She was such a wonderful human being. Surely she didn't deserve this.

She removed her sari pallu to show her chest.

"Look! See these marks? He beat me two days ago. It was terrible. I decided I couldn't live with him any longer." Rano began crying again.

"What about your aunt?"

"I went to her. She refused to take me in, the witch. She told me to go back to him as that was my home now."

I got up and fetched a glass of water for her. She gulped it down gratefully and smiled weakly at me.

"You have always taken care of me, Didi." Her eyes welled up again. "You think I should go back, Didi?"

"No, Rano! Why should you? To such a scoundrel? No way!" I surprised myself once again by my instantaneous reaction.

"Didi?"

"Yes, Rano?"

She looked down at the floor. "Can I ... can I...?"

"Can I what, Rano?"

"Can I come back and work here, at your home?"

Could she? This was indeed god answering my prayers.

"Didi, I'll do whatever you say. Give me work and some food, I'll be very grateful. I have nowhere to go, Didi. Please."

My heart leapt with joy. I hid the glow inside me as cautiously as a child hides his newly discovered treasure from prying adult eyes.

"Rano, you don't have to plead so much. I had told you, my doors are always open for you."

It was settled. I told Rano that I'd ask the "other maid" to leave and that she could take over immediately. It was heaven. My life was suddenly so simple.

Rano fitted back into the household seamlessly. My children were happy to have her back and my worries took wings and flew out. To express my gratitude, I got Rano some new clothes and belongings.

One thing marred this picture-perfect existence though. Rano's personal life was a mess. She had not received the happiness I thought she deserved and I felt sorry for her. It was her troubles in life which had gifted her back to me and the irony hit me in the face. A tiny speck of guilt took birth inside me. It grew bigger some day and vanished on others, but it remained and its presence pricked my conscience very often. I took solace from the fact that her lot in life had improved since she returned to me. However, there were moments when she would wear a lost expression and a tiny tear would trickle down her face. I knew she was missing her husband and home.

One Sunday afternoon, we hosted a lunch party for some friends. Rano worked efficiently and tirelessly to serve the guests well. Late into the day, they left one by one. After Rano cleaned up the kitchen and settled the children with me, I told her, "Now you go and take a nap. You must be very tired."

She sighed with fatigue and went upstairs to her cot in her room. When I went to check on her after ten minutes, the only sound I heard was her gentle snoring.

The doorbell rang.

I answered it. A man in his late twenties stood outside, shuffling his feet over the doormat. When he saw me he said, "Namaste. Is this Mrs Naina Rathore's house?"

"Yes it is. I am Naina. Tell me."

A look of relief crossed his face.

"I am Manohar, Rano's husband."

I stiffened.

"Yes, what is it?"

"I have come to meet Rano. Can you please call her?"

I looked him up and down. So he was the one who had made Rano's life miserable. I went two steps inside and took the keys off the hanger, then stepped out and closed the door behind me. I stood facing him just outside the threshold.

"Why have you come here? First you torture the girl and then you want to meet her! The poor motherless wretch! I saw the marks on her body. You should be thankful she didn't go to the police."

The man stood silently, head down.

"It is men like you who make women feel that marriage is useless! How dare you come here?"

Each word I spat at him was caustic and full of anger. I hadn't known I was capable of such bitter rage.

"What is it you want from her now?"

He cast a quick glance at me and then again fixed his sight on the doormat.

"I want to make amends, Didi. I realized my mistake when she had gone. So much misfortune has befallen me since she left. I know I didn't do any good to her. But I want to talk to her now and say sorry. If she forgives me, she might give me another chance."

"Another chance? Another chance, you say? For what? To make a fool of her? Why do you need her now? To use her like a doormat? To utilise her in bed? And then discard her when you're drunk?" I was almost shouting now.

He looked up. He was apparently taken aback. A split second later, I was asking myself why I needed to say all this to him.

His eyes were wet with tears of remorse, I could see that. Through my fury, I realised that he had every chance of winning Rano back. She could get back all the happiness she deserved, which I always said she did. Maybe for good. Her potential destiny was clawing at mine. In a flash, the threat of losing her to this man raised its head monstrously in front of me.

"Didi, please call her." Manohar's voice snapped me out of my thoughts. He had folded his hands together.

"How can I call her? She is not here," I replied abruptly.

"Not here? ... But..." Manohar's face was drained of blood it seemed.

"No! She had come to meet me after reaching Mumbai but said she doesn't want to be found by you. She left for some other place. She didn't tell me where." I paused briefly. "But I'm glad you came here. I've wanted to give you a piece of my mind for long. You really shouldn't have hurt her like this. She has suffered so much, poor girl."

He thanked me, hands still folded and eyes still wet. "If she calls you, Didi, please tell her that I had come and why. I will be grateful to you. She might give me a chance."

"Certainly. If she calls, I'll tell her."

Manohar left. I opened the door and went back inside.

Dusk had set in and the last patch of sun was fading away. Rano was still sleeping.

A dark sinister shadow fell onto the corridor floor. I drew the curtains and went to my children.

SUGAR AND SPICE AND ALL THINGS...

Which of us is lesser
Which the smarter one
Can you hear god's laughter
At the mirror having fun

When Amrita Varma put the phone down that morning, she was filled with dread. It was a call that she knew she would have to face at some time, and of course she had imagined it in her head several times, but now that it had happened, she felt as if the whole world around her stood still.

It was Brijesh-ji, her father's caretaker, calling for a second time. The first time, of course, she was in the middle of a conference call. She ignored her phone, thinking she could just speak to Brijesh-ji later. When he called again, however, she knew that something was wrong, and she was right. Her father, the famous journalist and author Hansal Pujari, was dying, and wanted to meet his daughter before he passed.

It had been a year since Amrita and her husband Gautam had driven down from Delhi to her father's house in the hills of Mussoorie. Retired for the last twenty years after publishing his last column, he had given up his life in Defence Colony for a more quiet and serene life in the mountains. Amrita would drive there every few months to check up on his steadily deteriorating health, and get an update from the ever-loving Brijesh-ji, who also made some of the best kachoris she had eaten in her life. The last time that she was there was his birthday. He had seemed well and happy, though he missed seeing his granddaughter. Now well into her rebellious teenage years and on the verge of college life, she had refused to accompany her mother for a "boring" trip to the hills.

But this whirlpool of thoughts and memories was interrupted by an urgent knock on the door. It was Vatsal, Amrita's young assistant and an intern with her marketing company.

Amrita was shaken out of her stupor, and realised that she hadn't moved an inch after putting down the phone.

"Sorry, Amrita Ma'am, this came in for you just now."

Vatsal walked in to hand over a sheet of paper that was still warm, and smooth, something that Amrita hadn't come across in a while. Of course, it was a fax from Brijesh-ji. Under normal circumstances she would have laughed at the fact that her old-school journalist father refused to set up an email account, but reading what was written on the piece of paper felt like a punch to the gut after that phone call. It was Brijesh-ji's handwriting:

Hansal Baba says to go to this address in Dehradun and pick up your sister, and bring her along, will explain later.

Sister? Amrita had grown up and been raised as an only child. What was going on? And then, she read the address; it was the Sahaya School for the specially abled in Dehradun. This was all getting a bit overwhelming, but at once, Amrita's crisis management skills kicked in. She gathered her things and stormed out of the office, almost running past Vatsal's desk. The time to process would come later.

"Ma'am...?"

"No time now. Clear my schedule for the next week, family emergency. Email me if it's important, call me if it's critical..."

She was in the elevator before Vatsal could even say that he got all of that...

*

Sister Rujuta, the head nurse at Sahaya home, was patient and kind, and had told Amrita that she would have to be very calm in dealing with Ambika. Amrita was made to wait in the office, where the "reunion" would happen, and in the meantime, was given the photographs and notes that Ambika had brought along with her when she had come in, nearly forty years ago.

Forty years, and she had never known that she had had a sister?

As she went through some of the photographs, a chill ran down her spine. She remembered some of the moments, vaguely, almost as if they were dreams, for they were from a time when she was barely two years old. It was like seeing a photo where there were two of herself. Her hands began to shake, as she wondered what it would be like coming face-to-face with the twin sister she never knew she had. She almost jumped as she felt a hand on her shoulder.

"Sorry, my dear, I didn't mean to startle you." It was Sister Rujuta. "See, my dear, I know how scared you are feeling, and remember, little Ambika is scared too, and she may not look it but mentally, she is a ten-year-old girl..."

"I can heaaarrrrr youuuuuuu!" came a voice from just outside the modest and slightly rundown office. It made Amrita's hair stand on end, like listening to a recording of herself, except as if imitating a child, emphasising every syllable of every word.

Sister Rujuta looked at Amrita as if to encourage her, but Amrita was clueless. Was she supposed to respond? As the weight of the silence threatened to drown her, Amrita said the first thing that came to her head.

"Come out, come out wherever you are!"

And as soon as she said it, she admonished herself. Hide-and-seek at a time like this? But somehow, it worked. Into the room jumped Ambika Pujari, and Amrita felt like she was going through some kind of dystopian out-of-body experience.

The woman who stood in front of her looked exactly like her, just less "proper". Amrita felt like she was looking in a mirror but she had to stop herself from pinpointing flaws like the unkempt eyebrows and the chapped lips that she would have made a to-do list of, to attend to. It was uncanny, and Amrita didn't know what to make of it. Ambika's hair was messy, her knee-length dress wrinkled and frayed at the seams, her skin a little rougher and tanned from spending as much time in the sun as the daily playtime permitted.

But while Amrita was struggling to put also this into perspective and move ahead, Ambika was smiling.

"Didi..."

Ambika rushed forward to embrace Amrita, who was surprised at the tears that followed. She hadn't given herself any time to process these emotions, or any emotions for that matter, since she had received the call from Brijesh-ji.

"Ambika..."

"Didi?"

"Do you want to say bye to your friends?"

"I already did, I know Papa is not well, we have to go, no ... They told me that my sister will come to take me to him ... but I did not know that you look like me."

Amrita was surprised to hear that. How much did Ambika know?

"Don't worry, Didi, it will be okay," said Ambika, as she embraced her sister. Amrita stood rooted to the spot, numb and not knowing how to react or what to say.

"Brijesh Uncle had told me that one day when Papa was not well, someone who looked like me would come to take me to meet him ... I didn't know it would be me, myself!" she continued, still embracing Amrita, "but he also said that that person would make it all okay like she always does..."

Amrita was letting this all sink in. In less than twelve hours her life had turned on its head, and she had a feeling it wouldn't end there...

"Should we go, Didi?"
"Yes ... Yes, of course."

*

The hour-long drive from Dehradun to Mussoorie was spent in silence. Amrita was struggling to process her feelings, but for some reason she was filled with anger, anger at being lied to, at being kept in the dark, and anger that her twin Ambika, sitting next to her, seemed least bothered that they might be going to see their father for the last time.

Hansal Pujari's estate was located on the way down from the famous Depot Hill in Mussoorie. He had always joked that if he shouted loud enough, he could call out to Ruskin Bond and have a chat over some chai. The gates opened automatically as Amrita's car approached. She had installed that feature last year when it became obvious that there could be a situation in the near future when maybe every second could be vital.

That didn't seem to be the case today, though, as Hansal came out to greet them, supported by Brijesh-ji. Hansal looked a lot paler and weaker than usual, but nothing about his demeanour and physicality suggested that he was a man living out the last of his days. At first, Amrita was filled with relief; she had lost count of the dreadful images that had flashed in her mind as she drove there from Delhi.

As she parked the car in front of the house, she glanced at her phone to check a message from Vivek, her husband.

Atika given detention for three days for bad attendance. Final warning from principal. Handled for now but must speak when you're back. Keep me posted, love you.

Argh! Her daughter Atika had been facing issues at school for the last year, constantly being caught skipping classes, and drawing graffiti on the walls of the school, acting out her rebellious years in the most immature ways. At a time when Amrita had been promoted to the CEO of her marketing firm, something she had been dreaming of her entire career, the one time she had needed the support and help of her family, her daughter had gone ahead and added to her worries.

But there was no time to think about that now.

Hansal held his hands out, and Ambika ran to embrace him. It was quite surreal for Amrita to watch this spitting image of herself. She had so many questions. Brijesh-ji walked slowly to the rear of the car, anticipating that the sisters would need help with their luggage.

"Just hers, Brijesh-ji, I won't be staying long…"

Mussoorie was a quiet place as the sun was setting, but Amrita's words seemed to echo in the air far longer than normal. Brijesh-ji stood still, looking at Hansal for instructions.

"Gudiya, come in, let's speak for some time, have a drink of sura with me, I know you have questions…" began Hansal, before he was rudely cut off by Amrita, who raised her finger at him for the first time.

"Don't 'gudiya' me anymore, Papa," she said, seething with anger. "I'm going to freshen up, and leave, and Brijesh-ji, please only take the gift-wrapped box from the car from my luggage."

As she stormed into the house, she passed Hansal and a scared-looking Ambika, who still had her arms wrapped around her father, holding his beard, just like the way Amrita would when she was growing up.

"Happy bloody birthday, Dad…" she said.

*

Dinner that night was had in silence, after Brijesh-ji had convinced Amrita to at least spend the night there to have a talk with her father. Hansal wasn't dying, or unwell, but he knew that his time wasn't very far off; he had called his daughters together because it was time, in his mind.

The walls were adorned with certificates and medals from Hansal's illustrious career, but front and centre on the mantlepiece above the fire were two little bronze trophies, obviously made to a modest budget befitting the convent school that Amrita went to. "For Outstanding Debating Skills," it said on the plaque, and just below in a string of holes that had been engraved by perhaps the Arts and Crafts teacher, "Amrita Pujari".

Amrita and Ambika sat across each other on the table, and Amrita spent more time watching, as watching her sister eat was like seeing herself when she was ten. Ketchup on everything, and of course the vegetables were ignored until someone else called her out on them. Till a few years ago, little Atika used to do exactly the same thing.

Hansal chewed his food slowly. He noticed that Amrita had barely touched hers.

"Gud..." he began before correcting himself. "Amrita, let's at least talk about it?"

"I'd, but honestly where do we even start?"

It wasn't like Amrita had lost her appetite; it was more because from the time she had come into her father's house, she felt as if she had a lump in her throat that she had been fighting every second. Ambika was so scared of her after her outburst on their arrival that she had avoided eye contact with her altogether, pouring more ketchup onto the aloo tikkis instead.

"It wasn't easy, beta, after Mom passed. I was struggling with my own sadness, and you ... I just instinctively felt that you were driven, motivated, and needed to be given the attention that would make you flourish, without being weighed down..."

As he spoke, Hansal reached out and held Ambika's hand, which was still clutching the spoon as she gobbled up the last of the little fried papad that Brijesh-ji served, crumbs falling all over her side of the table. Amrita tried hard to ignore the mess, but was getting increasingly anxious as she kept glancing towards her phone. This time there wasn't even a message from Atika saying sorry for being suspended, or sorry for anything at all; the nerve of the girl...

"And Ambu, she is special, she needed to be cared for in a way that I couldn't possibly manage."

Amrita understood what her father was saying, but how could he lie to her like that? Why would he?

"Forty years, Papa? It took you forty years to tell me the truth? And you give me nightmares by making Brijesh-ji send me stupid fax messages to make it look like you're dying?" Amrita was seething now, and she pushed her chair away from the table to get up.

"Beta, please, let's please sit down and talk, your mother had rules around mealtime..."

"Don't! Don't you dare talk to me about Mom. Not after what you've done."

Ambika had left her food, and was holding back tears, her didi was scaring her with her anger. She tried to pull her hand away from Hansal's grip to cover her ears like she had always done, but Hansal didn't let her. He looked at her as if to say, don't worry, it's going to be okay, but Amrita was angry, very angry.

"Why didn't you tell me?"

"I know, you're right. I should have. I kept thinking that whenever I did tell you, it would come to you as a shock and you'd need some time and space to deal with things, but you just went from strength to strength in your own life, and every time I came close to telling you, I just couldn't..."

"And all this time you thought it was fair to her?" demanded Amrita, gesturing towards her twin sister.

"I like my life in Sahaya, Didi, I have friends, they let us play, and watch movies on Friday, and they force us to eat vegetables but only that Sister Rujuta ... When she doesn't look I throw them away in the dustbin or pretend to drop them..."

"Oh just, please, Ambika ... You have no idea what you're talking about..."

"Enough!" shouted Hansal.

Amrita was shocked. It had been years since he had raised his voice, but it was all too much for Amrita. She glanced at her phone again for the fifteenth time in as many minutes, and still no message from her daughter. Ambika had covered her ears with both her hands and was on the verge of tears. Amrita turned on her heels and stormed outside, stopping to grab her car keys outside.

*

Amrita had forgotten how quickly the hilly air got cold after sunset, as she went about looking for Brijesh-ji so that he could unlock the door to the garage for her. She almost jumped as she heard her own voice call out, "Didi!"

Ambika had come out of the house without grabbing a shawl, and was shivering in the cold air of the August evening.

"Didi, please finish your food at least. Sister Rujuta says that you should not eat when you are angry, so I came to say sorry."

Amrita looked at her sister, not knowing whether to laugh, or cry, or scold her as she would a child.

"No! You don't say sorry to me. Don't do that. This is not your fault, you hear me? What Papa did was wrong, wrong to you and wrong to me. You have nothing to apologise for."

"But then why didn't you finish your food?" Ambika asked innocently.

"We can talk inside, you'll catch a cold…" said Amrita, taking Ambika by the arm and leading her towards the house.

"No! I don't want to go inside. I was so happy to see you, Didi, I didn't know about you at all, and when Sister Rujuta told me that there was a surprise for me I was so excited, but ever since you came to meet me, you have been angry with Papa, and angry around me. Papa says you're my sister, my twin sister, almost like we are the same. But we are not, you are just angry, all the time, maybe if you stand in this cool air it will help your mind…"

"It's not about the air, Ambika." Amrita felt strange, it was only the second time she had addressed her sister by her name. "It's about what is right, and what is wrong. What he did to both you and me was just wrong."

"But … Why?"

"Because … I mean, what do you mean why? He lied to us. To you. He didn't care for you or your happiness." Amrita was getting worked up again, and had to remind herself to calm down, and remember whom she was talking to.

"But, Didi, I was happy till you came to meet me…"

And just like that, Amrita felt like she had been punched in the gut, and something in her broke. That lump in her throat that she had been fighting finally won.

The tears poured forth, and seeing her sister cry, Ambika felt terrible and rushed forward to embrace her once again. This time, Amrita wrapped her arms around her sister, crying like she hadn't in years. It wasn't the injustice, or being lied to. She looked at her sister and for the first time in many years, felt helpless.

"I'm sorry, Didi, I did not mean to make you cry…"

"No, no, it's not your fault, Ambika," said Amrita through the tears.

"It's okay, Didi, you can cry if you want to…"

And as she cried her anger away, Amrita felt a connection she hadn't felt in years, and knew in that moment who, between them, would come and make it all feel okay again…

THANK YOU, PNEUMONIA

God hears when little girls pray
If only her parents would understand
What she prays for every day
And give god a helping hand

It was Sunday morning and one by one all the children were leaving the park. The hot noon sun beat hard on her head. There was no one left to play with now. Ten-year-old Nima thought of returning home too.

But ... she hoped things would not be as bad as they had been this morning. It had been like all other holidays. She had woken up to the arguing voices of Amma and Appa. And she knew that once things started like this they would only get worse.

Her heart sinking, she had witnessed the familiar scene all over again – Appa slapping Amma, who was shrieking hysterically. She dared not come between them, for the last time she had done that Appa had pushed her away. She just watched from behind the curtain, praying that it would end soon.

After an interminable period of time, it finally did, with Appa storming out of the house and Amma weeping into her pillow. Nima didn't try to console Amma. Somehow, it never helped, and Amma usually wanted to be left alone.

Nima had been loitering in the park all morning. The neighbourhood children came and went. She had played with a few of them, but most of the time she sat on the wooden seat of the swing, digging her toes into the warm sand, sleepy, worried and very, very tired.

Aunty Anju had walked up to her and asked, "I could hear a lot of noises next door. Anything happened at home, Nima dear?" Tears of shame had flowed down Nima's flushed cheeks. It always happened this way. The neighbouring grown-ups asked her so many prying questions which she never knew how to answer. Why did they enjoy upsetting her like this?

But then why did her parents have to fight like this? Why weren't they like her friend's parents? Sanju's parents took him out every evening to the park and Malini's family always went out for a picnic or movie every Sunday. She could hardly remember her last outing. In any case she'd never seen other parents fight like Amma and Appa.

Maybe someday a miracle would happen and her parents would become happy again. Maybe if she became a good child and prayed hard to god he would make her home as happy as those of the others. Didn't the nuns at school say so often that god always listened to a good child's prayers?

Thinking of school always cheered her up. How much better than home it was! Nima felt excited as she thought about tomorrow – there was going to be an interschool painting competition and Nima had been chosen to represent her school in the under-fourteen category again. Last year she had won the second prize, this year she was determined to win the first. That reminded her! She had to buy some new brushes for tomorrow.

Nima's heart sank again. Amma was in such a foul mood. How would she broach the subject of the new brushes? But then, they simply had to be bought today itself.

Nima walked back slowly towards the house. She opened the door and stealthily stepped in. Amma was in the kitchen, banging about furiously as she cooked. Nima slipped into the seat of her chair at the dining table quietly. She looked at Amma's face as she put a plate of food before her. She noticed that her eyes were swollen with crying.

Nima did not feel like eating anything but was afraid to incur Amma's wrath and so she forced herself. As she stuffed the last morsel into her mouth she noticed that Amma had already gone back to bed.

The kitchen was a mess. Appa would lose his cool again if he were to walk in right now. Nima tried her best to clean up as she stood on a stool to reach the kitchen slab. Then she proceeded to Amma's room.

Amma was not yet asleep. Maybe she was in a better mood, thought Nima, as she considered broaching the topic of the brushes.

"What is it, Nima?"

"Amma, I need new paintbrushes for tomorrow's competition."

Amma was glaring at her. "And you must tell me only now. You can't bear to see me rest a moment, can you? Why don't you ask that father of yours, instead of eating my head? The two of you together are bent upon ruining my life," she shrieked.

"Please, Amma."

"Stop pestering me and get away from here."

Nima turned back, tears streaming down her cheeks as her feet led her out of the house. She sat down on the porch steps. There was no point. It would be the same with Appa. Neither of them cared for her, they only cared for fighting and abusing each other. How long would all this go on, she wondered. She was always afraid that someday something awful would happen. Amma was always threatening to commit suicide and Appa too drove so recklessly when he was angry. Every night, before she slept, Nima thanked god that they were all alive, but every other day she was afraid again. Please, please, Amma and Appa, don't fight, she yearned to plead with them but would never dare to open her mouth. Many of Appa's and Amma's friends had tried to tell them this. But they never understood.

Nima was feeling so hot and tired. She thought of going inside and sleeping on the cot but she could hardly bring herself to get up. What was happening to her? Why was she so sleepy? She shouldn't sleep here ... must go inside ... in...

Soon she was fast asleep and dreaming. Dreaming of the rain – of cool drops that came first in a gentle shower and then in a spray of monsoon fury upon her burning torso. Delicious relief for many hours...

When Nima opened her eyes at last, she found herself lying on a bed. Her whole body ached miserably. But ... this was not her room ... what was this tube in her nose, and this needle stuck in her arm. Appa and Amma stood on either side of her bed, looking so cross and solemn. She saw a nurse enter the room and realised she was in a hospital.

As her eyes met Appa's she saw him go out of the room. He came in again with the doctor. She could only catch bits of their conversation.

"A case of pneumonia ... lucky she's come through sedatives ... should sleep well."

Nima closed her eyes. She felt so drowsy.

"Nima dear, you must eat and sleep well if you want to be all right soon," said the doctor, gently stroking her head while the nurse removed the tube from her nose.

Nima nodded weakly. If only she could tell him not to let Amma and Appa fight, she would be able to sleep without worrying. What if Amma did something stupid and Appa started beating her right there ... what if Appa ran away suddenly leaving Amma and her alone ... what if ... yes, sleep did conquer her at last.

But at the faintest sound she would open her eyes with a start, as though she had actually been awake all the while. And then relieved that things were still alright she would go back to rest, until the next start.

This time too she opened her eyes with a jerk. Appa and Amma sat on the same side of her bed. Amma was crying softly.

Nima's heart sank. He must have beaten her or he was going to ... Oh god! How could she stop them?

But ... what was this? He was giving her a glass of water! She stared. This could not be true. Amma and Appa? And now he was holding her hand. She had put her head on his shoulder.

Nima closed her eyes. This time she didn't want to open them, for fear that the scene might disappear and another more familiar one take its place. She must sleep, she could sleep now – a deep, restful, sleep...

THE HOMELAND

Where do I find my home
Who do I call my own
A lifetime we can roam
And in a crowd be alone

"Namaskar. We wish all our passengers a very good day. We are currently flying over Jaipur, which is known as the Pink City of India. In about thirty minutes from now we shall be landing, as scheduled, at Delhi's Indira Gandhi International Airport. Passengers may set their watches by IST at 3.30 hours at the present moment. Please stand by for the next announcement at 3.50 hours. We hope you are enjoying your journey with us. Thank you," said the voice over the intercom.

Natasha had been feeling drowsy all this while. It was the first time that she had flown for so many hours at a stretch. But as she heard the announcement and set her watch, she felt a tingle of excitement down her spine

Her mother had never been happy in India, even after Natasha was born. Natasha had been too small to remember what had happened. All she knew was that her mother had come back to Paris with her, when she was only two years old. The two of them lived with Natasha's maternal grandfather and had maintained absolutely no contact with her father, or other relatives in India.

They lived well, for Natasha's grandpa had a huge mansion for a house, most of which had been converted into a motel.

But Natasha had never really been satisfied. She missed having a father, especially when she realised that she did have one ... only that mother had deliberately kept her away from him. Allowing her to meet him was a distant question – Mother had not even allowed access to his address in India.

And Natasha had been so bitter about this.

She had argued, wept and fought but Mother had never yielded. She had simply said that she had forgotten the address as it had been more than eighteen years since she came back, but Natasha never did believe this. She had resorted to prying into her mother's drawers whenever the latter was away, in the hope of finding the address, or some sort of clue to the same. But she had never found anything that helped. She often fantasised about the country and its people as she read any and everything about India that she could lay her hands upon. Occasionally, she picked up colourful skirts and trinkets from the Indian emporium.

After she completed school, Natasha had moved out from her grandfather's mansion into her own apartment, one which she shared with her classmate Maria. Five days in the week she was at the university and on weekends she worked hard as a production assistant for the *Weekly Gazette* to pay for her expenses. Once in a month she paid her mother a brief visit and collected any mail that may have come in for her. It was a tough and busy life.

It was on one such day last year that she had noticed an unfamiliar blue envelope in the mail. She flipped it over. It was from India. With joy and trepidation she tore it open.

Dear Natasha,

I do not think you know who is writing this letter and I also doubt you will get to read it. Yet I am writing with the hope that it will reach you.

I am your uncle, Shiva, your father Damodar's brother. You were only two when your mother left India with you, yet I am writing to you and not to her, for I don't think she has forgotten the past enough to be able to share in this present.

I have to give you some bad news. Your father passed away a week ago. He had lost his sanity a long time back but we all tried our best for him. We found your grandfather's address yesterday while we were sorting out some of your father's papers.

We offer you our condolences and pray your future be as bright as your father would have wanted it to be.

Do write back if you feel like. We would love to hear from you.

With love and blessings
Your uncle
Shiva Saran

Holding back her tears, Natasha put the letter back into the envelope.

So this was how it was going to be. The piece of paper that she held in her hand had ended the little hope that remained in her that someday, somehow, she might see her father. For don't we all believe that it will never be too late ... until one day, it actually is?

If only Father had written to her earlier ... Why hadn't he? His insanity perhaps?

A few days later Natasha replied to her uncle's letter.

Over the next few months there had followed regular correspondence between Uncle Shiva's family and herself. Gradually, Natasha began feeling more and more a part of her uncle's family. Her uncle, aunt and cousin addressed their letters to Natasha Dugois, but they always referred to her as Nisha in their letters. For that, they told her, was the name her father had given her when she was born.

Today she was on her way to Delhi to meet the entire family ... to be with her father's people, her people. She had saved all she could over these months and had finally been able to afford this holiday. She often imagined how she might one day make this city her alternate home.

The voice over the intercom requested the passengers to fasten their seat belts; they were about to land. She soon felt her ears go "pop" as the plane descended. Then, even as she looked through the glass window, she felt the plane surge forward, gradually rolling to its halt. Homeland at last!

*

She clutched her bag tight as she exited the airport. There were scores of people waving at the entrance. Gosh, she hoped they would be able to recognise her. She had written to Uncle Shiva that she would be wearing this red skirt and white shirt. Ah! That must be him, coming towards her with a plump, pleasant-looking woman beside him.

"Nisha?"

"Yes ... Uncle?" she said, smiling.

It was a great homecoming. Her uncle, aunt and cousin made her feel more at home than she had ever felt. She spent the next few days chatting, shopping, sightseeing, horsing around with her cousin Shomu, looking at all the family photographs and devouring Indian food. Yes ... she really felt she belonged here!

And perhaps the greatest news of all was that Shomu would shortly be moving to Paris for some years to pursue a diploma in fashion designing. His parents had requested her if she could help him out with a spare room in her apartment – there was of course no question of him paying rent – he was the only brother she would ever have.

She enjoyed every moment of the two weeks that she spent. There seemed ever so much to talk about and yet in all their conversations there was hardly any reference to her mother. Whenever there was, an undercurrent of hostility was clearly perceptible. In fact, when they learnt that Natasha had moved out of her mother's home, and sensed that she and her mother were not on the best of terms, they had been very sympathetic. About her father, they seemed to be talking all the time ... what a lovely person he had been ... how much she resembled him, and so on and so forth...

By now she was even familiar with Delhi's streets and some of its more famous markets and shopping centres. She was always taken around by her uncle, aunt or Shomu. She had seen nearly all that was worth seeing. But there was still one place that she yearned the most to visit – her father's one-room tenement that she was told was located in one of the not-so-well maintained colonies of Delhi.

Natasha had often requested to be taken there ... yet it had been two weeks and somehow this trip kept getting postponed. Perhaps, she thought, they wanted to cushion her against any pain the experience might result in. Yet, for her it was so important to try and feel her father's presence amongst the things he used and the people he lived with.

Today, after many days, there had been no plans for an evening out. On impulse, Natasha went to her aunt in the kitchen.

"Aunty, may I go for a walk? It's such a pleasant evening," she said.

"Sure, Nisha. I'll ask Shomu to go with you," replied her aunt.

"No, Aunty, I'll manage on my own. I'm feeling a little adventurous, but I promise I won't venture too far and I'll be back soon. Please, Aunty," she pleaded.

"If you insist, my dear. But be very careful. Delhi isn't the safest place for a young girl to venture out after six," she said, her tone full of apprehension.

"I'll be careful, Aunty," Natasha assured her as she set off.

She hailed an autorickshaw at the street corner. She showed the driver the slip of paper on which her father's address was written. He seemed surprised that a well-dressed girl like her would want to go to this place, but he agreed to take her.

Fifteen minutes later they were there. It was a tiny, dilapidated one-room tenement. Natasha gave the front door a slight push. To her surprise it wasn't locked. She was soon to realise why.

There was hardly anything of value inside. A pile of old, dirty rags and a tin trunk were kept in the corner. The walls had peeled in so many places and the corner of the roof were thick with cobwebs. The smell of decay and neglect was everywhere.

Natasha opened the trunk. She rummaged through its contents in the hope of finding memorabilia to take with her ... an old tie, the Holy Bible, a book on basic French, an old saucepan.

"Who's there?"

She turned around with a start. At the front door stood a woman, looking at her curiously.

"I-I'm Natasha. My father used to live here," she explained.

"Oh," said the woman. Then after a pause she continued, "I'm sorry to have frightened you. I live next door and was wondering who it could be. Why did you come so late, my child?" She sighed. "There's nothing worth taking away, but we don't like strangers prowling around ... it's been like this ever since Damodar Bhai went. But ... how come you're here now?"

"It's a long story," replied Natasha.

The woman invited her for a cup of tea next door.

As they both sat sipping tea, Natasha explained everything. The woman was sympathetic and kind.

"Aunty, tell me something about Father," she asked, a little hesitatingly.

"Oh, Damodar Bhai? He was a good man, but very lonely. If only you had come a little earlier ... he might have died in peace. But then, how could you have? He didn't want to disturb your life ... that's why he never wrote to you though we told him so often to do so. You know, a lot of people thought he was mad. Yes, he was very miserable, mentally disturbed and disoriented too ... but he wasn't mad. After all, he stayed amongst us for ten long years ... we should know better, shouldn't we?"

Natasha was all ears.

"But his relatives, especially his brother Shiva, never bothered to do anything for him, though he often went to them pleading for help. They closed all doors on him and even appropriated his share of the family wealth. If his brother had helped him, he might have tided over the rough patch in his life. But they all preferred to proclaim him insane and leave him to his sad fate. He had a very hard time, for his health didn't allow him to work much, but the children in this colony still remember how often he played with them and brought them sweets ... poor man. There was nobody to look after him. No one even knew he was dead until a day later..."

Natasha had been sobbing for a long time now. Oh! how cruel fate had been ... how much she had wanted to do something for him ... if only....

"Don't cry, my dear. It's god's will. We all did our best, and it's not your fault. All we can do now is to pray for his soul to rest in peace," said the woman.

Yes, she couldn't do more than that, but Uncle Shiva could have. How wrong she had been in her perceptions about them. For, if they were being so good with her now, it was not so much because they cared. It was ... yes ... it was all falling into place now. It was because Shomu could do with her help when he moved to Paris.

Natasha wiped her eyes and bid the woman goodbye. She reached home as if in a daze.

At home her uncle's family sensed that something was amiss and prodded her to tell them what it was. But Natasha would not say a word as she slowly packed her bags.

Her aunt asked. "You can't do this. Why are you going? How will you manage? Where? What happened? What about Shomu?" she uttered in anguish.

Without a word she walked out.

Four days later, as she unpacked her bags in her apartment at Paris, there was a knock at the door. It was her roommate Maria.

"Hi! Back so soon? How was the trip to your homeland?" asked Maria, giving Natasha a hug.

Natasha pointed to the four walls of their apartment. "This is my only homeland," she replied with a weak smile on her face.

THE TALL TALE

What does a mother leave behind
For a child to remember her by
A friend both strong and kind
And lifelong memories that do not die

Bina lay on her bed, staring aimlessly at the ceiling and its every familiar wrinkle. She then looked down at the digital clock kept on the small wooden bedside table. Fifty-six minutes past three, it read. Precisely four minutes left, thought Bina, and decided to begin the arduous task of turning on her side, so that she faced Aditya when he walked into her room, and be ready for him to embrace her. It took her two minutes to turn, for half her body was paralysed.

At fifty-eight minutes past three, she noticed that while turning, she had shifted the bedcover at her feet, exposing the soft and bright pink foam of the mattress beneath. Bina grimaced as she straightened out the bedcover with her working left foot. Once again she stole a glance at the clock. Fifty-nine minutes past three, its large screen displayed. Just one minute left for the characteristically short peal of the doorbell (Aditya could not reach the doorbell, so he would jump and ring it, and hence...), her mind told her. She could already imagine her beloved Adi, walking up the staircase with his satchel on his back and his water bottle in hand. She waited with bated breath...

So she waited, and waited, but today Aditya simply would not come. She was now getting increasingly anxious. Every passing second made her more worried. Finally at six minutes past four, there was a quick ding-dong. Bina quickly pretended to be asleep. She could hear Sharda, the house help, open the door. Bina's heart was beating faster now, and louder too. She heard Aditya's footsteps drawing nearer.

Less than a second later, she heard it open. There was a quick scramble of footsteps, and then everything became silent. Bina knew that Aditya was very much near her. She always pretended to be asleep when Aditya came home from school, for she knew that he would come, sit down at her bedside, and, not wanting to disturb her, lightly plant a kiss on her cheek. She would then wake up, and greet him (or, more often, groan at the sight of his mud-stained shirt that had been a bright white in the morning), and then begin talking to him at great length about the day's events at school, while Sharda got him something to eat.

Aditya stood next to her bed, kissed her cheek, and she pretended to wake up. She saw his little three-foot figure, drenched to the bone. Yet he seemed to be extraordinarily happy, as was indicated by the smile on his face. And then she saw the puddle at Aditya's feet.

"Oh no!" said Bina. "Adi beta, you forgot to carry your raincoat again!" She knew well that Aditya had probably been aware that he should take it, but had left it at home on purpose.

"Sorry, Mama, I'll carry it tomorrow, I promise you."

"Why are you so late today, beta? You know that I worry about you..." Bina asked.

Aditya replied, "Relax, Mama, I am eleven years old now and I can take care of myself, you know that! I had forgotten my raincoat at home, and I thought that since I was in any case going to get wet, I might as well enjoy the rain for a little while longer." He chuckled.

"You're incorrigible, Aditya. Now be a good boy and go for a bath right away. Change into a fresh set of clothes. Ah, and before that, take all the books out of your bag and keep them out on the table to dry. Sharda has cut mangoes and kept them out on the table for you to eat. Hurry up, Aditya!"

"Mama, why can't I eat the mangoes and then go for a bath?"

Bina gave Aditya one of those stares that only a mother can give and make her son submit to her. That was enough for Aditya, who got the hint and after a little bit of grumbling, went for a bath.

Just as Aditya was out of earshot, Bina let out a little chuckle. Though she was supposed to be upset with Aditya, as any mother would and should have been, Bina had begun to enjoy these little arguments she had with him. In fact, she savoured any bit of interaction she had with him at all. After all, she did not know how much more time she had to cherish these little blessings.

Bina was a girl from a small village on the outskirts of Bombay. Her family was quintessentially rural, but well to do. When her father had saved enough money, he relocated to Bombay. Bina got educated in the city, and went on to pursue a career as a lawyer. She had an immense talent for arguing, and this was instrumental in her success. Once she was satisfied with her career, she got married to Nitin, a businessman, and about a year later, she gave birth to their son Aditya. She seemed to have the perfect life, for she had a beautiful child, a loving and caring husband, and had almost nothing in the world to worry about...

However, Bina's bubble was just about to burst. One day, when she was arguing out a case in court, she collapsed. She was rushed to the hospital, and after a few tests, doctors diagnosed her with a brain tumour. They said she had less than a year to live...

Now, the tumour was not only ending her life, but it was also impacting the quality of whatever was left of it. It had paralysed half her body, and had restricted the movements of the other half. She was now bedridden, with nothing to look forward to each day, save the arrival of her beloved Adi from school, and their little happy interactions.

Ten minutes later, Aditya had finished bathing and was sitting on a little foot-stool by Bina's bedside, gorging on his favourite, and no doubt delicious, Alphonso mangoes. Bina watched him, delighted, as he spilled fresh yellow stains on his shirt and pant. She was taking in every bit of this wonderful sight, before she realised that she must tick him off to be less messy. The juice continued trickling down his hands, onto his forearms, elbows, and finally his pants. She gazed at his round face, dimpled chin, and looked on fondly.

Patiently, Bina waited for Adi to finish eating the mangoes, lick his podgy fingers, and then asked him (as she did every day) about school.

Like always he first shrugged his shoulders, and said, "Nothing much, Mama, you know the usual ... Books and studies..."

Bina waited in keen anticipation, and, seeing her, Aditya's eyes lit up in excitement, as if he had forgotten to tell her something very exciting.

"You know, Mama, I almost forgot to tell you ... Something very good happened in school today! You know Pranay, no? He got into a fight with an older boy. I don't know why they fought, Mama, but I went in between and stopped the fight!"

Aditya went on to describe how he heroically took control of the situation and reported the duo to the principal, Father Pinto. He also said that because this, he was made the class monitor. Aditya paused, before adding, "Mama, do you feel happy when I tell you what a good boy I have been?"

Bina replied, "Not just happy, beta, I feel thrilled! You make all my pain go away!"

Aditya looked pleased. Bina smiled as she watched Aditya bubbling with excitement at the prospect of being given such importance. Moments like these drove away all the darkness and gloom in her life. It was almost as if she lived only for those minutes with Aditya. It seemed so wonderful that he was turning out to be such a good boy, in spite of her not being able to do as much as she would have loved to. She felt so proud of him. Over the last few months, she was living her life vicariously through him. He meant the world to her. It was almost as if god was compensating her big sorrow with small joys. Every day, Aditya would bring her stories of his tiny achievements at school. Tiny for the entire adult world, they meant everything to a child and his dying mother.

Bina and Aditya talked for over an hour. It was almost six o'clock. Then Aditya went to play cricket with his friends. Bina sighed, as she picked up a magazine and began to flip through its glossy pages. The beauty products displayed in the magazine held little interest for her, but it helped her kill time before Adi returned.

It was around forty minutes later that the doorbell rang. Bina was surprised, as Aditya would never come back home so early. Nitin, too, was going to be working late today, and was not going to be back home till eight o'clock. Who could this be?

Sharda entered Bina's bedroom and handed over to her a piece of paper. It was a visiting card. Bina read and reread it in disbelief.

Father Pinto!

She handed the card back to Sharda, telling her to call the man inside. She sat up as quickly as was possible in her state, and began to straighten herself up, wanting to look as neat and clean as possible, and also a suitable mother to the newly appointed class monitor. No doubt Father Pinto was here to congratulate her on her son's exemplary behaviour, thought Bina, but she still found it a little hard to believe that he would actually come and meet her in person.

Her thoughts were interrupted by the entry of a tall man into her room, with a curious Sharda just behind him. The man looked to be about fifty years old, dignified and distinguished. His demeanour was exactly as that of a principal of a missionary school should be – pleasant and completely in control.

"How are you, Mrs Sharma?" asked Father Pinto in a deep voice.

All Bina could manage was, "Yes ... well ... I'm getting along fine ... trying to enjoy the little time I have left..."

Father Pinto smiled. By now he had realised that Bina was a little perplexed as to the reason of his visit. "Well, Mrs Sharma, you must be wondering why I am here. I needed to tell you something about your son, Aditya..."

"Yes, yes, Father, Aditya told me everything about what happened today," Bina interrupted. "He is very happy, I assure you..."

Father Pinto looked a little bewildered. "Happy? Please, Mrs Sharma, can you tell me exactly what Aditya has told you?"

Bina went on to describe the story that Aditya had narrated to her. At the end of it, Father Pinto looked worried and puzzled.

"Well, Mrs Sharma, I know this will not be very easy for you to handle. I am sure that you love your son a lot, and I don't want to paint a bad picture of him, but you are his mother, and it is therefore imperative that you know this," said Father Pinto.

Bina was now worried. Had Adi done something wrong? No, it was impossible; it must be something else that Father Pinto was referring to. Her stream of thoughts was broken when he began speaking again.

"What happened today was entirely different from what your son has told you, Mrs Sharma. Aditya got into a fight with an older boy, and it was in fact Pranay who intervened and stopped the fight. If it had not been for Pranay, one of the two would have been badly injured, and it could have well been your son ... I appointed Pranay class monitor. I am sorry, Mrs Sharma, I know that in your present condition, it is unfair to ask you to handle such a situation, but as principal, it is my duty to inform you of your son's misbehaviour, and ask you to make him reform. He has been getting into these fights and has been very inattentive in class. Please try and understand, I would not like it if there is any more trouble in these difficult times than you are already facing..."

Bina was devastated, but she reined in her emotions. "Yes, Father, I do understand..."

Father Pinto took leave of her, leaving her alone and emotionally shattered.

For any other mother, this would have been a simple case of lying that demanded a solid reprimand. But not so for Bina. Bina's whole world revolved around Aditya, and for him to betray her meant that she was living a lie. She felt cheated, and it pained her when she thought that everything that Adi had told her of his so-called accomplishments in school was a big hoax, a lie.

All her life, she had been particularly drawn towards one quality more than anything else and that was honesty. It was her infinite belief in this quality which prevented her from accepting any case of a client she suspected was guilty, no matter how much money was in the offing. It was that quality which she found in and appreciated Nitin for. It was that quality which she expected from her son, and thought that he had in him, until now.

The more Bina thought about this, the more she became angry and upset. Then, as reason prevailed, she thought, why? Why had Aditya lied to her? Had she failed as a mother or had he failed as a son? All she wanted was for him to be happy, she thought, feeling sorry for herself, and this is what he gave her in return?

At that very instance, in a flash, she also realised that that was what Adi wanted for her too. All that he probably wanted was for her to be happy. And at eleven he had probably felt helpless about how to ensure this.

Bina knew what was to be done. Aditya would be home in around fifteen minutes.

As Aditya approached his house, he knew what awaited him, for he had seen Father Pinto entering his home. He did not know how he would ever be able to face his mother again, and felt like running away to avoid the confrontation. But that could not be done. All his life, his mother had told him to be honest no matter how harsh the punishment for being so might be, and if he had lied to her, the least he could do now is own up to her. He rang the doorbell.

Aditya walked into the house, sweaty and dirty, dazed. Usually, he burst into his mother's room and fed her with reports of what happened while playing cricket with his friends. It was usually something small but dramatically expressed, like the way Kshitij fell down and his leg began to bleed, or the way Aman's pants tore while he was running, and everyone had laughed. Sometimes he would tell her that he had scored a century, and she would smile, and tell him that one day he would be like Sachin Tendulkar. He would reply, "Mama, I don't want to be like Sachin, I want to be like Dhoni!" and she would laugh and run her weak hand through his untidy mop of hair.

But today their conversation was going to be of a more serious nature, Aditya knew. As he was about to enter her room, he felt like his heart was going to burst forth from his chest, for it was pounding very loudly now. Gathering all his wits about him, he entered...

Aditya looked at his mother, who was sitting on her bed. Her face was emotionless. He knew he was in for a tough time. She looked at him, and sensed his uneasiness, but said nothing.

"Err ... Mama, was somebody here?"

"Yes, Aditya, someone was. Do you know who it was? It was none other than Father Pinto, your principal!" said Bina.

Numb with fear, Aditya said nothing.

Bina smiled. "He came to ask me how I was, Aditya ... he is a very sweet man!"

"Did he say anything more, Mama, you know ... about me and the school and all that..." Aditya was shuffling his feet.

Bina paused, then shook her head.

Aditya let out a big sigh, relieved of the huge burden he had been carrying all this while. His joy knew no bounds. He was about to leave the room, when he heard his mother's voice again.

"Adi, I want to talk to you about something..."

Oh no! thought Aditya. She knew the truth after all.

Bina looked at him straight in the eye, and said, "Look, Adi beta, you are now the monitor of your class, and I want all the teachers in the school to have a good impression about you. Don't argue with me on this. Here, take this money, and go for a haircut now. You look like a ragamuffin. I don't want someone to think badly of you!"

Saying this, she handed him a crisp hundred-rupee note. Aditya said, "Yes, Mama…" He left the room, both puzzled and relieved.

As Aditya left the room, Bina looked at the clock. Twenty-eight minutes past seven, it read. She knew Aditya would be home before long, and with mixed feelings of despair and anxiety she looked up once again at the ceiling and its familiar cracks and wrinkles.

AFTERTHOUGHTS

For all those who fancy writing fiction, short stories were always the way to get started, at least in the pre-Google era when there were no courses to teach you how to write scripts. I too began that way. Moreover, I have always liked to write about women, because they interested me much more than men. Writing about them was like peeling the layers of an onion, due to their layered personalities and the complexities that inform various dimensions of their lives.

And so I indulged in this fanciful activity in the mid-1990s during the few hours I had, as my young kids took their afternoon naps. I was determined to not go back to journalism after this "momma break" of a few years. It was much too hectic for my mood at the time – the mood of wanting to spend lots of time at home with my new family.

My first collection, *Fragile Victories,* was born then, followed by *The Last Laugh,* a few years later. Incidentally, both the book titles were generic descriptions of the stories within the books, there were no stories named after the titles in the collections.

It's much the same with *Autumn Blossoms,* for I am a firm believer in the fact that women, and for that matter men too, bloom and discover strength in the autumn of their lives. As do many protagonists in these stories, where autumn stands as much for the vagaries of age as for what they are experiencing in life which gives them a new perspective.

Coming back to my story, what I thought was the autumn of my creative life, turned out to be a new beginning indeed. By the turn of the millennium I was sucked, lock, stock and barrel, into the audiovisual world, by virtue of living in Mumbai. For more than a decade I did lots of TV shows and then thought to challenge myself with writing full-length novels. I published four of them. In the rigours of writing for television and the time and engagement that novels required, my short stories languished.

Until that afternoon when Shantanu, while doing a piece on me, asked for the copies of my early fiction writing in order to understand my journey better. I handed him the now yellow-paged copies of my books, rather hesitantly I must add, and also told him that I had some more unpublished short stories filed in my computer.

By the next day the columnist in Shantanu had given way to the publisher. Our editor sahab had read them all and felt that they needed a new lease of life as the stories deserved to be read, along with the more recent ones. Shantanu also put my reservations to rest about going back to pure women-centric stories even for the new collection, for writing on women and their relationships was my forte and I should be unapologetic about this. I did see his point of view and started to revisit all the stories.

In fact, since the total number of stories was going to be higher in this collection, Shantanu suggested that we categorise them into three sections. The first would be the section about women's relationships with men. The second section would be women's relationships with other women. The third would be about women's relationships with themselves, by far the most complex of them all. Of course there are bound to be overlaps – these categories have permeable boundaries, so that it is possible for one story in one category to resonate in another. That too provides a sort of unity to the entire collection – apart from the overarching commonality of women being at the centre of each narrative.

Editor sahab also had me write a few lines as epigraphic inscriptions, a kind of short-hand for each story. As I discovered the closet poet in myself, I felt more energised, almost recharged, about this collection than I had felt about any of my books in all these years. In some ways I felt as if I was finally closing the "writing" bracket that I had opened two-and-a-half decades ago, and there was a sense of fulfilment perceiving it that way.

Up to this point, the exercise was fun, but when I started to read my earlier stories afresh, I faced another conundrum.

The truth is, I had outgrown many of my stories, in terms of the way they were written. Not only that, in a few cases I no longer identified with them in the form that they existed.

As I thought more about it, I felt that only if the author's voice needed to change should I rewrite or revise any of the published stories. Otherwise, it would be best to leave it to the reader to analyse how I had evolved as a writer over twenty-five years through my stories. Once I was convinced about this, I felt unafraid to expose my writing to scrutiny.

After analysing my early stories, I chose to make changes in four of them and I will share why I did what I did, especially for those of you who want to make the journey to writing and stick with it.

Screaming Silence: *The Last Laugh*

In the earlier version of the story, it did not seem woman-centric at all as the protagonist was a man, and the people opposing him were also mainly men. It has been changed to only women opposing the protagonist, and while doing that, it gave me a new interpretation to women's relationships with other women.

Your Guilt Or Mine: *Fragile Victories*

In the previous version of this story, a crucial turning point was not written in a manner that made it obvious as to what exactly had happened between the protagonist and another man. Maybe it was because I wasn't that bold enough at the time! So later on, towards the end, the reader could be left wondering and having to join the dots on their own. In the current version of the story, I decided to write the turning point in a clearer manner, where the reader has no room to doubt what really happened.

A Prayer Is Answered: *Fragile Victories*

Originally, the style of writing did not clearly describe the critical point of the story (this is in reference to the point where the protagonist ends up walking a bit too far into the water without having realised it). In the new draft, small changes have been made at this point of the story that highlight her state of mind and clearly indicate how the situation plays out the way it eventually does.

Not Man Enough: *The Last Laugh*

In the older draft, the central character's absolute fear of her body showing signs of womanhood were not impressed upon in a manner that justified the end, without making it seem random. The revised version of this story has been written in a manner where the ending is contextualised.

*

Finally, a few more interesting asides to some of the stories. Two of these stories are the script versions of audiobooks: "The Perfect Switch" and "#Couple Goals", so readers may be able to discern the difference in the writing style when books would have to be heard and not read.

Two more stories, "Not Man Enough" and "Two Gold Guineas", had been categorised as somewhat longer short stories. They are both from my second collection, *The Last Laugh*. But over the years the subjects of both these stories kept nagging me, and I felt that they deserved to be done justice to in the novel format. I had probably tried to cram them into short stories. But now, since I am familiar with long-format fiction, I felt I should write them thus.

So "Two Gold Guineas" grew up to become my third novel *Girls Don't Cry* and "Not Man Enough" became my first e-book, titled, believe it or not, *Not Woman Enough*. While the feel and basic characters of both the short story and the novel remained the same, a lot of adaptation and evolution had happened, some overt and some covert. This might be of interest to the readers who want to study the writing process academically. Others may just sit back and enjoy the stories for what they were at the time of conception.

As for the stories in this collection that have not been published earlier, well, it might be tough for me to recollect when in the intervening years which one was written. They were written only because one had been in the mood to write something apart from long format. As they say in Hindi: *Ainwayen*.

Happy reading.

COPYRIGHT ACKNOWLEDGEMENTS

Storytel

Couple Goals; The Perfect Switch

Fragile Victories, Har-Anand Publications

A Connecting Door; A Prayer Is Answered; Dawn to Dawn; Friends Indeed; It Happened One Day; Mother Comes Back; Not Now; Rewind; Thank You, Pneumonia; The Homeland; The Perfectionist; Your Guilt or Mine

The Last Laugh, Jaico Books

A Clean Slate; A Decision at Last; All for the Good Cause; Face-to-Face; Family Ties; Happily Ever After; Insane and Able; Not Man Enough; Screaming Silence; Such a Long Journey; The Final Act; The Guru; Turning Point; Two Gold Guineas; Virginal Fantasy; Waxworks